The Burning of
Rachel Hayes

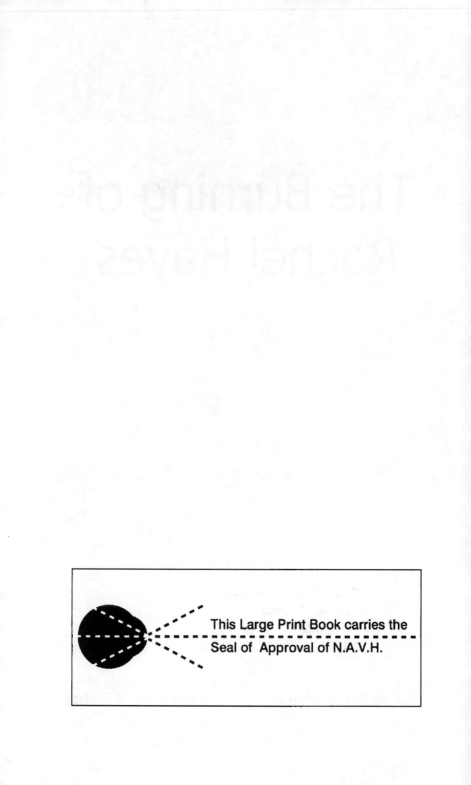

This Large Print Book carries the
Seal of Approval of N.A.V.H.

The Burning of Rachel Hayes

Doug Allyn

Willimantic Library
Service Center
1216 Main Street
Willimantic, CT 06226

Thorndike Press • Waterville, Maine

Copyright © 2004 by Doug Allyn

All rights reserved.

This novel is a work of fiction. Names, characters, places and incidents are either the product of the author's imagination, or, if real, used fictitiously.

Published in 2005 by arrangement with Tekno Books.

Thorndike Press® Large Print Mystery.

The tree indicium is a trademark of Thorndike Press.

The text of this Large Print edition is unabridged.
Other aspects of the book may vary from the original edition.

Set in 16 pt. Plantin by Al Chase.

Printed in the United States on permanent paper.

Library of Congress Cataloging-in-Publication Data

Allyn, Douglas.
    The burning of Rachel Hayes / by Doug Allyn.
      p. cm.
    ISBN 0-7862-7331-3 (lg. print : hc : alk. paper)
    1. Veterinarians — Fiction.   2. Michigan — Fiction.
  I. Title.
  PS3551.L49B87 2004b
   813′.54—dc22
                                    2004029222

The Burning of Rachel Hayes

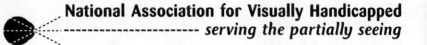

National Association for Visually Handicapped
serving the partially seeing

As the Founder/CEO of NAVH, the only national health agency solely devoted to those who, although not totally blind, have an eye disease which could lead to serious visual impairment, I am pleased to recognize Thorndike Press★ as one of the leading publishers in the large print field.

Founded in 1954 in San Francisco to prepare large print textbooks for partially seeing children, NAVH became the pioneer and standard setting agency in the preparation of large type.

Today, those publishers who meet our standards carry the prestigious "Seal of Approval" indicating high quality large print. We are delighted that Thorndike Press is one of the publishers whose titles meet these standards. We are also pleased to recognize the significant contribution Thorndike Press is making in this important and growing field.

Lorraine H. Marchi, L.H.D.
Founder/CEO
NAVH

★ Thorndike Press encompasses the following imprints: Thorndike, Wheeler, Walker and Large Pr int Press.

Prologue

Northern Michigan
October 8, 1871

A cold finger brushed Rachel's throat, jolting her out of a dream. She sat up, half-asleep, blinking in the red, pre-dawn glow, and realized her collie, Ginger, was nuzzling her. Whining. Frantic.

A prowler? Alert now, Rachel went utterly still, listening. Her Sears Barker shotgun was leaning against the nightstand within easy reach. Six shells under her pillow. Double-ought buckshot.

A woman alone can't be too careful. The Great Lakes lumber trade attracts rough types and she had a daughter to protect.

But Rachel made no move toward the gun. She knew every floorboard creak of the old farmhouse. The only sound was the ticking of the Beacon alarm clock on the nightstand.

Odd. The clock read two-fifteen. But it couldn't be. Morning glow was already brightening the bedroom, tinting the lace curtains pale rose.

Downstairs, the parlor clock began chiming the quarter-hour.

Two-fifteen? In the morning?

Then she heard it. Off in the distance. A deep, bass rumble of thunder. Rain? Please let it be rain. Hadn't seen a drop since July. The corn withered on the stalks, fit only for hogs or silage. A hard rain might still save the winter wheat.

Rising, Rachel slipped on a muslin dressing gown. Tall and spare, she was nearly forty now, coarsened by farm work. A handsome woman, nonetheless. Her smile could still lift a man's eyes and erase the years from his heart.

Hurrying to the window, she opened it wide to the breathless October night. Her parched fields stretched away to the Black River Hills, arid and empty.

But . . . they were moving.

The furrows were twisting and squirming, as though the soil itself was writhing in agony. Baffled, she stared at her land, trying to grasp the message of the shuddering earth.

It took a moment for the truth to register. The dawn glow was in the wrong quarter. The sun wasn't rising in the east. The light was from the south.

Bracing herself on the window ledge, Rachel leaned out as far as she could, trying to see. . . .

Dear God. The horizon was on fire. Miles of it. Flames blazing in the distant treetops, sparks and smoke roiling madly upward. The holocaust she'd warned her neighbors about had finally come. But it was far worse than she'd ever dreamed.

Rachel had seen forest fires in the years since she'd moved up to the lake country. But never anything like this. This firestorm was hurtling through the wooded hills like the devil's own cavalry, torching the land, burning it alive. Coming closer.

She shook her head to clear it. This was no dream. Hell was heading her way at a dead run.

"Hannah! Wake up!" Hastily pulling on her Pebble riding boots, she raced down the hall to her daughter's bedroom.

Her nine-year-old was sitting up, knuckling her eyes, golden hair awry, looking as rumpled and confused as Rachel felt.

"Hannah, get up and get dressed, dear. Right now."

"What's wrong?"

"There's fire in the hills, Hannah, we have to go. I'll be in the barn hooking up Beau. Hurry!"

Flying down the stairs, Rachel paused in the kitchen to light a lantern, then sprinted out the door with the ginger collie at her heels.

No cats or dogs greeted her in the yard. Ordinarily, a half-dozen mutts would be hanging around, hoping for a handout. Neighbors joked that the Hayes farm was a breadline for every critter in the county. It wasn't. Rachel worked hard to scratch a living from her land. But farming is a lonely life. And strays get hungry too.

Over the past few days they'd all vanished. Even her barn cats had fled. And now she understood why.

They knew. Somehow. They tasted smoke on the wind or heard some subsonic rumble inaudible to humans. And instinctively they knew a fire was coming. And it was time to go.

Opening the barn door was like stepping into hell!

Squealing hogs were gashing each other, trampling their piglets to death as they fought to scramble out of their pens. Her Guernsey milk cows were bawling, crashing mindlessly against their stall gates.

Damn it! Her animals were thrashing themselves to death with the danger still miles off. And they were all she had. Her

10

livelihood. Hannah's future. Years of sweat being smashed in a welter of blood and terror because the damned lumberjacks didn't clean up their trash. Littering the forest floor with timber slash, branches, and woodchips. Leaving it to rot. Or burn.

But even as she cursed the loggers and her luck she was unlatching the gates, freeing her stock. There was no help for it. Panic was killing her animals faster than any fire.

She hated it. Hated what it meant. Failure. Surrender. On the day she and Hannah moved onto the rocky, hundred-acre farm, she'd nailed a wooden plaque above her front door. One word. TENACITY.

Tenacity. A word to live by.

But not to die for. Daisy, her best milker, came stumbling out of her pen streaming crimson from her gashed foreleg, white bone splinters showing in the wound. Excited by the scent of smoke and blood, the ginger collie hurled herself at Daisy's flank, barking frantically, driving her out of the barn.

Only Beau, the roan gelding, remained now. Wild-eyed, flanks foamy with lather, the horse was stamping in his stall, daring Rachel to enter.

"Easy, Beau, eeeasy." Unlatching the stall door, she tried to slip inside. But Beau was too terrified, too quick. Lunging for the opening, he slammed her aside as he bolted into the corridor.

Leaping on Beau's neck as he swept past, Rachel desperately grabbed an ear and a fistful of mane! Bucking and twisting, the roan tried to shake her off but she clung like a burr, forcing his massive head down, wrestling him to a standstill by sheer force of will. And tenacity.

Panting, sweating, the woman and the animal stood locked together, straining, neither giving an inch. Rachel cooed to him quietly, pressing her cheek against his velvet forehead, telling him what a fine horse he was. What a handsome fellow.

Flattery with a purpose. She'd never get Beau hitched up if he kept thrashing about and without him they had no chance of outrunning the fire.

Persuasion won. As the gelding gentled down, she eased him around, slipped a hackamore over his head, then tied him to a stanchion.

Moving oh-so slowly to avoid spooking Beau, Rachel shooed the ginger collie out and swung the barn door closed, crooning all the while to the gelding. She eased the yellow-wheeled Stanhope buggy up behind him, gently sliding the shafts past his withers.

But as she tried to slip the breast collar over his neck Beau suddenly reared, throwing his head back, jerking Rachel completely off her feet!

Clinging grimly to the hackamore, Rachel managed to drag his great head down again. Beau was the gentlest animal she'd ever owned but he was only a hair's-breadth from wall-eyed insanity now, shivering violently, spraying her with flecks of lather.

Working feverishly, her hands slipping on the sweat-slicked traces, Rachel had almost finished the harnessing when Hannah burst into the barn with Ginger yapping behind her.

Beau panicked, rearing again, lashing out with his forelegs, hurling Rachel aside. The hackamore line snapped and he stampeded for the door. With Hannah directly in his path!

Rachel screamed but it was too late! Hannah froze as the gelding thundered toward her, banging the carriage off the stalls as he came.

But Ginger gamely stood her ground. Protecting Hannah, the little collie was beside herself with rage, dancing in the doorway, yapping furiously into the face of death.

And it worked.

Veering at the last second to avoid the dog, Beau slammed one of the Stanhope's wheels into a stall door, jamming it as the maddened horse lunged against the traces.

"Quick, Hannah, get in!" Leaping into the carriage, Rachel grabbed the reins and hauled the terrified girl up onto the seat beside her a split second before Beau yanked the buggy free and charged out of the barn.

Sawing desperately on the reins, Rachel fought to swing the horse and the careening carriage toward the gate.

She was winning, bringing the gelding under control. Once they were clear of the gate — with a crack like a lightning strike, the damaged wheel splintered! The buggy dropped with a sickening lurch, its axle gouging the ground like a plow, flipping the cab, spilling Rachel into the road.

Stunned, she clung doggedly to the lines as the crazed gelding dragged the buggy through the farm gate, slamming her body into a post, ripping the reins from her fists.

And then Beau was off, galloping madly down the rutted country road, dragging the wrecked carriage with Hannah still clinging desperately to the seat! Frozen. Horrified. Staring back at her mother.

"Jump," Rachel croaked, her voice barely a whisper as she struggled to her knees. "Forgodsake, Hannah. Jump!"

If the girl heard her she gave no sign. And then she was gone as Beau and the shattered buggy disappeared over the rise into the forest with Ginger yapping madly at his heels.

Rachel stumbled to her feet. Her left ankle was badly twisted, maybe broken. Grimacing, she staggered toward the gate after her daughter, barely able to stand.

She clung to the gatepost a moment, gathering her strength, but when she pushed away from it, her ankle gave way and she fell. Hard. Tasting blood and dirt in her mouth. And agony. Knowing she was too late.

The fire was crowning now, exploding through the treetops faster than a horse could gallop. The forest road had disappeared, obliterated by the inferno. God help them, Hannah and Beau were probably dead already.

Numbly, she hauled herself upright, clinging to the gatepost, trying to comprehend what was happening to her world.

Hell had burst open. The very air seemed

to be afire as the forest slash flamed skyward in a fiery torrent. All this destruction so a few timber barons could make a few more dollars.

So be it. Let them win. Let their fire come. Without Hannah, life was nothing. Death would be relief. Welcome.

Suddenly, incredibly, the ginger collie emerged from the swirling smoke. And for a wild moment Rachel thought Hannah had survived somehow. . . .

She hadn't. Ginger's smoldering coat and burned forelegs told the story. Panting, the dog limped up to Rachel and collapsed at her feet. Spent. More dead than alive.

And still the inferno came. Fireballs were rocketing through the wooded hills around the farm like a hail of comets, sparks and flaming debris howling up to the heavens.

In the fields, Rachel's cattle formed a final defensive ring, trying to protect their young. It made no difference. Dropping from exhaustion, the Guernseys bawled in helpless agony as the flames swept over them.

Cannon fire blasted in the forest, living trees exploding in the furnace heat. The farmhouse walls were already smoking as the blaze lurched toward her, unstoppable.

Armageddon. The end of the world.

Rachel stared into the fiery abyss, drew a

16

ragged breath, then knelt and gently picked up her wounded dog. They had no chance now. But Tenacity was her word of life. And the fire hadn't won. Not yet.

"Easy, girl, easy Ginger," she cooed to the collie as she limped toward her smoldering house. "Don't be afraid. We'll be all right."

It was a lie. But the dog didn't know.

Chapter 1

Lord, what a perfect spring morning. June sun grinning over the Black River Hills, wild tangles of lilacs sweetening the air.

In the meadow around Brenda Jozwiak's campsite, goldenrod and dandelions tossed their heads in the breeze, jostling for growing room in the greening grass.

Brenda took a long sip of Budweiser, rested the can on her generous breast, and leaned back in her deck chair beside the candy-stripe Jayco tent. Closing her eyes a moment, she luxuriated in the rosy glow on her eyelids, breathing deep.

Heaven would be like this. No husbands, no hassles. Just country sunshine, warm breezes, cold beer, and kielbasa in the cooler. Polack heaven. Brenda's heaven.

Her father's too, God rest him. He'd often brought Brenda and her brothers camping in these hills when they were kids. Planned to build a cabin here someday.

18

Never had. And never would, now.

Every breath of pine-scented air reminded Bren of her dad. Not all the memories were golden. Chaz Jozwiak was cranky when he drank and gloomy sober. Brenda learned to read his face for storm signals before she could walk.

But it was only his temper she feared. He'd never, ever raised a hand to Bren or her mother. Would have cut his arm off first. Sure he drank, but he sweated like a slave at Ford Rouge too. If life in the Jozwiak home wasn't the Brady Bunch, so fuckin' what? Chaz worked hard and did his dead-level best for his family. What more can you ask of your dad? Or anyone?

Until her own son was born, Brenda hadn't truly understood how much her old man had done for her. She cocked an eye now, squinting against the sun. Bobby was playing with his red Tonka truck, pushing it through the grass a few yards from the tent. Her fairhaired boy. Literally. A blocky little squirt with a blonde crew cut, eyes as blue as Windex. Light of her life.

Bobby's father? A total shit. Dumped her a month before the boy was born, always late with his child support, seldom bothered to see the kid. Thank God she hadn't married the prick.

Her own dad dodged PTA meetings but he never missed the boys' softball games or Bren's tennis matches, though she knew damned well he never understood the scores.

Best of all, he included her in his camping weekends.

Brenda was no daisy. Chunky in high school, she was pushing two-fifty now. Not fat. Beef. That's what her brothers called her, Beefy Bren. Unless the old man was within earshot. Around him, they had treated her like a lady or got the back of his hand.

Still, he could have made the north country treks a guys-only thing, taken her brothers, left her behind. But he didn't. Never once.

Chaz Jozwiak's gift of campfires and friendship revealed his heart to Bren more clearly than a carload of candy samplers. He loved these northern Michigan hills and he shared them with her. So he must love her too, even if he wasn't much of a hugger.

Then suddenly he was gone.

Coronary. Dropped like a rock on the job, third shift at Ford the day after Christmas. Working overtime to pay for these empty acres. Land the boys sold off to pay for his funeral.

So Brenda brought Bobby north on the first warm June weekend. Maybe when he was a little older she could explain how much these hills meant to his grandfather and . . .

She blinked awake, disoriented by the solar glare. Yawning, stretching like a she-bear, she sat up and glanced about for her son.

"Bobby?"

Shading her eyes, she scanned the meadow. He'd been playing with his truck a little ways from the tent. Had she nodded out? Checked her watch. She'd dozed a minute or two. No more.

"Bobby, honey, where are you? If you're hiding, the joke's over, okay? Allee allee in free!"

No answer. But he couldn't be hiding. She could see two hundred yards in any direction from her campsite. Nothing was moving but the grass and goldenrods swaying in the breeze.

Uneasy now, she got up and checked the tent and her station wagon. Both empty. What the hell? A gull wheeling high above the hills screamed and Brenda fought down the urge to do the same.

Movement. In the distance, a ground squirrel bustled across the hillside, clearly visible a hundred yards away. If she could see a squirrel that far off, how could an eight-year-old boy vanish?

A flash of red caught her eye. A Tonka fire truck, upside-down, forty yards away in the middle of the field. But no Bobby. Not a trace.

"Bobby, answer me! This isn't funny, young man! Bobby!"

Chapter 2

I don't like heights. High places where you can slip, trip, and break your neck.

Airplanes are no problem. Flying is safe. More or less. Big jets are rock solid, built of chrome steel and titanium. Statistics say more people die falling from ladders.

A fact I remembered too clearly as I climbed up the ancient wooden extension ladder. Clutching my paint bucket and brush. One damned rung at a time. All the way to the peak of the old barn.

Thirty-two feet above the concrete driveway. Felt like thirty miles. Sweating like a seal in a steam bath. My guts in knots. Too stubborn to quit. And too broke.

Bottom line, I couldn't afford to hire a pro. I was stuck with this job. And stuck with the fact that my dad taught me to paint walls properly. Begin at the top, work your way down.

Which meant starting at the barn peak. So

I climbed the damned rungs and began slathering on the paint, with my knees locked around the ladder in a death grip.

I knew I was safe. I wouldn't fall unless I let go of the ladder and there was noooo chance of that.

And the ladder couldn't break. I found it in the barn when I moved my gear in. Hand-made of ash, it was probably stronger than steel. I'd lashed it to the bumper of my Jeep in the driveway so it couldn't slip or kick out from under me.

Theoretically.

But every time I glanced down, the damned thing seemed to be bowing like limp linguini. An optical illusion. Had to be.

At least the view up here was terrific. From the peak I could see across the Black River Hills all the way to the turquoise surf of Lake Huron on the horizon — Someone screamed.

I froze. Listening.

Wasn't sure what I'd heard. A cry. A hawk? I'd seen one wheeling overhead — no, there it was again. Faint and far away. A woman. Screaming.

Locking in on the sound, I slowly swiveled, trying to figure which direction — the ladder lurched! Whoa!

Clinging desperately to the rails, I

watched my paint can cartwheel down to smash on the pavement below, splattering the driveway and my Jeep a bloody barn red.

Damn it! I'd nearly twisted myself into a broken neck — The scream came again. Definitely a woman, definitely in trouble. I scrambled down the rungs two at a time, cursing all the way.

Skidding through the pool of paint, I untied the ladder from the bumper, fired up the Jeep, and roared off down the country road, heading south, toward the sound of the voice.

With the top down, I couldn't hear anything over the wind blast. Still, the sound had come from this general direction. Maybe I could get a fix on it from high ground.

Pulling off the road at the crest of a hill, I killed the engine and stood up in the seat, listening. Nothing. With my ears still ringing from the road noise I couldn't — no. There it was again! I scanned the distance for some sign of her. No one in sight. The rolling meadows were as empty as the back of the moon.

Cranking up the Jeep, I charged off again, hoping I'd guessed the direction right. Two miles, three. No sign of anything or anyone. Pulled off again, waiting for my hearing to adjust to the summer silence.

"Help! Please!"

Damn. Her voice seemed to be coming from just over the next rise. But the road led off in the wrong direction and the hill was too rough for the Jeep.

Grabbing my cell phone out of the glove box, I sprinted up the slope toward the sound of the screaming.

Cresting the hill, I looked around wildly. Spotted her. A heavyset woman in a blue denim sunsuit. On her knees in the middle of a meadow, clawing desperately at the earth. A red Ford Escort station wagon was parked forty yards away with a striped tent pitched beside it.

"Lady? Are you all right?" She didn't answer, kept digging, her hands bloody from the effort. What the hell was up? I trotted down the slope to her.

She was younger than I'd thought. Mid-twenties. Coppery hair twisted into a thick braid. Barefoot. A tattoo on one beefy shoulder. HARLEYS RULE!

She looked up, her red face tear-streaked, eyes wild. "My son!" she stammered. "He fell down this fucking hole! Help me dig!"

A hole. In the middle of a field. My heart stopped.

"Ma'am, listen to me. You've got to back

26

away from there. Right now. It could be a sinkhole."

"What the hell are you talking about?"

"A sinkhole, ma'am. They open up sometimes in this part of the state. Underground streams gouge out caverns. If you don't back away, you could cave the roof in on your boy and bury him. Can you see him?"

"He's — down there a ways. He landed in water but he's on a rock now."

"Okay, that's good, come on now, back away. I'll get us some help." Popping the cell phone's antenna, I dialed 911.

"Emergency Services, how may I direct your call?"

"I'm Doctor David Westbrook. I'm on a country road somewhere south of Algoma —"

"What address, sir?"

"Lady, where are we? What road are we on?"

She looked around wildly. "I don't know! I don't live around here!"

"Look, operator, we've got a kid down a sinkhole. We're west of US 23 ten or twelve miles south of Algoma. My vehicle is a tan Jeep, it's parked by the road. We need some help out here, a fire truck or —"

"Sir, we can't dispatch emergency vehicles without an address —"

27

"But there aren't any road signs! We're directly south of the McCrae estate on whatever road that is. My Jeep is parked —"

"I'm sorry, but we can't dispatch —"

"Then send the police! Send somebody!"

"Sir, unless you wish to report a crime —"

"Crime? How about I hunt you down and punch your lights out! Would that be crime enough for you? Damn it, get somebody out here! Fast!" Tossing the phone aside, I hurried to the woman. "What's your name?"

"Brenda. Brenda Jozwiak."

"I'm Dave Westbrook. Have you got any kind of a pad in the tent? Something to spread our weight on the ground?"

"I've got an air mattress."

"That should work." I was already running for the tent. Tossing her sleeping bag aside, I yanked the mattress out and raced back to the hole. "Okay, I'm going to inch out to him and —"

"Let me do it!"

"Lady, no offense, but I'm probably a hundred pounds lighter than you are. What's your son's name?"

"Bobby," she said, swallowing. "He's eight."

Laying the mattress down a few yards from the hole, I stretched out prone on it, then nudged myself and the mattress ahead with the toes of my work boots. The opening was a rough oval, two feet across by eighteen inches. Bloody gouges in the earth showed where Brenda's efforts had widened it.

"Bobby? Can you hear me?"

"Mom?"

"No, I'm a friend. My name's Dave. We're gonna get you out of there, buddy, but I need you to tell me a few things. It's real important, all right?"

"Okay." His voice sounded faint. And fading. Damn.

"Are you in the water, Bobby?"

"Partly. I'm halfway on a rock now. My arm hurts bad. And I'm cold. It's really cold."

"Hang in there. It may get dark for a minute. I'm gonna look down." I inched warily out over the hole. Utter blackness. Couldn't see a thing. Then a faint orb seemed to glow in the darkness. A boy's face. Fifteen or twenty feet below at the bottom of a narrow shaft. "Hi. Can you see me?"

"Yes."

"The water, Bobby. Is it moving, like a stream?"

Hesitation. "No. It's more like a pool. I think it's a well or something. The walls are real steep."

"What kind of walls?"

"Stones. Close together. Slimy. I'm slipping. I can't hold on."

"Oh God," Brenda groaned.

"Bobby, stay very still. Help's coming." I backed away from the hole to Brenda. "Okay, here's where we are. Bobby says it looks like a well and he could be right. If it's not a sinkhole, that's good. But he's slipping. We can't wait for help. Do you have any rope?"

"No, I —"

"Okay, we'll make do with the tent. Are you as strong as you look?"

"Damn straight I am."

"Good. Give me a hand." I hurried to her tent and began unsnapping its cables.

"What the hell are you doing?"

"The tent's nylon, it'll bear my weight. We'll stake it at the top, I'll shinny down, tie Bobby to it, and you can haul him up. Sound like a plan?"

"Yeah, okay. Hurry!" Kneeling, she tore one of the stakes out of the ground with startling ferocity. We collapsed the tent and pulled it free in a matter of seconds.

Hurrying back to the hole, I began twisting the nylon into the equivalent of a bedsheet ladder while Brenda hammered two pegs in the ground and tied one end of the tent to them.

"You ready?" I asked.

"I was born ready, jack, just get your ass in gear!"

"Right. Bobby? I'm coming down for you. I may kick some dirt loose so close your eyes. Okay?"

"But it's dark!" His voice was close to panic.

"Bobby, I haven't got time to argue. Close your eyes now, understand? And don't move, even if some dirt falls on you. I'll find you, okay?"

"Okay, okay, they're shut!"

"Good. We're dropping the tent first. Here it comes." I slid the twisted tent into the hole and carefully let it unfurl. My eyes met Brenda's a moment, then I slithered my legs into the hole and began shinnying down, hand over hand, down into the darkness under the earth.

Roots clawed at me as I squeezed my shoulders through the narrow gap. Hollow splashes echoed from below, loose dirt dropping into the water. After the morning glare, the pit was black as a demon's heart. I couldn't see a damned thing and the air was rank as a cesspool.

"Bobby?"

"Down here."

Blinking rapidly, I tried to peer through

31

the dimness. "Okay, buddy, I see you. Here I come." I let myself slide, clinging to the slick nylon for all I was worth. As my eyes adjusted, the walls gradually materialized. Stones. Hand-fitted field stones. The boy was right; thank God, it wasn't a sinkhole. It was probably an old well, roughly circular, six or seven feet across. Looked solid. But the stones were too slick to offer handholds and it was a helluva long way down.

The last foot of the tent was dangling in the water. I hung in mid-air a moment, getting my bearings. The boy was a yard or two below me, hunched over a stone that had buckled out of the wall.

And a few feet off to his right, there was a corpse. Or what was left of one.

Sweet Jesus. I blinked, swallowing hard, trying to be certain the shadows weren't playing tricks with my imagination. No. It was definitely a corpse. A skeleton, draped over a rock, much as Bobby was, half buried in muck from the fractured wall.

The boy didn't seem to be aware of it yet. Good.

I slid the final yard down the tent, wincing as the icy water slithered over my legs to my waist. God it was cold! Gritting my teeth, I let go, then dog-paddled over to the boy, easing alongside, blocking his view of the corpse.

Stocky kid, hair in a coppery blonde brush cut. Freckles.

"Hey, Bobby, how are you doin'? Can you move your arms and legs?"

"Sure. I swam over here. But I'm cold. And it stinks."

"It sure does. What do you say we head back up to the sunshine?" I kept my tone light, but I didn't like the look of him. An animal's eyes can mirror its pain when there are no other symptoms. Bobby's eyes had a wounded look: vague, inwardly focused.

Waist deep in the frigid water, he was blue-lipped and shivering, his little face bloodless as a beached trout. Probably in shock, almost certainly hypothermic. I'd only been in the water a few moments and my calves were already going numb. We had to get him out quickly.

"Brenda? Can you hear me?"

"Yeah! How's Bobby?"

"He's a little banged up but he's okay. Listen up. It's not a sinkhole, we're in some kind of an old well. I'm going to tie the tent around him, then you haul away, okay?"

"Just hurry the hell up, goddammit!"

"Yes ma'am." But as I took the boy's left hand to slip it around my neck, he gasped and went ashen.

"Ow, that hurts! My chest really hurts."

"Where?" I examined him quickly, running my hands gently over his torso. If he'd broken a rib, moving him could puncture a lung. Nothing felt out of place though, and the boy didn't flinch at my touch. Not a rib then.

Collarbone? His left arm was limp as a noodle. I traced the line of his clavicle, found a lump and some unnatural softness in the center. Fracture. Damn! But there was no help for it down here.

"Brenda? We've got a problem. Bobby's collarbone is broken. I'll strap his arm down but be extra careful as you haul him out. And don't forget to toss the tent back down, okay?

"Bobby, listen to me. Your mom's going to pull you up. Your arm may hurt a little, but you have to stay very still. Don't wiggle and don't be afraid. We'll have you out of here in a minute."

The boy nodded mutely. Definitely shocky. Stripping off my belt, I strapped Bobby's arm to his torso, then wrapped the tent around his waist and knotted it firmly.

"Okay Brenda, haul away!"

The boy rose slowly toward the halo of light overhead, slowly rotating, a little human piñata. Dirt rained on me as Brenda pulled him through the gap. And then he was gone.

And I was alone. Well, almost.

I shifted around to get a better look at the skeleton. Couldn't see much. Too dark. Hell, maybe it was just a weird tangle of roots after all. I found the idea comforting. Especially since I might be joining him if I didn't get some help from above. It had only been a few moments but it already felt like a month.

Then the light flickered as the tent came slithering back down to me.

Using the moist stones for footholds, I clambered slowly up the tent, hand over hand, until I shouldered through the gap into sunlight that seemed painfully bright. And very, very sweet.

Chapter 3

I kept the Escort's gas pedal matted all the way to Algoma, its little Ford engine whining like a lawn mower. Brenda cradled Bobby in her arms, crooning to him, tears and snot dripping from her sunburned nose. A police car gave chase at the village limits but I didn't slow down. We rolled into the emergency room driveway with the prowl car right behind, flashers blazing.

Everything shifted to fast-forward. Two nurses and an intern quickly took Bobby from Brenda's arms, laid him on a gurney, and rushed him into a curtained examination cubicle.

Covered with filth from the well, I waited near the admissions desk for the cop, a lanky, Algoma County deputy in an impeccable tan uniform. Jessup, his name tag said. Gaunt as a vampire and just as grim.

I gave him my driver's license and a quick recap of what happened. Jessup listened without comment, told me to stay put, took my license back out to his patrol car, and got on the radio.

Alone for the moment amid the bustle of the emergency ward, I noticed my hands were trembling. Reaction to the rescue? Fear of the police? Maybe both.

A second patrol car pulled up beside Jessup's. *And here we go,* I thought.

The new cop was older, mid-forties, square as a concrete block with an attitude to match. He bulled through the double doors with Jessup in his wake.

"Mr. Westbrook? I'm Sheriff Wolinski. Did you make a 911 call at 11:08?"

"About then, I guess."

"Did you also make a verbal threat to the operator?"

"A kid had fallen down a well. We needed help and she wouldn't send it without getting my shoe size. Maybe I . . . overreacted?"

"If you needed assistance so badly, why didn't you wait for it?"

"I didn't know if help was coming. The boy was half in the water and barely hanging on."

"So you decided to play hero instead? You could have caused that boy a serious injury by moving him —"

"What the hell's goin' on here?" Brenda Jozwiak, two hundred and forty-five pounds of sweaty, disheveled motherhood, shouldered her way between us. "You shitheads aren't really gonna give us a speeding ticket for rushin' my boy to the hospital, are ya?"

"No, ma'am, we're —"

"Then what's this crap? This guy saved my son's life! Climbed down a fuckin' well and got him out. What are you bustin' his balls for?"

"Ma'am," Wolinski sighed, "we're just trying to clear up —"

"Miss Jozwiak?" a nurse called. "The doctor needs to see you a moment."

"I gotta go," Brenda said, leaning into Wolinski, smearing his uniform with mud from her massive breasts. "But if you give this guy any shit at all, you're gonna have to deal with me, Officer. And you don't wanna deal with me. Trust me on that." She stomped off, meaty bare feet slapping on the tiles.

"Friend of yours?" Wolinski asked, brushing off his shirt.

"Never saw her before this morning. Look, I was working, I heard a woman screaming. I managed to find her and tried to get help. If I got out of line with your operator, sorry about that. I was a little stressed at the time."

"You also identified yourself as a doctor."

"I am a doctor. A veterinarian. David Westbrook, DVM."

"Never heard of you."

"I'm just moving to the area. I leased a barn on McCrae Road. I'm converting it to a clinic."

"Or you think you are. Did you rent it from Mrs. McCrae?"

"No, a real estate company. Why?"

"Did you tell them you were a felon on probation when you filled out your lease, Doctor Westbrook? Don't look so surprised. It's the age of computers. There's no place to hide anymore, not even in a little backwater town like Algoma."

"I'm not hiding —"

"That's him," Brenda Jozwiak interrupted, "that's the guy who saved my Bobby."

A pert sparrow of a woman was with her, wearing a black Eddie Bauer safari jacket, black denims, and sandals. And carrying a camera. Her finger and toenails were painted the color of raisins, chestnut hair cropped close as a boy's.

"Hi," the girl said, offering her hand. "Megan Keyes, with the *County Herald*. Sheriff Wolinski, nice to see you. Looks like a story with a happy ending for a change. Can I get a picture of all of you together?"

"Hold off, Meg," Wolinski said. "I need a few minutes with Mr. Westbrook —"

"Why?" Brenda demanded. "You'd best not be thinking about arresting him for a damn thing, sport. Unless you're ready to check into this place yourself."

Wolinski hesitated, eyeing the two women. Megan held up a small microphone and switched on the recorder on her belt. "Are you considering charges, Sheriff? If so, what would they be?"

"No, I guess not," Wolinski said, covering the mike. "Mister Westbrook made an error in judgment, but considering the circumstances, we'll let it pass. No pictures of me with him, though, Meg. He's your story. Especially if you do your homework. I'm glad things turned out okay for you, ma'am. Let's go, Jess." The two lawmen wheeled and walked away.

"No pictures of me either," Brenda said. "Not till I get cleaned up some. Me and my buddy here look like we been hauled through a knothole ass backwards, which is damn close to the truth. Lemme find a john. I'll be right back."

"I'll go with you," Megan offered, hurrying along in her wake. "We can talk on the way. Don't leave, Mr. Westbrook."

I didn't. Instead I stood there a moment, thinking, common sense warring with conscience. Common sense lost.

"Sheriff, wait up a minute. There's something else you should know."

"Yeah?" Wolinski and his deputy turned, waiting for me to catch up. "Like what?"

"There was a body down there. In the well."

"What kind of a body? Man? Woman?"

"I don't know. It was a skeleton, actually. Tangled up in some roots."

"Are you sure it was human?" Jessup put in. "Could it have been an animal, maybe?"

"I'm a vet. I'd know the difference."

"You say it's tangled in some roots?" Wolinski said, chewing the corner of his lip. "Are you sure it was there at all?"

"It was dark, I had no flashlight, and I was worried about getting the kid out. It's possible I could have been mistaken."

"But you don't think so," Wolinski asked, reading my eyes.

"No. I'm pretty sure of what I saw."

"Do we have anybody missing, Jess?"

"No sir. Just the usual wants and warrants."

"Any idea how old this thing might be, Westbrook?"

I considered that a moment. "Old, I think. I didn't see any clothing on it, not even rags. But it was dark."

"Yeah, I guess it was," Wolinski said, eyeing me thoughtfully. "Just so we understand each other, I'm going to ask you one time, straight up. When some guys get out of the joint, they like to jerk cops around. Sort of a payback. Is anything like that going on with you, Westbrook? If there is, you'd best say so now."

I shook my head.

"Okay," Wolinski nodded. "Where are you staying?"

"At the barn on McCrae Road. There are living quarters upstairs."

"I know. You said you were working when you heard Miz Jozwiak yell?"

"I was on a ladder, painting."

"At the McCrae place?"

"That's right. Why?"

"Because the McCrae property must be ten miles from where we found your Jeep. That lady's got a helluva set of lungs, but ten miles? Nobody can yell that far. How do you explain that?"

"I don't know. A trick of the wind?"

"More like a miracle than a trick," Wolinski snorted. "Still, I guess it worked out. As for the rest of this, you stay close to home, you hear? We'll be in touch. Real soon."

After the law left, I found a men's room and promptly scared myself. Whoa. No wonder Wolinski figured me for one of America's Most Wanted.

I'm no male model at my best. Five-eleven, lanky, with a face my ex-wife once described as "more interesting than handsome." In my grimy painting duds with my mop matted with mud, I looked like a Wookie on a bad hair day.

Shucking my shirt, I began soaping my arms in the basin.

The door boomed open.

"Hey, are you decent?" Brenda said peering in. "Yeah, you look decent to me." She lumbered into the bathroom, grabbed me around the waist, hoisted me off the floor, and waltzed me around the cubicle. In the doorway, Megan Keyes raised her camera.

"Hold it." Megan shot a couple of quick flash photos.

"Hey, come on," I protested. "Snapshots in a men's room?"

"I promise to crop out the urinal if we can do the interview now."

"Give us a minute," Brenda said, looking up into my face. "Look, I feel really stupid, but in all the craziness I've forgotten your name."

"David Westbrook. Dave."

"I'm Brenda. Thank you, Dave. Thanks for helping me." Lowering me gently to the tiles, she gathered me into a brawny hug. We stood in silence a long moment, sharing body warmth, both shakier than we'd realized.

"It sounds corny as hell but I really don't know how to repay you," Brenda said, stepping back. "There's no way."

"No charge." I swallowed. "I'm just glad I could help. You've got a great kid there. Never cried, kept his head the whole time."

"It happened so fast," she said wonderingly, as much to herself as to me. "I closed my eyes a second, and he was just . . . gone. Like he'd been snatched down under the earth or something." Her voice was quivering, a hiccup away from hysteria.

"He came through it okay," Megan said hastily. "Don't make yourself crazy, now. What did the doctors say?"

"He's gonna be fine," Brenda said, brightening. "His collarbone's broke so he'll be in a cast awhile, but otherwise he's okay, thank God."

"How did he fall?" Megan asked.

"Weren't there warning signs around the well?"

"Signs? Hell, there wasn't even a well," Brenda said. "I've played in that meadow a thousand times with my brothers. Tag, football, soccer, we stomped over every damn foot of that ground. There was no hole there."

"It was only a few feet across and covered with debris," I said. "Bobby just had the bad luck to step in the wrong spot."

"But it's an empty damn field," Brenda insisted. "I wouldn't of let Bobby play there if I thought for a second there was any danger. What's a well doing in the middle of noplace?"

"Maybe we'll turn something up when we research the story," Megan offered. "I'm more interested in what happened today."

"A miracle happened," Brenda said fervently, punching me in the shoulder. "This sumbitch pulled off a fuckin' miracle."

Megan grinned up from her notes. "Do you mind if I paraphrase that? Just a little?"

Chapter 4

Sweat dripping in my eyes, I squinted at the bubble in the center of the level. There. The two-by-four stud was exactly vertical. Bracing my boot against it, I was tapping a casing nail in at an angle when the room darkened.

A tall man was in the doorway, the sun at his back, blocking my light. "You the new vet I been readin' about in the paper? The hotshot hero?"

"I'm Dr. Westbrook. Can I help you?" The voice was oddly familiar but the face was so weathered it took me a moment to place it. "Uncle Bass?"

"I'm surprised you remember." He didn't offer to shake hands. Nor did I. "You've grown some. Last time I saw you was after some high school race. Cross-country. Ten years ago?"

"Something like that. I don't remember the year but the race was a three-mile, cross-country. I finished second. How are you?"

"Not bad. At least I'm not in jail."

"Neither am I. Not anymore. And I'm kind of busy so . . . was there something you wanted?"

"I wouldn't say no to a beer."

"That's not what I meant."

"I know." He sauntered in, eyeing my handiwork. Half a head taller than me and just as lanky, dressed for labor: blue flannel shirt, jeans, sweat-stained John Deere cap. A three-day stubble bristled sharply silver against his workingman's tan. Gaunt, angular face, ice blue eyes narrowed by the sun, pinched in the corners. My father's half brother. And his only enemy.

"You do pretty fair work. Ever swing a hammer for wages?"

"I worked construction to help pay for college and I'm in the middle of something here, so . . . ?"

"Your dad called me," he said abruptly. "A couple months before he died."

"Really? What did he want?"

"I don't know. I told him to fuck off. I was half in the bag at the time. Figured he'd call back but he never did. I didn't know about him havin' cancer. I'm sorry."

"About what? That he's dead or that you blew him off?"

47

"Both. But mostly about the phone call. We hadn't talked in a lot of years, so it had to be important for him to call me. I been thinkin' on it since. Figure he wanted me to look out for you."

"Why on earth would you think that?"

"Because you've always been a wild dog. Like me. You even wound up in jail like me. About the only thing you've got goin' is you're good with animals. Like me."

"I didn't know you'd done time."

"It's not something a man brags about. I did three years in a prison camp in Vietnam, Hanoi Hilton. Spent a couple stretches on the county too. I know a little about jailin'. Like it's a lot easier to stay in than stay out."

"Not for me. I made a stupid mistake. I had a long time to think about it. I'm not going back."

"Glad to hear it. Looks like you could use some help here."

"The way you helped my dad when he called?"

"That's how it was with us. Bad karma, bad timing, whatever. Look, I can't make things right with your old man. Too late. Maybe you and I can do better."

"Why should we?"

"Because it's what your dad wanted."

"You don't know that. And I don't need a babysitter."

"Do I look like a babysitter to you, stud?"

No. He looked more like a roughneck, blue-collar saloon brawler. Which is what he was. Or so I'd been told.

"The thing is, Uncle Bass, my dad didn't like you much. And he was a pretty fair judge of character."

"Can't argue with that. Your old man was always sensible. Maybe that's why he stayed home while I went off to save America from the North Vietnamese or whoever."

"Was that the trouble between you two?"

"That doesn't matter now. It's over. You're an educated man, been to college and all. Didn't they teach you about lookin' a gift horse in the mouth?"

"I don't think we covered that, no."

"Then it's time you did. Look, you came north for a new start. Maybe I need one too. You're my nephew and you can use some help. I'm offerin' to do what I can, when I can, no charge."

"I don't like owing people."

"Christ on a bicycle, David, you don't — all right, all right." He waved off my objections. "Tell you what, I've got a farm at the west end of the county. I keep a saddle horse and some huntin' dogs. I'll help you get started here, you treat my animals for free until you figure we're even. That fair enough?"

"Yes," I admitted. "It's more than fair."

"Good. I drive truck for a living so I'm gone a lot, but I'll work between runs. What's all that fuckin' blood in your driveway? Looks like a cow fell off your roof. Helluva way to attract customers."

"It's red paint and I don't have any customers yet."

"You got one now," he said, glancing over his shoulder as a V-8 engine rumbled to a halt out front. "Whoa. Maybe not. Are you in some kinda trouble, boy?"

"Not that I'm aware of. Why?"

"Because the law just pulled up," he said. "My, my, you do work fast."

Chapter 5

A gleaming black pickup truck screeched to a halt beside the prowl car just as Wolinski climbed out. The pickup was macho-ed to the max: blackout windows, oversized tires, a roof rack of halogen lights over the cab. A tough truck, something an outlaw biker might drive.

Or a reporter. Megan Keyes hopped down from the pickup like a pixie popping out of a tank turret. Same correspondent's uniform: safari jacket, shorts, sandals, sunglasses. Cute as a speckled pup.

The woman with her climbed out more slowly. Taller, older, chestnut hair showing a little gray. Pain lines around her mouth. Blue blouse and slacks, L.L.Bean walking boots. Her silver-headed cane wasn't a fashion accessory. She used it with every step.

Wolinski looked like business as usual, steely brush cut cropped boot camp short, tan summer uniform with knife-edge creases. Cop's eyes.

I stepped out, brushing the sawdust from my hands. "Hi, folks. What's up?"

"You, if you're not careful, Westbrook," Meg said with mock annoyance. "Why didn't you mention you saw a body down that well? In this town, corpses do qualify as news."

"Brenda was upset about her son. I didn't want to make it worse. Sorry about that."

"Apology accepted. As long as we can talk about it now."

"What about it?"

"That's what we need to know," Wolinski said. "Mind if we step inside?" It wasn't a request.

"Not at all, if you don't mind sawdust." I held the door as they trooped in. Wolinski winced when he saw Bass.

"You hiring out for construction work now, Bascomb? Or do you know the Doc here from . . . somewhere special?"

"David's my nephew."

"Why am I not surprised?" Wolinski sighed. "We'll cut right to it, Westbrook. This lady is Daryl Keyes, the editor of the *Herald*."

"My sister and also my boss," Meg put in.

"Hi." Daryl's handshake was a feather

touch. Knuckles distorted by arthritis.

"The newspaper's been here longer than the town," Wolinski said. "My office doesn't list any current missing persons but Daryl came up with two possibles from her back files. You don't mind answering a few questions, right?" Again, not a request.

"Ask away. I'm a little curious myself."

"Let's begin with the well," Daryl said. "You're sure it was a well? Not a root cellar or a foundation?"

"Definitely a well. Six or seven feet across, built with fitted fieldstones. The boy was clinging to a rock that had bulged out at the waterline. He was one lucky kid."

"How far down would you guess the body was?"

I thought a moment. "At the same level as the boy. Ten to twelve feet. Seemed deeper at the time."

"I'll bet it did. Were any artifacts near it? A rifle, perhaps. Or steel traps?"

"I didn't see anything like that but it was dark, I could have missed it. I was more concerned about getting Bobby Jozwiak out of there. Why?"

"In the late fifties, a trapper disappeared in that area. A man named Zeke Chabot. He was a poacher, probably running an illegal trap line. His wife said he went out one night to check his traps and never came back. They did a thorough search at the time but didn't find a thing. His wife said Zeke was carrying his rifle and some steel leg traps."

"I would have noticed a rifle, I think. There was nothing else near the body."

"Good," she smiled, "because my other candidate is a lot more interesting. There was a farm on that land at one time, a house and barn built during the Civil War. In the 1870s a woman named Rachel Hayes bought the property and worked it with her daughter, Hannah. Until they disappeared. Do you know anything about the Great Fires?"

"Just odds and ends from school. Forest fires, right?"

"Forest fires burn trees. The Great Fires burned everything. Two and a half million acres in Michigan went up, including most of this county. Forty towns were leveled, more than a thousand people died."

"Good lord," Wolinski frowned. "That many?"

"That estimate is probably low. When the towns burned, all records were lost, so there was a lot of guesswork afterward. Plus, there were a great many transients in those days, migrant farm workers, lumberjacks. If the

54

fires caught them in the open, there was no trace of them afterward. The Hayes farm disappeared in the fire of October, 1871. Rachel Hayes and her daughter vanished with it."

"Burned?"

"Probably. No one actually knows what happened to them. There were no phones or radios in those days, no way to warn anyone or call for help. And the fires moved with incredible speed."

"What caused them?"

"Greed. When the lumber barons logged off the forests, they didn't bother to clean up their litter. Millions of acres were littered with slash, branches, and sawdust. The kind of tinder you'd use to kindle a campfire, as flammable as gasoline. A lightning strike, sparks from a train, and the slash exploded into firestorms that tore across the country faster than a horse could gallop. The heat was so intense that boats a mile offshore burst into flames. Railroad tracks twisted like pretzels. At Metz, a rescue train derailed and fifteen women and children in a metal freight car were roasted alive — My God! What on earth is that!"

A small, twisted feline stood unsteadily in the doorway, fangs bared, hissing at us. He was minus his right foreleg and a patch of scar tissue covered his right eye.

"This is Frankenkat," I said, scooping up the battered tom. "He doesn't see too well. Makes him edgy around strangers."

"Franken— ?"

"Frankenkat. Named for obvious reasons. He was run over by a car, lost a leg and an eye, but I stitched him back together and he's still all cat. Aren't you, fella?"

Frank cocked his head, hissed at me, then tried to squirm free. I scratched the scar over his eye and he relaxed, nestling in the crook of my arm. "Please go on about the fires," I prompted. "I had no idea they were that bad."

"It's hard to imagine now, but in rural areas, people like Rachel Hayes just disappeared. Her neighbors couldn't even find the road to her farm afterward, much less her house. All the landmarks were gone. Photographs from those days look like Hiroshima after the bomb. Scorched earth and ashes for hundreds of miles. Total annihilation. And the odd thing is, Rachel Hayes warned people it was coming."

"How do you mean, warned them?" Bass asked.

"She was apparently the local, one-woman version of Greenpeace in those days. She wrote letters to the paper, spoke out against the loggers at village council meetings. It was a risky position to take at the time, especially for a woman. Logging was the biggest industry in the area and the timber companies had a lot of clout."

"How much clout did they have after they burned down half the state?"

"Quite a bit. Apparently they had spin doctors back then too. The loggers blamed Rachel for the fires. Claimed she started them to prove her point and got caught when they burned out of control."

"Was there any truth to it?" Wolinski asked.

"Not likely. The fire began twenty miles south of her farm. Still, she was a woman alone, an outsider speaking up against the county's biggest companies. It was easier to blame her than look in a mirror. Even today, when there's an unexplained fire, locals still joke about Rachel Hayes."

"Some people ain't joking," Bass put in. "Drive around the back country, sometime. You'll see a lotta burned-out farms."

"Vandals," Wolinski snorted. "Nothing supernatural about it."

"The thing is, Doctor," Daryl said, her eyes locking on mine, "that well you found is the first trace of the Hayes farm anyone's seen in over a century. And when the fires overran them, some people took refuge in their wells."

"Their wells?"

"Everything was burning, where else could they go? They hoped the water would save them. A few survived, but most died of smoke inhalation or drowned. In their wells."

"I see." And I was beginning to. "So you think the body I saw might be this . . . Rachel Hayes?"

"It's at least possible. Perhaps her little girl is there too. Or maybe it's the missing poacher, Zeke Chabot."

"That's assuming he actually saw anything," Wolinski said.

"Well, when can we find out?" Meg asked impatiently. "How soon can you recover the body, Stan?"

"I can't recover it at all, Meg," Wolinski said mildly. "Cold corpses are even more trouble than warm ones. We have to determine the race of the remains —"

"Race?" she interrupted. "What difference does that make?"

"If the remains are Native American and there's no evidence of foul play, jurisdiction passes to the Three Fires Council."

"You've lost me," I said. "What do the tribes have to do with this?"

"Under Michigan law, all Native American remains are protected by statute. Years back, people used to dig up Indian graves and sell the relics to museums or curio shops. Called it archaeology, but it was grave robbing, pure and simple."

"But this isn't a grave," I pointed out. "The body's down a well."

"Which is where it'll stay until I can organize a proper recovery. The county coroner has to sign off on the age of the remains, I have to determine no crime is involved, the tribes' cultural archaeologist has to certify the bodies aren't Native American, and the state has to take an infra-red aerial photo of the site to make sure we haven't blundered onto an old cemetery."

"It's a well, Stan," Meg repeated.

"Meg, it wouldn't matter if it was a freaking pyramid. Recoveries of historical remains have to be supervised by a state-certified anthropologist. A prof named Tipton from the University of Michigan handles most of them, and he's a pain in the ass unless everything's strictly by the book."

"But it's been at least fifty years and maybe a hundred," Megan protested. "Why not get them out and sort out the paperwork afterward?"

"Because any site with unidentified remains is a crime scene until determined otherwise. Granted, this sounds more like a job for Indiana Jones than a coroner, but that's not my call to make. Or yours."

"Point taken, Stan. When can you move on this?"

"Give me a couple of days to contact everybody. And Doc, I want you there to show Professor Tipton exactly what you saw. A recovery like this is an expensive operation. I don't want any misunderstandings."

"Sorry, but I've got too much work to do here."

"Think of it as a civic duty, Doc. The paper's made you a local hero for rescuing the Jozwiak kid. You don't want to disappoint folks now. Especially me. And I really think you should help out."

"He'll be there," Bass said, stifling my objection with a look.

"Glad to hear it. I'll give you a call when the arrangements are set. Gotta go, take care folks."

Megan was eyeing me curiously.

"What?"

"Nothing," she said. "Not a thing."

Chapter 6

After they left, Bass and I had words. But not many. He apologized for volunteering my services as a grave robber. And I conceded it was the right thing to do. The publicity would be good for the clinic. And whoever the corpse was, the poacher or Rachel Hayes, the bottom of a well's a bad place to spend forever.

On the bright side, my remodeling job promptly picked up speed. Bass showed up early and worked hard. Drove his nails true and ran electrical cables with perfect ninety-degree turns, wired exactly to code. No shortcuts, no cobbling.

No chatter either. Bass was no talker. Nor am I. Not anymore. Mostly we worked in silence, communicating with nods or an occasional grunt. Not necessarily a bad thing. You learn more about people from the work they do than anything they say.

Talk is cheap, as the saying goes. And no

good deed goes unpunished.

Wolinski called two days later. The county's official effort to recover the bodies was set. He also said half the agencies in the state would be there. I thought he was kidding.

When I arrived at the well site, a county cruiser was blocking the entrance and a lanky deputy impatiently waved me off. I waved back, then drove around him into the field.

And into a mob scene. An Algoma Fire Department Emergency van was parked near the well, flashers blazing. Having an EMT tech on hand was a wise precaution, but I couldn't imagine why its strobes were on. The bones in the well wouldn't be needing mouth-to-mouth.

The van was flanked by a hearse, a police cruiser, two school buses, a white NewsChannel 6 van, and a dozen more civilian vehicles. Rachel Hayes and the poacher may have died alone but one of them was coming back in high style. All we needed was a roller coaster to make the carnival complete. With coffins for cars.

An unruly mob of high school students was clustered around the well, joshing around while a harried teacher tried to keep order. Meg was standing with Sheriff Wolinski in a group near the hearse watching a TV reporter from NewsChannel 6 interview a heavyset Native American. A contrast in styles.

The newsman was impeccably decked out in a Channel 6 green blazer with matching tie, his coif sprayed neatly into place, not a follicle moving despite a brisk breeze.

The Indian was in faded denims, his gray mane tied back in a ponytail, a turquoise necklace draped around his bull neck.

Meg waved me over as the TV crew finished filming.

"And here's the man who started it all," Meg said, taking my arm, introducing me around. "Dr. Dave Westbrook, this is George Black Elk, the state cultural archaeologist. The carrot-top who looks like Huck Finn's cousin is Toby Mallette, a funeral director who also doubles as our county coroner —"

"Excuse me. Can we get started before these gawkers trample everything? I'm Carter Tipton, Professor of Anthropology, University of Michigan, Dr. Westbrook." Short, balding, with nearly invisible eyebrows, Tipton used a handshake to steer me away from the others. "I understand you discovered the remains?"

"More or less."

"What's the physical scene like below? I scanned it but couldn't see much."

"It's a well, lined with fieldstone, maybe twelve feet to the waterline —"

"Thirteen feet, five inches, actually. Quite a deep well for that era. They dug them by hand, fitting the stones as they went. Dangerous work."

"It'll be tricky today too. The walls of the well are dank and slippery. I brought a ladder so we can —"

"No need for it," Tipton interrupted. "I plan to rappel down. Less impact on the site that way."

"Bad idea. I've done some rock climbing. The well opens up below the surface. A line will dislodge debris from above every time you move."

He considered that a moment, then nodded sharply, like a bird nipping a seed. "Very well, we'll use a ladder. Did you disturb the remains? Move the body at all?"

"No. It was about four feet from the boy. He wasn't aware it was there, so I kept clear of it."

"Well, that's something at least. I may be able to date the site from peripheral evidence. Amateur diggers are more destructive than grave robbers."

"I wasn't digging for anything," I said

mildly. "We were trying to rescue a kid. Look, the sheriff asked me to show you what I found. If you've got a problem with that, take it up with him."

"I've no objection to your assistance, Doctor. As long as we're clear on the chain of command. I have full authority from the university to make this recovery. With or without amateur help. You're welcome to tag along if you do as you're told. Do we understand each other?"

"Absolutely. Except for the part where I tell you to lighten up on the attitude. I didn't ask for this job and you wouldn't be here if amateurs hadn't found the site. If you don't want my help, fine. I'll take my ladder and go home."

Reddening to the top of his fringed dome, Tipton was one second from ripping into me when he realized we'd attracted an audience. Meg, Wolinski, and the TV people were looking on.

"No need to get testy, Westbrook," Tipton said, visibly suppressing his temper, "perhaps I was a bit abrupt. But if this corpus dates from the nineteenth century, it could be an important find. Let's get on with it, shall we?"

I waited.

"Please," he added, almost spitting the

word. He probably didn't use it often.

"No problem. What do you want me to do?"

"You can help with the equipment, that sort of thing. We'd better get dressed."

Stalking over to a blue Ford Safari with U of M plates, Tipton began climbing into a full-blown scuba diving outfit: neoprene wet suit, goggles, and life jacket.

I stripped down to a T-shirt and cutoffs and swapped my work boots for tennis shoes. George Black Elk gave me a hand lifting the ladder off my Jeep and carrying it to the well.

"Don't mind Tip," Black Elk said, as we carefully lowered the ladder down into the dark. "He can be a little stuffy but it's not personal. He's just —"

"A pompous asshole?" Meg put in.

"Pretty much," Black Elk grinned. "But he's damned good at his job."

We ran out of ladder before we reached the bottom. Black Elk's eyes met mine a moment. "How deep is this sucker, anyway?"

"Thirteen feet to the water. Below that, I don't know."

"Better hope you don't find out," he grunted, lashing the top rung to the tent stakes. He double-checked the knots. So

66

did I. Rock solid. Good.

"Would you mind taking a few shots while you're down there?" Meg asked, draping a waterproof Minolta digital camera around my neck. "Just aim it and press this button. And don't drop it, please. It cost more than my car."

Tipton waved me over to hold a wire mesh collection tray while he attached a pulley assembly to it with nylon line.

"Is that what you're wearing, Westbrook? We're headed underground, not to Daytona for spring break."

"The well's pretty rancid. You might have trouble rinsing the stench out of that suit."

"That's why God created grad students," he sniffed. "You're going to get chilly down there. The water's nine degrees Centigrade at the surface, seven at the bottom."

"I don't plan on getting wet. This is your show, sport. And the body's high and dry at the waterline."

"Always best to be prepared," he said, tugging on a bright yellow neoprene helmet that coordinated with his suit. "Shall we have at it?"

He didn't wait for my reply. Sliding a halogen headband helmet lamp over his forehead, Tipton clipped the pulley to the top rung of the ladder, then started down, carrying the tray. I gave him a minute, then shoved Meg's waterproof camera under my shirt to keep it from swinging, took a deep breath, a last look at the sky, then followed Tipton down before I could change my mind.

Down and down, into the underworld.

Chapter 7

Roots brushed at me near the surface, but quickly thinned out. Climbing down the ladder definitely beat slithering down a nylon tent hand over hand. And it also helped that I knew what to expect. Sort of.

The fieldstones were fitted to one another so tightly I doubted you could slide a scalpel between the seams. Slick as a brick outhouse. Or a tomb, I suppose.

After pausing to snap a couple of quick pictures, I continued down toward the bulged wall section where Bobby'd clung to life. Below me, Tipton's lamp flickered eerily, reflecting multiple rays off the damp stones.

He stopped at the waterline to look over the site, then eased into the water and thrust himself to the outcropping that held the remains. So much for needing me as a guide.

I stayed dry, waiting where the ladder met the water a few feet from the corpse. Too close for comfort. In the greenish halogen glow, the skeleton looked like a nightmare, the bones stained from decades of dripping sediment, teeth shattered.

"Fractures," Tipton said softly, indicating breaks on the leg and lower mandible. "Broke his leg and dislocated his jaw in the fall."

"His jaw?"

"From the size of the humerus and phalanges, I make this an adult male in his late twenties at time of death. Can't see enough of the pelvis to be absolutely certain, but he's probably the missing poacher. Damn."

"What's wrong?"

"I was hoping to find the woman. Nineteenth century skeletal remains undamaged by preservatives like formaldehyde or alcohol are very rare."

"There's something next to his left ileum, buried in the mud," I said, pointing. "Looks like metal. See it?"

Tipton wiggled the object a moment, then lifted it clear. A rusty steel trap, its chain dangling.

"Leg trap," I said. "Fox, beaver, or coyote. Cruel, but effective. Assuming the animal doesn't ruin the pelt by chewing off its own ankle to escape. You're right, it's the poacher."

"Ironic, isn't it?" Tipton said.

"What?"

"He fell down this old well, couldn't climb out or even call for help. Nothing to do but wait to die. I wonder how many help-less animals he put in the same situation?" Tipton wiggled the leg trap for emphasis.

"I don't care much for trapping either, but people don't run trap lines for sport around here. It puts food on the table."

"I wonder if he thought lunch was worth it?" Tipton snorted.

"Probably not. They said he had a rifle with him. I'll check for it below."

"Go ahead. I'll have our poacher out of the mud in a few minutes. No need to stand on ceremony, there's nothing special about him." Using a small trowel from his tool belt, Tipton began loosening the bones from the soil.

I played my light around the ledge, then began working it down methodically, one row of fieldstones at a time. The water had a coppery tint, transparent as a picture window. Its clarity made the depth decep-tive. By counting fieldstones, I could tell it was roughly twelve feet deep but the bottom seemed much closer, almost shallow enough to stand in.

Unfortunately, the water's mirror surface

reflected too much light. I couldn't see the bottom clearly. I'd have to go lower. Damn.

Climbing down to the bottom rung, I winced as the bone-chilling water crept over my calves, then up to my waist.

I locked an elbow around a rung, leaned out, and pointed the flashlight beam directly below. The well pit leapt up in bold relief.

I'd expected a jumble of trash but it looked oddly pristine. A fuzzy layer of brown silt covered the bottom like shag carpet, dimpled in spots where debris had tumbled into it, probably rocks I knocked down during my first visit. Otherwise, it appeared to be unmarked, perhaps undisturbed since the Great Fire sealed it off.

Not much to see. A circular shape that looked like the bottom of a bucket, a few branches, that was about it.

A wave of relief suffused me, but it was tinged with regret. I guess I'd been hoping to find them, the lost lady and her little girl. But they weren't here. I wondered what really happened to them all those years ago? Had the fire trapped them in their house? Or perhaps swept over them as they fled . . .

A ragged tangle of branches against the northern wall caught my eye. It didn't resemble human remains, but something about its shape seemed oddly familiar. Couldn't see it clearly. Too much silt.

Bracing myself on the ladder, I swung my feet free and kicked hard for a minute or two, churning the water to a froth.

Tipton glanced curiously at me. I shook my head and he went back to his work.

The bottom vanished as the swirling cloud of silt roiled upward. I held my position on the ladder, hovering above the murk like a ghost.

Gradually, the silt began settling again, revealing the shapes on the bottom more clearly than before. The ring was definitely the base of a metal bucket. The odd jumble . . .

Sweet Jesus!

It was a skull. Human. Teeth bared in a final grin, lying on its side, eye sockets staring into infinity. But what on earth was the rest of it? Swallowing hard, I peered down through the clouded water, trying to get a better angle, to make sense of what I was seeing.

Because the torso wasn't human at all.

"Is something wrong?" Tipton asked.

"Yeah," I said, swallowing. "You need to take a look at this."

Shifting around, Tipton read my face first, then peered below. Adding his helmet lamp to my flashlight glow didn't change anything. The skeleton wasn't distorted by shadows. The skull was clearly human but the torso was outsized and monstrously twisted, crouching on the floor of the pit in the deep-December darkness.

I've had extensive classes in both human and animal anatomy, but I couldn't make this shape compute.

"My God," Tipton breathed, his eyes alight. "What do we have here? The elephant man? An alien?"

"I don't know." A sudden shiver snapped me out of my daze. My legs were going numb. The icy water was getting to me. Or maybe the shape on the floor was.

"Take some photographs," Tipton ordered. "I want a record of this. We'll get the other stiff up and out of the way. Then I'll see to this one."

Right. Raising the camera, I set the strobe and began photographing the creature on the bottom from varying angles. Tipton hastily wrenched the poacher's skeleton out of the soil, piling the bones on the tray.

"Hurry it up, Westbrook. I need a hand with this."

I took one last shot, then grabbed the pulley rope and began hauling the tray upward while Tipton kept pace with it on the ladder, steadying the load.

At the top, Tipton thrust the tray out through the opening, then scrambled after it.

I took one final photograph before starting up. It seemed important to record this moment properly. It was an historic occasion.

The body count for the Great Fire of '71 had just risen by one.

The question was, one what?

Chapter 8

A jostling mob was already clustered around the poacher's skeleton when I climbed out of the hole. Mallette and Black Elk were kneeling by the remains, looking it over carefully.

Meg joined me at the edge of the crowd, eyes shining with excitement. "Pretty macabre. Are you okay? You look a little green."

"I'm fine. What's going on?"

"George and Toby are taking measurements to determine the race of the skeleton. Tipton said there's another body down there? Rachel Hayes?"

"I honestly don't know what it is, Meg. I —"

"Doctor Westbrook? Could we get moving, please?" Tipton said, handing me a second recovery tray. He'd already strapped on a scuba air tank and a face-mask to go with his wet suit. A bantamweight Jacques Cousteau.

I almost told him where to stick his tray. I'd had more than enough of that hole and of him.

But I was curious about the body in the well too. Lost woman, Martian, or whatever, it didn't belong in that reeking pit.

So I waved off Meg's questions, trotted after Tipton like a pet puppy, following him back to the last place in the world I wanted to be.

Tipton was already at the waterline when I started down. Pausing on the bottom rung, he adjusted his face-mask and checked the draw on his air tank. He clipped the floodlight to the ladder, switched it on. And stepped off. Free-falling slowly down to the pit of the well. I stopped just above the waterline, holding the wire mesh tray. Below me, the floodlight lit up the well floor like a museum displaying a grotesque work of art.

Title: Soul in Agony.

If Tipton was affected by the distorted humanity of the corpse, he gave no sign. Adjusting his flotation jacket to neutral buoyancy, he began waving the loose silt away from the skeleton with his hands.

The water around him clouded, leaching out the color, giving the scene the grainy look of an old black-and-white film. He waited patiently for the roiled silt to settle out, then began brushing soil from the bones with a small whisk. Grim work. And slow. But as more of the body emerged from the mire, the mystery of its alien shape only deepened. For a moment, something about it flickered in the back of my memory. A sense that I'd seen it before somewhere. Which was damned unlikely. And yet . . . nothing. Couldn't put a finger on it.

I settled for taking a few photos, then made myself as comfortable as I could on the ladder and settled in to wait.

Totally focused on his tedious job, I doubt Tipton even knew I was there.

Fifteen minutes passed. Twenty. Tipton kept grimly at it, working like a machine. But after nearly half an hour of hanging from the ladder like a bat, I was beginning to stiffen up.

Tried flexing my shoulders and shifting around to keep warm. No help. The chill of the damp stones was settling into my soul. It had to be far worse for Tipton, immersed in the icy water.

Only his hands were moving, rifling the soil beneath the bones with a thin plastic probe, then carefully whisking it away.

"Yo! Professor Tipton? Are you all right?"

No response. Perhaps he hadn't heard.

Perhaps he was being a dork.

"Professor?" Tipton waved me off impatiently without looking up. I decided to give him another five minutes before bailing out to get warm. No point in both of us dying of hypothermia down here — Tipton eased away from the skeleton and gently thrust himself to the surface.

"Marvelous condition," he said, spitting out his mouthpiece. "Absolutely pristine."

"Terrific. What the hell is it?"

"That's the best part. I'm not sure. It's clearly human, probably female, but beyond that?" He gave a shrug that turned into a fierce shiver that racked his shoulders. His cheeks were bloodless and his lips had an unhealthy bluish tinge.

"Are you sure you're okay, Professor? Maybe we should take a breather before —"

"If you're cold, go back up," he snapped. "I don't really need you anyway. Now give me the damned tray and let's get on with this. My air tank's running low."

His common-courtesy tank wasn't exactly brimming either, but I was too cold to argue. I passed the mesh tray down to him instead. His hands were trembling as he took it. Excitement or hypothermia? Hard to say. Resetting his mouthpiece, he sank beneath the surface again.

"You're welcome," I called after him. And realized my voice was as shaky as his. Tipton might be tougher than he looked, but I was definitely crowding my limits, shivering like a hen in a hailstorm. And not just from the cold.

The fetid air and darkness were beginning to weigh on me. Reminding me how many years of my life I'd wasted in places I really didn't want to be.

After carefully positioning the tray next to the skeletal remains on the bottom, Tipton worked his hands beneath the bones, then shifted them onto the mesh with exquisite care.

He glanced up, and even through the mask and roiling silt I could read the triumph in his eyes.

Tweaking the CO_2 cartridge on his vest to increase his buoyancy, he floated slowly up from the shadows, carrying his grim prize on the tray like a ghoulish waiter.

They broke the surface together, Tipton's face only inches from the skull. "Take a photograph," he panted. "I want a record of this."

Raising the camera, I took two quick shots, then lowered it again. The skeleton was intact. The skull seemed normal but the torso was terribly distorted, bulging below the collarbone. If this was Rachel Hayes, I couldn't imagine what she'd looked like in life.

Tipton didn't look much better. His face was chalk white and his eyes were closing involuntarily. Borderline hypothermia. We'd been down here too damned long.

"Time to move out, Professor. You go first. I'll carry the tray."

He started to object but didn't have the juice. "All right, but please be careful," he said, reluctantly passing the tray over. "The structure is extremely fragile."

"So are we. Let's get up in the sun before somebody sends a tray down for us." Bracing myself against Bobby Jozwiak's rock, I let Tipton climb past me. And found myself face to face with Rachel Hayes.

Or rather, face to skull. An unnerving moment, staring into pits where eyes had been.

"Hey, Rachel, I'm Dave. Nice to meet you. I know this sounds like a line, but I think I know you from somewhere."

Tipton glared at me. Rachel was glaring already.

As we made our way upward, I grew more concerned about Tip. Every rung took him a bit longer, and at the top he barely had the energy to drag himself out.

"Let me go, I'm all right!" Tipton yapped like a terrier, when Black Elk tried to help him up. Crouching on his knees, he waited impatiently for me to emerge with the tray.

A hush fell over the group when I finally lifted the lost lady into the light. I didn't blame them. Even though I'd been observing the body for the past half hour, sunlight made the grotesque shape of the dripping bones even more shocking.

The crowd's silence had nothing to do with reverence for the dead. It was fear, raw, elemental. Fear of death? Partly. But mostly fear of . . . The Other.

Snatching the tray from me, Tipton carried it to the plastic sheet beside the poacher's remains.

I climbed out, stretching, grateful to feel sunlight again. Then followed the crowd to the hearse.

The TV newsman shoved a microphone at Tipton, asking him how he felt about opening a century-old tomb. Ignoring him, Tipton hovered over George Black Elk and the coroner as they examined the remains inch by inch.

Black Elk had a set of chrome calipers in his fist but made no move to use them. Instead, he simply stared into the eyeless sockets, much as I had, as if reading some message in them.

"Well?" Sheriff Wolinski asked. "What is it?"

"Caucasian," Black Elk said, getting slowly to his feet, still eyeing the skeleton. "Female. I think. Damn. What happened to her?"

"Nothing," Tipton breathed, his face flushed with excitement. "The skeleton's intact. She was born this way. What do you know about the Hayes woman?" he barked, whirling on Meg. "Did she have scoliosis?"

"Scoli— ?" Meg echoed, surprised.

"Scoliosis, kyphosis, rheumatoid arthritis," Tipton said, exasperated. "Any disease that could have distorted her frame like this?"

"I don't know —"

"Don't you have any photographs of her?"

"No, we didn't know that —"

"You haven't even looked? My God, don't you realize the importance of deformed skeletal remains? I expect incompetence from undergraduates, but you people are supposed to be professionals."

"Whoa, hold on a minute," Meg said. "I don't work for you."

"She looks okay to me," I said quietly.

"Don't venture opinions outside your area of expertise, Doctor," Tipton said, turning on me. "Clearly, she's —"

"It's not a she, Professor. It's a they. And this is my field of expertise."

Tipton stared at me, baffled. "What on earth are you talking about?"

"That bulge at mid sternum? It's an occipital plate. The back of a skull. On the righthand side, where her ribs seem to bulge out? That's actually a second rib cage. Canine."

"Canine?" Black Elk echoed. "What are you saying?"

"It's a dog. Or part of one. I thought it looked familiar. It should. I spent four years studying every bone of it. What we're seeing is a partial canine skeleton, fused to the female subject at the sternum. The lower extremities are missing. The spine apparently separated below the thorax and disintegrated. Possibly it was broken when she — excuse me — when they fell."

"I don't understand," Wolinski said. "How did she get tangled up with a dog?"

"They're not tangled, Sheriff, she's holding it. She probably died holding it. She jumped into the well to avoid the flames and their bodies sank to the well floor together. Over the years mineral deposits have fused them so seamlessly you can't tell where one ends and the other begins."

"What about it, Professor Tipton?" Wolinski asked. "Any truth to that?"

"He's . . . right," Tipton nodded, unable to hide his disappointment. "I found an animal hipbone in the silt but I ignored it. Superfluous. But once you lose the preconception of the single thorax, you can see where the second structure joins the first. An animal thorax."

"A dog," I put in. "From the narrow skull, probably a collie or a similar breed."

"A female Caucasian. And one small dog," Black Elk nodded. "The remains appear to be historic, a century old, perhaps more. Toby?"

Mallette nodded, his mouth a grim line. "I concur. At least a century."

"We're all in agreement then? The first set, adult Caucasian male. From the evidence and a quick check of the dental work, it's most likely the remains of Zeke Chabot, missing since 1955. This second set, Caucasian, female. Possibly the remains of one Rachel Hayes. God rest them both."

"God?" Carter Tipton snorted, with a rictus of a grin. "Don't you mean Manitou, George?"

"Screw yourself, Tip," Black Elk said quietly. "There's nothing remotely funny about this."

Tipton's reply was drowned out by the blaring of a car horn. A Mercedes convertible pulled into the field past the prowl cars. The driver vaulted out and shouldered his way angrily through the crowd. He was wearing a corduroy sport coat and jeans. His thinning blonde hair was military short. So was his temper.

"What the hell is going on? What are you people doing here?"

"Step back, please," Tipton snapped. "You're in my light."

"You step back, Shorty. You're trespassing on private . . ." His voice trailed off as he saw the skeletons on the ground. "Mother of God," he said softly. "What is all this?"

"Do you own this property?" Wolinski asked.

"My company does. My name's Sinclair, I manage a gravel pit just across the county line. The Osterhaus pit. We bought up this section a few months ago. What's all this about?"

"An anthropological recovery," Tipton said, rising. "You've apparently purchased an historic site, Mr. Sinclair. I'm Professor Tipton, University of Michigan. I trust we can count on your cooperation."

Sinclair ignored Tipton's hand. Or maybe not. Sinclair's own right hand had been replaced by a chromed utility pincer. "Let me get this straight, you're digging up bodies on my land without even asking?"

"We didn't dig for them, Mr. Sinclair," Tipton said. "We recovered them from an old well. One of them was probably a fire victim near the end of the last century."

"Fire? What the hell are you talking about?"

"If you'd paid attention in grade school, you'd know," Tipton sniffed. "Now if you don't mind, I have to get my specimen out of the air."

"Yeah, well I do mind," Sinclair said, blocking Tipton's path. "Maybe you didn't hear me, sport. My company owns this land. We didn't authorize any school projects and nobody's taking off with anything until I say so."

"The county doesn't need permission to recover bodies, Mr. Sinclair," Sheriff Wolinski said. "Any area where remains are found is technically a crime scene."

"But not anymore, Stan," Black Elk put in mischievously. "We've already declared the remains historic."

"All the more reason to examine them

under controlled conditions," Tipton said, exasperated.

"An autopsy?" Sinclair said, incredulous. "It's a little late for that, isn't it?"

"Not an autopsy, a biochemical analysis," Tipton snapped. "Bone composition, DNA analysis, and calcification tests can provide valuable insights into nineteenth century nutrition and disease. Even an illiterate should be able to grasp that!"

Sinclair eyed Tipton a moment, then shook his head slowly. "Maybe you can get away with talking to your students like that, Shorty, but we're not in school. Step aside, please. I'd like to see what all the fuss is about."

Tipton was rude but not crazy. He let Sinclair pass.

Kneeling beside the tray, Sinclair examined the skeletons more closely. He reached out, as if to cup the woman's cheek with his good hand, but didn't quite touch it. Then he rose slowly, shaking his head.

"Look at them," he said softly. "You can almost hear them screaming. This is wrong. These people don't belong in a lab."

"Not people," Tipton snapped. "They're skeletal remains. Specimens."

"Mister, I had friends who came back from Desert Storm in smaller pieces than this. We still buried them properly. And if they're only specimens, then they're mine, not yours. You're on private property."

"Don't be ridiculous. Why on earth would you want them?"

"I don't, but they were people once. If they have kin, then that's where they belong. Buried in a proper grave with their own around them. Not getting whacked apart in some laboratory."

"He's got a point, Carter," Wolinski said. "As soon as we confirm Chabot's identity, his remains will be turned over to his family for burial."

"U of M already has more stolen Ojibwa bones than your museums can catalog, Tip," Black Elk added. "If you want historic Caucasian bones, dig up a couple of alumnae. This lady waited a hundred years to be found. Why not let her rest?"

"Superstitious nonsense!" Tipton snapped. "Sheriff Wolinski, would you please inform these people that I've been authorized to take possession of the remains!"

"I can't. She's not a Jane Doe, Professor, she's been tentatively identified as one Rachel Hayes. The situation's a bit like a contractor plowing up a family plot. The remains are either reburied in place, which isn't an option here, or transferred to a mortuary pending notification of next of kin."

"That's absurd! I recovered this specimen and I'm taking it. Anyone who objects can take it up with the University's attorneys!" Kneeling, Tipton seized the tray of Rachel's remains. But as he rose, he wobbled, losing his balance.

And lost the skeleton as it slid off the tray. I grabbed for them as they fell, too late. The remains spilled into the dirt, and a connection that endured a century of darkness shattered into a grisly jumble of bone fragments. Gashing my wrist for good measure.

Tipton paled, so shaken I thought he might collapse.

"I'm sorry," he stammered. I couldn't tell if he was apologizing for my bleeding wrist or to Sinclair or the bones.

"Let it go, Tip," Black Elk said, wrapping an arm around the smaller man's shoulders, holding him up. "She's beyond caring. But you look a little shaky, my man. Come on, I've got a thermos in my car."

Toby Mallette, the freckled mortician, glanced at the sheriff. "I take it this . . . jumble just became my problem?"

"Hold Chabot's remains for his family," Wolinski nodded. "Store the other one the usual six months. Unless you're claiming her, Mr. Sinclair?"

"No, I don't want it, I just didn't . . . do

whatever seems right, Sheriff. I have to get back to work."

"Okay," Wolinski nodded, "she's all yours, Toby. I'll fax you the paperwork tomorrow. That's it, folks! The show's over and apparently we're on private property, so let's move along. Drive safely now."

Pulling on a pair of plastic gloves, Mallette unfurled a green rubber body bag and swept the bones into it like so much dog doo, then carried it to his hearse with the News 6 cameraman filming all the way. I felt like punching somebody, but didn't know who and hadn't the energy anyway. Instead I stalked to my Jeep, stripped off my shirt, and tossed it in back. Checked the gash on my wrist.

"Are you okay?" Megan asked.

"Hell no," I said, wincing as I smeared Bacitracin ointment in the cut. "You'd think after a hundred freaking years we could have handled this better."

"It was Tipton's fault, not yours. I thought for a second Sinclair might punch the little jerk's lights out. Pity. Would have made a boss story. Local landowner decks U of M dweeb. What did you make of Sinclair?"

"Probably okay if you like the rich, rough, and ready type."

"Rich?"

"Anybody who drives a Mercedes and runs a gravel company is rich by my standards. He's minus a wing. Did you notice?"

"I pretty much noticed everything about Mr. Sinclair," Meg said slyly. "I'd better interview him, up close and personal. I'll need some face time with you too, David."

"Me? What for?"

"About the well. What it was like, all the down and dirty details."

"We hauled up some old bones and dumped them in the dirt. Is that a story?"

"Of course." Dropping her voice an octave, Meg mimicked a hyper-earnest TV talking head. "Missing for more than a century, social activist Rachel Hayes suddenly reappeared today amid considerable controversy. Violence erupted as two schmucks nearly came to blows over her corpse, but in the end she was smashed to smithereens and bagged up like last week's trash."

"Along with her dog," I added.

"It's a perfect metaphor, David. In her own time Rachel couldn't vote or drink in a bar, and a hundred years later she's still getting kicked around."

"Right," I said, pulling on a clean T-shirt. "I know exactly how she feels."

Chapter 9

Driving south toward Ann Arbor in his University SUV, Carter Tipton felt ragged and raw. Exhausted from his hour at the bottom of the well digging out the skeleton. But most of all, angry.

What a fucking shambles! To work so hard on the recovery, such a valuable one, then end with nothing. Damn it!

A farm woman and a nineteenth century pet, remains uncontaminated by embalming fluid. A fantastic find! The skeletons could have generated overlapping grants for a half dozen studies: rural diet, arthritis, mineral retention, work-related injuries . . .

Lost. Thanks to the bungling of a few inbred rednecks. Who were probably related to the halfwit in the battered red pickup who'd been tailgating him for the past mile. Flicking his damned headlights for passing room. Idiot!

As the pickup pulled out to go around him, Tipton mashed the SUV's gas pedal. The big Ford surged ahead, easily leaving the pickup truck behind. But not for long.

Angered at being blown off, the pickup driver didn't slow or pull back in. Instead he stayed in the outside lane, goosing his gas pedal, giving Tipton the high beams as he came up behind him again, closing the gap.

Typical northwoods macho moron. Stupid enough to risk being killed or maimed playing tag on a two-lane highway. Ordinarily Tipton would have eased over and let Mr. Pickup Truck go right on by. Not tonight. He'd taken enough guff from mental defectives for one day.

The University's big SUV had speed to spare, enough to outrun any rattletrap truck ever built. Tipton used it, watching the digital readout climb to seventy, seventy-five, eighty.

But the pickup stayed with him, matching his speed and his mania, continuing the lunatic game, pedal to the metal, mile for mile. Until finally the pickup fell behind, pulling back into his own lane. But not quitting the contest. Tailgating him. Hanging off Tipton's rear bumper less than half a car length behind, furiously flicking his headlights.

Cretin! It was taking every iota of Tipton's concentration to keep the big Ford under control. But even at eighty, fighting to keep the vehicle on the road, he sensed his attention drifting. Back to the well. To the darkness and the bone-deep cold. And the grisly blended skeletons.

At the time he'd kept his horror in check. The deep, gut-churning revulsion he'd felt to the marrow of his bones. But now it came creeping back. Galvanized by the excitement of the chase, he could feel his throat closing with fear, the hackles on the back of his neck rising. As though some unseen presence had slithered into the car with him.

He could still see that eerie, twisted shape. A grotesque fusion of female and canine forms. Dog-woman. He'd met a few women at faculty mixers who looked part pooch, but Rachel Hayes was the real thing. My God, he could almost smell her, the beastly reek of her bones, filling his senses with — The pickup driver blared his horn, snapping Tipton back to reality.

Eighty-five! Good lord, he was doing eighty-five fucking miles an hour, racing with a halfwit maniac who was still tailgating him, leaning on his blasted horn!

Frightened now, Tipton tried to slow

down. Couldn't. The damned pickup truck was too close. At this speed even a minor bump would send both vehicles hurtling into the trees.

No choice. Had to get his speed down somehow. Too tired. Couldn't control the SUV much longer. Swallowing, he eased off the gas pedal, just a hair, no more.

Instantly, his rear window blazed with the pickup's headlight glare as the truck surged closer, banging into his rear bumper. And still the idiot didn't back off! Stayed where he was, drafting the big Ford like a demented super-stock driver, only a half-inch from destruction for both of them.

But even as he wrestled the wheel, his eyes flicking frantically between the road ahead and his rear view mirror, Tipton couldn't shake the sense that the dog-woman was somehow near. Her stench, rising from his diving togs, seemed to be growing stronger, more acrid, making his eyes water. Tried to blink the tears away. Didn't work. Risked a quick swipe with the back of his hand — and realized something was moving in the rear of the SUV!

His wet suit was stirring, writhing as a haze rose from it, roiling, blocking out the pickup's headlight blaze, taking shape!

Babbling in terror, Tipton stomped the

SUV's brakes, fighting the wheel to keep the Ford from flipping. Trying desperately to get off the road and get out — too late!

The swirling maelstrom of darkness behind him suddenly surged over him, searing his eyes and sinuses, burning him alive even before the big Ford plunged off the road, slammed into an overpass, and exploded, flames flowering upward like a napalm bomb!

Panicked, the pickup driver locked up his brakes, skidding through the fireball's smoke, finally plowing to a halt on the shoulder of the road a hundred yards beyond Tipton's burning SUV.

The pickup driver opened his door to go back, hesitated, then carefully closed it again.

No point. The big Ford was blazing like an oil rig in hell. Nothing could live through that.

Chapter 10

The blacksmith's quarters above the clinic are crude but airy, with plenty of space. Which suits me just fine. I've spent too much time in tiny rooms. With barred windows.

Furnished in early Salvation Army, the sprawling living room and three large bedrooms could house the whole Walton clan with room to spare for the Brady Bunch. My personal gear, consisting of three milk crates and a cat carrier, barely dented one corner of my bedroom.

Normally I prefer showers, but after a hard day of grave robbing, the thought of a long sudsy soak in the ancient claw-foot tub drew me like a magnet.

Stripping as the bathtub filled, I tossed my jeans into the soapy water before climbing in, saving a trip to the Laundromat.

The gritty tub probably hadn't been used since the Korean War, but as I settled into the bubbling suds, my spirits lifted, rising with the steam off the bath.

Knots in my shoulders and thighs began unraveling as I slid deeper into the water's warm embrace. The perfect prescription. A breather. A few quiet moments to consider what had gone wrong at the well. And how I felt about it.

Resting the nape of my neck on the tub rim, I closed my eyes, replaying the afternoon on the slide projector of my memory.

Tipton, a pushy little prig. And a driven man. Working like a dog at the bottom of that well, scrabbling at the muck in the murky water to free Chabot and the Hayes woman from a century of sediment and slime.

But we'd stayed down too long. Tipton was so exhausted and shaky that he fumbled the . . . remains? Rachel Hayes? What should I call them?

Nothing. Not anymore. Tipton smashed them to bits. And the pompous twit was so upset I actually felt sorry for him. Well, maybe a little.

I felt sorrier for Rachel and her dog, angry that everything turned out so badly for them. They'd waited down there so long, clinging to each other in the dark with only a dead poacher for company.

Considered him a moment. Chabot. The trapper. What his last hours must have been like. Leg broken, face broken, dying in agony in that stinking hole. Jesus, what a way to go. It all seemed so damned grisly. And unfair. Especially for Rachel.

Wasn't sure why she bothered me more. Maybe because she died trying to save that dog. That was something I could understand. But beyond it, I didn't really know Rachel Hayes. Never would now. Black Elk was right, bones are beyond caring.

Maybe what really troubled me was the final, fatal truth of it. That in the end, a pile of bones in the dirt is all any of us amount to. Hopes, dreams, and a lifelong struggle? Just bones in the end. Like dogs.

Like Rachel. Who seemed to be about half-dog. Which wasn't so bad. Often as not, I prefer dogs to people. Cats too. Humans may be at the top of the food chain, but as a race, we need a lot of work.

My shoulders ached from hanging on the ladder and the cut on my wrist still burned. Considered popping a couple of Excedrin but couldn't summon the energy to climb out of the tub. This is what old age would feel like. Old bones. I could still hear the godawful clatter of Tipton dropping them. . . .

The bathroom door opened softly and someone switched off the lights. A woman. I could tell by the shape of her body as she dropped her robe to the floor. And then she stepped into the tub.

"Megan?" I said, knowing the woman was too tall, too heavily built. And then her hands were on my shoulders pulling me close, her naked ribs against my chest. Two sets of ribs.

The chill of her icy heart was freezing mine. Her arms slid slowly up my chest, circling my neck, pulling me down into the water, deeper, down and down into the dark —

"Rachel?"

A splash snapped me awake! Icy water was covering my face, filling my mouth! I was trapped in the well, drowning as Rachel pulled me down. I broke free, thrashing my way to the surface, gagging, gasping for air, trying to fight free of —

Nothing.

I was in the bathtub. In my quarters at the barn.

No Rachel. No Tipton. No fucking skeleton. I'd dozed off and slipped down in the soapsuds, that's all. Except that the bathwater had cooled and I was freezing.

The room was dark. Staggering upright, shivering so fiercely I nearly fell, I switched on the bathroom light, blinking at my watch, trying to focus on it.

What the hell? Eleven-twenty? I'd been asleep in the cast-iron tub for hours. And felt every aching minute of it.

Wrapping myself in my faded terrycloth robe, I wobbled into the bedroom, skin shriveled, soul chilled to the core.

Crawled under the covers still wearing my robe, shivering, the gash on my wrist throbbing. Couldn't seem to get warm. . . .

The phone rang. I blurred slowly awake, groggy, fuzz-brained. But I was almost comfy now, didn't feel like getting up to answer it. Waited for the answering machine to beep.

"David? It's Megan Keyes. It's a little after twelve. Something's come up. Please call me, it's important." She left her number and rang off.

Started to doze off again. Whatever she wanted could wait until morning — damn!

I snapped fully awake. It was morning. Sunlight was streaming into the room.

Megan said twelve. Noon, not midnight. I'd slept the clock around. Why hadn't the alarm sounded — because I hadn't set the damned thing after zonking out in the tub.

Stumbling into the bathroom, I gulped a couple of Excedrin and splashed water in my face, trying to wake up.

The image in the mirror looked familiar. Unshaven, hollow-eyed. I remembered it too well from my drinking days. Looked like the picture Dorian Gray stashed in his attic. The well must have bled me more than I'd realized.

Even the narrow gash on my wrist seemed wider, with an angry border. I carefully checked the cut and my forearm above it for any traces of septicemia, the telltale scarlet filigree. No sign of it. Just a cut with an attitude, nothing more. But to play it safe I reapplied some antiseptic ointment and covered it with a gauze pad to keep it clean.

Thought about taking a cold shower to wake myself up. Blew the idea off. I wasn't quite ready to get back in that bathtub. Never might be too soon.

I was shaving when the phone rang again. "Hello?"

"David? It's Megan. Are you okay? You sound odd."

"Overslept. What's up?"

"Nothing good. I wanted to tell you before you heard it on the news. Carter

Tipton was killed last night."

"What?"

"He's dead, David. Look, I'm down-stairs. Can I come up?"

I glanced out the window. Meg's black outlaw pickup was parked below in the driveway. "Yeah, maybe you'd better."

Chapter 11

"Finish shaving, for pete's sake," Meg said, "you look like the Phantom of the Opera."

I'd answered the door in jeans, barefoot, no shirt, face half-lathered. "What happened to Tipton?"

"Single-car accident." She paced the living room nervously as I shaved, talking toward the open bathroom door. "He was headed back to Ann Arbor on 23 South. Apparently nodded out at the wheel. His car left the road at high speed, piled into an overpass, and went up like a Roman candle. Burned down to the frame. They haven't released his name yet but they've positively identified the body — damn! Will you please put a bell or something on that cat, David? He scared the hell out of me again!"

Eyeing Meg balefully, Frankenkat yowled at me, then wobbled off to the kitchen to await his breakfast.

"Ease up, he likes you. I think. It's tough

about Tipton. We stayed down that hole too long. I was half frozen and I wasn't even under water. He was shaky when we came up, probably borderline hypothermic. That's why he dropped the tray. I should have warned him, Meg."

"Not to speak ill of the dead, but the late professor wasn't much on taking advice. I hit him with a couple of questions as he was leaving and he bit my head off. He looked healthy enough if you don't count having a hard on for the world, which was probably normal for him."

"Hypothermia's tricky, though. The symptoms are barely perceptible. You get tired, get stupid, then nod out. I was so whipped when I got back yesterday that I took a bath and woke up in the dark drowning in frozen soapsuds. If Tipton was half as tired, no wonder he bounced off an overpass."

"We don't actually know that he fell asleep at the wheel," Meg interrupted. "There were no witnesses. Could have had a coronary or swerved to miss a deer. Bottom line: he hit an abutment at eighty miles per. It happens every day. Know what's really bugging you?"

"What?"

"You thought Tipton was an arrogant

jerk so now you're wondering if you didn't bother warning him because you didn't like him. How's that fit?"

I paused with the Bic double-edged razor in mid-air, then continued shaving. "Pretty close. What are you, a shrink passing as a reporter?"

"Nope, but I've spent enough time in therapy to qualify for an honorary degree. Look, I didn't like the little twerp either, David. He was pushy and patronizing. But I didn't wish him any actual harm and neither did you. Maybe Rachel did him in."

A dark shape sat bolt upright in the back of my memory. A woman. With two rib cages.

"What is it?" Meg asked.

"I don't know. I think I dreamed about her last night. Can't remember exactly. But it was . . . ugly. We were in the well. Nut-job nonsense."

She stopped pacing, eyeing me through the doorway as I toweled off the last scraps of lather. "I'm amazed you're not totally freaked. After seeing those skeletons up close, I can't believe you two stayed down there as long as you did."

"Considering what happened, we probably shouldn't have."

"That wasn't your fault, David. It wasn't

anybody's. On a brighter note, remember the guy who broke up Rachel's coming-out party? Chris Sinclair? I interviewed him last night. God, I love my job. He's old-timey polite, built like an Eddie Bauer model, and he can actually smile when he lowers his shields a minute. Plus he's an honest-to-God war hero."

"Which war?" I stalked into the bedroom looking for a clean shirt.

"Desert Storm. Yeah, yeah, I know it's the oldest pickup line on the planet, but I didn't hear it from Chris. He's like you, Westbrook. Mysterious. So naturally I ran down his background. He was a pilot, won a Silver Star."

"Is that how he lost his arm?"

"No, that happened a couple of years ago. Cracked up a plane in Panama, got banged up, had to quit the Air Force. He was stationed at the old Oscoda SAC base once, liked the north country so much that he bought into a sand and gravel business. A dirt farm, he calls it."

"Jet pilot to dirt farmer? Quite a swap."

"After all he's been through, he's just glad to be breathing. I'm having dinner with him tonight. No interview, just . . . dinner."

"For a polite guy, he doesn't waste much time."

"Get real," Meg grinned, "I asked him. Knew he'd be too nice to say no. I hope you're the same way."

"About what?"

"I've got this idea, David, for a story. Maybe a series! Listen, a woman disappears in a terrible fire. A century later, a kid falls into her grave, you go down after him and find the lost lady. The nineteenth century single mom angle makes it a natural for *Redbook* or *Atlantic*. Plus, a woman who loved dogs so much she died holding one? Too perfect. Who doesn't like dogs? We could wind up on the cover of *TV Guide*."

"Whoa up. Who said I want to be on the cover of anything? We need to talk about this."

"We're talking now."

"No, you're talking and I don't like what I'm hearing. I don't want to get involved in some big production."

"You're already involved. You're the connection. You found her!"

"No I didn't, Bobby Jozwiak —"

"Fell down a well," she broke in impatiently. "But you're the one who heard a woman calling, pal, a good ten miles away. And when I interviewed Brenda at the hospital, she couldn't remember shouting for help at all."

"Nuts. Maybe she didn't realize she was yelling, but she was. I heard her."

"Really? Funny, but Brenda doesn't strike me as the hysterical type."

"Where are you going with this? Brenda didn't call for help? I heard someone else? Like Rachel? C'mon, that's a fairy tale and you know it."

"No I don't. But I know a good story when it lands in my lap and this one's got more weird twists than a rubber boa. With a little research on Rachel I can make this a dynamite piece for a national rag or even TV. Not just a fishwrapper item in the *Herald*."

"I wish you luck. Count me out."

"Why? Is there something in your past you're worried about, Doctor? Like jail time, for instance?"

I froze, opened my mouth to argue, then closed it again. Gut instinct said deny everything. Lie like a carny barker. Until I read her eyes. Lying wouldn't help. She knew.

"Just because I come on like a Valley girl doesn't mean I'm a lightweight, David. You were the man of the hour at the hospital, but Stan didn't want his picture taken with you. In an election year. It tripped my trigger, so I checked you out."

"You didn't mention it in the story you

ran about the rescue."

"It wasn't relevant. You got rowdy in a small town bar, slugged the cop who arrested you, and did two years in Milan for assaulting a police officer. You may not be Wolinski's favorite citizen, but you're no ax murderer. Know what? That little tidbit could have spiced up the boy-in-the-well story a lot. I'm a good reporter, but I try not to trash my friends."

"Friends? Is that what we are?"

"Almost. I think we could be. If you ever get out of jail."

"What are you talking about? I am out."

"Not completely. I think part of you is still locked up. Your heart, maybe. You're a nice guy, David, and not just because you risked your neck going after that kid. It's in your eyes when you look at that crippled cat. I know you had to be tough to survive in prison, but eventually you'll have to trust people again. Why not start with me?"

"It's not that simple." I moved to the window, stared out. Across those hills was Algoma, a quaint little Michigan tourist town nestled in the Black River Valley. Beyond it, the big lake. Huron. The Sunrise Side.

I hadn't lived there since I was a kid. But I still remembered every street name.

111

In jail, Algoma was my grail. If I could just get back here, start over, everything would come out right. Maybe it was only a fantasy, but I needed to believe in something. And Meg was right. If I really meant to stay here, I'd need a friend. And I don't lie to my friends. If I can help it.

"Okay," I said, taking a deep breath, "here's the thing. When I got into that scuffle, I was drunk. I'd been loaded for a year, maybe longer."

"An alcoholic?"

"Probably. A shrink in Milan claimed I wasn't an addictive personality. His diagnosis was post-traumatic stress syndrome."

"What kind of stress?"

"The worst. I married my girlfriend in college. We had a daughter, but . . ." I swallowed, hard. "We lost her. Leukemia. I fell apart. Went on a bender, stayed wasted 'til I bottomed out in jail."

"Sounds like a rough time."

"Tougher for my wife. When she needed me most, I bailed. Dried out in the slam, got my head screwed on straight, more or less. After I made parole I went home to try to patch things up with Lin. A little late. She'd moved on, found somebody else. It was for the best, but I copped an attitude and we argued. She drove off in a huff and . . ." I

112

swallowed. "She ran over Frank."

"Frank?"

"My daughter's cat. Slept at the foot of her bed every night of . . ." I swallowed. "Of her life. And we'd smashed him to hell. He was still breathing, so I took him to a clinic and patched him back together. Sort of."

"You mean that one-eyed, three-legged . . . ?"

"Cat, right. Frankenkat. He looks a little rough, but he's a miracle to me. Seeing him up and bumbling around was the first time I'd felt good about anything in years. Reminded me why I became a vet in the first place.

"One of my old professors at State hired me as a research assistant and part-time janitor. I saved every cent, borrowed the rest. And moved up here to make a fresh start."

"That's quite a story."

"It's not a story at all, Meg. It's my life, and my former wife's, and our daughter's. It's private. I don't want it laid out like a damned comic book."

"I understand that, David, truly. But nothing's really private anymore. Not medical records or e-mail and definitely not a prison record, especially in a town this size. Sooner or later your past will come out. The only question is how and when. And how much damage it will do. And maybe I can help."

"I'm listening."

"You've got your sad story, here's mine. I grew up writing for the *Herald*, moved to L.A. fresh out of college. Got into a . . . bad situation out there. So I ran home to Algoma to work for my big sister again. A loser. One hot story can change all that and this is the one. I'm going to write this, David. I have to."

"Even if I say no?"

"It's too late for that. You're part of the story, whether I write it or someone else does. The difference is that I'll try to protect you. I think I'm a good enough writer to work around your past, especially if you give me other material to use."

"Like what?"

"Hopes and dreams. The stuff stories are made of. With some research, I know I can humanize Rachel. She's such a strong character I can probably keep most of your private life out of it. The question is, do you trust me enough to let me try?"

Good question. The truth was I hardly knew her at all. Pert, with a sprinkle of freckles across her nose. Cute as a wren. But there was bulldog tenacity there as well. And street-smart ambition. It had been there all along. I'd missed it because I liked her. Sometimes we only see what we want to and disregard the rest. And sometimes that's enough.

"Well?" Meg prompted. "Deal?"

"Okay. Deal."

"Good. Thank you." She gave me a quick peck on the cheek with a grin so infectious I found myself smiling too.

"Gotta go," she said, stepping back. "So many men, so little time. Have to call my agent and some TV people I know before my hot date."

"Have fun."

"Why don't you come with us tonight? Have a few beers, meet some people. It'll do you good."

"I'm busy, broke, and down deep you don't really want a chaperone anyway."

"Gimme a break, we're only going to dinner. My virtue's safe enough."

"I'm more worried about his."

"You should be," she said, giving me a rubber-faced leer. "I've got a good feeling about this, David. That well's going to be lucky for us. You'll see."

She hustled off, a perky package of irresistible energy.

I hoped she was right about the well being lucky.

But it occurred to me that it hadn't been very damned lucky for Zeke Chabot. Or Rachel Hayes. Or even her dog.

Chapter 12

After Meg left I fed Frank, then trotted downstairs. Bass had been hard at it while I was off robbing graves, running electrical cables through the partition studs. I picked up where he left off, installing new outlet boxes at eight-foot intervals.

Ordinarily I like working with my hands; the scent of raw lumber and sawdust smells like hope. Building a new room, a new life, one board at a time. But even as I measured and cut the paneling, Tipton's image kept popping up. Hadn't liked him much, but he had guts and — a horn beeped out front. UPS delivery.

I signed for the large, flat parcel, carried it inside, and laid it across two sawhorses. Carefully, I slit open the box, taking my time, savoring the moment.

A sign. A positive sign, for a change. Two-and-a-half feet by four, hand-carved then sandblasted, raised letters in Old English print gilded with twenty-three-carat gold against a forest green background.

Westbrook Veterinary Clinic. And in smaller letters below it: Dr. David Westbrook, D.V.M. I caressed the lettering with my fingertips, swallowing a sudden lump in my throat.

The invoice was taped to the box. Eighteen hundred twenty-three dollars and change. Ouch! That maxed out the Visa card.

It was a much nicer sign than I needed and definitely more than I could afford.

And worth every damned penny.

There was no hurry to hang it. I was at least three more weeks of break-neck work before I could open the clinic for business. But after the shambles at the well and Tipton's death, I was hungry for something hopeful. I wanted to see this beauty shining in the sun.

The old ladder was still lashed to the Jeep's roof bar, so I untied it and propped it against the wall beside the office door.

Climbing the first few rungs, I started to lift the sign above the door, then hesitated.

The wall was freshly painted a cheery barn red. But above the door, the paint was smudged. Darkened. As though something beneath it was bleeding through. It appeared to be lettering. A family name? Maybe a business sign from the old blacksmith shop? Definitely a word. I tried tracing it with my fingertip. T-E-N . . . Ten something? Couldn't be a house number. The address out here was 6577.

Curious now, I climbed down the ladder and backed away from the barn, trying to gain some perspective. T-E-N, a blurry spot, C-I-T . . . Y.

TENACITY. Couldn't imagine what it meant. Odd that I hadn't noticed it when I painted the facade. Maybe the fresh paint activated some dormant chemical in the original lettering, giving it new life. Because it seemed to be growing clearer as I watched. Tenacity. An unusual word to paint over a door. Not a bad word though. Better than gang symbols or expletives.

Almost seemed a shame to cover it up. But I had a sign of my own to mount. Climbing the ladder again, I shifted my new sign around, centering it, then nailed it firmly above the clinic door. Or what would be a clinic door in a few weeks.

Westbrook Veterinary Clinic. Dr. David Westbrook, D.V.M.

Folding my arms, I leaned back to admire it, waiting for a surge of satisfaction. Instead I got a sudden flash of the well, the stench of old bones. It was so vivid, so oppressive, I glanced around, half-expecting to see the dog-woman from my dream standing behind me. She wasn't. But I could almost — no, I actually could smell the well stench.

It was the ladder. The bottom of the damned ladder was still damp from the well, still reeked of death and darkness. Enough of this!

Laying it in the middle of the driveway, I hosed it off, then toted it back to the barn's main corridor and left it where I'd found it.

Afterward, I tried to recapture the initial lift the sign gave me but it was gone. The gilded letters looked pretentious. And I really couldn't afford them. I could just as easily have painted my name over the door. Or better yet, kept the original name.

Tenacity. A good word to keep in mind. Especially for a guy with a ton of work to do. But even as I tore into the day's labor, I couldn't shake the nagging feeling that I was overlooking something important. That something heavy was headed my way.

And I wondered if Tipton had the same feeling just before he crashed into that over-pass.

Chapter 13

I woke the next morning sore as a punching dummy after karate class. I'd worked half the night trying to make up for my lost morning. Trying to make myself so tired that I'd sleep without dreaming.

It didn't work. Every creak and groan of the old barn shifting in the night snapped me instantly awake. Even Frankenkat was restless, prowling the living room, sniffing, exploring. Hunting.

Maybe it was an old habit returning. Inmates sleep light. A single footfall can rouse half a cell block. Maybe Meg was right, and I wasn't entirely free of all that.

Nuts. At least I knew what to do about it. When the going gets tough, run.

John Wayne might not approve, but it works for me. As a kid, when things started closing in, I ran. In high school and college, running cross-country earned me a letterman's jacket and a pass from phys ed classes. I'm no Carl Lewis, but I won a few meets and placed in a few more.

In jail I ran even harder. Milan has a 1500-meter track just inside the wire. Running flat out with the wind in my face was the only freedom I knew for nearly two years.

Hadn't done much running since coming to Algoma. No time. Didn't really have time today either, but I needed to clear my head and break a sweat. Okay, a mile or two, no more.

Once outside though, with the sun climbing over the hills and the cool air as sweet as country wine, I just kept going. Running free.

Jogging along the shoulder of the road in shorts, I could feel aching muscles loosen up then fall into place as I found my stride. The Lope That Lasts Forever.

Running in prison I'd kept my eyes slitted, nearly closed, pretending I was back in high school, hearing the crowds at the finish line as we sprinted home. Now, running with my eyes wide open, I drank in the beauty of the countryside: every tree, every flower, every roadside weed.

Behind me in the distance, a red pickup parked by the roadside fired up. I listened as I ran, waiting for it to overtake me, but when I glanced back it hadn't moved. It was still sitting there, motor idling. Lost sight of it between hills. When I crested the next rise it was gone.

A half-mile from the barn I passed a striking home on the crest of a bluff. Modern style, cathedral ceilings, lots of glass and odd angles, constructed of stone and cedar. Nice. So were the Benz wagon and the gleaming silver Jaguar parked in front of the stables.

The mailbox read McCrae. My mysterious landlady? Had to be. The fields behind the house shared a distant fence line with the pasture behind my barn/clinic.

Just beyond the McCrae place, an upscale subdivision began that stretched all the way to the outskirts of Algoma. Swinging away from the houses, I kept to the country roads, taking a roughly circular route that eventually headed back to the barn.

I was feeling the pace now, aches and strains kicking in. Nothing fatal. I could already see the barn's silhouette in the distance, the sun rising behind it. And the sheer beauty of it struck me like a punch over the heart.

Couldn't make out my new sign yet but knew it was there. And I found myself picking up the pace again. Running hard for

. . . Home. A feeling I hadn't known for a very long time.

As I topped the last hill, I could see the barn clearly, my new sign gleaming over the door, a thin plume of smoke coiling lazily from the roof peak.

It looked so peaceful it took a moment to register. Smoke? There shouldn't be any smoke! What the hell?

Pounding up the driveway, lungs bursting, legs turning to rubber, I jerked open the clinic door. Smoke billowed out but there was no fire, no flames. I charged through the office to the back door and yanked it open.

Heat hammered my face like a fist! Clouds of thick smoke were roiling in the corridor. Dropping to my knees, I tried to peer beneath it. The stack of lumber and materials in the center of the aisle was ablaze. The flames hadn't reached the walls yet, but sparks were spiraling upward to the hay bales stored in the loft above. It could spread in a matter of seconds.

There was a phone in the tack room midway down the aisle but it was too close to the blaze. Slamming the door, I sprinted up the stairway to my apartment.

"Frank! Here Frank!" Grabbing the phone, I dialed 911 and reported the fire while I rushed through the smoky apartment searching for my cat. No sign of him. Damn it! I'd been letting Frankenkat roam free in the barn, couldn't remember if he'd been in the apartment when I left for my run. If Frank was trapped in the barn on the far side of the flames . . .

But as I sprinted back down the stairs I spotted Frank backing down the stairs, one careful step at a time, already halfway to the bottom, making his labored escape. Probably bolted through the door as I came in.

Cocking his head, Frank peered up at me with his good eye, as if asking what the hell I was waiting for? Good question.

"Thanks for the warning, pal." Scooping Frank up, I raced out to the Jeep and shut him safely inside. Then I grabbed the hose, rushed back into the barn, and began wetting down the flames.

Couldn't get close, too much heat. Tried spraying the bottom of the fire first, Boy Scout style. Instead of dying, the fire blazed, as though feeding on the water.

Anyone with half a brain would have backed off and waited for the firemen, but I couldn't. I was fighting more than a fire. Every hope I had was going up in flames. And so I kept charging in, hosing down the stack for as long as I could stand the heat.

Then I'd back out, wet myself down, and try again.

I had the worst of it under control when the first fire truck rolled in.

Chapter 14

It didn't burn long. It didn't have to. The firemen backed their truck into the barn's rear bay door and quickly doused the blazing lumber stack. In fifteen minutes they were already coiling their hoses to head out. I thanked each of them and offered free checkups for any pets they'd care to bring. A few said they would. But it didn't matter.

As I toed the smoking ashes of lumber and paneling, I knew I was finished. Every dime I could save, beg, or borrow was tied up in those materials. I was busted flat. Tap City.

I'd just started raking up the debris when a prowl car roared up to the open bay. Sheriff Wolinski and a lanky old-timer in civvies climbed out. Balding, with a fringe of reddish hair, rumpled suit, rumpled face, he looked like a Bassett hound with glasses.

"Hold on, Westbrook," Wolinski said. "Don't touch anything."

"Why not?"

"Because every trouble call I get lately turns out to be you. This is Dick Anderson, the sector fire marshal. He'll be taking a look around."

"Doc," Anderson nodded, eyeing the rubble. "Looks like quite a blaze. How did it start?"

"I know where, but not how. Building materials were stacked here in the corridor. They're all that burned. I went for a run, saw the smoke as I came back. Called 911, grabbed a hose, and got part of it out. The firemen finished the job."

"When you sprayed it, did the flames go out or spread and flare back up?" Anderson asked, strolling around the wreckage.

"You mean like a gasoline fire?"

"Why do you ask about gasoline?"

"Because I've worked in gas stations. Spraying water on a gas fire spreads it. This fire didn't spread like that, but it didn't go out right away either."

Anderson nodded, then peered into the open tack room. "What's in those barrels against the wall?"

"I don't know. All that gear was there when I rented the building. Other than occasionally borrowing a tool, I haven't been in there."

Anderson lifted one of the metal barrel lids, sniffed, and wrinkled his hound nose. "Caustic lime," he said, dropping the cover back into place.

"Quick lime?" Wolinski echoed. "What's it doing here?"

"It's a disinfectant," I explained. "Sprinkled around a horse stall, it kills germs and neutralizes uric acid from the droppings."

"It'll burn your skin if you get it on yourself," Anderson added. "Is that how you burned your wrist?"

"This isn't a burn, it's a cut."

"Nasty one," Anderson winced, taking a closer look. "You oughta see a doctor, son."

"I am a doctor. It's not serious."

"It's your arm," he shrugged. "You've been painting. Did you use rags or cotton waste to mop up paint thinner?"

"The paint's water-based latex. No paint thinner, only lumber and paneling." I broke off as a silver Jaguar sedan screeched to a halt beside Wolinski's prowl car in the open bay door. A woman in jeans and a denim jacket scrambled out, trailed by a tall, dapper type in a gray business suit.

Scowling at the damage as she came, the woman marched up angrily to us without waiting for her companion. "What happened here, Stan?" she asked brusquely. A compact five foot-three or so, she was probably pushing forty. Heart-shaped face, a shaggy mane of dark hair, and even darker eyes.

"Vonnie, Les," Wolinski said, nodding to the newcomers. "That's what we're trying to find out. Only the good doctor here isn't much help."

"Why not?" she said, turning on me.

"Whoa up, lady, I don't even know who you —"

"Yvonne McCrae," she said, cutting me off. "I own this building. I take it you're Dr. Westbrook? Would you mind telling me how a barn that's stood for ninety years suddenly catches fire a month after you rent the place?"

"Six weeks, actually."

"Whatever! And it was my understanding you were only renovating the blacksmith shop. What were you doing out here?"

"I kept building materials in the aisle to keep it out of the weather."

"How did the fire start?"

"We're not quite clear on that, ma'am," Anderson said. "It began in this lumber pile, but I don't see an obvious cause."

"This is Dick Anderson from the fire marshal's office," Wolinski explained.

"How do you know it started here?" Mrs. McCrae asked.

"The Doctor said so and the flame patterns confirm it. The building materials burned, but while the walls are charred on both sides of the aisle, they didn't ignite. The fire began in the center and was spreading out. Lucky the Doc caught it in time."

"Is it?" Yvonne said, giving me a dark look. "Somehow I don't feel particularly lucky."

"No, ma'am. I assume you're insured?"

"She is," her tall companion put in, "but as I recall, the policy on this building has a twenty-five-hundred-dollar deductible."

"Too bad," Anderson said. "You're out two and a half grand and I just lost my best motive. The easiest way to spot arson is to check insurance policies or company books. Red ink burns more buildings than napalm."

"Whoa," I said, "are you saying someone set this deliberately?"

"I'm still working on that. Do you smoke, Doctor?"

"No."

"Had any trouble with anyone?" Wolinski asked pointedly. "Maybe an enemy from the old days?"

"No, and I doubt this was arson anyway. If somebody wanted to burn this place, they would have touched off the hay in the loft. The whole building would have gone up."

"True," Anderson admitted. "Unless the burn did what it was supposed to. Maybe the lumber pile was the target."

"Why would anyone do that?" Mrs. McCrae asked.

"The doctor's the only one who can answer that."

"I did answer it," I said. "No one had a reason to start this fire, least of all me. I'm not insured."

"Too bad," Anderson said, kneeling to probe the ashes with a pencil, "because it feels like arson to me. A fire in the center of an aisle? No combustibles, not even electrical service near it. I don't smell any accelerant residue though, no gasoline or nitrates. Which leaves propane, acetylene, possibly oxygen. Doctor, do you —"

"No," I snapped. "We use a kerosene heater to dry paint, but it's in the clinic. No gasoline, no nuclear bombs either."

"Okay, okay," Anderson said, holding up his hands for a truce. "Just asking. I smell something sour, though. An animal carcass maybe?"

"Animal? No, there was nothing . . . The ladder."

"You mean this thing?" Anderson toed the unburned section.

"That's only the top section. The bottom half was waterlogged, smelled pretty bad . . . That's odd. Only the bottom half burned."

"The wet half? That is odd. Still, it was a hot blaze and fires do funny things. Some tell their stories straight out. Others gobble up the evidence just to play with my head."

"You make them sound human," Yvonne said.

"Oh, any old firedog will tell you fires have personalities. This one feels coy. Like a woman. Or maybe I'm missing something. Does anything seem out of place, Mrs. McCrae?"

"I haven't spent much time here lately," she said, looking around. "With all the mess, it's hard to say."

"Well, if you think of anything, call me at this number." He handed us each a business card. "I'll fax Stan my report later today for your insurance claim, Mrs. McCrae. Since there's no hard evidence of arson, I'll list it as origin unknown. If the adjusters give you any static, have them call me. Any questions?"

"I have one," I said. "Why did you say a

woman caused this fire?"

"I didn't mean a real woman, it's just my sense of it. Some fires are imps. Some are killers so evil you want to hang 'em. Why? Do you have a lady friend angry at you?"

"No, but . . . never mind. It's nothing."

"Then I'm off. I've got another burn to see before lunch. I'm sorry we didn't meet under better circumstances, Mrs. McCrae. I heard your husband speak at a United Way banquet once. He seemed like a fine man. I'm sorry for your loss."

"Thank you."

"We should be going too, Yvonne," her companion said. "Our reservations are for one."

"Go on without me, Les. I'd have to change now, and I don't feel much like lunch anyway."

"But we're meeting Judge Reardon and —"

"I know. Give them my apologies. Please."

"As you wish," he said stiffly. "I'll call you later." Giving her a quick peck on the cheek, he stalked back to his Jag and roared off.

Yvonne McCrae was eyeing Sheriff Wolinski.

"What?" he asked.

"That's what I'm wondering, Stan," she

said evenly. "Why did you bring the fire inspector to a dinky little barn fire?"

"It's his job to check out suspicious fires, Von."

"What made this fire suspicious?"

Wolinski started to speak, then hesitated. "The Doc will have to tell you that. Or not. I have to go. Sorry about your trouble, Von. And Doc? You'd better sleep outside tonight."

"Why?"

"Didn't your mama tell you? Play with fire, pee the bed? See ya." He sauntered out, chuckling.

"Good lord," Yvonne said, looking around, "what a mess. Is there much damage up front?"

"A little smoke, nothing serious. But it doesn't matter. My plans burned with the building materials, Mrs. McCrae. I'm not insured and I maxed out my credit and blew my savings to buy those materials. I can't afford to replace it. I'm sorry."

"Being sorry isn't much help," she said, nudging the top section of the ladder with the toe of her hand-tooled western boot. "What's your problem with Stan Wolinski?"

"Problem?"

"Don't waltz me around, Westbrook. Something's obviously wrong between you two. Is it personal or what?"

I considered fibbing but there was no point. Not anymore.

"He doesn't like me much. Probably because of my prison record."

"Your what?"

"Record. I did two years in Milan for punching out a police officer."

She was looking at me like I'd grown a second head, an odd moment to notice how intensely dark her eyes were. And how magnetic. I realized I was staring and looked away.

"Great," she said softly. "This is just marvelous."

"Sorry."

"Stop saying that!"

"Look, Mrs. McCrae, I'll make this easy for you. I'll give you my i.o.u. for next month's rent, we'll cancel my lease, I'll clean up this mess and clear out of here tonight."

"And go where? I thought you were broke."

"I've been broke before. I'll get by."

"Good for you. How am I supposed to rent this building with the remodeling half done?"

"What do you want me to do? Tear it out?"

"No! I want you to stand by our agreement and finish it."

"I can't do that. I don't have the money."

"That's not my problem. We have a deal."

"Our deal just went up in smoke! Along with a month of damned hard work. You're not the only one who got burned here, lady."

"But I'm not — okay, okay, hold it! Beating each other up won't help anything. You're right, we both have a problem here. Any suggestions?"

"Sure. Front me the money to finish the job. I'll pay you back when I open."

"And why would I do that? Because your prison record makes you such a terrific credit risk? By the way, you should have told me about that."

"It was a lease agreement, not my life story. If I'd told you up front, would you have made the deal?"

"Hell no! I — look, it doesn't matter now. And I'm sorry if I bit your head off. I played in this barn when I was a girl. Neighborhood kids would meet out here and swing from the pulley ropes like Tarzan and Jane. I really hate seeing it like this."

I started to say I was sorry, caught the warning in her eyes, and stopped. And we both smiled. She had a quirky smile that erased years from her eyes. Those very dark eyes.

"Look, let's call a truce, Mrs. McCrae. Neither one of us asked for this mess, but we're stuck with it. I'm willing to do whatever I can to make it right, but my options are pretty limited. Let me give you a ride home. I'll get this mess cleaned up; you can decide what you want to do and let me know. Fair enough?"

"I . . . guess it'll have to be." She glanced around, taking a last wistful look at the damage. And for a moment I glimpsed the girl she'd been, playing in the hayloft. She must have been a darned cute kid. Still was.

Chapter 15

Outside, she climbed into the Jeep and Frank promptly scrambled onto her lap. But instead of flinching, Yvonne looked at him with wonder.

"My gosh, you poor little guy. What on earth happened to you?"

"He lost an argument with an Oldsmobile."

"He lost more than that. An eye and a leg for openers. Is he yours?"

"He is now. I sort of inherited him. His name's Frank. Frankenkat, actually."

"Frankenkat. Perfect name for a perfect guy." She stroked his throat and Frank basked in the attention. A rare thing. He barely tolerated me, perhaps because he associated me with pain. Or maybe he just preferred a woman's touch. Couldn't blame him. Yvonne McCrae was a very attractive woman.

Very. She was probably ten years older

than I, definitely not my type, but she was having a distinctly unsettling effect on me.

Chemistry? Oedipus complex? I had no idea. But something was going on. With me, at least.

"He must have been terribly injured," she said, caressing the scar tissue over Frank's injured eye. "Why didn't you put him down? Most vets would have, I think."

"It's a long story. Let's just say it was important for me to save him. And he was worth it. He's a real character."

"He seems like one." She scratched his belly. "Can I ask you something? Without getting your back up, I mean?"

"You can try."

"How serious are you about making a go of this place?"

"It means . . . a lot to me. A second chance, a fresh start. A lot. Why?"

"So, the fire wasn't just a roundabout way of getting out of your lease? Look, don't get angry. The inspector said it was —"

"Arson," I nodded. "Okay, you've got a right to be suspicious. I actually do know a little about arson from my . . . travels. For instance, arson's usually a crime for profit. Did you make any money from the fire?"

"Of course not."

"Neither did I. In fact, I lost my shirt. I

140

had no reason to do this and I didn't do it. Are we clear now?"

"Okay," she said, still watching me. "I read about you in the paper. Rescuing that boy? That was . . . a wonderful thing to do."

"That's me, Mr. Wonderful. When I'm not Mr. Arsonist."

"Are you always sarcastic? Or only with people you dislike?"

"I don't dislike you, Mrs. McCrae, you seem nice enough. This just isn't a day I'll want to relive in my golden years."

"Nor I." We rode in silence the rest of the way. I wheeled the Jeep into her driveway.

"Drive around back to the barn, please."

The barn at the rear of the house was the opposite of mine. Smaller, with an architectural design that matched the house, it was built of stone and cedar. A white show corral backed up to it and the pasture beyond looked as neatly manicured as a championship golf course.

"One last question," she said, "a medical one. Are you a pretty good vet?"

"I try to be. I was tops in my class at State. My patients bark at me sometimes, but they never write nasty letters."

"You have a strange sense of humor."

"Thank you."

"That wasn't a compliment. Come

inside, please, there's something I want you to see." She climbed out, still cradling Frank in her arms.

The barn's interior was snow white, floor to ceiling, immaculate as an Amish kitchen. Two rows of stalls faced each other across a central corridor. Yvonne opened the upper gate of the first stall. A golden palomino stallion whickered a greeting, leaning his great head against her cheek. I thought Frank might object, but he seemed perfectly content in her arms.

"This is Twenty Gold, my saddle mount. A few months ago he started bleeding from the nose, not much, just a little, but his nares looked quite raw."

"Any other symptoms?"

"None. His temperature was normal, he didn't go off his feed. I had him examined, the vet put him on antibiotics for a week, but the bleeding continued. Then traces of blood started showing up in his manure." She was watching me, waiting.

It wasn't fair. The symptoms could indicate any number of things . . . but she'd know that. Which meant it had to be a trick question.

Stalling for time, I moved beside her, looking over the stallion. He was in magnificent condition. So he'd been cured. But of what? He was the only horse here, so it couldn't be anything contagious, and the building was clean . . . And that was it. The place was spotless. Which meant someone kept it that way. So I gambled.

"Warfarin," I said.

"What?"

"Rat poison. You keep feed for this fella somewhere around here, right? Oats and Omalene attract rats. I'm guessing your stable help set out some small boxes of supermarket rat poison to get rid of them. The active ingredient in those packages is Warfarin, an anticoagulant, mixed with rice dust to attract vermin. Unfortunately, horses like it too. Is that what happened?"

She nodded, eyeing me thoughtfully.

"Then your animal was never in real danger. Next time use mousetraps. They're messier but your stud won't chew on them more than once."

"That's very good. It took my vet three visits and a second opinion to figure it out."

I shrugged, doing my best to look nonchalant. She tousled the palomino's mane, then led me back out into the sunlight.

"I may have a possible solution for our — problem," she said abruptly. "If you're game, that is?"

"At this point, I'm up for just about anything."

"Fair enough. Do you know anything about greyhounds?"

"The dogs or the bus?"

"The dogs, and don't be —"

"— a jerk," I finished. "Right. Greyhounds: narrow frames and jaws, sixty to eighty pounds on average. An ancient breed, six thousand years give or take, descended from coursing hounds. Originally bred for hunting, more recently for racing. Overbreeding in this country has introduced genetic dysfunctions like hip dysplasia and albinism. Have I won anything yet?"

"Maybe you have. A few months ago the police raided a drug lab near Midland. They found eight greyhounds roaming around on the property. Maybe you read about it?"

"I kind of avoid police news. What about it?"

"After the trial, the hounds were slated to be destroyed. The Algoma Humane Society, which I happen to chair, offered to adopt them, but the shelter said the dogs would need professional care and training before they can be placed in the community. Is that something you could handle?"

"I suppose so, but —"

"Good. I want you to volunteer for the job. Pro bono."

"For free? Look, I can't even —"

She waved off my objection. "In return for caring for the hounds, you can charge whatever materials you need to finish your clinic to my estate account. Within reason, of course. How does that sound?"

Our eyes met and held. An oddly intense moment. She was a little wide in the hips, wearing no makeup and dressed like a ranch hand. Yet I was drawn to her. It made no sense at all.

"Is something wrong?"

"I'm just thinking it over. That's a very generous offer."

"You bet it is. Do we have a deal?"

"Almost. I have a question. I can see why you'd want to save the dogs, but since you obviously don't need the rent money for the barn, why are you bothering to help me?"

She considered that a moment, scratching Frank's ears. "I'm not," she admitted. "I'm helping me. My late husband was a terrific guy. Too terrific, in some ways. He managed our finances and did a great job. But since his death, I've had to learn it all from scratch. Renting this barn was my first solo business decision. I don't want it standing empty to prove to . . . some

145

people that I can't manage my own affairs."

"By some people, you mean your friend in the Jag?"

"That's really none of your business."

"You're right, it's not. Fair enough. Saving some stray dogs in exchange for construction materials works for me. Deal." I offered my hand, felt a jolt when she took it. Static electricity. Probably from petting Frank.

But she glanced up, startled, actually looking me over for the first time. With those dark, intelligent eyes.

I was soot-smeared, wearing a raggedy sweatshirt and shorts, definitely not ready for prime time. But if she was revolted, she hid it well. I realized I was holding her hand and let it drop.

Leaning into the Jeep, she gently placed Frank on the seat. "He's beautiful, isn't he?" she said, scratching him under the chin.

"Most people don't think so. He is to me."

"It's nice we finally agree on something, even if it's only a one-eyed cat. I'll send somebody over to give you a hand cleaning up."

"Thank you. By the way, what does 'tenacity' stand for?"

She stared at me blankly. "Tenacity? Willpower, you mean? Stubbornness? Why?"

"The old sign above the barn door."

"What sign?"

" 'Tenacity,' in capital letters. It bled out through the new paint. You said you played in the barn as a girl, I thought you might know about it."

"No, I don't recall seeing a sign there, and we played there quite often."

"It's not important. There are worse things to have over your front door. 'Men's Room,' for instance."

"A very strange sense of humor," she repeated, shaking her head. But she was smiling as she turned and walked into the house. A nice smile.

And she wasn't as wide in the hips as I'd thought. More like exactly the right size. I couldn't have met her at a worse time. And yet . . .

I found myself whistling as I drove back to the barn. Frank eyed me suspiciously.

"Shut up," I said.

Chapter 16

Chris Sinclair was hanging on for dear life as Megan Keyes raced her outlaw pickup truck into the clinic driveway. Throwing it into a power-skid that ended inches from the clinic door, Meg vaulted out of the truck, rushing into the building while Chris was still unfastening his seatbelt.

"Yo, David? Are you alive?" Meg called, charging through the empty clinic out to the barn.

"Go away, you're a jinx." I was sooty and surly, raking the last of the ashes into a neat pile. Relieved to see me in one piece, Meg rushed to give me a hug.

"Daryl caught the squeal about the fire on the scanner," she panted. "I was afraid — well, anyway. You're sure you're okay?"

"I'm fine," I said, mussing her hair, pausing when I realized we weren't alone. Chris Sinclair had followed her into the barn. In a teal polo shirt and creased khakis

148

he looked buff, solid as a steel beam.

"Unhand that woman before I snap your spine," Chris said. Kidding, I think. Smiling anyway.

"David, you remember Chris?" she said, stepping back.

"The party-crasher from the well," I said, accepting Sinclair's left hand. He seemed looser today. Meg's perky magic at work. She only came up to his shoulder, but it was clearly a mismatch she could live with. She was almost glowing.

"No hard feelings over all that, I hope," Chris said. "It was a jolt finding a mob digging up bodies on land I'd just bought."

"No need to apologize, you were right. After a hundred years in the dark, they didn't belong in a lab."

"Maybe we should have left them alone," Megan said, surveying the damage. "From the looks of this place, I'd say Rachel resents getting jerked around."

"What happened?" Sinclair asked.

"The fire investigator thinks it was arson. I don't. Either way I doubt any ghosts were involved."

"Arson?" Meg said sharply. "Why would anybody want to burn this place?"

"Exactly my point. No reason. It's a barn, forgodsake."

"What did the sheriff say?"

"Wolinski suspects me of everything since the hit on JFK. If he really thought it was arson, I'd already be in jail."

"Then it must be a ghost," she quipped. "They never leave traces."

"Unless the evidence went up in the fire," Chris said.

"Spoilsport. What's the matter, you don't believe in ghosts?"

"I've never met one."

"I've never met anybody from Peru," Meg countered. "That doesn't mean nobody lives there. Do the math. The late Rachel dies in a fire, we dig her up, and suddenly things start burning. Professor Tipton dies in a fiery crash and now David's place gets toasted? Too weird."

"You mean like the Mummy's Curse?" Chris offered.

"More like a mommy's curse. Revenge of the dog-woman."

"You're a hoot, Meg," I said. "Notice I'm not laughing."

"That's okay." Meg's smile faded as she examined the fire-scarred wall. "I'm not sure I'm kidding. The police came up with a witness, a long-haul truck driver who saw Tipton's SUV just before he crashed. The trucker said he was doing eighty at least.

Racing, or being chased, the guy thought."

"Chased by what?"

"The witness said a pickup truck was right on Tipton's tail. Red, maybe."

Something tugged at my memory. I swept the cinders into a dustpan, trying to remember.

Meg was eyeing me. "Anything wrong?"

"No," I said, choking on a cloud of soot. "Everything's just terrific."

Chapter 17

For the next few weeks, I pushed the whole ugly business of Tipton, Rachel, and the fire out of my mind to focus totally on finishing the clinic.

With summer coming on, Bass was spending more time on the road and couldn't help as often. But Yvonne McCrae proved as good as her word. Chubs Meachum, a local contractor, came in to repair the fire damage and finish rewiring the building.

Grizzled and minus a couple of teeth, Meachum wore bib overalls with no shirt. No underwear either, judging from the way he kept scratching his crotch. And he moved like molasses. Underwater.

But he was also a careful craftsman who never had to do anything twice. Watching him was a lesson in life. Slow down a little. Get it right the first time.

Together we had the fire damage repaired

in a week, leaving me free to concentrate on the office. Lengthening my days, I worked dawn to dusk and often beyond.

Once the wiring was finished, I hung the interior doors, nailed up prefab paneling, beige linen above, fake oaken wainscoting below. And suddenly the place looked more like a clinic and less like a junkyard after a bomb blast.

Simultaneously, the first medical supplies began to arrive. Pet food supplements, rubber gloves, syringes. Everything had to be inventoried, then stacked in the corners to keep it out of the way while I frantically built shelving and cupboards to hold it all.

Megan dropped by a couple of evenings a week to pump me for background information for her series on the death and rescue of the late Rachel Hayes.

In theory, our talks were interviews, but they soon turned into old-fashioned college dorm riffs on life, love, and What's It All About, Alfie? The things friends kick around when they find time.

Beneath her tuff-girl banter, Meg was bright as a sparrow and just as mischievous. She had a gift for laughter but she was also a scalpel-sharp observer. She didn't miss much.

She knew life is tough — she'd fought

through some bad patches herself — yet she was tenaciously upbeat. A survivor. She reminded me that life was fun and funny once, and could be again. A simple message, and one I really needed to hear.

We liked each other. A lot. So, naturally, she asked why I never hit on her.

"Fear of death," I said. And we both laughed.

The truth was simpler. We didn't have that kind of chemistry. We hit it off so well it would have been very easy to blunder into an affair. But it would have wrecked something valuable. Real friends are as rare as lovers. And sometimes they're harder to find.

And soon Meg had a lover. She and Chris Sinclair were seeing a lot of each other. *An unlikely match,* I thought.

Meg was chatty, Chris wore silence like a bulletproof vest. A private man. But with a wry sense of humor that popped up at odd times.

Sometimes he massaged the surgical scars on his neck, his eyes darkening as he did so. Pain? Or anger? Maybe both. I sensed a box-cutter edge in Chris that wasn't far from the surface.

He couldn't hide his feelings for Meg, though. Sometimes their eyes would meet and the hunger and heat would flash like chain lightning.

I envied them. My own social calendar stayed at zero. I settled for pumping Meg for tidbits about my intriguing landlady.

Yvonne McCrae was nine years older than I, not big rich but very well off. A widow for three years, she'd recently gotten engaged to her attorney, Les Hudspeth, the slick in the silver Jaguar. Their Christmas wedding would be the highlight of Algoma's social season.

Terrific. Not only was I attracted to an older woman totally wrong for me, she was already taken by a snob in her own set. The whole idea was nonsense. A crush. Or whatever.

Forget about it.

So I tried. But she kept popping into my thoughts at odd moments. Annoyance flashing in her eyes. That dark mane of hair. I wondered what it would look like wet. Or tied back.

I even climbed up into the back loft of the barn a few times. With the bay door open, I could watch the lights across the meadow where Yvonne McCrae and Les Hudspeth were probably yukking it up with friends, discussing stock options and the bloodlines of thoroughbred horses and thoroughbred kids.

I didn't feel like The Great Gatsby. More like a Great Moron. Gatsby had cash for champagne breakfasts and a Duisenberg. I barely had gas money for my Jeep.

But luck is a funny thing. It can turn in a heartbeat. Either way.

Chapter 18

Bass and I were taking a late afternoon breather when Meg's outlaw pickup roared up out front and she came racing through the door, eyes alight.

"Yo, drop what you're doing, Westbrook. I just got a call from the mortuary. One of Rachel's relatives is claiming her body. Daryl's already on her way. Let's go."

"I can't, I'm not —"

"Go ahead," Bass said. "I can run the Reddy-Heater to dry the woodwork while you're gone. Besides, you've been so surly lately, kissin' a stiff might cheer you up."

Meg was hauling me out before I could argue. "You don't want to miss this. It would be like losing a book in the middle of the last chapter."

"Just so it is the last chapter," I muttered.

Daryl was waiting in the lobby. Matching our pace to hers, we made our way to Toby

Mallette's office. Very posh. Carpet thick enough to mow, carved mahogany furniture. Acres of room for grieving families and their checkbooks.

Mallette, the freckle-faced mortician who'd bagged Rachel at the well, was chatting up a fiftyish type who looked like Sean Connery after a hunger strike. Seamed face, wary eyes, a steel-gray brush cut that matched his pricey tweed overcoat.

"Hi," Meg said, briskly seizing the newcomer's hand, "I'm —"

"Megan Keyes, *County Herald*," he finished for her. "You're probably too young to remember, but I'm Gerald Whitfield. I knew your father."

"Of course I remember, Mr. Whitfield. Government service, right? In the first Bush administration? I thought you lived in Washington."

"Part of the year. We also have a vacation home on the big lake near Oscoda. What brings you here? I didn't know I still rated press coverage."

"Some people are always news, Mr. Whitfield. How is your family related to the late Rachel Hayes?"

"Distantly. Mr. Mallette said there's already been some furor. I'd prefer to avoid any more publicity."

"It's a bit late for that. You should have seen the crowd at her coming-out party. In any case, the *Herald*'s already involved. My sister Daryl tracked down Rachel's farm and this is Dr. David Westbrook, who found her remains."

Reluctantly, Whitfield shook hands. Firm grip, wary eyes.

"How did you learn about Rachel?" Meg asked, switching on a mini-recorder.

"I've known about her all my life. I was just going to show Mr. Mallette a genealogy chart that traces the Whitfield line back to sixteenth-century England."

Retrieving a manila envelope from a brief-case at his feet, Whitfield unfolded a chart the size of a road map, the Whitfield/ Gooding family tree.

"Very interesting," Meg frowned, scanning it. "But I don't see where Rachel Hayes fits into it."

"She doesn't," Whitfield said. "She's not a Whitfield by blood, thank God. She joined the family briefly in 1868 when she married Erasmus Whitfield, my great-grandfather."

"Why did you say 'thank God' she isn't a blood relative?" Daryl asked, easing stiffly into a chair beside the desk.

"Every family has skeletons in the closet; Mrs. Hayes is one of ours. As you're probably aware, my great-grandfather was a wealthy man by the standards of the time. Timber, a paper mill, land development."

"A lumber baron?" Meg interjected.

"That's the pejorative term, yes. In any case he was elderly and in poor health when he married Mrs. Hayes, who was thirty years younger. His children opposed the marriage. Most of them were older than Mrs. Hayes and she'd been a servant in their home. She was a bog trotter, a shanty Irish immigrant with a young daughter, probably illegitimate. A handsome woman, though, if you like the type. I have a photograph taken on their wedding day . . ."

Retrieving a picture in an antique frame from his briefcase, he gave it to Meg. She eyed it a moment. Then passed it to me.

And there she was. At long last. Rachel.

Standing stiffly at the shoulder of a portly gentleman with gray muttonchop whiskers, her dark hair was pulled up in a tight bun. Narrow faced, pretty in a vixenish way. Erasmus looked a bit befuddled. Not Rachel. Her gaze lanced through the fuzzy sepia tint with such intensity that I found myself tilting the photo to avoid it.

Yet despite the grim stare, I felt a rush of relief. Because I'd never seen her before.

I'd half expected to recognize Rachel. I

160

was afraid she might be the fantasy figure who visited me so vividly the night Tipton died. The dog-woman from the well.

She wasn't. The real Rachel didn't look anything like the phantom from my nightmare. Thinner, prettier. No resemblance at all.

Which meant the dog-woman was only a bad dream. Nothing more. A subconscious twitch born of stress and exhaustion.

"If this was a wedding picture, I'd hate to see them at a funeral," Meg said. "They look like they've been sipping vinegar."

"It was an unhappy match," Whitfield agreed. "And a brief one. Apparently my relatives were right to be concerned. Erasmus fell ill soon after the wedding. He joked about the strain of marriage to a younger woman. His children suspected something more direct, like arsenic or belladonna. During his illness, Mrs. Hayes seized control of his finances. He died a few months later."

"Didn't his children order an autopsy?"

"There was no body to examine. Erasmus Whitfield burned to death in a fire at the family home at New Paris in May of 1869. A fire that his new wife and her daughter miraculously escaped."

"Another fire?" Meg breathed, glancing

at me, then checking her recorder to be sure it was running. "What happened?"

"It was probably arson, but Mrs. Hayes wasn't available for questioning. She cleaned out the family bank accounts and disappeared with her daughter before the funeral, never to be heard from again. Until a friend noticed her name in a genealogy site on the web. I phoned Mr. Mallette and flew back from Washington to settle things."

"This is great stuff," Meg said. "I take it you believe Rachel murdered her husband?"

"It happened over a century ago, but from letters written at the time, it's clear his relatives believed she killed him and her actions support that view. As does her own death."

"Her death?" Daryl echoed. "How so?"

"She died in a fire herself," Whitfield said smugly. "I'd call that poetic justice."

"Her daughter and a thousand other people died in that same fire," I said. "Was that poetic too?"

"No offense, Doctor, but I've been hearing about the wicked Rachel since I was a boy from relatives who fairly spat when they spoke her name. It was decent of you to recover her remains, but you needn't have bothered. She was already where she belonged."

"The bottom of a well is hardly the place for a lady," Mallette said smoothly.

"She was no lady," Whitfield snorted. "But since she was briefly connected to my family, I feel obligated to settle her affairs for good and all. Can I reimburse you for your efforts, Doctor Westbrook?"

"No, thanks. I can't take money for this. I didn't do it for you."

Meg arched an eyebrow, well aware of my financial status or lack thereof.

"You're sure?" Whitfield persisted.

"Dead sure." Dead sure I was brain dead.

"Then all that remains are the remains," Whitfield said, smirking at his own wit. "Cremation seems appropriate. Can you arrange that, Mr. Mallette?"

"We have a crematory on the premises and a number of moderately priced receptacles. A tasteful religious ceremony —"

"No ceremony, no casket," Whitfield said, cutting him off in mid-pitch. "The woman was a thief and a murderess who came to a bad end before we were born. Burn her remains and dump her ashes or fertilize your lawn with them. I just want the matter closed."

Meg drew me aside while Whitfield settled the arrangements. "No wonder Rachel toasted his great-grandfather," she whispered. "Two minutes with this twit and I wouldn't mind torching his shorts myself." She turned back to the older man. "Mr. Whitfield? When you're finished could you spare a few more minutes? The *Herald* is planning a series of articles on Rachel Hayes and —"

"I told you I prefer to keep this private," Whitfield said evenly. "It may seem old-fashioned, but my family name still matters to me. Any attempt to smear us and your little backwoods tabloid will have serious legal consequences. Are we clear?"

"Tabloid?" Meg sputtered. "Who the hell do you think you're talking to? The *Herald* may be a small paper but —"

"I hate to be impolite but I have a flight to catch. Sorry we couldn't have met under happier circumstances, ladies, Doctor." He stalked out. He didn't offer to shake hands this time. Neither did anyone else.

"Wow," Meg said. "Talk about anal retentive. He's threatening lawsuit over a piece I haven't even written yet."

"He can't win, can he?" I asked.

"He won't have to," Daryl said. "We'd still have to retain counsel and defend ourselves. Win or lose, lawsuits cost."

"Are you saying we should back off?" Meg asked, bristling.

"What I think doesn't matter," Daryl said, rising stiffly. "You'll do as you please, as usual. I'd better get back to the office. While I still have one." She limped out.

"Gee, that went well," I said.

"No big thing. Dar and I have been scuffling since I was six. Rachel's the one getting screwed. Again. I can't believe Tipton died and you risked your neck just so Mr. Blueblood can finish the job the fire started a hundred years ago. Toby, isn't there some way to — ?"

"Don't ask, Meg," he said, waving her off. "I'm legally obligated to follow Mr. Whitfield's instructions."

"Okay, but he said he doesn't care where you dump her ashes."

"So?"

"So he couldn't object if we dump her in a nice urn and bury it properly."

"No, I suppose not," Mallette said, brightening. "I have some very nice urns for under a hundred dollars —"

"And a stone," I added, mentally kicking myself for buying into this. "She should have a marker with her name on it."

"We can do a very tasteful stone, including engraving, for around five hundred dollars. Say five-fifty for the stone and the urn together?"

"Works for me," Meg said. "Bill the paper, Toby, we'll divvy up the tab later."

"Excellent," Mallette said. "To be honest, I didn't care for Mr. Whitfield's instructions either. Some people dismiss funeral arrangements as malarkey —"

"But they must matter or they wouldn't cost so damn much," Meg said brightly. "Do you want me to sign anything?"

"Not necessary. What would you like on the stone?"

"Her name, Rachel Hayes, and her daughter's I suppose, since they died in the same fire," Meg said. "The girl's name was Hannah. October, 1871. Anything else?" She looked at me.

"I don't know. Free at last?"

"Most appropriate," Mallette agreed, making a note. "It takes four to six weeks to have the stone carved and delivered. I'll notify you when it arrives. Are you staying for the cremation?"

"You mean now?" Meg asked.

"He said immediately. Since you're buying the stone . . . ?"

"I'll stay," I said, surprising myself.

"Sure, why not?" Meg agreed. "Will it take long?"

"A complete burn — ah, cremation, takes a couple of hours. Most folks just stay long enough to say their final farewells. This way, please."

He led us down a flight of concrete stairs to the basement, blathering all the way. Rolling her eyes, Meg had me smiling in spite of our surroundings. Which were pretty grim.

Toby ushered us into a concrete storeroom with dozens of coffins stacked against the walls, floor to ceiling. Pine boxes, burled walnut, hammered copper, even a few that gleamed like solid gold. Variety is also the spice of death, apparently.

The main attraction was a stainless steel appliance that looked exactly like what it was: an oversized oven big enough to cater a cookout. For cannibals.

"Very impressive," Meg whistled, taking out her notebook. "Does this thing have a name?"

"The Jarvis Power-Pack Cremator II," Mallette said proudly. "Gas-fired with an operational temperature ranging between 1800 and 2200 degrees Fahrenheit."

"Retort?"

"Burn chamber. Would you care to view the interior?"

"I'll pass. No offense, Toby, but isn't the decor down here a bit . . . industrial?"

"Clients seldom see this room, Meg. The

altar's above us. At the end of a traditional ceremony the casket is lowered hydraulically from the dais into the flames of the retort. A very dramatic effect."

"I'll be. Can we get on with this? I can think of places I'd rather be."

"Sorry, didn't mean to babble, but people seldom ask about my work." Taking a cardboard box the size of a small suitcase from a shelf, he placed it on the metal roller ramp in front of the cremator.

"That's it?" Meg asked. "That's all that's left of her?"

"The remains from the well were shattered, which reduced their size considerably. Would you like to examine them? Mr. Whitfield looked her over quite carefully."

"Probably looking for family loot," Meg snorted. "I'm not that curious. Dave?"

"I've already seen more of them than I care to, thanks."

"As you wish." Mallette slid the cardboard box into the oven, closed the door, and tapped several buttons on the control panel. There was a soft whuff as the oven came on.

Folding his hands, Toby lowered his head reverently. Meg and I followed suit. And found myself saying a silent prayer for Rachel Hayes. And her daughter Hannah.

And a small dog whose name I didn't know. Goodbye. Good luck. When I looked up Meg's eyes were misty. Mine too.

"It's so unfair," she whispered. "Caught in the middle of nowhere with no way out. Holding her dog till the very end. And beyond. I don't know what happened with Whitfield's great-grandfather but —"

A small bell began chiming from the cremator control panel. Frowning at the gauge, Toby tapped it with a fingertip.

"Is something wrong?" Meg asked.

"The burn's running a little hot, that's all. Probably because the remains are desiccated. It's self-regulating so the heat will normalize in . . ." The warning bell's tempo sped up and a low rumble began vibrating the concrete floor, as though a giant engine was idling in hell. An amber light winked on above the oven door.

Clearly worried, Mallette yanked open a six-inch viewing port in the center of the oven door. His face was instantly bathed in a flickering emerald glow that gave him a leprous look, as dead as his clients.

"Toby, what the hell's happening?" Meg demanded.

"There's . . . something moving in there," Mallette said, wonderingly. "I can —" Suddenly the amber light flashed red, the warning bell raced to a machine-gun clangor, and there was a sharp hiss from within, like the opening of a pneumatic door.

"The gas shut off automatically but . . ." He stared into the retort, transfixed. "She's still burning! Hotter than before." The temperature gauge needle was buried in the red zone and the warning light over the door was flashing to the beat of the bell's clang.

Mallette slammed the view port. "We have to get out! Something's wrong. I've never —" He froze as someone began hammering on the oven door. From the inside!

Mallette stumbled back from the thundering door, unable to tear his gaze away, waiting for it to open. . . .

The pounding stopped. As suddenly as it had begun. The red light slowed, then blinked out, and the bell fell silent. A long, ragged sigh filled the room.

A sound I knew well. Last gasp. Death rattle.

"What the hell was all that?" Meg asked, swallowing. "What happened?"

Shaken, Mallette reluctantly checked the view port. "She's . . . gone," he gulped. "I mean, they're both gone."

"What do you mean, gone? You said this would take hours."

"It usually does, but . . . there's nothing left but ash."

"Isn't that the point of the operation?" I said, trying to calm him. "Ashes to ashes, dust to — ?"

"Don't be an idiot!" Mallette snapped. "A burn takes two and a half hours minimum, not two freaking minutes! And reduction is never total. Bone fragments have to be crushed in the pulverizer. But there are no fragments. I've never seen anything like this."

"You said something was moving in there," Meg said quietly.

"Smoke. It must have been smoke."

"Smoke would be normal, wouldn't it?"

"Damn it, Meg, it had to be smoke! It just — well it was swirling a little strangely, that's all. It looked like —"

"Like what?" she pressed.

"The bones were moving!" he blurted. "Like they were — writhing in agony."

"Water vapor cooking off?" I offered.

"And somebody pounding on the door?" Meg pressed. "Water vapor?"

"The retort is stainless steel," Mallette said. "Maybe the metal was expanding or contracting. I've never cremated remains this old before. And I damn sure never will again!"

Driving home, neither of us spoke for awhile.

"I don't know about expanding metal," Meg said at last, "but I know people. Toby was scared spitless. I think he saw something in that oven."

"Like what? A ghost?"

"I don't know, but definitely more than smoke. I think if I were Rachel Hayes, and got cremated twice, it would really tick me off. What do you think?"

I almost told her about my recurring nightmare of the dog-woman and the well. But it was too crazy. Like a kid being afraid of monsters under his bed.

"Whatever it was, it's definitely gone now, Meg. Up in smoke. Up the flue. It's over."

"You hope," Meg said.

Chapter 19

Bass picked me up at seven the next morning for the two-hour drive down to the Quad County Animal Control Shelter. Hung over, surly, and silent. Good. I was in no mood to talk either.

I was awake half the night chewing over what happened at the mortuary. In the gray light of morning it all seemed simple. The remains burned hot, overheated the oven, which caused the racket. Simple.

I don't believe in ghosts or much of anything else. As an undergrad I studied anatomy, physiology, chemistry, medicine, and a half dozen related sciences. I'm a rational man, most of the time.

But I've held animals in my arms as they died. I've felt their spirits . . . leave. One moment they're living, the next they're inert. Something changes, some vital energy moves on. Any basic science text will tell you energy can't be destroyed, so where — ?

"Don't like dog pounds," Bass grumbled, breaking my train of thought as he swung his battered van into the Animal Control Shelter parking lot. "Too much like a jail. San damn Quentin for pets."

The shelter wasn't so bad. A beige brick building in its own cul-de-sac off US 10 north of Midland, it looked like an ordinary office complex. But I knew what Bass meant. Sadness hovered over it like the haze above a crematory.

Lost, strayed, or abandoned, the animals in shelters have one thing in common. They'd rather be somewhere else. A feeling I knew all too well.

I seldom visit shelters. Control officers can deal with most routine animal ailments. Anything complicated or contagious is cured even more promptly. Permanently. By lethal injection.

I understand the necessity. I also understand hunger in Bangladesh. That doesn't mean I have to like it.

The shelter was opening as we entered, workers, mostly women, filing in. A rangy, uniformed officer, bald as a cueball with a graying goatee, glanced up from behind the information desk.

"Can I help you?"

"I'm Doctor Westbrook. We're here to

pick up some dogs for the Algoma Humane Society?"

"Right, Mrs. McCrae called. Well, you've come to the right place, guys. If there's one thing we've got, it's spare dogs. And cats, a few exotic birds, and an iguana. I'm Liam Sullivan, Sully to my friends and everybody else. I'm the director here. Right this way." Sullivan escorted us to a locked metal door marked SECURE AREA. DANGER! NO ADMITTANCE!

Bass gave me a raised eyebrow. Sullivan smiled, unlocked it, and waved us through.

"Welcome to death row, gentlemen."

He was dead serious. The room was the pound's maximum-security lockup. Instead of chain-link kennels, the dogs were caged in individual concrete cells. Pit bulls, Rottweilers, Dobermans, all of them bearing the savage scars of fighting.

"I thought fighters were always destroyed," Bass said.

"These dogs are evidence. Belong to a dope dealer named Kiki Garces. The Feds are using them as chips to bargain with Kiki's lawyers. When the plea deal's done, so are these fellas."

"Don't seem fair," Bass said, stopping to rumple the cropped ears of a Doberman. "Killin' 'em for what we've made 'em."

"There's nothin' fair about the way folks treat animals. Check out the lady Labrador there by the table."

A chocolate Labrador Retriever female was shivering beside a stainless steel examination table against the wall. She appeared to be two to three years old, eighty pounds, sleek, healthy, and well cared for. A beautiful dog.

That's what made her scars so impossible to understand. She'd been branded. Someone had burned a swastika into the flesh of each of her shoulders. The Lab cowered as I knelt to examine her. I didn't blame her.

The scars were layered, burns upon burns. Whoever did this had taken his time. Recently. Some of the lesions were still raw.

"Easy girl," I murmured, stroking her gently as I moved around her. Shifting her tail, I examined her vagina, then knelt to check her mammary glands. No burns or other injuries. There were abrasions around her muzzle and just above her paws, though, indicating her legs and jaws had probably been tied. While she was being tortured.

As I reached for her collar, I noticed my hands were shaking. I wanted to strangle somebody.

"Who did it?" Bass asked. He'd spoken

softly but several fighting dogs rose to their feet in their cages, eyeing him. Recognizing the danger in his tone.

"We don't know yet. Vixen here belonged to a Jewish family named Feiger. A history teacher at Saginaw High. Somebody stole the dog, branded her, then tied her to the porch for the family to find. Probably some halfwit teenybopper with a hard-on for the world."

"That doesn't narrow it down much," I said, rising, scratching Vixen's chin. "Hard to believe a kid did this."

"Hitler and Jack the Ripper were kids once," Sullivan said. "Any chance her pelt will regenerate?"

"No, the lesions are too deep. Once she heals, we can do skin transplants to camouflage the scars but it'll be a drastic series of surgeries. I take it the Feigers gave her up?"

"They've got little kids. A thing like this is terrible enough without being reminded of it every day. Maybe she'll get lucky and someone will want her."

"She's a little short on luck, you ask me," Bass grunted. "Where are the dogs we came for?"

"Here, in the last eight cages," Sully said, leading the way. At the end of the row, eight greyhounds rose as one, snake-like heads weaving, seeking our scent. Not backing off a bit. Bass knelt in front of one of the gates, eye-to-eye with a black male hound. Narrow-chested with legs like a gazelle, he eyed Bass, then displayed a full array of fangs in a silent snarl.

"These hounds aren't fighting dogs. Why do you have 'em on death row?"

"What did Mrs. McCrae tell you about them?"

"Only that they were seized in some kind of a raid," I said.

"Methamphetamine lab, run by some college boys from Dearborn. Bought the hounds from racing kennels figurin' to launder their drug profits at the dog track. Stupid bastards blew up the garage where they were cooking the meth. One kid's scarred for life, the rest are in the slammer."

"Tough," Bass grunted. "So?"

"So they didn't know dogs any better than chemistry. They kept them in an oversized chain-link corral. Ten acres or so. Left them loose in there, tossed their food over the fence, let them scuffle for it."

"Damn," I said softly. "How long were they penned up like that?"

"Couple of months. Long enough to bond."

"As a pack, you mean."

"That's why I couldn't put them out for adoption. They've never really been domesticated. No way to know how they'll react to separation from the pack or to being around people. Couldn't risk the liability of a civilian getting hurt. You, on the other hand, are a professional."

"That's what my diploma says."

"They're probably going to be trouble. You know that."

"I know. But their only crime is keeping bad company, and that shouldn't be a capital offense. I can't leave them here, so let's get them aboard before I change my mind."

Sully loaned us muzzles for the greyhounds and helped load them in the van. They were edgy, milling around, growling uneasily.

Bass gave me a look that said it all.

"It's not too late to change your mind," Sullivan offered.

"Not likely," I said. "What will happen to the Labrador?"

"Vixen? County regs don't allow us to keep dogs more than six weeks. With those scars . . . To be honest, I doubt we'll be able to place her."

"I'll take her, then. After she heals, I can do the transplants, put her back together again."

"We have no budget for surgical fees, you know."

"Putting her right will cover it."

"You sure?"

"The man keeps a one-eyed, three-legged cat," Bass grumbled. "A branded Lab will fit right in."

"Then have a safe trip, gentlemen. And good luck with those hounds."

Chapter 20

The problems began as soon as we got back to the clinic. The cavernous old barn had space to spare, but it was designed for horses, not hounds. Domesticated dogs would have been content in cages but this lot would need more room. The horse stalls would have to do.

Hauling a wheelbarrow out of the tack room, I began sweeping up the dregs of straw and dried manure in the empty stalls. Bass followed right behind, closing off the space above the gates with vinyl-coated fencing. Horses can't vault a stall gate but greyhounds can leap six vertical feet to get a better look at a butterfly.

And then we freed them.

The dogs exploded out of Bass's van in a canine stampede, barking, yawping, frantically racing up and down the corridor, noses to the ground, seeking a way out. A wild mix of colors: black, white, fawn, brindle. Only two were actually gray. Vixen, the branded Lab, joined in the excitement, running with the others, already a part of the pack.

"Beautiful," a woman whispered. Yvonne McCrae was watching from the far end of the hall. In all the racket, I hadn't heard her come in.

She was dressed for riding: boots, denim breeches, and a muslin blouse, her dark hair tied back with an amber scarf. No makeup. No need for any.

I was dressed for shoveling shit. Torn T-shirt, jeans, and work boots, tastefully trimmed with dried horse manure. "Vonnie," Bass nodded. "Good to see ya. Is this your idea? Makin' these hounds into house dogs?"

"You don't approve?"

"I don't see the point. That pound is full of leftover pets. These hounds grew up in a damn cage. Look at 'em slink around, tails down, growlin.' Ever seen a cross wolf?"

"Cross wolf?"

"Half wolf, half dog, half nuts. Ojibwa hunters stake a husky or shepherd bitch near a wolf trail. If the pack doesn't tear her apart, a male mates with her and the pups are cross wolves. Great guard dogs. But you can't ever trust 'em. They never lose that wolf wildness. These dogs got that same look. First time some kid pokes a thumb in a hound's eye, he's liable to get his little hand bit off."

"Greyhounds aren't wolves," Yvonne countered. "They're racing dogs."

"Actually, they're not," I said. "The fans think they're watching a race but the dogs are trying to run down that robot rabbit to kill it. They're coursing hounds. Born hunters."

"These dogs have never hunted anything."

"No, but they've been bred for the chase for ten thousand years. Their pictures are on the walls of Egyptian tombs. Hunting's in their genes. A few generations running around a track doesn't change that."

"Are you trying to back out of our arrangement, Doctor?"

"Not at all. I just want you to understand that retraining them will be tricky business. Bass is right, they've been in an abnormal environment, but that doesn't make them a lost cause. With care and some training, I'm sure they can be socialized."

"My God," she gasped, "what happened to that Labrador?"

"Bad people," I said simply. "Don't worry, she's not part of our agreement. I'll take care of her."

"You oughta be more worried about that brindle bitch," Bass said. "The one over there, growlin' when anybody comes near her. Looks mean as a snake."

Apart from the others, the brindle was eyeing us with an eerie calm, measuring us with ebony eyes. Darker than the rest, almost liver colored, she was willowy with a deep, narrow chest and long legs. I doubted she weighed sixty pounds.

One of the bounding hounds bumped her and she snapped at him. He backed away, cringing.

"She's the alpha," I said.

"Say what?"

"Pack behavior. Wild dogs, wolves, jackals, always hunt in packs. Even mixed-breed strays will instinctively form a pack and these hounds aren't strays. They're hard-wired for it. That little female is the alpha bitch, the boss dog. She dominated that male, even though he's bigger than she is."

"Aren't boss dogs always the strongest?" Bass said.

"Actually, we're not sure how dogs select alphas, but size isn't the dominant factor. Alphas are the brightest and most aggressive. They're born to lead and the others recognize it intuitively."

"So what you're saying is, we've got a pack of wild dogs here?" Bass asked.

"At the moment, something like one," I admitted. "That's not necessarily bad. Packs are just extended families. Like tribes."

"Or gangs," Bass snorted. "Oughta take 'em straight back to the pound, save us all a lot of trouble. I've got a window frame to finish out front. You need me for anything?"

"Not if Mrs. McCrae can spare a few minutes," I said, trying to sound casual. "The dogs need a quick exam."

She gave me a look, but shrugged. "I can help if it won't take too long. Go ahead, Bass."

I could've handled the dogs alone, but working with Yvonne would be a lot more interesting. For me, at least.

I began with the biggest black male, the one the little brindle had warned off. Kneeling beside him, I murmured to him a moment, then took off his muzzle and asked Yvonne to hold his collar.

She didn't hesitate, cooing to the hound with no fear as I checked him over, her face only inches from his. And mine.

She had faint smile lines in the corners of her eyes and a small scar above her lip she

185

could easily have concealed with makeup, but didn't. I caught the scent of her hair. Jasmine, I think, which made me instantly aware that I probably smelled like sweat and horse hockey.

"What are you looking for?" she asked as I lifted his lips to examine his mouth.

"General condition. We'll check their gums for anemia, eyes for jaundice, coats for flea nests or dehydration. This guy's a little underweight and has a couple of minor wounds, probably cage scrapes. Nothing that needs stitches. Overall, he's in good shape." Releasing the black, I caught one of the grays. Singly, they were docile enough; maybe this would work out.

"And you can tell all this with a one-minute once-over?"

"Sure. I haven't lost a patient for almost three years."

She eyed me curiously, as I checked over the gray. "Would you mind smiling or something when you're kidding? I can't always tell."

"Just assume I am. You won't be wrong very often."

"But that last crack was about being in jail, wasn't it? How can you joke about something like that?"

"It's how I cope. Joking in self-defense.

The truth is, jail wasn't fun. Surreal some-times, but never fun. How do you cope?"

"By riding, I guess. Things look simpler from a saddle. You feel like you can outrun your troubles, even if you can't. Do you ride?"

"No, I love horses but I usually try to outrun my troubles on foot."

"Maybe that's why you keep getting caught."

"Touché. By the way, you're very good with animals."

"I've been around them all my life. Grew up on a farm."

"A farm? I thought . . ."

"What?"

"You were a senator's wife, I assumed you were born big rich."

"Hardly. My father was a doctor. He moved to Algoma looking for peace and quiet after serving in Korea. He found it. Our farm was only a hobby, but he loved it and so did I."

"And your fiancé? Does he like animals?"

"Les isn't really the outdoor type, he's — why did you ask that?"

"Just making conversation."

"Really?" She scanned my face, an un-comfortable feeling. She was very close. And very shrewd. "You know, I really am running late," she said abruptly. "Can you manage the rest without me?"

"I think so. Thanks for helping out."

"No charge, it's been . . . interesting." As she rose, she absently reached over and brushed my cheek. Not a caress, just a touch.

"Piece of horse pucky under your eye," she explained. "Good luck with the dogs." And then she was gone. To lunch. With Les. Her fiancé.

Horse pucky. My cheek still felt warm from her touch. What the hell was going on here? She wasn't my type. Linda, my ex-wife, is a willowy blonde. And we were the same age. Yvonne McCrae was not only older and out of my league, she was engaged to somebody else. Being drawn to her made no sense at all. None.

"What happened?" Bass yelled from the clinic doorway.

"Nothing, why?"

"Von went tearin' out of here like a scalded dog. Thought maybe you goosed her or somethin'."

"She's late for a date."

He lounged in the doorway, watching me work. I'd saved the little brindle female for last. The others had been relatively easy to handle, jumpy, but grateful for the attention. Not the brindle. The trouble with alpha dogs is, they know they're superior beings. And that you're not.

Eyeing me suspiciously as I approached, she snarled when I reached for her collar, baring her fangs. A serious warning. Back off!

Instantly the other hounds were on alert, hackles up, growling, circling us, totally focused on me and their boss lady, poised to attack.

"Need any help?" Bass grinned, waiting for me to disappear under a snarling army of dogs.

"Everything's under control." A lie. I'd left the hounds unmuzzled after checking them and they could chew me into vet-burger in a New York second.

But quitting now would be fatal. To work with them I needed their trust. And respect.

Kneeling beside the brindle, I held out my hand to give her my scent. A moment of truth. Would she bite, or back down?

She did neither. Instead, she sniffed my hand, then lowered her head and began licking my wrist, avoiding my eyes.

Odd. It wasn't a perfect posture of submission but it was close enough. Taking their cue from the alpha, the others relaxed and went back to exploring the barn.

The brindle let me check her over without further complaint.

"How'd you know she wouldn't take your freakin' hand off?" Bass asked.

"She's a lady. She just wanted a little courtesy."

"Is that your secret? Treat dogs like ladies? How do you treat your ladies?"

"I wouldn't know. I'm out of practice."

"It's like ridin' a bike. But a lot more fun." He went back to work in the clinic out front, leaving me with nine space cadet hounds and a troubling image of Yvonne McCrae up close. Wondering why she'd touched my face.

Horse pucky? That's probably all it was. Which summed up the situation nicely.

It was only later that I realized why the brindle licked my wrist. She was cleaning the half-healed gash on my wrist I'd picked up trying to catch Rachel's bones.

Which made her behavior doubly strange. Ordinarily a wound will trigger aggression in an alpha. Instead, Rachel's mark seemed to break the ice between us. I wasn't her new best friend, but we weren't enemies either. I'd settle for that.

But her reaction to that cut was still damned odd.

Chapter 21

For the next few weeks, working and caring for the greyhounds gobbled every second of my time. Vixen already had a reindeer name, so I named the greyhounds after Santa's sleigh team, Dasher, Dancer, Prancer, etc. They didn't recognize their new handles, of course, but it helped me to keep track of them.

The brindle, I named Milady De Winter. She reminded me of Faye Dunaway in *The Three Musketeers*. Cool, sleek, and dangerous. Yet Milady became my ally. Sort of. I let her out of her pen first and kept her near me while I fed the others, hoping some of her authority would rub off. It seemed to. After a few days they quit growling at me.

By the second week I could turn them loose in the barn together and examine them without getting nipped. Vixen's scars were healing, protected by a baby blue shawl that Yvonne McCrae left for her. It would be months before I could begin the series of transplants to camouflage her scars, but meanwhile she adjusted to her new life as an apprentice greyhound with the openhearted enthusiasm only dogs can muster. Despite her scars and the savagery she'd endured, I envied her unquenchable spirit. The essence of tenacity in a baby blue blanket.

Exercise turned out to be the biggest problem. Hounds need to run every day. There were hundreds of empty acres between the barn, the road, and the McCrae estate on the hill, but I couldn't let them run free. They didn't know their names and had no sense of home about their pens in the barn. On their own, they'd simply vault the corral fences and be long gone and lost.

My solution was to trot them on a leash a few laps around the pasture every day, then back to the barn. Since they bolted and lunged at every scent or odd shape, I could only handle two hounds at a time, which meant I was spending several hours every afternoon exercising dogs.

I was getting into great shape, but the hounds were barely maintaining muscle tone and it was taking too much time away from the remodeling. At this rate I'd be lucky to finish by Christmas.

And then a fall changed everything.

I was running the last two hounds, Milady and the big black male named Dancer, when I tripped and fell. Hard. And lost Dancer's leash.

Instantly, he was off in a flash, nose in the wind, heading for the horizon. Scrambling to my feet, I called him but he paid no attention, overjoyed to be running free.

He was sprinting for the fence beside the road. With no chance of catching him, my only hope was to run Milady back to the barn, get the Jeep, and try to grab Dancer up before he disappeared or got himself run over by a cattle truck.

But when Dancer realized Milady was heading back to the barn, he hesitated, then wheeled and raced back to us, falling into position just off her left shoulder. I grabbed his leash, end of problem. And the beginning of an idea.

I had no illusions that Dancer came back because I'd called. He just didn't want to abandon his alpha. Perhaps he couldn't. And I wondered if the others would react the same way.

For the next few days I took turns running the other hounds with Milady, keeping her on a leash while releasing them to run free. And it worked. They'd dash across the fields, stretching out and covering ground at a breathtaking pace, but when I trotted Milady back to the barn, the others came running to rejoin her. Every time. Pack instinct.

I tried turning them loose two at a time and got the same result. Then three. And then four. A revelation. The more dogs I loosed, the closer they stayed to Milady. They sprinted around like rockets but always kept her in view.

Running free worked magic on their personalities as well. They were more playful with each other. Happier. If they hadn't quite accepted me yet, they were thoroughly bonded to Milady and each other and that was a start.

Even Bass noticed the difference. Said they were turning into real dogs, might be worth saving after all. Coming from him, it was a major thumbs-up.

I wasn't immune either. Running through the fields with Milady while the dogs raced each other, crisscrossing the pasture searching for scent, the greyhounds were an incredible sight. Their lithe beauty literally took my breath away, lifting my spirits in a way I thought I'd lost forever.

The day my daughter was born was the happiest of my life. The day she died . . . my heart slammed shut so tightly I didn't think I'd ever care about anyone or anything again.

Saving Frankenkat reminded me that I didn't have to save the world in order to do some good in it. But running with those hounds reminded me what it was like to feel young again, and free. Happy. The kind of happiness that comes when you're doing something exactly right.

It affected me even when I wasn't running. The image of the chase stayed with me. I found myself smiling at odd moments just thinking about it.

Bass had the perfect explanation. "Blood," he said.

"Say what?"

"You didn't teach them hounds to run like that, right? It's in their blood, their genes, whatever. After half a million years of huntin' in packs, they're wired up to do it automatic."

"Genetically speaking, that's right. So?"

"So for fifty thousand years, people have been livin' with dogs, huntin' with 'em, sleepin' with 'em to stay warm, keepin' each other alive. If they're wired to hunt in a pack, what makes you think we're not? Best be careful, young stud. Keep runnin' with them dogs, next thing you know you'll be carryin' a stone ax and haulin' women around by their hair."

He was kidding, I think. But that didn't make him wrong. Jokes can be as true as textbooks. And the truth was that running with the hounds was a wonderful release, as relaxing as a week at the beach.

I was still broke, in debt to my eyeballs, and brooding about a woman who barely knew I was alive, but for an hour a day I was in the wind, a truly free spirit. And in that hour, I wouldn't have swapped lives with a pharaoh.

Chapter 22

One Friday afternoon Meg was leaning against the fender of her pickup at the clinic when I trotted in with the hounds.

"I saw you running," she said, trailing me into the barn as I put the hounds in their pens. "It looks like your life's going to the dogs."

"You say that like it's a bad thing." I tousled Vixen's ears as I closed her pen gate. "Where have you been hiding?"

"Locked away like a nun, writing all day and half the night. Rachel's pretty much taken over my life."

"Are you okay? You look a little peaked."

"Thanks for noticing. I um, I brought something for you." She hesitated, as if unsure of herself, then slapped a folded newspaper in my hand. I checked the date.

"Saturday's *Herald*? I get tomorrow's news today?"

"Something like that. Open it."

I did. The second page headline: The

Cremation of Rachel Hayes. Our eyes met.

"First copy," Meg said evenly. "Hot off the press."

"Am I going to like this?"

"I hope so. I had to use more of your background than I originally intended."

"I thought we had a deal."

"I honored it, David. Or tried to. I kept your family out of it for the most part, but there are too many parallels between your life and Rachel's to ignore."

"What parallels?"

"You're both loners, you both love animals —"

"How do you know she loved animals?"

"She raised livestock. With Whitfield's money in hand she didn't have to work, so she must have wanted to. Neighbors complained because her farm was a crash pad for every stray dog and cat in the county. Her place was as isolated as this barn and for the same reason. You both moved up here after trouble in your lives."

"You're right, I'm not sure I'll like it."

"But it's not really about you. It's Rachel's story, or as much of it as I can find. Except for Whitfield's lousy wedding picture, odd tidbits in old newspapers are all I've turned up."

"How so?"

"She dropped the Whitfield name when

she moved up here, but Hayes wasn't her family name, it's from her first marriage. Without her maiden name or her first husband's Christian name, there's no way to trace her. I've got snippets of information from local county records and I've downloaded a ton of research I haven't even scanned yet. Daryl wanted to bag the whole idea after we got a threatening letter from Whitfield's lawyer."

"He was serious about the lawsuit?"

"Apparently. His great grandpa murdered a million trees and he figures it makes him royalty or something. Rich prick. Personally, I think he's bluffing. He hasn't got a legal leg to stand on. But the *Herald*'s a small paper with shallow pockets and he knows it. Daryl thought we should play safe and protect the paper."

"But she printed it anyway?"

"Her choice was run the story or lose me. We're still sisters, even when we're fighting. Besides, in my not so humble opinion it's the best thing I've ever done. I'm throwing a celebration bash at the Algoma Inn tonight. I want you to come."

"Even if I don't like the piece?"

"Did they lobotomize you in jail, Westbrook?"

"No."

"Then you'll like it. Did I mention the food is free?"

"I'll be there."

"Good. Bring a date if you like. I'm bringing Chris."

"Sounds serious."

"We could be, if we don't blow it. We're both busy and even when we're together sometimes Chris is somewhere else. In a bomber at Mach 2, maybe. I'm a tough chick, but it's hard to compete with that."

"If it's a contest between you and a stealth bomber, my money's on you, kiddo. You're sneakier."

"Thanks so much. Don't be late, okay? I guarantee it'll be interesting."

"Is that a threat?"

"You bet."

I was whipped from running the hounds and needed a shower. Instead, I climbed up to the loft, settled down against a hay bale, and read Megan's piece through from start to finish.

"'The Cremation of Rachel Hayes" filled a foldout section in the center of the paper. No doubt about it, it was terrific. I'm no lit critic, but I've been an omnivorous reader all my life, and I know good work when I read it. Using threads from my past and Rachel's and Brenda Jozwiak's, Meg had knitted a narrative as rich as a medieval tapestry.

It was an odd feeling to see my life in print but I couldn't fault a single line. She mentioned my daughter but deftly avoided the specifics of what happened afterward.

The primary focus was on Rachel and Brenda, and how one mother's desperate cry for help must have echoed another call, a hundred years before. And in a way, I'd answered them both.

Everything was accurate, yet it had more meaning. As though our lives actually mattered in the grand scheme of things. Which was something I hadn't believed in a very long time.

There was also something troubling about it that didn't register until later. Meg was right, there were quite a few parallels between my life and Rachel's. Troubled background, love of animals, even coming to the north country for a new start.

She was a hardworking, self-reliant woman. And she'd ended up dead and forgotten in the bottom of a well. Three men had been in her well since: Chabot, Tipton. And me. And I was the only one still breathing.

It was all just a coincidence. I knew that. But it wasn't much comfort.

Chapter 23

Stepping into a noisy dining room filled with well-dressed civilians was more of a jolt than I expected. In the joint, mess halls are chancy places. A bump or a sidelong look can leave you bleeding in an instant. Animals tend to be touchy when they're feeding, hounds and hominids alike.

No one seemed on edge here though. The Inn was country elegant: linen tablecloths, a massive fieldstone fireplace, black oak beams overhead, and heavy oaken tables. Most of the men were wearing ties. I have a tie but couldn't find it, so I settled for a tweed sport coat and jeans. Impoverished veterinarian chic.

I spotted Meg sitting at a long table with a dozen guests — "DAVEEEEE!" Brenda Jozwiak roared, turning every head in a room as she barreled through the crowd. Hoisting me off my feet, she whirled me around like a rag doll.

"Man, it's good to see ya! You look great! How you doin'?"

"Good, Brenda." She'd dressed for dinner in a denim cowboy shirt, jeans, and biker boots. And a grin so wide I couldn't help matching it. Meg hurried through the crowd to join us.

Meg was actually wearing a dress, the first time I'd ever seen her in one. A navy shift, lace collar, plain enough to pass for a school uniform. Dynamite. She looked like a coed on her first date, flushed with excitement. Or maybe booze.

"Glad you could make it."

"I'd crawl to Timbuktu for free food. You both look terrific. Are you old enough to be out this late, miss?"

"I turned street legal in the last century, wiseass. Turn him loose, Brenda. Everybody's waiting for us."

Brenda gave me one last pirouette, and as the room whirled past I realized Yvonne McCrae was watching me from a few tables away. Her hair was coifed, she was wearing an off-the-shoulder peasant blouse, and I was making my way to her the moment Brenda put me down.

"Mrs. McCrae, how are you?"

"Fine, Dr. Westbrook. You remember Les Hudspeth, my fiancé? And this is Judge

Reardon and his wife Miriam." Reardon nodded, Hudspeth eyed me like an unwelcome interruption. Which I probably was. Which was fine by me.

"Dr. Westbrook's the new veterinarian I've been telling you about. John and Miriam have American Saddlebreds."

"But you won't be handling horses, will you Doctor?" Hudspeth interjected. "That old barn's hardly the place for it."

"I won't be doing large animal surgery there, but saddle horses seldom require it. And I make house calls."

"He's wonderful with animals," Yvonne said. "I've been watching you run the greyhounds. It's quite a sight."

"Keeping an eye on your investment?" Les asked acidly.

"No, I just . . . anyway, it's nice to see you, David."

"And surprising," Les added. "Wouldn't think this would be your sort of place."

"You're right. I usually prefer to eat with dogs. No ties required. And in some ways, they're more courteous than people. Don't you think so, Mrs. McCrae?"

"I suppose so," Yvonne said uncertainly. "Would you care to sit —"

"I think the doctor's lady-friends are getting impatient," Hudspeth interrupted.

"And a gentleman never keeps a lady waiting." Our eyes locked a moment. He was impeccably dressed, groomed, and almost matinee idol handsome by most standards. But he looked away first.

"Right again, Les, I'd better get back to my friends. Stop by the clinic anytime, folks. You too, Mrs. McCrae. Anytime at all."

"What was that about?" Meg asked as I rejoined them. Brenda led the way and we trailed in her wake. "Was Les Hudspeth giving you a hard time about something?"

"Nothing I can't handle." But she was staring up at me, her impish smile widening. How do women know these things? It's not fair.

"My God, David, you've got a thing for Yvonne McCrae, haven't you? Sheesh, what's up with that?"

"Nothing."

"Bull. It's all over your face, but . . ."

"But what?"

"Well, she's a bit older for one thing."

"She's also classy and engaged to a guy who spends more on manicures than my total net worth. I know all that. Let it go, Meg."

"Are you kidding? This is priceless . . . or maybe not," she said, reading my mood.

"Sorry, I'm the last person to cop a giggle over anyone's love life. God knows, I've bitched mine up often enough. So? Have you made any moves?"

"Sure, I invited her to my barn for an Alpo sandwich and a Dixie cup of sweet red. Don't be an idiot, nothing's happened, nothing's going to."

"Hey, sometimes the best love affairs are crushes. I had a major thing for Mel Gibson once."

"No kidding? How did it work out?"

"I turned fifteen and got over it. I never actually met Mel, but at least we didn't have to divide our stuff after the breakup. Stay with the crush. It's less painful."

Meg parked me between Brenda and Daryl. I gathered most of the guests were connected to the paper one way or another. I didn't catch many names. My focus kept wandering, glancing across the room to Yvonne and party. They seemed to be having a great time. Damn.

"Hey, sport, you're a million miles away. What's up?"

"Sorry, Brenda, how are you doing?"

"Really great. Bobby's healin' like a Highlander. He should be. Been checked over by half the doctors on the planet."

"Why? No complications, I hope?"

"Nothin' like that. That Chris fella, Meg's one-armed wonder? His company doctors double-checked everything the hospital did, all free, part of their insurance coverage. Said Bobby's in great shape, should be good as new in a month or so."

"That's terrific."

"Yeah, it is, thanks to you. When I think about what was down there . . ." She shook her head. "Jesus, I need a drink. How about you?"

"No, I'm good, thanks."

"Your ass, pal. I'm buyin' us a drink and we're drinkin' it. Got me?"

She headed for the bar. I didn't need a drink, but one wouldn't kill me and Brenda was on edge. So was I. And I wasn't the only one.

A young black guy across the table was checking me out. Not a jailhouse stare, more like curiosity. Late twenties, hard and squat as a keg of nails, he was wearing tinted glasses, an aqua sport coat over a black Oakland Raiders T-shirt. An urbanite among the rubes. I definitely didn't know him. I would've remembered. He reached across, offering his hand.

"Dr. Westbrook, I'm Reggie Laws. I'm looking forward to working with you. Ever consider wearing a beard? Might give you more definition on camera. A Shelby Steele look, you know?"

"I've never given it much thought," I said, glancing at Daryl for help. Laws caught the look and turned on Megan.

"You little twit. You haven't told him, have you?"

"I haven't told anyone, Reg," Megan said, smug as a cat in a canary bar. "I was saving you for an after dinner surprise. Yo, everybody," she tapped her water glass with a fork, "I'd like to introduce my special guests of honor, Dr. David Westbrook and Mr. Reggie Laws. Most of you have read about David rescuing the Jozwiak boy in the *Herald*. Reggie's not quite as heroic. He had the dubious honor of being my boss at the L.A. *Examiner* before he sold out to TV. You can explain the rest, Reg."

Laws rose. "Folks, what Meg is too modest to say is that my company does joint productions with Public Television, and we've optioned her new project for a PBS documentary. I wanted to call the series 'Revenge of the Crispy Critter' but the network preferred Meg's title so, a toast." He raised his champagne glass. "To the Public Television mini-series and, hopefully, the best-selling book of the same name, 'The Burning of Rachel Hayes.' "

Reggie's speech had silenced the entire dining area, and the applause that began at our table quickly echoed around the room. Laws beamed his thanks to his wider audience, a born ham.

"What book, Meg?" Daryl asked. "I've only seen a single piece. How many more are there?"

"Actually, sister mine, I've been writing almost around the clock the past few weeks. I'm at forty thousand words now and it's growing like cancer. The book's almost writing itself."

"Rachel's story smells like a hit to me," Reggie put in. "An ecology freak before her time, an independent woman socially and politically repressed. The book can share historic stills with the TV series and synergy could move a million units hardcover, triple that in soft."

"Let me get this straight," Daryl said, eyeing Megan coolly. "What Mr. Laws is saying is that if everything goes exactly right . . . you can pay me the fifty bucks you owe me?"

It wasn't that funny, but it broke the tension. Meg and Daryl hugged, friction forgotten. Success not only has many fathers, it has sisters too.

"You said you were looking forward to

working with me?" I asked as Reggie sat down. "On what, exactly?"

"You're part of the show, Doc. Your back-story's perfect for TV: family tragedy, jail time. *Les Miserables* in the boondocks. You and Rachel both hit the sticks to outrun your past and start over. She disappears and a hundred years later you find her? It'll grab a twenty share at least. Our average viewer's crowding sixty and seniors love sob stories."

"Whoa up, pal, I didn't agree to any of this."

"Meg said she talked to you about it."

"About a small-town newspaper series. Nothing like this."

"Well, if you're seeing dollar signs, here's a reality check. Since it's a documentary, we don't actually need your permission or anyone else's. Freedom of the press and all that. But we aren't looking to hurt anybody. It'll be in good taste and we'll spread a little bread around."

"And if I don't want to be part of it?"

"Then lay out," Reggie snapped, his voice rising. "Your background's a matter of public record —"

"Dial it down, you two," Meg leaned over Reggie's shoulder, cutting him off. "Reg, why don't you get with Chris about the sites we need? He knows the back country. I need to talk to David. Alone."

Grasping my arm none too gently, she led me away from the others. "Damn it, will you chill out? Don't spoil my big night."

"We had an understanding."

"We still have one."

"Reggie doesn't think so."

"He's a producer, he breaks balls for a living. I'm the chick who's writing the scripts and I'm your friend. Trust me, okay?"

"And trust Reggie, too? Anyone else I should trust?"

"I promise we'll work it all out when things get rolling, just don't rock the boat now. This deal —" She broke off, startled by Reggie's voice raised in anger. "My God, now what?"

"Are you nuts, man? You can't do that!" Reggie and Chris Sinclair were nose to nose. "It's a fucking historical site!"

"It was a safety hazard!" Chris snarled. "Two people died in it and a kid fell down the damned thing. Our insurance rep said fill it or they'd cancel our liability coverage."

"Guys, guys," Meg said, pushing between them. "What's the problem?"

"Nothing heavy," Reggie snapped. "Except that your boyfriend buried our prime shooting site. It'll be like filming The Civil War without freakin' Gettysburg."

"It was a hole in the ground, not King Tut's tomb," Chris retorted. "If anyone else got hurt there, I'd get sued from here to breakfast. It was just business."

"Damn poor business, sport," Reggie said, shaking his head. "You just cost yourself a nice piece of change."

"I don't work for change, sport," Chris said coldly. "Losing a wing doesn't mean I hang out on corners with a tin cup."

"Ease up, I didn't mean it that way."

"I don't give a rip what you meant. The next time you make plans for other people's property, try telling 'em about it first." He wheeled and stalked out.

"What's up with him?" Reggie said, lifting his shades to watch Chris go. "Is he always that touchy?"

"He's usually the mellowest guy on the planet," Meg said. "I've never seen him go off like that."

"Hell, I didn't mean to run him off, Meg, I was just ticked about losing the well. No big deal, we can find a lookalike site."

"I'd better go after him," Megan said. "Look, dinner's on me, everybody. Have a good time, okay?"

After Meg left, our little group made

uneasy small talk for a few minutes, then Brenda begged off, saying she didn't like leaving Bobby alone, Reggie followed, and the other guests started bailing out like rats from the Titanic. In short order Daryl and I found ourselves alone.

Across the room, Yvonne, Les, and friends were calling it an evening too. She smiled a polite goodbye at me over the heads of the diners. Then Les touched her bare shoulder and she turned away. Terrific.

"That was quick," Daryl said gloomily. "From a celebration to a wake in five minutes flat."

"Nothing connected with Rachel has ever gone right. Why should tonight be different?"

"Did you know anything about this book or TV business?"

"Not until tonight. I haven't seen much of Meg lately."

"So . . . you don't know she's started drinking again?"

"An occasional taste? Or a lot?"

"How much is a lot? She's an alcoholic, David."

"She said she had a problem once. I thought it was history."

"It was. She's been stone sober since she came home. I thought she left the booze behind in L.A. with her troubles."

"What kind of troubles?"

"The usual. A messy affair. She got involved with a married cop, his wife overdosed on sleeping pills. Meg blamed herself and fell apart. Something you might know a bit about."

"I guess I've been there. Sort of."

"Then maybe you can help. Meg has a tough-kid front, but she's more fragile than she seems. This project is too much, too soon."

"Are you asking me to talk her out of it?"

"I doubt that you could. The way she's rushing into this thing, a TV deal for a project that's not even finished, blowing off a potential lawsuit —"

"She thinks the lawsuit is a bluff."

"The point is, she charged ahead anyway. Win or lose, a suit could finish the *Herald* and she doesn't care. She's not thinking clearly. Booze or ambition, I don't know. But I can't talk to her, we've got too much history. She needs a friend."

"I think Chris has that covered."

"Being her lover doesn't make him her friend. You, on the other hand, have a three-legged cat."

"What's that got to do with it?"

"Everything."

Maybe she was right. Daryl and Meg were polar opposites, but they were still sisters. She was clearly worried about her. Which worried me.

"If booze is a problem, I can't break her arm, Daryl. She'll have to realize it on her own. But I'll do what I can."

"That's all I ask. Good God, this thing started with a little boy down a well and it's been spreading like some kind of evil oil slick ever since. I've got a really bad feeling about it."

"Meg thinks it's her big chance."

"What do you think, David?"

I considered that a moment. Tipton's SUV exploding, the fire in my barn, century-old bones shattering in the dirt. A stainless steel oven roaring like a rocket launcher.

"You don't want to know."

Chapter 24

At noon the next day Bass and I finished the final rough carpentry in the clinic. Phase one, over and done. All I needed now was, well, almost everything. Carpeting, overhead lighting in the surgery, examination tables, a drug safe, an intercom, bulletin boards . . . Two more weeks of work at least, maybe three. But not today.

It was Saturday and we'd earned a break. And some excitement.

"You sure you want to try this?" Bass asked. "If one of these hounds takes off, we'll have a helluva time runnin' it down."

"I don't think they will. I've been working with them individually on voice commands: come, sit, stay, the usual. For the most part they obey."

"The most part?"

"Their background makes them a little . . . eccentric. But I've taken four hounds running with Milady with no trouble. The pack instinct binds them together. I think they'll be all right."

I didn't mention that Yvonne McCrae had been watching the dogs run and I wanted to impress her with something really special. Eight hounds in full flight. Plus one Labrador.

Letting Milady out first, I hooked a leash on her collar to keep her at my side as Bass and I released the others. Then we trotted them down the corridor. Bass scrambled up on a fence for a rodeo seat, whooping as the full troop of greyhounds boiled out of the barn into the sunlight.

Always wired, the hounds were bounding in the air like grasshoppers on a griddle, eager to be away. Even Vixen had the fever, as wired as the rest. An apprentice greyhound in a baby-blue blanket.

Keeping Milady on a short lead, I guided her onto the faint cow path that ran parallel to the fence. She immediately set the pace, hauling me along. The other dogs fanned out in a wide semi-circle with Milady at its center. And we were off.

Greyhounds were all around me, flowing over the ground like an airborne army, floating rather than running. A breathtaking vision, like suddenly seeing the world in three dimensions.

Three of the dogs were cruising ahead of the main body, hunting for scent, casting back and forth in intersecting arcs that efficiently covered every foot of ground within fifty yards of the pack.

Dancer, the black male, slammed into Blitzen, a smaller gray male, bowling him over. Blitzen immediately bounded to his feet, snarling, eyes alight. Facing off, fangs bared, the two circled each other, growling deep in their chests while the rest quickly formed a ring around them. A cycle I'd seen dozens of times in the joint.

Just what I needed. A dog riot. They'd chew each other up and finish me off for dessert. Milady was showing an interest in the confrontation so I stepped up my pace, forcing her into a lope to keep up.

Which ended the scuffle. As soon as they realized Milady was pulling away, the spectators began peeling off to follow. Without an audience, the combatants gave it up too, sprinting to overtake us.

Unfortunately, the pace was overtaking me. The past weeks had gotten me into great running shape but keeping an eye on so many dogs was throwing me off balance, breaking my stride.

And yet, on some crazy level I was really beginning to enjoy myself. Running at the center of the pack felt so natural, so elemental that my blood was pulsing with the power of it. Maybe Bass was right. Maybe numberless centuries of humans and dogs sharing food, shelter, and the hunt had marked both races.

If so, my mark needed a touch-up. We'd only covered half the usual distance and I was already fading, throat on fire, my knees wobbling. Running a few dogs at my own pace was one thing, keeping up with a pack of exuberant hounds was quite another. I couldn't find the right gear and my fuel was running low.

In the distance, the McCrae estate came into view atop a long rise, the sun behind it giving it an enchanted glow. Couldn't tell if Yvonne was watching. Hoped so, but I had other things to worry about.

As we neared the corner where the pasture abutted a gravel road I swung left, running Milady parallel to the chain link fence. She followed my lead and the others veered like a flock of birds, sprinting past us on the new heading.

From the corner of my eye, I glimpsed a silhouette figure, a shadow on horseback coming from the McCrae stables, riding toward us on the road. Yvonne? Couldn't make out who — Milady jerked to a halt, yanking me off my feet!

I hit the ground like a refrigerator dropped from a roof, breath exploding in a *whuff*, rolling, my wrist tangled in the leash. Thorny claws raked my face as I crashed through a bush that ripped my arms and clothing like barbed wire, snagging me to a halt.

Stunned, I stood up, only to be slammed down again as Milady lunged against her collar, trying to twist her way out of it. The rest of the pack had already bolted, boiling away like a school of sharks. Racing after the horse!

They'd spotted the mount and rider in the distance and were giving chase, heads down, scrambling up and over the fence or clearing it outright with great leaps, sprinting off down the road.

Milady was plunging frantically, jerking my arm half out of its socket with every leap, desperate to join the runaways on their damned adventure.

Struggling to my knees, I dragged Milady out of the underbrush but I'd barely staggered to my feet when she hit the end of her leash at a bad angle, pulling me down into the briars again. And I lost the leash!

Milady rocketed off, racing after the others. Vixen and Prancer, the smallest hound, hadn't made it over the fence yet and Milady joined them, all three dogs leaping at once. Vixen nearly cleared it but her shawl caught, throwing her off balance and she slammed into Milady, sending her sprawling.

Pulling free of the brambles, I charged after them, diving at the leash just as Milady jumped, pulling it out of my reach. I hit the ground hard again, empty-handed.

"Shit!"

And she did. Sort of. Instead of bracing for another try at the fence, Milady promptly sat down. Fidgety, fairly jumping out of her coat with excitement, but she sat. And the other two dogs joined her, aping the alpha. All three sitting, eyeing me.

Grabbing the leash, I stared at them, dumbfounded. The training worked. Shit? Sit? Close enough. I drew Milady to my side, barely resisting the urge to slap her silly. Wiping the sweat from my eyes with my forearm, I squinted into the distance trying to spot the others. No sign of them. Nor of the horse and rider. Damn it!

Milady and her companions were anxious to follow the pack, wherever it was. So was I, but I had no idea where they'd gone and no illusions that I could catch up with them on foot. I had to get this lot back to the barn, then chase down the renegades in the Jeep.

"Lady, come on." I tugged hard on the leash to start her back but she whirled on me, planting her feet, baring her teeth in a silent snarl. The other two circled closer, their neck ruffs rising, fangs showing, and suddenly the lost pack seemed like a very small problem. I had to get Milady moving before the other two moved in on me.

And so tried the only thing I could think of. I gave her my arm. Showed her the gashed wrist. And it worked. Again. She lowered her head to the healing wound, licked it, then looked up at me, waiting. "Okay," I said, slacking off on the leash. "Let's go."

As though she'd understood, Milady immediately circled left, heading in the general direction the horse and rider had gone. Trailing in her wake, I let her lead me for thirty yards or so, just long enough to get the other two running with us. Then I tugged her gently into a long, curving loop away from the fence that gradually brought us around in the right direction, headed for the barn.

If she realized what I was doing, she didn't object. But I was still six dogs short and God only knew what happened to the horse and rider. Terrific.

My stamina was nearly gone, sweat stinging my eyes, breath coming in gasps. It was all I could do to keep running and keep the hounds from hell under control. If she pulled me down again, I decided I'd just lay there and let the pack rip out my giblets.

How far to the barn? Two hundred yards? It looked like two miles. We were running through low foothills now. To the south, rolling woodlands seemed to climb to the sky. And though my lungs were breathing liquid fire, I was moved by the beauty of it.

Was the pain easing a bit? Maybe. Second wind? Yes. Definitely. My stride was settling down, the gears and sprockets of my legs somehow meshing together again. I was still hurting but it was bearable now. Another hundred yards through the hills, then one last turn and —

Four hounds. I suddenly realized I was running with four dogs, not three. One of the runaways had rejoined us. Another suddenly appeared on the far side of the fence. Donner. Head down, tail tucked, he vaulted the fence easily, streaking toward us, a taupe torpedo. Then he veered away again and I glimpsed something small and brown scrambling desperately a few yards ahead of him.

Donner leapt for it, missing, tumbling

over a rise and out of sight.

Milady picked up her pace as we neared the barn. Sucking up every ounce of willpower I had, I lengthened my stride to keep up with her and stay on my feet.

Five hounds now. Then six. The hunting pack was gradually reforming around us, dogs drifting back like ghosts, taking up their stations, moving at their effortless lope, spreading out and casting again. Floating over the ground, flying low, mouths agape, tongues lolling.

But not from exhaustion. I swear they were . . . Smiling.

Born in cages, raised to chase a mechanical rabbit to amuse faceless mobs, running as a pack was the first natural thing they'd done in their entire lives. No wonder they were grinning.

If not for the rider they would have stayed together the whole run. I tried to count them to see if any were still missing, but they kept shifting positions and I was so exhausted I could barely focus on my next step.

Donner came streaking back into view, barreling through the pack, carrying something in his jaws. He offered it to Milady but she snapped at him and he sheered off to take a position at the rear of the main body, skulking, avoiding the others.

Were there seven dogs now? Maybe. They were floating around me like biplanes on patrol as I thumped along, burning the last of my reserves. The barn was just ahead now but it was shrinking as my vision narrowed down to a tunnel.

Blackout. I knew the signs. I was hitting my limit.

I could see the barn door now with Bass lounging against it, watching us come. The sight of him gave me an angry shot of adrenaline. I'd be damned if I'd fall on my face in front of him! Besides, if I crashed now, the hounds would probably finish me off.

Somehow I stayed upright, stumbling into the yard with the pack boiling around me.

"Hell, don't stop," Bass yelled. "Take 'em on back to their pens."

Unable to speak, I managed a nod and forced myself to jog into the dimness of the barn. Made it. Sweet Jesus, somehow we'd made it. The hounds sprinted into their cages without being coaxed. Bass had their dinners waiting beside their water dishes.

He helped me latch the gates behind Dasher and Vixen. Donner stopped to nuzzle my hand before going in, leaving me a warm, furry bundle. I stared at it, baffled, trying for a crazy moment to figure out what it was, what kind of an animal had only two legs — and realized it was half of a squirrel. The front half. Donner'd bitten it cleanly in two.

And then I was on my knees, retching, spewing onto the floor. Sensing Bass watching, I forced myself to rise, wiping my mouth on my sleeve.

"You okay?" he asked, grinning.

"Terrific." I gagged back a surge of bile that rose in my throat.

"Thought so. Only asked cause you look like the scratchin' post in a fuckin' lion cage. Fall down, did ya?"

"Once or twice. How many dogs am I short?"

"Two. What happened?"

"Somebody rode out of the McCrae place on horseback and the hounds took off after them."

"Damn, that must have been Yvonne on Twenty Gold. That stud's a handful even without the hounds of the fuckin' Baskervilles chasin' him. Where'd she go?"

"Don't know. I lost sight of them over the hill."

"Subdivision's over that way. I'll check that out. Take your Jeep cross country into the north pasture, look for Yvonne there."

He was out the door before he finished speaking.

I stumbled out to the Jeep, fired it up, and roared around the barn into the field, bucking and bumping over the uneven ground, heading for the McCrae place.

Couldn't see anyone but it was hilly and she could be anywhere. The land sloped upward toward the wooded hills beyond. And that's where I saw her, limping slowly out of the trees, leading her palomino stallion.

Gunning the Jeep around so sharply I almost flipped it, I rocketed toward her. Twenty Gold heard me coming and raised his head, dancing nervously. Too jumpy. Braking to a halt, I leapt out and hurried up the hillside on foot.

Yvonne looked dazed. Her nose was bleeding and one cheek was smeared with mud that matched her ruined blouse and jeans.

"Mrs. McCrae, are you all right?"

She started to speak, then just nodded. "Can you hold my horse? I need to sit down —" She was already falling. I managed to grab both the reins and the lady, easing her to the ground.

Kneeling beside her, I quickly ran my hands through her hair, checking for injuries. No blood, no obvious trauma. A muddy smudge on her temple was scraped raw, but there was no edema and hopefully no concussion . . . she was looking up at me.

"What are you doing?"

"Giving you a quick physical. What happened?"

"I um, rode out to watch the dogs. Got a better look than I expected. Twenty Gold bolted into the trees. A branch knocked me off. I'm all right. A little shaken up."

"More than a little. You've got a welt on your temple and your nose is bleeding. Did you hit your head when you fell?"

"No, I rolled when I landed. I got more scraped up trying to grab Twenty in the trees. Stupid, really stupid."

"It wasn't his fault, the dogs —"

"I didn't mean the horse," she said with a flash of spirit. "I meant me. I should have guessed how the dogs would react. Shouldn't have ridden Twenty out."

"Why did you?"

"They were so . . . beautiful, running free. I've never seen anything like it."

Her eyes were liquid pools. And I kissed her. Hard. On the mouth. Pure impulse. Just did it. Soft, warm lips. Salty with the taste of her blood. She pushed me away.

"What are you doing?"

"Sorry. I've wanted to do that for a long time."

"I haven't known you a long time. You're out of line," she said, struggling to get up. "I don't know what you're trying to pull —"

"Don't do that."

"Do what?" she said, exasperated.

"Make it ugly. I don't want anything from you." I helped her up. "But you're right, I was out of line. Sorry. Am I fired?"

"I don't know. Help me mount."

"Your horse is still skittish."

"If I walk him back, he'll think throwing me is a new game we play. Now hold his head. Please."

I held his halter and she pulled herself into the saddle, wincing as she sat upright.

"Are you sure you're okay?"

"Fine. You've got blood on your mouth."

"I think it's yours."

She touched her chin gingerly with her fingertips. They came away bloody. She glared at me, utterly baffled. I had no idea what she was thinking.

She wheeled Twenty Gold, spurring him to a trot, and then a full gallop, leaning over his neck, racing him home, the two of them flying over the ground like a centaur.

She never slowed, never looked back. And I wondered if I'd blown my chance.

Not likely. I never really had a chance.

I trudged back to my Jeep, fired it up, and set off in search of my runaways.

I didn't find the hounds. They found me. As I cruised the circular lanes of the upscale subdivision, an Algoma County patrol car came up behind and flicked his flashers. I pulled over. Wolinski stepped out and motioned me back to his car.

"These your dogs?" Dancer and Cupid were in the back seat, wired, bright eyed, and entirely pleased with themselves.

"I'm afraid so. Where did you find them?"

"In Mrs. Loftus's back yard. They killed one of her cats, ran the other one up a tree. I wouldn't try apologizing to her anytime soon. Give her a couple weeks to cool off. If you're still around in a couple of weeks."

"Why shouldn't I be?"

"Because it seems like every 911 call lately has your name on it, Westbrook. I'd run you out of town right now on general principles if Mrs. McCrae hadn't adopted you as a pet project. But the minute I think you're a problem for Yvonne or anybody

230

else, you'll be gone in a New York minute, clinic or no clinic. You read me, convict?"

I nodded.

"Good. Now get these fuckin' dogs out of my car."

Chapter 25

I was lugging a couple of gallons of paint out of the Algoma Hardware when a silver Jaguar whipped in behind my jeep, blocking it in. Les Hudspeth climbed out.

He looked good, had to admit it. A handsome man and well aware of it. Patrician looks, a touch of gray at the temples that matched his suit, Sulka tie just loud enough to whisper nonconformity. Made me feel like a roughneck with a cow college degree. Which is pretty much what I am.

"We need to talk, Westbrook. I have a proposition for you."

"I think one of us is the wrong gender, Les."

"Not that sort of proposition." He managed a smile. Barely. "I've been looking into your financial situation. And your background."

"Why?"

"As Yvonne's attorney and fiancé, her investments and safety are my business." His smile faded. "I'll be blunt, Doctor, you're undercapitalized and you're an ex-convict. A bad risk on both counts."

"Mrs. McCrae already knows I have a past. And you'd be surprised how little dogs care about it."

"Their owners will, when it comes out. And I can promise you it will. And your arrangement with Mrs. McCrae is very temporary. We're going to be married in a few months. Did you know?"

"I heard that. You're a lucky guy."

"Some people might think Yvonne was the lucky one."

"Some people watch wrestling on Pay-Per-View. What do you want, Hudspeth?"

"Suppose I could offer you enough money to make a proper start? I have a client who's interested in buying your business: lock, stock, and lease agreement, plus a modest profit."

"Buying what? The building's not finished yet."

"His son's in veterinary school and he's concerned that if your practice becomes established the boy will choose to locate somewhere else. Algoma's really not big enough for two vets."

"No? Seems like a nice-sized town to me.

How many lawyers does it have?"

"Our businesses are hardly equivalent."

"You're right. I fix broken animals. I'm not sure what you're trying to fix."

"A bad situation," Les said smoothly. "In a fair way. Or perhaps on a fairway. Do you play golf?"

"I don't play at anything, much. What's the offer?"

"Bearing in mind that you don't actually own your office space —"

"Skip the smoke and cut to the pitch. It's your deal, not mine. What's the bottom line?"

"Mid-forties."

I blinked. "Forty thousand?"

"Let's say forty-five thousand even. Cash. With an understanding that you won't open another clinic in the area. Do we have a deal?"

"I'll have to think about it."

"My client has other options, you know. He can open a new clinic and hire an experienced veterinarian to give his son a practice to take over. I doubt your little clinic could survive that kind of competition."

"I said I'd think about it."

"How long? My client isn't a patient man."

"A couple of days should do."

"Good. I'll have the papers drawn up."

"I didn't say I'd take it."

"You will," Les said confidently. "You're a bright young fella and only an idiot would turn this offer down. You have no real ties here, Westbrook. Take the money."

"And run?"

"Exactly." He didn't bother to conceal his contempt anymore. "Take it and run. Call my secretary for an appointment. We'll work out the details." Figured he had me now. By the balls. And maybe he did.

Didn't push it, though. Just slid into his silver Jaguar, flipped me a mock salute, and drove off with an elegant grumble.

Chapter 26

I watched him go until he disappeared around a distant corner. Then I stowed the paint in the back of the Jeep and slid behind the wheel. Didn't fire up the engine. Just sat there awhile, thinking.

For a lawyer, Hudspeth was a pretty fair liar. But I've spent months locked in small rooms with guys who tell lies for a living. Hudspeth had broken the liar's prime directive: get your story straight, chapter and verse. Improvisers always screw up.

The doting dad buying a clinic for his kid was a workable lie, straightforward, logical. But when I said I'd think about it, Hudspeth overreacted. And got pushy.

Buying me out would get the fictional dad a half-remodeled barn that I didn't even own. Opening a new clinic, on the other hand, would cost a little more, but it would give the kid a going concern to take over.

Why would somebody consider buying a

half-baked barn when opening a shiny new clinic would have the same effect?

He wouldn't. Which meant Hudspeth's client probably wasn't real.

Unfortunately, I could only think of two candidates who might want me gone and had money enough to pay for it.

I'd just talked to one. Maybe it was time to clear the air with the other.

Bass was waiting at the barn for the paint but I was too angry to stop. Instead I drove directly to the McCrae house.

A housekeeper directed me to the show ring behind the stable, a small, circular corral where Yvonne McCrae was exercising her stallion. Standing in the center of the ring in a T-shirt, jeans, and riding boots, hair tousled, her eyes hidden by designer sunglasses, she was the picture of cool competence, revolving slowly as the big palomino trotted in circles around her at the end of a long lead. A faint bruise on her temple was the only visible souvenir of her fall.

Climbing up, I perched on the top fence rail, watching.

"Must've been some kiss," I said.

She glanced up, didn't reply, continuing to work the horse.

"Les Hudspeth stopped by to see me.

Was that your idea?"

"No, why would it be? Les doesn't care for you much, though. Did you two have an argument?"

"Not at all. In fact, he made me a heck of an offer. To leave town. He says one of his clients wants to buy me out."

"Which client?"

"He didn't say. I'm not sure he really has one."

"Why not?"

"His story didn't hang together. So I'm wondering if Les is the one who wants me gone? Or you are?"

"Dr. Westbrook, if I wanted to get rid of you for some reason, I could just padlock your building. Nor can I think of any reason Les would want you to leave."

"I thought after what happened the other day —"

"I got thrown by a horse the other day. I've been thrown before. I've been kissed before too. In any case, I didn't tell Les about it and I doubt that he knows."

"Why?"

"He would have said something. He's not the silent type. And he certainly wouldn't offer to buy you out over a kiss. No offense, but Les wouldn't consider you a rival."

"That hurts."

"You'll survive. Is it a good offer?"

"Very."

"Then I suppose . . . you'll be leaving." It wasn't a question.

"I told him I'd think about it. What do you think I should do?"

"I think you'll do what you want."

"So it doesn't matter to you one way or the other?"

"Of course it matters. You and Bass have worked very hard on the barn and the dogs are doing well. I'd hate to see it all come to nothing." She was shortening the lead line as she spoke, pulling the stallion to her in ever shrinking circles until he stopped, head down, nuzzling her. I dropped off the fence and walked to her. She turned to face me, reading my eyes.

"What do you want from me?" she asked quietly.

"I honestly don't know. Nothing. Or maybe everything. Don't look at me like that, it doesn't make sense to me either. But there it is."

"There what is?"

"I seem to have a thing for you, Yvonne. A crush, whatever. Believe me, I'd lose it if I could. It's messing up my life."

"Then get over it. I'm ten years older than you are and I'm engaged."

"Only nine years, I checked. And your fiancé has serious bucks and a new Jag, and if I wanted to bring you a rose I'd have to steal it off a grave."

"That might seem very touching. If we were really talking about a schoolboy crush."

"I'm not a schoolboy."

"No, you're an ex-convict. I talked to a friend. Not about you specifically, about a — hypothetical situation. She called it Cadillac eyes."

"Cadillac what?"

"Eyes. It's an Ojibwa saying: 'Cadillac eyes, pony money.' "

"Ah, I see. I'm a gold-digger, right? And you're what? A Cadillac?"

"What I am is unavailable, so . . ." Cupping my neck with her free hand, Yvonne pulled my head down and kissed me full on the mouth. And held it a moment.

"That was for the other day," she said. "We're even now. Want some advice? Take Les's offer, David. It's probably the smart thing to do." She turned and walked away with the stallion trailing obediently behind her.

"I'm not that smart. Can we talk about this?" She waved me off without turning. So

I stalked back to my Jeep.

But I found myself whistling on the drive back to the barn. "Unchained Melody," I think it was. True, the lady just told me to get lost. But she'd also kissed me.

And she'd asked a friend about a hypothetical problem. Which meant she had a problem worth asking about.

Good. I don't mind being a problem. I have a natural talent for it.

Chapter 27

"Forty-five thou's a lot of money," Bass said. He was leaning against a sawhorse, sipping a Miller Lite, while I finished painting the back office wall. "You gonna take it?"

"I should. I could pay you for the work you've put in and still have enough left for a better start than I can make here."

"I never asked you for wages. We made a deal."

"That doesn't mean I don't owe you."

"Funny, whenever somebody offers me free money I start lookin' for a foxhole to dive into. Why would Hudspeth want you gone? Jealous?"

"Yvonne says he wouldn't consider me — what?"

Bass was staring, his beer suspended in mid air. "Hell, I was just kiddin'. But you're serious, aren't ya? Have you got something goin' with Yvonne?"

"No."

"But you've got eyes for her? That's crazy."

"Crazy runs in my family. Look in a mirror sometime."

"Mirrors scare me. You doin' anything about this great love affair?"

"Like what?"

"Flowers, candlelight dinners, moonlight limo rides?"

"Up yours. There's an old Indian saying, never needle a guy with a paintbrush in his hand. How well do you know her?"

"Von? Known her most of her life. Me and Scotty McCrae were buds, served in 'Nam together. Good man. Yvonne was a nice girl, good family. Her old man died broke when she was fifteen or so. Her mom fell apart, so Vonnie pretty much ran things after that. Sometimes I wonder if she married Scotty to make things right for her family."

"Married him for his money, you mean?"

"No, not like that. He chased her, not the other way around. But maybe Scotty havin' serious bucks didn't hurt."

"Were they happy?"

"How can you tell? They seemed to get along all right. Scotty spent a lot of time in Lansing playin' senator, Yvonne stayed here raisin' horses."

"No kids?"

"Scotty had kids with his first wife. They're grown now, only a few years younger than Von. I don't think he wanted another litter."

"Where did Hudspeth come in?"

"A partner in Scotty's law firm. Seems like a natural match: same background, same cliques, and he doesn't need her money. He's the highest priced attorney around, strictly blue chip. So is Yvonne. She's out of your league, sonny."

"I know that. So what do I do about it?"

"How the fuck would I know? I'm the last guy in the world you should ask about women. If I were in your young boots I'd go out, get hammered, and hope things make some kinda sense in the morning."

"The last time I tried that, I wound up in the House of Many Doors."

"You were lucky," Bass said, crushing his beer can in his fist, tossing it toward a trashcan. "I wound up in Vietnam."

Chapter 28

I worked late after Bass left, trying to square my thoughts as neatly as he aligned wiring. The choices were simple.

Stay. For what? Hudspeth had the juice to drive me out of business, Wolinski had me on his short list, and for all I knew the ghost of Rachel Hayes had me in her sights.

Or go. Yvonne was right, moving on was the smart thing. I'm reasonably bright, better at schoolwork than at life, but not an idiot. For once maybe I should Do The Right Thing. And go.

The problem was, it felt all wrong.

Bottom line, I liked this town, liked the hills and the wind of the north country. I liked this barn, liked the idea of working in a place I'd built with my own hands. I even liked the hounds, God bless 'em. And I had strong feelings for Yvonne McCrae. Mixed up feelings, maybe, but powerful nonetheless.

Love? Infatuation? What was the difference? Actually, it didn't feel like either one. It was more like . . .

Hunger. Just to be with her, to be around her. I'd never felt anything like it before. Hunger. Bass was probably right. I was spending too much time running with hounds.

I knocked off about ten, dog-tired, but too edgy to sleep. Instead I climbed up to the loft and opened the loading bay doors to the night breeze, watching the lights of the McCrae place atop the rise across the meadow.

Yard lights only. No one home. Or she was already asleep. With Les? No. Well, maybe. But don't waste time thinking —

One of the yard lights winked out, then back on.

Something had passed in front of it. Too far off. Couldn't tell what it was. Yet somehow I knew. And so I waited, watching the skyline at the crest of the long slope. Until I saw movement against the stars. A shadow. A stallion, walking.

Easing out through the bay door, I lowered myself to arm's length and dropped the last six feet to the ground. I rolled and came up running, loping through the pasture grass in the dark, my heart pounding as though I'd already covered a mile.

I turned at the fence, jogging along it until I found the gate, then onward. I could see them now, Yvonne sitting sidesaddle on Twenty, except that he wasn't wearing a saddle, only a blanket.

I slowed to a walk as I approached, afraid I might spook the horse. Or the rider. No need. She shifted position as I neared, watching me come.

"Hi," she called softly. "It's a beautiful night."

"Every night's beautiful out here. Is that why you came?"

She looked away, and I thought I'd misspoken, said too much — She turned and held out her arms.

"Help me down."

I caught her waist as she slid off the stud's back but didn't bother to slow her fall. I let her body carry us both down to the grass, holding her on top of me, sliding my hands up her shoulders, pulling her mouth down on mine.

No taste of blood this time, only heat, as our lips sought each other's secrets, melding, her fingers in my hair, holding on, her tongue probing mine.

The night, the stars, all washed away, lost in the intensity of those first moments. Running my hands over her shoulders, her back, my lips on her cheek, her chin, her throat.

We paused, panting, clinging together, still unsure of each other. Then we began again, as the uncertainty faded and our passion rose until there was no mistaking it, no turning back.

I fumbled clumsily at the buttons on her blouse, couldn't manage them, too eager.

Brushing my hands away, she sat up, tugged her blouse free of her skirt, then pulled it up over her head. Shaking her hair free, she unsnapped her brassiere in front, loosing her breasts in the starlight, alabaster, with large aureoles, dark as a mystery.

I buried my face in them, her body heat enveloping my cheeks, tracing her sternum with my tongue, down to her navel, tasting salt and jasmine.

Couldn't wait. I began unbuttoning her skirt. And she stopped me. Held my hand in place a moment. Then rose, a silhouette against the stars.

She picked up the stallion's reins. My heart was hammering in my throat. Afraid she might walk away . . . Pulling off the saddle blanket, she unclipped the reins and slapped him on the rump. He snorted, then galloped off into the dark, heading for the barn.

"I don't think we want an audience."

Naked to the waist, she stared down at me a moment with a quizzical smile, as if she couldn't quite believe she was here. Or what was happening.

Nor could I. Spreading the blanket on the ground, she knelt on it and reached out to me.

Surer now, less frantic, we kissed and fondled and probed as we slipped out of the rest of our clothing. And then she was beneath me, her thighs opening, welcoming. She was already wet when I entered her, as though we'd been together a thousand times with ten thousand more to come.

And then we were rocking, thrusting together with such force that I was gasping, forgetting to breathe. And I had a fleeting memory of that first day, when I'd thought her hips were a bit wide. Wrong. They were perfect. Exactly the right size.

Too much. Her skin, hair, her mouth, wetness. I exploded much too soon but it triggered a response in her, and another in me, an orgasm so intense I couldn't tell if it went on for a month or a moment. But after, I was spent, as though I'd sprinted a 10k race flat out.

Nestling together in the dark, the breeze cooling our bodies, she cradled her head in the crook of my arm, gazing up at the stars while I gazed at her. Horse scent from the blanket mingled with the jasmine in her hair. Appropriate. Exquisite.

"Yvonne?"

"Don't talk." She pressed a fingertip against my lips. "Don't . . . make any promises."

"I think ruhh ruhhh rooboo," I mumbled against her finger.

"You idiot," she grinned. She moved her finger aside but covered my mouth with hers before I could speak, and her breasts were against my skin and her thighs on mine and the premature explosion didn't matter. The marvelous roller coaster surge was beginning again. . . .

Chapter 29

Cold. Shivering, I tried to fold myself tighter for warmth. Then snapped awake. I was in the field. On a saddle blanket. With my shirt draped over my shoulders. Alone.

Sitting up slowly, I looked around. The sliver of moon was setting over the hills and I watched it awhile, thinking. Remembering.

Then I pulled on my jeans and boots, and sauntered slowly home in the starlight. Whistling all the way. Same dopey song as yesterday. "Unchained Melody." "Oh, my love . . ." Something like that.

I felt as loose as a teenybopper, that glow when everything feels new, everything's still ahead of you. Felt almost young and limber enough to make the ten-foot jump back up through the open bay door.

But not quite. Instead, I strolled around to the front door. And froze. Even in faint light I could make out the shape of a strange vehicle parked in front of the office. A truck. It grew more familiar as I approached. Meg's outlaw pickup. With its smoked windows, I couldn't tell if anyone was inside or not. Stepping up on the running board, I tried the door latch. Locked. But the interior light switched on automatically at my touch and I could see Meg slumped against the doorpost. Startled by the light, she sat up, looking blearily around.

"Meg? Are you all right?"

"Hey," she said, as her window hummed open. "How are you doin,' David?"

"Better than you are, I think. Are you loaded?" It was a rhetorical question. The reek of booze rolled out of the truck like a wave.

"I had a few," she admitted. "Didn't mean to get tanked, it just kinda snuck up on me. Sorry to wake you up. Hey, can I crash with you tonight? If I go home I'll hassle with Daryl and I'm just not up to it. Not tonight."

"No problem. You're in no shape to drive anyway. Come on, I'll fix up a spare room."

"Thanks. 'Preciate it." She eased out of the truck, moving very, very carefully. I took her arm as we climbed the stairs for safety's sake.

"Just for the record, this isn't a subtle attempt to have my way with you. Probably should be though. Oops." She stumbled against me. "Sorry. Damned stairs are wobbly."

"I'll level them tomorrow."

"Good idea. We'll get everything straight tomorrow."

"What do you mean, everything? What's wrong?"

"Nothing. Nothing a vet can fix, anyway. I'm not a pet."

"If you were I'd put you down for being a nuisance." I helped her into the living room, eased her down on the sagging couch. "Wait right here, I'll have a bed ready for you in a jif."

"We can double up in yours," she called after me. "I don't take much room."

Ignoring her, I hustled up some blankets from a closet and quickly made up a bed in one of the spare rooms. Meg had toppled over and scrunched into a fetal curl, snoring softly. She only groaned when I tried to rouse her, burrowing deeper into the cushions.

Hell, the couch was probably as comfortable as the bed anyway. Slipping off her sandals, I slid a pillow under her head and covered her with a blanket. She murmured something but didn't wake. God, she looked so young. But the booze odor was too familiar to me, recalling memories better forgotten.

I stumbled off to bed, laid there a moment trying to recall the texture of Yvonne's skin in the moonlight. . . .

And woke clear-headed, with the morning sun warming the room, feeling better about life and the world than I had in . . . I couldn't even remember how long. Too long.

Snuggling down in the blankets, I luxuriated in the glow, remembering Yvonne and the night. And Meg's arrival. Until it dawned on me that unless I was hallucinating, I could smell bacon.

Pulling on my jeans, I eased the door open. No need to be quiet. Meg was in the kitchen, humming over the stove.

Barefoot, she was wearing one of my work shirts over panties and . . . nothing else. Her blouse and slacks were in a crumpled pile at the foot of the couch.

"Morning," she said brightly. "I was just going to call you."

"What's all this?"

"Breakfast, what's it look like? Sit down. How do you take your coffee?"

I stayed where I was, eyeing her.

"I borrowed one of your shirts. Hope you don't mind."

"It looks better on you than me, Meg. But the last time I checked, the buttons worked."

"What's the matter?" she said, facing me, the shirt open to the waist. "Don't you like the view?"

"The view's terrific," I said honestly. "But it's not what we're about, so why don't you button up that little number and tell your buddy Dave what's up?"

She colored, her eyes snapping. Then stalked out to the living room, buttoning my shirt on the way. I poured two cups of coffee and carried them to the table. When Meg returned, she was wearing her slacks.

She sat across from me, staring into her cup, reading something in its dark depths.

"He's married," she said abruptly. "Chris is married."

"Oh." I sipped my coffee. "Sorry."

"Not as sorry as I am, damn it. I should have known. The nice ones are always married."

"Thank you."

"Get stuffed, Westbrook, you know what I mean."

"You liked him a lot?"

"Present tense. I like him a lot. Thought we might have a chance for the real thing. But I'm not going to get involved with a married man, damn it. I just don't know what to do about it."

"How married is he?"

"Separated, he says. She's in Georgia staying with her folks. They have two kids, boy and a girl. She must be crazy."

"Why?"

"Because she's got what I'd give the world for: Chris and kids and a home. And she's throwing it away. He thinks it's because of his arm. She just can't deal with it."

"That's possible. Sometimes people refuse to pick up pets that are scarred. That's how I got Vixen, the little Lab that wears the shawl. It hides some nasty scars."

"So she was dumped because she isn't perfect?"

"Scars are ugly, especially hers. But mostly I think the injured pet scares people, reminds them how chancy life is."

"Is that what Frankenkat does for you?"

"Frank? No, he's the opposite. He reminds me that there's always hope if you don't quit. Or something like that. Animals are easy for me. I've never met one I didn't like. Sometimes — I don't know — I can almost sense what's wrong with them. Like we're on the same wavelength. People are a lot tougher for me to figure."

"So pretend I'm somebody's pet mouse.

How do I handle this thing with Chris?"

"It depends on how you feel about him, down deep. I can't help you with that. I can dissect hearts, but I can't read 'em. One thing I can tell you though, getting hammered won't help."

"Last night was . . . an overreaction. I can handle booze."

"So could I. Right up to the second I took a swing at that cop. End of lecture. Let's eat. What have you got there?"

"Scrambled eggs, toast, Canadian bacon, bagels and, wow, lox? Where did you find lox in Algoma?"

"Find it? I didn't, I thought you went out to. . . ."

But even as I said it, I realized what must have happened. Someone had brought me breakfast. As a surprise. Someone who could let herself in with her own key. Damn!

Meg must have read the consternation in my eyes. Her face lit with an imp's grin.

"Oops," she said.

Chapter 30

After a quick shower, I shaved, pulled on clean jeans and boots. Meg was wearing my best shirt, so I settled for a Detroit Pistons tee.

Driving to Chez McCrae I tried to come up with a plan, an approach, anything. Nothing came. It didn't matter. When I pulled into Yvonne's driveway, there was no place to park. Cars were lined up clear out to the road.

So much for the quiet tête-à-tête I had in mind. Had she collected a lynch mob? Wouldn't blame her.

Parking on the shoulder, I trotted up the driveway to the house. Rang the doorbell, glancing around. It really was a handsome home, fieldstone and cedar. Somebody had taken a lot of care to — The door opened. Tall woman, fiftyish, café-au-lait with cornrowed hair and a doe's liquid eyes. Mauve silk blouse, dark slacks.

"Hi, I'm Dr. Westbrook, is Mrs. McCrae in?"

"Speak of the devil, we were just talking about you. I'm Amanda Hawley. Come in."

Baffled, I followed her down the flagstone hallway to a sunken living room, rustic modern, a stone floor decked with Navaho rugs, Norse furniture of bent oak and tanned leather, and a stack-stone fountain against one wall with an honest-to-God birch tree growing up into a skylight that lit the room.

A half dozen well-dressed women and one older gent were seated at a long dining table. I scarcely noticed them.

Yvonne was at the head of the table, hair casually coifed, wearing a navy suit with a puritan collar and reading glasses, a vision of prim and proper. A flash of her in the moonlight flicked across my memory. As different as . . . night and day. The straitlaced outfit should have accented her age. It didn't.

"Hey, David," Daryl Keyes said, waving a hello, "meet the County Humane Society board." She quickly rattled off their names, none registered. "Doctor Westbrook's the famous tomb raider, coming soon to a supermarket tabloid near you. He's also managing our adopt-a-dog program. For free."

259

"Hear, hear," the older gent beamed, leading a small round of applause. Which Yvonne didn't join, I noted.

"Sorry to interrupt, can I see you for a minute, Mrs. McCrae? It's important."

She smiled tightly, excused herself, and I followed her out onto the back deck.

The view was marvelous, rolling hills, my barn in the distance, and a major thunderstorm brewing in Yvonne's eyes.

"Your timing stinks, David. I have guests."

"This can't wait. We need to clear some things up."

"No, we don't. I had no right to barge in this morning. I wanted to surprise you. And got surprised instead."

"I can explain that."

"You don't have to. I was upset at first, but in a way I'm glad it happened."

"If this is glad, I'd hate to see you ticked off."

"All right, I'm not glad, damn it, but it was definitely a reality check. It highlighted everything that's wrong between us, the difference in our ages, our lives —"

"Whoa. For the record, Meg showed up out of the blue last night, loaded. She was in no shape to drive home so she crashed on my couch. End of story."

"Does this happen often? Girls dropping by to sleep over?"

"Nope, Meg's the very first. I guess it's a little early in our relationship to ask you to take my word for that."

"David, we don't have a relationship. We had — I don't know — an incident. A moonlight incident. Chemistry, hormones, whatever. But it was one night. It wasn't real life."

"It felt very real to me."

"But I'm not like that. I don't . . . have flings."

"Neither do I."

"Maybe you should explain that to the girl in your room."

"She wasn't in my room, she was in the living room. On the sofa."

"This is pointless. It simply can't work. Those people in there are my dearest friends and most of them are old enough to be your parents."

"But you're not. Look, I'm coming out of a bad time, scrambling hard to make a fresh start. I didn't plan on meeting you, I know the timing couldn't be worse. And I'm still glad I did."

"Emotionally? Or financially?"

That stopped me. I stared at her as though I'd been slapped. "Wow. That's cold."

"Sorry. I had a wonderful night. A terrible morning after."

"And now we're back to . . . what? Cadillac eyes or whatever it was?"

"We're not back to anything. That's what I'm trying to tell you."

"Okay," I said with a shrug.

"Okay?" A trace of uncertainty wobbled her tone. Good.

"It's Catch 22, Yvonne. I can't convince you I'm honest if you think I'm not. Anything I say could be a lie, right?"

"I didn't mean —"

"Hey, given our situation, it's a logical assumption. Dead wrong, but logical. Maybe it comes down to this. Do you really believe I'm some kind of a con man? Is that it?"

"No. I mean . . . God, I don't know what I think. But I don't see how it can work and I'm afraid it will end badly."

"Maybe it won't end at all. Waking up this morning felt like every Christmas I ever had as a kid. I'll admit things have happened quickly and we're probably not Dear Abby's idea of a perfect match, but I've lost enough in my life to know when something good happens, you'd better grab it. And you're the best thing that's ever happened to me."

"That's a very nice thing to say."

"Thank you. Have dinner with me to-night. I'll think up a few more nice things."

"I can't."

"I promise I won't pressure you, we can just talk and —"

"It's not that. I have a — previous engagement."

"Ah. With Les?"

She nodded, looking so miserable I wanted to wrap her in my arms and promise everything would work out. But crowding her would have been a mistake. She was not a lady to push.

"Okay," I said.

"You keep saying that."

"I don't know what else to say. Are you in love with him?"

"I . . . care for him. He's been very good to me. I thought I had my future all worked out, David. It was all very . . . sensible. Very logical. Then you come crashing in and turn everything upside down. Including me," she added wryly. "I need some time and space to think things through. A few days. Is that too much to ask?"

"No, of course not. Not if that's what you need. Can I ask a favor?"

"What?"

"Kiss me goodbye."

She hesitated, and I thought she might

just walk away. Instead she lifted her face to mine and kissed me. No fireworks exploded, the earth didn't move. But we just melted together as seamlessly as two drops of mercury flowing into each other. As though we'd kissed a thousand times before.

After a time she drew back, looking into my eyes. "I think I'm in a lot of trouble," she said quietly.

"I certainly hope so."

"I have to get back to the others. I don't want Les to hear about . . . whatever's going on with us from a stranger. My God, what am I going to tell him?"

"Goodbye?"

"You're no help. He'll probably have me committed. And he'd be right."

"No," I said. "He'd be wrong. This is right."

"I don't know what this is."

"But it's something, isn't it?"

"Yes. It's definitely something."

I watched her walk away, wondering what she'd do. She had more to lose than I did: reputation, social position. All I was risking was the lift I felt whenever I saw her.

But it felt like a lot. And I was tired of being a loser. I wanted to win again. Whatever it cost.

Chapter 31

Marty Lachaine goosed the gas on his battered Ford pickup, blaring his horn at the moron broad in the blue Toyota who was dawdling, looking for a parking space.

"Bitch!" he shouted out the window. "Watch where the fuck you're goin'!" Flushing, the elderly woman glared at him as he wheeled the pickup around her. Marty flipped her the finger.

"Chill out," Kurt Hemke said, "the Caddy's still in sight. Ain't likely to lose him in this one-horse town."

They were cruising Algoma's business district, two roughnecks in flannel shirts, tailing a coffee-colored Cadillac half a block ahead.

"Fuck you," Lachaine grunted. "I know I ain't gonna lose him. I'm just tired of fuckin' around. I say we catch him alone, kick the livin' shit out of him, and be done with it."

"Fine by me. Except nobody paid us to whup nobody." Hemke eyed Lachaine warily, gauging his mood. Marty was risky business to cross, as likely to stomp a buddy as a stranger.

"Whoa, where the fuck's he goin' now?" Lachaine slowed as the Caddy pulled into a small shopping center. Hemke followed it with his eyes as they cruised past.

"Video store," Hemke said. "He's parking down on the end, away from the other cars. Probably worried about somebody puttin' a door ding in his new Caddy."

"I'll ding the motherfucker," Lachaine nodded grimly, gunning the pickup into the mall's second entrance, weaving through the lot to a delivery alley that circled around behind the shops. Racing the length of the strip mall, he screeched to a halt in the shadows at the far end of the buildings, only twenty feet from the Cadillac.

Both men piled out. Hemke glanced around, checking for witnesses. No one was near.

"Only thing I hate worse'n a spook is a spook in a brand new pimp-mobile," Lachaine snarled, grabbing a tire iron from the back of the pickup. "I swear, some jobs I'd do for nothin'. C'mon, let's fuck this baby up!"

Chapter 32

Halfway back to the clinic, I quit worrying about Yvonne long enough to worry about Meg. Wondering if she'd still be there and in what condition. Daryl warned me she was drinking too much. Apparently she was dead right.

When I wheeled my Jeep into the clinic drive, it was worse than I'd feared. Meg's pickup was still there. And Chris Sinclair's Mercedes convertible was parked beside it. He was leaning on the fender in a tweed sport coat and khakis, arms folded, looking like a time bomb about to blow.

"Is Meg here?" he snapped as I climbed out.

"I don't know, I've been out."

"But she was here?" He straightened. "Last night, I mean."

"She crashed on my couch, sure."

"On your couch? We have a misunderstanding, but instead of working it out she goes running to you? Is there something you want to tell me, Westbrook?"

"Sure. If you show up late some night, you're welcome to crash on my couch too, Chris. But it won't make us a couple, if that's what you're wondering."

"I haven't got time for this, I've got a plane to catch. I have to see Meg."

"Try knocking."

"No answer."

"Then either she's not here or she doesn't want to see you. Same difference."

"Not to me. Suppose we take a look and see if she's here."

"Whoa, you mean look under the bed, something like that? I don't think so."

"You think you can stop me?" His eyes lit up. He was angry, needed somebody to hit. I knew the feeling all too well. I was halfway there myself. But the last thing I needed was more trouble.

"What I think is, if you try to go up there, we'll go around," I said evenly. "Maybe you can stomp me into next week. Maybe not. Either way, you'll get blood all over your jacket. And we'll still be outside."

He chewed that over, measuring me with his eyes. Déjà vu. I'd been in this jam a dozen times in the joint. Chris was rock solid, combat-trained. No doubt he could whip me in a fair fight. But I quit fighting fair my first week inside.

"For pete's sake," Meg said, stepping out on the landing. "Anybody who still believes in evolution should check out you two. Chris, what on earth do you think you're doing?"

"Nothing," he said, lowering his hands. "I just want to talk to you."

"And you figure to get on my good side by beating up my friends?"

"No, I — sorry, Dave. Didn't mean to come on like a goon."

"No problem. Look, I've got work to do in the clinic. If you two want to talk —"

"We can talk on the way," Meg said, trotting down the steps. In her salmon sunsuit she looked fresh and perky as a speckled pup, no trace of a hangover or blues in the night. "I'm supposed to drive Chris to the airport and keep his car. Assuming you still trust me not to run it off the nearest bridge, Sinclair."

"Like you said, we'll talk about it," Chris said, obviously relieved that she was speaking to him at all. A moment ago he'd been ready to hand me my head. A few words from Meg shifted him from full-attack mode to semi-sheepish. Easy to see what Meg saw in him. A tough customer,

269

but basically a nice guy.

He held the driver's door open for Meg. Instead of being impressed, she slid behind the wheel, fired up the 'Benz, and slammed it into reverse, forcing Chris to scramble into the passenger's seat.

"Buckle up, buster," she said, giving me a wink. "You're in for a bumpy ride."

She roared off with Chris still struggling with his seatbelt. I almost felt sorry for him. But even sorrier for me.

Yvonne had asked for a few days. It already felt like a very, very long time.

Chapter 33

"Can we at least talk about this?" Chris asked. They were in his Mercedes, Meg driving, wind tousling her curly mop, her eyes hiding behind her sunglasses.

"Talk about what? That we've been seeing each other for weeks, sleeping together. And you forgot to mention having a wife and kids? No problem. Believe me, I understand."

"I don't think so."

"Sure I do. I've been here before, remember? I even told you how it turned out. His wife overdosed. Nearly died. I'm not doing this again, Chris."

"I'm not asking you to."

"Good, glad that's settled. It's a lovely day, isn't it?" And it was, a bright summer sun tinting Algoma's small town streets into a picture postcard of home, the big lake glittering on the horizon like a diamond necklace.

"Meg, please," Chris said, trying again. "I didn't mean to lead you on. I never expected things to get this serious."

"That's your defense? You wanted a quick lay? Didn't want to complicate things by telling me the truth?"

Chris hesitated, then shrugged. "Yeah. Actually, that's pretty much how it was."

Surprisingly she laughed. "At least that's straight up. Well, if wham, bam, thank you ma'am is what you wanted, Sinclair, congratulations. You got it. So did I. And it's over."

"But that's not what I want now. Look, I admit when we started it was just chemistry. I had the hots for you. I still have. I wasn't looking for anything serious between us. I'm not sorry it happened, I'm glad. I just didn't expect it."

"That's too bad. It's also too late. Drop it, Chris. We had a fling; it didn't work out. It happens every day. No big deal."

"Fine," he sighed, reclining his seat, closing his eyes. "Then I guess I'll skip the part where I beg and plead and tell you how much I care about you, right? Wake me up when we get to the airport."

And he dozed off. Just like that, in the middle of the freaking argument. The sonofabitch! Meg was half-tempted to smack him awake but wouldn't give him the satisfaction of showing how furious she was. And how hurt.

Damn it, how could he do this, knowing how she felt about him? Unless wham, bam was all they really had? No, she was sure that — ahh, hell. Maybe he was right. Better to let things cool off and sort it out later. Assuming there was anything left to sort out.

They were leaving the city limits now, passing the town cemetery. An odd movement caught Meg's eye. A woman . . . moving among the tombstones . . .

Good God! Her throat seized up, couldn't swallow, couldn't speak. Could only stare as the figure drew closer.

"Meg!" Chris shouted, too late. With a screech of metal the Mercedes glanced off the rear fender of a parked car. Desperately, Meg locked up the brakes, sending the car into a skid, sliding broadside down the quiet street, tires howling like demons from hell.

Chapter 34

I'd just gotten back to work, still chewing over Yvonne's definition of "time and space," when Reggie Laws drove up. He was dressed for a safari, khakis with a knife-edge crease, a black muscle tee to show off his iron-pumper's build. Eddie Bauer hiking boots. Impeccable. All he lacked was an elephant gun and a faithful guide.

"Kind of a low-rent setup isn't it?" he observed. "For a doctor's office, I mean?"

"Dogs don't worry much about decor."

"Dogs don't pay the bills, champ, owners do. One thing you learn in my business, keep an eye on the money. Speaking of which, I need to rent you for an hour or two."

"To do what?"

"I covered more ground than Daniel fuckin' Boone yesterday, couldn't find the famous well. Half those country roads don't have signs and I can't navigate by tree moss or however the locals do it. I'll pay for your time, say a hundred bucks an hour?"

"Are you serious?"

"Don't I look serious?"

Actually, Reggie looked halfway to an attitude, but I definitely needed the money. Losing my Cadillac eyes image meant finding cash of my own. So I shrugged off the warning signs and went along.

Grabbing a duffel bag out of his midnight blue Cadillac, Reg tossed it in the back of my Jeep and climbed in. We didn't talk on the drive into the Black River Hills. I asked how the project was going but he didn't answer.

Fine by me. I had troubles of my own to think about. At least we had a beautiful day for it, clear and brassy, gulls wheeling in the cloudless sky above the rolling countryside.

I thought the well site was branded into my memory but as I slowed the Jeep to a halt by the roadside, I couldn't spot the hole. In the end I had to find it by driving across the shallow ditch into the field, following tire tracks that led to . . .

Nothing.

A square meter of raw earth in the middle of an empty meadow was all that remained. The well had been filled, raked smooth, and new grass was already growing. A few weeks and all traces of it would be gone.

"This is the place," I said, climbing out, "or it was. Not much to see now."

"They did a number on it, all right." Reggie nudged the new grass with the toe of his pristine boot. "I wonder why?"

"Chris said their insurance company ordered it. Two people died in this well and Bobby Jozwiak nearly bought it too."

"Right, but to duck liability they only had to fill in the hole. It's in the middle of a fuckin' empty field. Why bother to rake and seed it? Didn't make sense yesterday, still doesn't."

I glanced at him. "I thought you said you couldn't find it."

"Actually, I lied about that. Wanted to talk to you alone. Couldn't think of anyplace more private than this."

"Okay, we're private. What's on your mind, Reggie?"

"Cars, for openers. Did you notice the Caddy I drove to your office was blue?"

"So?"

"That's because the coffee-colored one I rented at the airport got trashed yesterday. Somebody seriously worked it over. Maybe with a Louisville Slugger." Reaching into the Jeep, he unzipped his duffel bag and pulled out a baseball bat. "Something like this one. Poked out its eyes . . ." He jabbed the bat into one of the Jeep's headlights, smashing it.

"Hey! What do you think you're doing?"

"Back off, Doc. I played ball in college. Hit .321 my senior year. How far do you think I can drive you?"

I hesitated. For a crazy moment I was almost angry enough to tackle Reggie, bat and all. It passed. Barely.

"What the hell's up with you, Reggie?"

"That's what I wanna know. Somebody wrecks my car, I gotta ask myself why. I have no enemies here, most people don't even know who I am. So it comes down to the series, doesn't it? Who doesn't want the series made? That's a short list. The story's mostly about two people. One of them croaked a hundred fuckin' years ago. The other one is you."

He waited. So did I.

"So I ask myself why the good doctor wouldn't want the series made, do some checking, and surprise, surprise, my man's done time. Nothin' heavy, but probably enough to bury his punkass new clinic if word got around this two-bit town. How'm I doin'?"

"You're not even warm. Meg knows about my background. She promised not to use it in the series."

"Yeah? Well I didn't promise and my company's invested a hundred thou in this project. Why didn't anybody tell me about it?"

"It's got nothing to do with Rachel or the well."

"I think the guy with the bat should decide that. Point is, I know about you now, Westbrook, so if you figured to chase me off by bustin' up my car, you blew it. All you did was piss me off."

"I didn't work over your car."

"No? Then who did? One of your ex-con runnin' buddies?"

"Not a chance."

"Wrong answer." He swiveled a half step and slashed savagely at the Jeep's front fender with the bat, smashing a chunk out of the fiberglass. "Damn that feels good! Trouble is, if I wreck this piece of shit, I'll have to walk back to town. Maybe I'll work on you instead. Unless you start givin' me some straight answers."

"Try asking me something I know."

"Okay. You know Meg's a juicer. Got jammed up in California over it. Most writers drink. Occupational hazard. So when a reporter gets canned for drinking —"

"If you want to talk about Meg's problems, talk to Meg."

"I'm talking to you, Doc. If this series flies it could make serious bucks. Since it's at least partly about you, maybe you want a piece of the action."

"I never wanted it to be about me. I still don't."

"So you say. But there could be another reason you aren't asking for cash. Because you've already got it. Like if Meg paid you to keep your mouth shut."

"About what?"

"The truth. Truth's a slippery thing. I worked on a show once about child prostitutes, schoolkids swappin' their bods for high style clothes and drugs? A Baltimore paper ran the series. Graphic stuff, perfect for television. Ever see it?"

"No."

"Neither did anybody else. Four months and a million bucks into development, it crashed and burned. I was just a production assistant, but the fallout was so heavy I didn't work for two years."

"What happened?"

"There was nothing to film. Kids may be peddlin' their asses somewhere, but we couldn't find one verifiable case in Baltimore. The reporter heard rumors about kiddie hookers and went on a crusade, stretched the facts and filled in the blanks with bullshit. He was so hot to save the world, he wrecked his career and nearly trashed mine. I used to dream about catchin' that motherfucker alone, just me and my Sammy Sosa slugger here. Maybe I will yet." He took a practice swing, his eyes locked on mine.

"I've never been to Baltimore."

"But you know what truth is, right? And you were involved in the incidents Megan's writing about. How much of it is true?"

"In the pieces I've read, things were exactly as they happened. Only better."

"She punched it up?"

"No, she just laid it out so it made sense. When I went into the well after that kid, I didn't know Rachel was down there. She'd waited over a hundred years for someone to come. I didn't realize how incredibly sad that was until Meg wrote about it. She gave it perspective, but her facts were absolutely straight."

"She's one helluva writer," Reggie conceded grudgingly, "I'll give her that. What about at the mortuary? The mortician, what's his name?"

"Mallette."

"Right. He claims it was just a minor malfunction. The oven overheated a little and you and Meg panicked."

"Sure we did. Alarm bells were ringing, something was pounding inside that oven like King Kong trying to break out. If there'd been any furniture I would've been under it. Mallette was more spooked than we were."

"That's not his recollection."

"The eyewitnesses at my trial weren't unanimous either. I still did the time."

"So you did," Reggie conceded. "And Mallette ain't the most macho guy on the planet. So that brings us down to the lady. Rachel Hayes. What do you know about her?"

"Nothing. I'm no historian. Ask Whitfield, he's her only relative."

"Colonel Whitfield," he snorted. "Interesting guy. Heavy Washington connections, vacation home here, an estate in Virginia. Granddaddy was a lumber baron. The colonel part is real enough, he's Air Force reserve. Tying his family history into the project would give the story real style. Dirt on the Rich and Famous."

"So why don't you get it?"

"Because he's bucking the program. Whitfield won't confirm or deny anything. All I've got is what he told you. Rachel and his great grandfather were married and maybe she croaked him. Anything more is an invasion of privacy according to his lawyer. Says Rachel's an embarrassment, doesn't want to publicize the family connection. Won't be interviewed on camera. Blew us off."

"So?"

"So I can't verify his story. All the paperwork went up when Rachel torched the family digs. Wedding license, deeds, the works."

"But if they were married —"

"They were married by a Justice of the Peace at the courthouse in New Paris, Michigan, 1868. The whole damn village of New Paris burned to the ground in 1871, along with forty other Michigan towns in the same fire that took Rachel off. For all I know, everything Whitfield told you is a crock."

"Why would he lie?"

"Why does anybody lie? But if they are, I'm the one gettin' hung out to dry. All we've got are bits and pieces. They seem to fit, but something doesn't feel right. I don't like it."

"Rachel's been dead a long time."

"The 1870s weren't the Dark Ages. People left traces, records, relatives, something. Not Rachel. Did she really murder her husband and skip? Damned if I know.

And it's my job to know."

"What's this got to do with me?"

"I'll spell it out, Westbrook. Right now, this project is a few pieces in a small town newspaper. We can all back away from it and nobody gets hurt. Not Meg, not you, especially not me. You can even earn a kill fee, say five grand? But I need the truth. My gut says something's wrong, I just don't know what it is."

"Five grand?"

"Cash money. Today."

"Fair enough. Some moron bangs up your ride, you're having trouble finding facts about a hundred-year-old dead woman, and you figure it's a big conspiracy? Offhand, I'd say the problem is you, sport. You got burned once and now you're paranoid. Personally, I'd love to see you bail out. But I don't know what happened to your car and Meg is writing the flat-ass truth. Is that worth five grand?"

"Not hardly."

"Didn't think so. But you're gonna pay me for this wild-goose chase and for my headlight and the ding in my Jeep. It's a long walk back to town. Sport."

Chapter 35

"Again," Meg said, catching the bartender's eye.

He nodded and started assembling a tequila sunrise. Her third. Her last, she promised herself.

She could already feel the buzz from the first two, relaxing her shoulders, cooling her down. Leaning back on the barstool, she breathed in the familiar scent, old smoke, new scotch.

Rod Stewart on the jukebox. "Young Hearts." She didn't feel like a young heart. More like roadkill. Which she nearly was, banging Chris's Benz off that parked car. Over . . . what?

What the hell did she see? A woman. Definitely. But only for an instant and not very well. So why did it spook her into a fender-bender?

Because she wasn't really there.

She was mist, or smoke. Transparent.

Which meant . . . what? That she saw a ghost? Or she was cracking up?

Jesus, what she really needed was to crawl into bed and sleep for a week. It was all too much. Working around the damn clock on Rachel's story. Chris turning from Mr. Right into Mr. Married Cheater. And then seeing . . . whatever the hell that was.

Rachel? No. Hadn't seen her clearly but the woman didn't look much like her. Only caught a glimpse, though. Too busy bouncing off a parked car.

Damn. Chris was so ticked about his dented Benz he drove her straight back to her place and dropped her off.

But the last thing she needed was to face an empty apartment. What she really needed was a drink. Maybe two. In a place where people didn't treat you like a junkie for taking an occasional taste.

She was losing it. Knew it. It was turning into L.A. all over again — no! Damn it, it wasn't! She was more experienced now, smarter. Tougher. Wouldn't fall into that trap again.

This time she'd handle it. Nail this story. Write Rachel's project so well Reggie'd kiss her ass to buy it.

Chris? She'd sort him out later. Talk it through or walk away. Whichever felt right.

Rachel, then Chris. First things first. And the first thing was to pull herself together.

One last drink, to take the edge off —

"Hey babe, you're Megan Keyes, ain't ya?"

Big guy, flannel shirt. Smelled of stale sweat. "Do I know you?" she asked

"We've met. Marty Lachaine. You interviewed me once. Buy you a drink?"

"I've got one coming, thanks, Mr. . . . ?"

"Lachaine."

"Right. Look, I've had a rough day and I'm really not looking for company, okay?"

"No problem. Maybe some other time." The big guy sauntered down the bar. He looked vaguely familiar but Meg couldn't place the face. He paid the bartender for her drink and brought it to her.

"Look pal, I told you —"

"Hey, no strings. Drink it in good health, Miss Keyes. Like I said, maybe I'll see you around." Backing away, Lachaine joined an equally scruffy buddy in a corner booth, both of them eyeing her hopefully.

Terrific. Courtship, northwoods saloon style. Time to take off. Nodding politely at her benefactor, Meg slugged down the sunrise, then rose. Felt the floor tilt a little.

"Whoa," she muttered, leaving the bartender a tip. "Better start drinking more often. Definitely out of shape."

The floor rocked even more as she headed for the door. No problem. Someone steadied her arm and she glanced up gratefully.

The big guy. And his buddy. Damn, still couldn't place his face.

Chapter 36

Bass and I worked the last few hours of the afternoon in silence. I kept losing focus. Hadn't heard from Yvonne. And what was going on with Meg? Booze? Probably.

Distracted, I slammed my thumb with a hammer! Damn it! Threw the freaking hammer across the room, bouncing it off the floor into a panel. Punching a dent into Bass's handiwork.

Kneeling, he gave me a look and began collecting his tools. "Must be quittin' time."

"You can quit any time you like."

"What's buggin' you?"

"Nothing."

"Which is why you're bouncin' hammers around?"

"Sorry. That won't happen again."

"Good. Has this got somethin' to do with Yvonne?"

"No. Yes. I don't know."

"Sounds about right. You want to talk about it?"

"No."

"Your call," he shrugged. "I got a short haul truckin' job, should be back tomorrow afternoon. With any luck we can finish this off next week. If you don't keep wreckin' the place."

"I said I was sorry."

"Yeah. Look, I'm not all that clever but I've got a few more miles on me than you do. So what's wrong?"

"Everything. For instance, when a woman says she needs some space it's usually a polite way of blowing you off, right?"

"There ain't no 'usually' with women. Every blessed one's different." He tossed a screwdriver into his toolbox. "We talkin' about Yvonne now?"

I nodded.

"Wouldn't hazard a guess. She's complicated. And she's too good for you anyway. If you're gonna run them dogs you'd best get to it. Looks like rain. Want me to lend a hand?"

"No, go ahead. I can manage."

"It's your funeral."

I looked around the office after he'd gone. He was right. We were nearly done. And

289

nicely done. Once the vinyl flooring was down, I might actually attract a client or two.

Meanwhile I had to take care of the only customers I had. Closing the barn doors, I turned the hounds loose in the long corridor to gambol and scuffle with while I mucked out their pens. Vixen was playing as happily as the others, scars and pain forgotten. The blessings of a short memory.

After filling their feed bowls, I collected Milady out of the mob, snapped a lead on her collar, then trotted her out into the afternoon with the pack milling at her heels.

I hadn't risked running the hounds together since they'd chased Yvonne's horse, but she wouldn't be riding today. Bass was right, the sky was darkening, charcoal thunderheads rolling down from the north as we headed out. A quick trot around the fence line and with luck we'd be home before the rain caught us.

Starting at an easy lope, I settled into the rhythm we'd developed over the past weeks, a comfortable, mile-eating trot. The hounds fanned out around me, casting, crisscrossing, snuffling over each tuft and hummock, charging and feinting as they ran. And smiling. Grinning at the sheer wolfish pleasure of doing work they'd been born to.

And in spite of everything, Yvonne, Rachel, and Meg, and the rest of it, my spirits began to lift. Running with that pack, coasting across a meadow surrounded by my savage, playful cronies, it was simply impossible to stay blue.

Even when dogs collided, tumbling through the grass snapping and snarling, the spats were momentary. Seconds later they'd be sprinting off together, family again. Not a bad paradigm.

The rain overtook us halfway to the roadside fence, a cool, misty drizzle that actually made running more pleasant. The hounds ignored it completely. My only adjustment was to turn my collar up.

By the time we rounded the first turn at the corner of the property to run parallel with the chain-link fence, the grass was getting slick and tricky, making me run a step at a time, focused on keeping up with Milady and staying on my feet.

I kept her near me, snubbing up the leash to prevent any sudden lunges, but I was losing track of the others. Even Vixen's blanket was hard to spot and the hounds were nearly invisible in the drizzle, materializing out of the mist, ghost dogs with dripping pelts and snapping jaws, gleefully trying to bowl me off my feet. Playful or not, fangs slashing at your ankles tend to keep you alert.

Suddenly the chain-link fence whanged, jerking, vibrating like harp strings. Damn! A hound must have banged into it in the rain. Pulling Milady up short, I peered back through the haze. And realized the corner of the fence had been knocked flat.

A pickup truck had skidded off the road and smashed into the fence. Entangled in the mesh, the driver was rocking back and forth, tires howling, fighting for traction to break free.

It was Megan. Her outlaw pickup was unmistakable. What on earth was she doing out here? Loaded? Had to be. Damn.

My first thought was to help her, but I feared the dogs might bolt through the gap in the fence and scatter. The problem solved itself as the truck surged forward, slewing wildly as it rumbled into the pasture.

The field around me brightened to an eye-stabbing blaze as Meg switched on the truck's roof rack of halogen floodlights. Flashblind from the glare, I didn't realize for a moment that the truck wasn't just building up momentum to recross the fence. It was plunging ahead, parallel with the fence line, bucking over the uneven ground. Heading straight at me!

Sweet Jesus! She had to see us, the damned halogens were lighting up the field like a freaking football stadium! Caught in the outer limit of the spotlight glare, Vixen was watching the truck come, cocking her head, trying to decide what all the noise was about.

The truck suddenly veered left, centering the dog between its headlights and accelerating. Vixen froze, dazzled by the lights, her blue blanket glowing in the halogen blaze.

She was still standing there, blinded by the glare, when Meg's outlaw pickup ran her down, smashing her body into the turf.

"Nooooo!!!" Instinctively I charged toward the fallen dog only to be jerked up short by Milady's leash. And she was right. The damned truck had swerved back, hurtling toward us again, picking up speed as it came. There was no helping Vixen now. And we were next. The trees! Our only chance was to make it into the trees before the crazy bitch ran us all down. Yanking Milady sharply to the left, I sprinted off at a ninety-degree angle to the charging pickup.

Didn't know where the trees were, couldn't see them through the drizzle, but any doubts about the truck's intent vanished as the driver cranked its wheels hard over, throwing it into a power slide to follow us. It spun halfway around on the wet grass, then plunged ahead, engine roaring.

Sprinting flat out with Milady leading me at the end of her leash, I focused on the ground directly ahead, watching for holes or hummocks. The footing was uneven and if I fell . . .

I risked a glimpse over my shoulder. No freaking way we could outrun the pickup to the trees. It was only forty yards behind now, gaining rapidly. Only the rain-slicked grass had kept us alive this long — I slipped, skidding to one knee, using the leash to keep from going down.

Scrambling to my feet, I nearly fell again as Milady lunged to the right. The ground slanted upward that way. Instinctively, Milady was heading for higher ground, for turf the pack could defend.

No chance. The steel monster at our heels was too fast and much too close. The grass around me suddenly blazed into light as the pickup bore down on us. The ground was rising now, getting steeper. If we could only make it over the crest — but it was too late. The truck would be on us in seconds.

I veered sharply left for three paces, just long enough for the headlights to swerve after me as the driver reacted, then I lunged hard to the right, throwing myself bodily down the slope, dragging Milady with me.

The truck howled past, missing us by inches, bucking and bouncing across the slippery hillside as the driver fought for control. Sliding to a halt at the bottom of the rise, I watched, praying it would flip.

It didn't. Meg straightened it out on the flats, then wheeled around, heading back at us.

Still blind from the lights, I wasn't sure which way to move but Milady knew, lunging frantically, dragging me back up the rise. I glimpsed vague shapes moving through the mist as the other dogs rejoined us, one at a time. My throat was on fire, legs wobbling, but there was no stopping now.

In the flats below, the truck was weaving back and forth. Searching. Apparently she'd lost sight of us. But not for long. Blitzen, a rangy gray male, dashed across the outer perimeter of the headlight beams, heading directly up the hill to rejoin the pack.

Gunning its engine, the truck immediately veered to follow him, gaining on the hound as it came. In the glare, I glimpsed more hummocks beyond the one we were climbing.

We were already in the foothills, the trees could only be sixty or seventy yards ahead.

But which way? I couldn't see squat through the damned rain. My only hope was that Milady would lead us to high ground again, into the cover of the woods. Slackening the leash, I gave her free rein, concentrating on the ground underfoot. It was taking everything I had to keep up with her. Couldn't risk a look back. But I glimpsed a hound to my left, then another. The hunting pack forming around us again, ghostly shadows running in the rain. And then the dogs sprang into sharp relief as the headlights caught us.

Any of them could have sprinted ahead to safety, leaving Milady and me to face the black outlaw's charge, but they held their positions in the pack, fanned out, running together.

We were climbing steadily now, passing occasional alder saplings. The tree line was coming up, thirty-five yards ahead. But the truck was gaining too. It would be on us in twenty paces. Maybe less. And then my luck ran out.

I tripped on a rock, stumbled, and went down. And made my decision. Releasing the leash, I scrabbled frantically in the dirt, trying to loosen the stone.

The headlights caught me there, blinding me. But I wasn't alone. Dancer, the black male, had also turned to stand and fight. Crouching beside me at bay, his shoulder mane ruffed, eyes ablaze in the headlight glare, he bared his fangs, growling defiance into the face of . . . He had no idea what he was facing. And didn't care.

Ripping the rock free, I staggered to my feet. For a split second I glimpsed an image reflected in the truck's windshield. Not a face. Just eyes. Focused on me. Desperately, I raised the rock over my head — but Dancer moved first.

Snarling, he launched himself at the pickup's steel throat. Striking it head on, directly between its headlight eyes, he caromed off the hood and crashed into the windshield, shattering it with his broken body.

Cranking the wheel to avoid the hound's charge, the driver skidded wildly off across the face of the hill, bucking and rocking, fighting for control. Bouncing off a hummock, the pickup went airborne for twenty yards then crashed down broadside, tumbling end over end down the hill.

And vanished as its lights winked out.

Dazed, I lowered the rock to my waist, peering frantically into the rain, trying to spot the truck. Couldn't see it. It had traveled fifty yards or more before it had gone over. Couldn't tell where it was now.

Every fiber of me was screaming for vengeance, to charge down the hillside and smash whoever I found. But first I had to gather the pack. If they scattered and were lost now, it would mean Dancer threw his life away for nothing.

And suddenly Milady was beside me, trembling, glancing up at me, then in the direction the truck had gone. Eager to hunt it down as I was. As though she'd read my mind.

The others were gliding out of the trees to us. Shifting my rock to my right hand, I took her leash and began working my way across the hillside.

We found Dancer halfway down the slope, twisted and broken, his jaws open in a silent snarl, eyes staring into infinity. I knelt beside him a moment in the rain, resting my hand on his brow. His body was still warm. But his spirit was gone.

The pack sensed it too. Milady nuzzled him briefly, then turned away. Whatever Dancer — who — ever he was, that essence wasn't here anymore. All that remained was a broken bundle of fur and bones on a muddy hillside.

Rising stiffly, still toting my rock, I followed Milady into the dark. She led us directly to it. A hundred and twenty-yards across the torn, slippery turf, we found the outlaw pickup, battered, overturned on the passenger's side.

The pack fanned out, circling it, snarling, but I could see no sign of life. The truck looked as dead as Dancer. Crouching by the spider-webbed windshield, I peered inside. Empty. Nothing moving. But I had to be sure.

Clambering up the chassis onto the wreck, I yanked the driver's door open and squeezed through to check the interior. Nothing. Had the driver been thrown out? No. The windows were intact. Must have climbed out the same way I'd climbed in.

Standing atop the wreck, I squinted into the rainy darkness. Couldn't see a thing. Below me, Milady began growling, a barely audible rumble in her throat, her nose twitching as she sniffed the air near the truck.

Could she follow the driver's scent? Jumping down, I walked her around the wreck, looking for a footprint, blood. Anything.

Immediately sensing my purpose, Milady put her nose to the ground, then headed off to the east following a spoor utterly invisible to me. Ten yards, twenty — she lunged!

Snarling, she grabbed something in her jaws, savaging it.

A glove. A brown jersey work glove. Extra large. Stuffing it in my pocket, I followed Milady into the dark. But not far.

A few yards on, she began whining, casting back and forth, confused. Apparently she'd lost the scent in the downpour. It was a miracle she'd followed it this far. No way to find the driver now. Whoever it was.

Chapter 37

The black-and-white Algoma patrol car crawled along the dirt road, stopping at the flattened fence section where the truck smashed through, flashers winking in the drizzle.

Two cops got out. I didn't recognize either of them. A tall, lanky type with a black mustache and an economy-size woman, five-ten, two hundred-plus pounds. Muscle, not flab.

Hatless, her thick blonde hair was plaited into tight braids coiled above her ears, a Dutch milkmaid look. Popping an umbrella open, she knelt and examined the tire tracks with a flashlight before stepping carefully across the fence.

"Hi there." Her accent was as thick as pecan pie and just as southern. "I'm Sergeant Raedean Keeler. My partner here's Officer Gillette. You're Westbrook?"

"Yeah. The truck's over there, about two

hundred yards toward the trees. Nobody's in it."

"Tell you what, why don't we follow the tracks back," she said. "It'd be easy to get turned around in this drizzle. You're welcome to share my umbrella if you like."

"I'm already wet." I fell into step beside her.

"So what's this about, David? 911 said you were pretty excited on the phone."

"I was exercising my dogs; the truck came crashing through the fence and tried to run us down."

"Why?"

"I have no idea."

"Who was driving?"

"I don't know that either. It was empty when we got to it."

"Nobody around?"

"No, but it took us awhile to find it in the rain."

"You keep saying 'we.' Was someone else with you?"

"I meant the dogs. One of them's right here."

She knelt beside Vixen's broken body, straightening her muddy blanket as she glanced back along the tracks. "Swerved," she said. "Almost looks like he did it deliberately."

"It was deliberate," I said.

"Why do you think so? Since you don't know who was driving."

"I saw it swerve. It was no accident."

"Maybe," she said, rising. "Or maybe the driver just lost control of the vehicle for a moment."

I almost bit. I opened my mouth to argue, but a reflex ingrained by years of slam time closed it. Never argue with a cop. Ever.

My first impression of them had been hick city, small town small-timers. But there was an edge behind the woman's accent, an ironic intelligence. She was playing dumb and playing me like a fish, trying to make me react. And say something stupid.

"The other dog is farther on," I said.

Following the tracks, we found Dancer's smashed body and the scarred earth where the truck had skidded across the side of the hill.

"Lost control here, then rolled it." It was the first time Gillette had spoken. "Why the hell did he swerve like that?"

"The dog jumped at the truck," I said. "He bounced off the hood into the windshield."

"Jumped at it?" he said doubtfully. "You're saying the dog took on a damn truck? More likely he was just trying to get out of the way."

"No," Raedean said positively. "He jumped at it all right. Read the tracks. The pack was further on up the rise there. This one turned to fight. Hounds'll take on God Almighty to save their own. Helluva shame to kill a dog over a lover's spat."

I caught the implication, but let it pass. I led them down the hillside to the truck.

"My goodness, what a mess," Keeler said, shaking her head. "I recognize this truck though. And so do you, Westbrook. Come on, this is between you and your girlfriend, right? Megan Keyes? You gotta know this is her truck. There isn't another one like it in the whole damn county. Funny you didn't mention that."

Scrambling up on the cab, Gillette retrieved the registration papers from the glove box and passed them down to Keeler.

"Megan Keyes. But you already knew that, didn't you, David? What's up here? You two having some problems? Maybe a lover's quarrel that got a little out of hand?"

"It's nothing like that. Meg and I are just friends, we're not involved. One of the dogs found a man's jersey glove a little ways off. It's too big to fit Meg."

"O.J.'s glove didn't fit either. So your

story is you don't know why her truck's out here?" Keeler pressed. "You're just friends, as in, 'hey baby it's over, but let's be friends?' Jeez, I hate it when guys who dump me say that. Maybe Meg felt the same way."

"Nobody dumped anybody. We aren't lovers."

"From the looks of this truck I'd say you're not friends anymore either. It also looks like whoever was drivin' must've gotten banged up some. Do you know where Megan is now?"

"No idea."

"She's at County General. We picked her up an hour ago, dazed, disoriented, and bleedin' some. Like she might have been in an accident."

"Is she all right?"

"After what she tried here, why should you care? Since you're not lovers."

"Is she all right or not?"

"I really can't say. Let's take a ride to the hospital, Westbrook. To visit your . . . ex-friend?"

Chapter 38

She looked like death. Against the sterile hospital pillowcase Meg seemed as bloodless as a corpse. Only the faint pulse of her temporal artery offered proof of her vitality.

Her sweat-dampened hair clung to her skull like a rumpled cap and her eyelids appeared bruised, with purplish smudges beneath.

This is how she'll look in her casket, I thought. *Or when she's very old.* Yet there were no wounds, no cuts on her face to indicate she'd bounced off a windshield or rolled down a hillside in a truck. Either she'd been damned lucky or . . .

No. I'd known it the moment I saw her lying there. Perhaps I'd known since I glimpsed the reflection in the windshield. She hadn't been driving that truck.

A nurse touched my elbow. "Could you step into the hall please? We need a moment with the patient. You too, ma'am."

Daryl rose stiffly from the chair in the corner of the room. She looked almost as bad as Meg: red-eyed, disheveled, and drawn. And very, very angry.

"Hang in there." I gave Meg's hand a squeeze. She didn't respond.

In the corridor, Daryl slumped against the wall, bracing herself with her cane. "I can't do this anymore," she said quietly.

"What happened?"

"One of the deputies called me. A patrol car found her in the street. Drunk, stoned, or both."

A doctor in surgical scrubs joined us. Tall, dark, and balding, he looked harried, and much too young.

"I'm Dr. Caldwell. Are you the family of Miss" — he checked the name on his clipboard — "Megan Keyes?"

"I'm her sister. How is she?"

"Reasonably well. She's out of danger. We're going to keep her overnight for observation. She's suffered some minor contusions and lost a lot of blood."

"Blood?" Daryl echoed, paling. "But I thought she'd only stumbled."

Caldwell hesitated a heartbeat, then shrugged. "I'm sorry, there's no delicate way to say this. The injuries she incurred in the fall are relatively minor. The blood loss is the result of an apparent miscarriage. Her physical condition is good. It was early in the pregnancy, six to eight weeks. She should make a full recovery in a few days. Frankly, that's the least of her problems. Do either of you know what she's on?"

"On?"

"Her drug of choice? She was brought to emergency seriously intoxicated. She smelled of alcohol but a breathalyzer test came out point zero two, so her problem's more than booze. We did a tox screen for cannabis, cocaine, and heroin, all negative, but mixing alcohol and drugs can have nasty consequences. Any idea what she might have taken?"

"No," Daryl said. "None."

"Are you sure it wasn't exhaustion?" I asked. "She's been working around the clock."

"Fatigue doesn't dilate your pupils. She was incoherent when they brought her in, no idea where she was or how she got here. She mentioned being in an accident earlier, but there's no evidence of injuries that could cause a blackout. Which leaves us with drugs. Unless you can offer another explanation?"

Daryl glanced at me helplessly. I had no answer either.

"If you're concerned about legal repercussions, Sheriff Wolinski has already recorded her admission as a medical assistance run, so no criminal charges are pending —"

"If we knew, we'd tell you," Daryl snapped. "We don't."

"Please, I meant no offense, Miss Keyes, I have to ask. It should be in her medical records in case of a recurrence. If you can get her to talk about it, please keep us informed. It'll be held in strictest confidence."

"I understand," Daryl nodded. "Can we talk to her?"

"Not tonight; she's sleeping and rest is the best thing for her now. Come back in the morning. We'll take good care of her. By the way, I enjoy your paper very much, Miss Keyes. This Rachel Hayes thing? Wonderful stuff. Now if you'll excuse me . . ." He hurried off, checking his clipboard.

"A miscarriage?" Daryl said quietly when we were in the elevator on our way down. "Did you know she was pregnant?"

"No. I don't think she did either. She's mentioned wanting a kid more than once. She wouldn't have gotten loaded if she'd known."

"Unless she cared more about getting wrecked than about her child."

"That's a lousy thing to say."

"This isn't my first ride on this particular merry-go-round, David. What a waste. She has everything. Talent, energy, legs that work. All I have is a country newspaper and a cane. Arthritis puts me in this hospital so often I know the nurses by their first names. I'd give anything to have Meg's ability. And she doesn't give a damn. Never has."

I let it pass. Daryl was tired, upset, and possibly right. I've known dopers who'd pimp their children for a quick buzz.

Reggie Laws was standing at the information desk when we stepped out of the elevator.

"I came as soon as I heard," he said, hurrying over. "How is she?"

"It was just a fall," Daryl said curtly. "She'll be fine. They're keeping her overnight to be on the safe side."

"Good, glad it's not serious. Will she be able —" He swallowed the question, reading Daryl's eyes. "I guess business can wait. I'll stop by tomorrow. You guys take care."

"Reggie?" I called after him. "How did you hear about this?"

"A message on my answering service. Why?"

"Who left it?"

"I don't know. Someone from the sheriff's department, I guess. What difference does it make?"

"Maybe a lot. Why would they call you?"

"How should I know? I'm just glad to get the straight scoop for once. See ya, Doc."

"What was that about?" Daryl asked.

"I just wondered who tipped him. And why? Did you call him?"

"To wreck my sister's big chance, you mean? No. Why would I bother? She's doing just fine on her own. I think I'll hang around the coffee shop awhile in case anything comes up. Care to join me?"

"I'm sorry, I really can't. I have to be someplace."

"At this hour?"

I didn't try to explain. I'm not sure I could have.

I suppose going out to find Dancer and Vixen in the rain didn't make much sense, but then their dying didn't either.

I'm not a religious person. Until this business with Rachel Hayes I probably hadn't spent ten consecutive minutes in my life wondering what happens after we die. Heaven always seemed too good to be true. But after some of the things I saw in prison, hell's not that much of a stretch.

Still, it wasn't faith that told me not to abandon the two dogs to the night. It was something stronger. More elemental. Something I'd learned from them. Loyalty. To the pack. To the death.

Taking a spade out of the tack room, I trudged out along the path we'd followed.

With a rising wind bullying me along, I found Vixen where she'd been run down. Wrapping her blue blanket about her, I carried her broken body across the field to Dancer's hillside. Both dogs were locked in rigor now, their frames smashed, spirits flown. Scarcely recognizable as the vital creatures they'd been.

I buried them together on high ground, just below the crest of the hill where Dancer had thrown away his life defending his friends. The spot was sheltered from the wind with open fields and rolling hills to the south. Not that the view mattered.

But perhaps it did.

It seemed to me that these two had come too far and survived too much to have died here for nothing. If there's any justice in this world or the next then they're running . . . somewhere.

Together.

Through hills like these.

When I'd finished, I smoothed the earth

over them and set a stone to mark the place. I tried to think of something to say but nothing came. It was just as well. Dogs are an older race than men. They probably have gods and dreams of their own.

But as I rose, an eerie, chilling sound raised the hackles on the back of my neck.

Back at the barn, the greyhounds were keening, their ululations echoing across the hills. Pouring out their souls, mourning their friends.

And for the first time, I truly felt like a member of the pack. I knew exactly how they felt. I ached for their loss too.

If I knew how to howl, I would have.

Chapter 39

"Do you think I've flipped out, David?"

Meg was sitting up in her hospital bed in one of those ridiculous backless gowns. Her wee wren's face looked haggard, but composed. She was herself again. More or less.

"No, of course not."

"You're not a very good liar."

"Thank you."

"I'm serious. The nurses keep checking me out like they're sizing me for a strait jacket. Daryl and Reggie talk down to me like I'm a chimp with a learning disorder. Reg wants me to take a month off to recover."

"Would that be such a bad idea?"

"If I do, he'll dump me and the project too. Half of it only exists in my head. There's no way a new writer could meet the deadlines. The studio will pull the plug, Reggie will walk away, and I'll take the blame. Bottom line, it's my concept, my show. And in all modesty, I'm the only one who can make it work."

"And yet here we are."

"That's my point. I can't get anything done in here. Which brings me back to question one. Do you think I'm nuts? And don't bother fibbing to spare my feelings. I need to know."

I could see she did. Which was too bad, because my first instinct was to lie like a pol on election night. But she was right, I have no talent for lying. Especially to friends. And it's not a skill I want to develop.

"I don't know, Meg. I'm a vet, not a shrink. Dr. Caldwell said you were incoherent last night."

"Yeah." She bit her lip. "I've um, been wracking my brain since I woke up this morning. I can't remember squat about what happened."

"What do you remember?"

"I remember driving, being angry with Chris. And then . . . I saw something."

"What?"

"That's just it, I'm not sure. Things are . . . garbled after that. I banged up Chris's car, he dropped me off at my apartment." She looked away a moment, gathering her thoughts. "I think I stopped off at a bar . . . but I really can't remember."

"Nothing?"

"Only . . . feelings. Being afraid. Really scared."

"Of what?"

"I don't know. Of something . . . awful."

"Did you get loaded?"

"Not on booze. They told me my blood alcohol was only point zero two. If I'd done any serious drinking, it would have been a lot higher than that."

"Do you remember driving your truck?"

"No. Sheriff Wolinski asked me about that earlier this morning. He said somebody took a joyride in it? And chased you?"

"Something like that."

"Well, I doubt it was me since I apparently couldn't even walk straight."

"Any idea who it could have been? Were you with anyone? Reggie, say?"

"Reggie'd be the last guy I'd drink with. He already thinks I'm a lush. I don't know what happened to my truck. Maybe I left the keys in it."

"Maybe. Which brings us back to question one. But I can't answer it, Meg. You'll have to."

"Fair enough," Meg said, taking a deep breath. "I've had troubles with booze and pills before. I've told you that. I've even had blackouts, but only when I was tooted out of my gourd. And in those days I was knocking

316

back tequila sunrises for breakfast. I can't explain what happened yesterday, seeing . . . whatever it was. I've been working hard, but that's never bothered me before. Damn it, I don't think I'm a head case. Do you?"

"If you had kennel cough or mange, I could treat you. Your mental condition's outside my area of expertise."

"Thanks a bunch." She fell back on her pillow. "One thing I'm sure of, I can't stay here. I've done the hospital thing before and I don't like it. Too much time to think. If I'm not crazy already, a few days in this place will do the trick."

"Your doctor —"

"— said he'd cut me loose as long as I wasn't alone. I can't stay with Daryl. Too much baggage. Can I crash with you for a few days? You live in a barn with orphan dogs and a three-legged cat. Can you make room for one more stray? Please?"

I almost said no. Probably should have. But she looked so vulnerable. Like a puppy waiting to be kicked. And I've got a weakness for puppies.

"Sure, if your doctor okays it, you're welcome."

"Good. I promise I won't make any more passes at you. I'll even sign an affidavit to that effect for . . . well, for anyone who might be interested."

"If you mean Yvonne, I doubt she'd care if I moved in with an all-girl topless tuba band. I called to tell her about the dogs, left a message. She hasn't called back. Anyway, we definitely can't have you getting crazier than normal. The world's not ready for it. When do you want to leave?"

"Twenty minutes ago," she said, showing a flash of her old spirit. "Give me two minutes to change and we can bail me out of here. And David? I owe you big for this. You're a lifesaver."

"I'd better be," I said.

Dr. Caldwell didn't do cartwheels over the idea of releasing Meg, but he conceded there was no pressing medical need to keep her. We compromised. Meg promised to rest, I promised to thrash her soundly if she didn't, and we both promised she'd check in with Caldwell in a few days. So he signed her out.

A nurse brought her down to the lobby in a wheelchair. A precaution, they said. Meg looked like she belonged in it, so pale and drained I almost changed my mind. She marched grimly out to the Jeep on her own, though, wearing a game face. One tough babe, no doubt about it.

We drove to her apartment to pick up some clothing and her computer. In silence. I guessed she was probably more whipped than she'd thought. I was wrong.

"Did Dr. Caldwell tell you what happened?" she asked quietly.

"He said you fell."

"Did he tell you I was pregnant? That I miscarried?"

"Yeah. He did. I'm sorry, Meg. Really."

"There's nothing else to say, is there? Except that it's a lucky thing Chris buried Rachel's well. Right now a hundred years in a dark hole sounds pretty good to me."

Her eyes were as vacant as a death mask. Two narrow tear tracks trickled silently over her lips. I doubt she knew she was crying.

Her flat was on the ground floor of a ten-unit Spanish inn that enclosed a central parking lot. Her parking spot was empty. The police were holding her outlaw truck in impound.

Following her in, I bumped into her when she froze a few steps into the living room. Her apartment smelled like a saloon. A cantina, actually. Aroma de Tequila. *Muy* funky.

A liquor bottle was smashed on the kitchen floor. Meg nudged a piece of glass with her foot.

"I must have had a better time than I thought. This isn't even my brand."

"You don't have a brand anymore. Get what you need. I'll clean this up."

I swept up the glass and blotted the stain with paper towels, keeping an eye on Meg. She stopped in the bedroom doorway, staring.

"Are you all right?"

"No," she said, her voice shaky, "I — don't remember any of this, but . . ."

"What is it?"

"I don't know. This place feels . . . awful to me. I keep an overnight case packed in my bedroom closet. Would you get it for me please? I'll grab my laptop and we can go."

"Sure." Tossing the towels in the trash, I found the case just as Meg gave a yelp of dismay.

"What's up?"

"My freaking laptop is fried. Looks like I spilled something on it. It's dead as a coal bucket."

"Did you lose anything important?"

"A week's work, maybe more," she said grimly. "Nothing I can't rewrite from memory. And I will. Know something? Ghosts or demons or whatever, I'm going to finish this story if it kills me. I'd kill Rachel, but the psycho bitch is already dead."

She noticed my stare.

"Sorry if I sound whacked, I've had a bad week. Am I scaring you?"

"A little."

"Good," she said. "That makes two of us."

Chapter 40

Having Megan in the house was like being married again. In the worst sense.

The last year of my marriage was a train wreck fueled by scotch. Working, drinking my lunch, bagged by midafternoon, stopping off on the way home to make a new friend, shoot pool, any reason at all to avoid going home to Linda. And the terrible pain in her eyes.

Toward the end, with the booze out of control, it dawned on me that she was seeing someone else. It hurt. But I also felt a surprising rush of relief. Because I knew it would be over soon. Lin was too honest to cheat on me for long.

With Megan, I had the opposite problem. I was afraid to leave her alone. Afraid she'd . . . what? Cut her wrists? Jump out a window? I had no idea. But I knew how narrow the ledge along that particular cliff was. And how tempting it could be to try to fly.

But if Meg was on the edge, she didn't show it. She bought a new laptop, moved into one of the empty bedrooms, unpacked in twenty minutes, then commandeered the kitchen table and went to work.

The first few days I made excuses to pop up from the clinic every hour or so. Sometimes less. Meg was amused at first, then annoyed. But before long she hardly noticed.

Whenever I checked, she was typing, her face glowing green in the reflected light of the monitor, gazing through the screen like a window to the past, totally engrossed. I think Rachel Hayes was more real to her than I was.

Still, she was eating, her color was improving, energy level ramping back up. I left her to it. If it ain't broke . . .

A week after Meg moved in, Chris stopped by. I heard him drive up and met him out front.

"Dave," he nodded, climbing out of his Benz. Tweed jacket, khakis. Sunglasses masked his eyes but he looked sallow, hollow-cheeked, and needed a shave. "I called the house. Daryl said Meg's living here now."

"Staying here," I corrected. "She needed a quiet place to work."

"Right. Working together on the big story, are you?"

"I mostly keep out of her way. And the answer to your next question is no, we're not."

"Not what?"

"Involved."

"Oh." He digested that a moment. "Can I see her?"

"She's sleeping now. Pulled an all-nighter. She was still working when I got up at seven, didn't crash until after lunch."

"Up all night? Don't you see how crazy that is?"

"She's committed to her work, Chris. That doesn't make her crazy."

"Damn it, she's seeing things, drinking again! Any idiot can see she's having a breakdown. She belongs in a hospital, not working all night in a rattletrap barn."

"She's been in a hospital, Chris. Her doctor cut her loose to come here. She's not drinking, her strength is coming back. She's been through a bad patch, but working is how she copes. Hell, she looks better than you do, pal. Are you all right?"

"I'm fine, I just . . ." Removing his sunglasses, he massaged his eyes. "God, this is such a mess. I was hoping it would work out, that we could have something good."

"Maybe you can."

"No chance. Even if we could get past the personal stuff — ah, hell. Look, if you're her friend, you've got to get her off this Rachel Hayes thing. It'll wreck her, if it hasn't already."

"Why should it? I thought you didn't believe in ghosts."

"I don't! But I'm not the one who's seeing 'em. I don't know if she's being haunted or cracking up, but writing about it will only make it worse." He punched his metal pincer into the palm of his good hand. "Believe me, I know how bad things can go." He climbed into his Mercedes. "Tell her to call me. Please. And you look out for her, Dave, or I'll be lookin' for you. Understand?"

He gunned the Benz out of my drive without waiting for an answer. Which was okay. I didn't have one anyway.

I told Meg about Chris's visit over supper, or what passed for it: nuked pizza, orange juice, and coffee. Meg was wearing a black jersey running suit with Chinese characters down one leg. Hadn't combed her hair in a day or two.

"He's worried about you. He thinks you're overworking, that this Rachel business is risky for you."

"And he wants me back in the hospital? Another day in that place and the cops would be talking me down off the roof."

"Even if he's wrong about the hospital, he may have a point about the project being too heavy a load. What do you think?"

"What I think is, I'm two-thirds finished with the best work I've ever done. The fires, the people like Rachel and her daughter who died so horribly, rich bastards like the Whitfields who raped the land and left it to burn. You're damned right I'm caught up in it. But I'm not obsessed. It's a helluva story but that's all it is. A story."

"A ghost story?"

She wiped a bit of pizza goo off her chin, thinking. "It can't be. I'll admit some strange things have happened. The bones superheating in the mortuary oven and whatever it was I saw in the cemetery. But anything about ghosts would kill the story as a documentary. Even if it's the flat-ass truth."

"Do you think it is?"

"I don't know. The mortuary can be explained away, I guess. And I can't remember what I saw that day, only what it felt like. Thinking about it doesn't help, it's got me half crazy."

"That's what Chris is afraid of."

"Why? Half crazy's normal for me."

"He wants you to call him."

"I can't deal with him now. It's too complicated and too damned painful. I'll finish the project first, then figure out what to do about Chris. If he's still interested."

"He will be."

"Good. How did he look?"

"Terrible. Like he hasn't slept in a week."

"Even better," she said with a flash of her old spunk. "I hope he's eating his heart out. Maybe we've got a chance. But first I'm going to finish off Rachel. Unless she finishes me."

I couldn't tell if she was joking.

Chris was at least partly right. Recreating the grim life of a dead woman had to be a downer. But just because Meg didn't want me underfoot didn't mean she had to be alone.

I started bringing Milady up to the apartment evenings, as company for Meg. Or vice versa.

No luck at first. Milady wasn't interested in being anyone's pet. Who could blame her? To us she was a dog. To her pack, she was a queen.

Still, she had to learn to tolerate people so I kept her with us at night, letting her crash on the couch.

Gradually, she accepted the routine. A run with the pack, dinner, then quiet evenings with me reading, Meg writing, and Milady regally ignoring us both.

Oddly enough, it was Frankenkat who broke the ice. I kept Frank and Milady separated at first, afraid she might mistake him for lunch. Instead, she seemed to adopt the broken cat, trailing him around, lounging near him when he napped. Watching over him.

A surrogate puppy? Possibly. Anyone who spends time with animals knows that beyond their obvious hungers for food and affection, we haven't the vaguest notion of what motivates their secret hearts. Any more than we understand our own.

I was in the barn feeding the hounds when Meg stepped out on the landing.

"David? Yvonne McCrae called. Something about a horse?"

"What about it?"

"I'm not sure. I was working and it takes me a minute to come out of the fog . . . anyway, she wanted to talk to you about it. Okay?"

"Sure." But it probably wasn't okay. Terrific, Yvonne asked for some space and the first time she calls, Meg answers. Still, at least she called.

After shaving quickly, no mean feat with a five-for-a-dollar Bic, I finger-brushed my hair into semi-respectability and found a clean shirt. Meg was too busy writing to needle me, which was just as well. I wasn't in the mood.

Finding Les Hudspeth's silver Jag parked in Yvonne's drive with the trunk open didn't improve my outlook. Considered coming back later but what the hell. I'd been invited.

I rang the buzzer. Les answered, stepping outside, half-closing the door behind him.

"Ah, the good Doctor. I prefer to talk business at my office but since you're here —"

"I'm not here to see you. Mrs. McCrae called. Is she in?"

"She's changing. Is there something I can —"

But I was already pushing past him. "Yvonne?" I stumbled over a suitcase in the hallway. There were three of them.

"Wait a minute." Hudspeth grabbed my arm, half spinning me around.

"It's all right, Les," Yvonne said, coming out of a bedroom, putting on an earring. She was wearing a teal and black jogging suit and loafers, her hair tied back in a pony-tail. Traveling clothes.

"I asked David to stop by. He'll be looking after Twenty Gold while I'm gone. Take the bags out please, I'll just be a minute. This way, David. I have a list for you in the study."

I followed her in. A man's room: massive desk, leather chairs, a fieldstone fireplace with an elk mounted over the mantel.

"What's going on, Yvonne?"

"Lower your voice, please," she said, closing the door. "I'm going away. If you can look after Twenty Gold I'd —"

"Is that why you called? To talk about your horse?"

"No, not exactly. I heard about what happened with the dogs —"

"Really? From whom?"

"The sheriff, and Daryl Keyes. They said Megan or one of her friends chased you in her truck —"

"That's not what happened. It's not even close."

"But Daryl —"

"— and Megan may be sisters but they're not friends. If you wanted to know what happened, why didn't you ask me?"

"I tried. Well, I called."

"Ah. And Meg answered, right?"

She nodded. "You're living with her, aren't you?" A wisp of hair dropped over her eye. I reached out to brush it back but she turned away. A gesture that told me more than I wanted to know.

"She's staying with me. And you assumed . . . well, why not? I'm still the guy with Cadillac eyes, right? And now you're going away. And our special night was what? A wild thing? Everything's back to normal?"

"Believe me, there was nothing normal about what happened with us that night."

"It was special to me too. But that was then. You said you needed time to think. I take it the time's up or Les wouldn't be here."

"Les is only here because —"

"— he fits into your life and I don't? Is that what you're trying to tell me?"

"No, I —"

"Sure it is. And if you can go away with him after what we shared, then maybe you should. It's the smart thing to do. We both know I can't offer you much more than a fling. So I'll make it easy for you. I'll take Les's buyout offer. When you get back I'll be gone, no forwarding. Enjoy your little getaway and —"

She slapped me sharply across the mouth! I stared at her, stunned.

"I'm sorry. I — shouldn't have done that. I um, I'd better go." She stopped in the doorway, turning to face me, her eyes swimming. Pain or rage, I couldn't tell. "For the record, Les is only driving me to the airport. My sister's second baby is due in a week and I'm going out to help. I thought it would be the perfect place to do some thinking. But you're right. It might be simpler for both of us if you're not here when I come back. Don't bother about Twenty Gold. I'll make other arrangements."

I followed her out, touching my lip gingerly. Hudspeth was waiting in the doorway with an overnight case. Yvonne marched past him without a word. He glanced after her, then back at me, grinning like a Cheshire cat.

"Trouble over the horse? Doctor?"

"Screw you."

"Now just a minute —"

"And stick your offer. I'll be staying on."

"You're making a big mistake," he said, blocking my path.

"I could write a book on big mistakes. And unless you want to be the next chapter, you'd better get out of my way."

He set himself, raising his hands to a boxing stance, waiting for my move, not bothering to conceal his contempt.

And I almost fell for it.

I stepped in, locked and loaded, ready to

erase the smug look from Hudspeth's face — but at the last second I realized he wanted me to hit him!

One punch and I'd be back in the slam. Probation revoked, buried under new charges. Out of the picture. One punch. And even if I knocked him into next week, he'd win.

It would almost be worth it. But not quite. So I brushed past him instead of putting him on the deck. But it was a near thing. A very near thing.

Chapter 41

"David! Wake up! Fire!"

Groggy, I sat up, groping for the bedside light. Switched it on. Nothing happened.

Blinking, I glanced around the room trying to clear my head. And realized I wasn't alone. A figure was standing near the window in the moonlight.

"Meg?"

But it wasn't. She turned toward me, a hazy figure with a sad smile. A woman I'd seen before. The night Tipton died.

I knew I had to be dreaming but it didn't feel like it. She looked real enough to touch. I could even smell the stench from the well — no! It wasn't the well. It was smoke. The gauzy shape at the window wasn't a woman at all, it was a roiling cloud of smoke!

"Meg!" I yelled, leaping out of bed, pulling on my jeans. "Meg, wake up!"

Barefoot, I charged into the living room. Smoke everywhere. Milady sat up on the couch as I hammered on Meg's door and switched on her light.

She was propped up in bed, sound asleep with her computer on her lap. "Meg! Wake up! Come on!"

I grabbed her arm to haul her out, but she shook me off. "Wait!"

"Wait hell! We've got to get out. What are you doing?"

"Dumping this to memory!" she said, frantically typing. "I'm not gonna lose another damn word if the whole place burns down around my head."

"Meg, come on!" But she was up, yanking the computer's power pack out of the wall, wrapping the cord around it as she ran for the door.

"Which way?"

"Down the back stairs into the barn. Less smoke in that direction. Go ahead, I'm right behind you!"

Grabbing the cell phone I dialed 911, reporting the fire as I headed for the back stairs. I was halfway out the door when I remembered Milady and Frank. Hurrying back inside, I scooped Frank up from the couch. Milady stretched, then trailed me out as I raced down the wooden stairway into the dark belly of the barn.

I switched on the overhead lights. No sign

of fire down here; the air was cool and clear. Only the rustle of the dogs stirring restlessly in their pens.

And the sound of sirens wailing in the distance.

"What the hell happened?" Meg asked, looking around, dazed. In her oversized flannel pajamas she looked all of fourteen.

"I don't know. I woke up, the room was full of smoke — Milady, get down here!" The hound was still sitting on the landing, watching us. I called again, and she made her way down the stairs, taking her royal time.

"Keep her here," I said. "I'm going to check outside."

Grabbing a fire extinguisher from its rack by the door, I hurried out, circling the front of the building, looking up at the windows. The shades were drawn, but I couldn't see any flickering of flames behind them. No smoke pouring out either. I opened the office door. It was clear inside. Good.

I was heading up the covered stairway to the apartment when a fire truck roared into the parking lot, sirens dying as it crunched to a halt.

"What have you got?" a fireman yelled, piling out of the truck.

"I don't know. There's a lot of smoke —"

"Okay, stand aside and let us handle it," the fireman said, grabbing an extinguisher and an ax, hurrying up the steps past me. "Is anyone inside?" He tried the door. Locked.

"No. No one's in there."

"Key?"

Damn. "It's inside."

"Shouldn't be too bad. Knob's cold." Tapping a fist-sized hole in a corner of the door glass with the handle of his ax, he reached in and unlocked it.

"Stand back, please." He opened the door a crack, then stepped warily in. A second fireman brushed by me, stopping just outside the door on the landing.

"Tom?" he yelled. "What's up?"

"Nothing yet."

A police car skidded to a stop by the truck below, flashers ablaze. A deputy stepped out. The tall gaunt type who'd been with Wolinski at the hospital. Jessup.

"Clear," the first fireman said, stepping out. "Sir, where's the fire?"

"I don't know," I said, following him into the room. "I woke up, the room was full of smoke . . ." I stopped. The living room was absolutely clear, no fire, no smoke. Nothing.

"Which room? Where was the smoke?"

"In this room. And my bedroom, over there."

"I checked it, no fire there." Kneeling by the kitchen sink, he opened the cupboard doors, checked inside, then rose, facing me. Young guy, brow like a chimp, snaggled teeth. "What kind of smoke was it?"

"What do you mean?"

"I smell something, but not smoke. Carbon monoxide, I think. Do you have a heater or a grill?"

"No, not up here. There's a kerosene Reddy-Heater downstairs in the clinic, but we aren't using it now."

"Better check it just the same." We trotted down the back stairs together. "Doorknob's warm," he noted. "Better stand back."

But there was no need. There was no fire in the clinic. The heat was from the kerosene heater, cooking away.

"Wow," the fireman said, opening the front door and windows. "You're lucky to be alive. Another hour of this and you'd be dead, mister. You should never run these things in a closed room. The monoxide can kill you."

"I know that. We weren't running it."

"No? Somebody was."

"I'm telling you, we had no reason to —"

His beeper went off. Waving me silent, he unclipped a cell phone from inside his slicker. "Ninety-eight. Go."

He listened a moment. "Okay, we're clear at this location. On our way." He flipped the pocket phone closed.

"Look, mister, I don't know what happened here, dumb mistake, bad joke, whatever, but we've got another call, gotta go. Just be a helluva lot more careful with that heater. Next time you might not be so lucky."

I followed him out to his truck. Meg was with the deputy, her face stricken.

"David, I have to go. There's a fire."

"It was carbon monoxide, Meg, it'll be clear in —"

"Not here! It just came over the radio. The newspaper's burning!"

Chapter 42

I hate police cars. I've never ridden in one that took me anywhere I wanted to go. But when the deputy offered Meg a lift to the fire with lights and sirens, I jumped in, unwilling to let her go alone.

Back seats are for prisoners. No door latches, a grill separating you from the driver, d-rings in the floor for leg shackles. Meg didn't seem to notice. I couldn't think of anything else.

"My God, my God," Meg whispered as we rocketed down the long driveway. Even the quick glimpses through the trees showed ugly flickers of flame, fire trucks, arcs of water.

"It's not too bad," I said, "seems to be limited to the garage."

"It's a carriage house, David. It's where we make up the paper. All the computers, scanners, photo equipment . . ." Her voice trailed away. . . .

340

As our car pulled up beside a fire truck, we could see that the carriage house was a total loss. The building was still burning, but only the front wall was standing. The roof had collapsed into a shambles of smoldering wreckage.

Meg rushed to Daryl, who was in her bathrobe, her face smeared with soot. Meg tried to embrace her but Daryl grabbed Meg's wrist and led her away from the others, clearly furious.

I hung back, checking over the site. The carriage house had burned to its foundation. One fire crew was already rolling its hoses as a second truck wetted down the rubble with mist. Lumps of melted goo and twisted metal were all that remained of the computers and office equipment.

Sheriff Wolinski had a quiet word with the deputy who drove us over, then stalked over to me, hatless, his eyes red-rimmed, irritated from the smoke. Or from seeing me.

"Doc, another fire and here you are. Why am I not surprised?"

"What happened?"

"Arson, no question this time. Gasoline splashed around, touched off. Old building, wooden walls. Sprinkler system kicked on but since it was burning from the outside in, it didn't help much. Jessup tells me you had some excitement at your clinic too. What was that about?"

"I woke up, the room was full of smoke. Meg and I got out, but when the firemen arrived we found a kerosene heater running. It could have killed us both."

"Jess said there was no smoke when the firemen arrived. Couldn't even smell any. And Reddy heaters don't smoke."

"I know. But there was smoke when I woke up. And I definitely didn't leave that damned heater running. We haven't used it in weeks."

"Still, it's kind of funny you smelled smoke. When the fire was all the way over here."

A blue Cadillac pulled up. Reggie Laws climbed out, heading toward Meg, but Wolinski cut him off.

"Hold it, bud, I need a minute with Meg. A few questions."

Reggie shrugged and backed off. I moved in to listen.

"Do you recognize the guy standing over by the red pickup truck, Meg? The big guy in the plaid shirt, three-day stubble?"

"I know who he is," she nodded. "His name's Lachaine. Marty, I think. I did a story on him once. Police beat."

"A story? That's the only way you know him?"

"I may have run into him around town. Why?"

"Because Marty says he knows you. In fact, you, the Doc, and Marty have a lot in common with that Hayes woman you're making the fuss over."

"Meaning what?" I asked, joining them.

"Fires, Doc. Seems like fires follow you folks around like one of your psycho grey-hounds. Or you invent them. Know what I think happened tonight?"

"I can hardly wait."

"I think you reported a false alarm to give yourselves an alibi for this fire, Doc. To prove you weren't here. Leaving that heater running was just a diversion."

"That's crazy. We had nothing to do with this."

"It that right, Meg? You claim you don't know anything about it either?"

"Of course not! What the hell are you talking about?"

"Arson, Meg. We picked Marty Lachaine up a half-mile down the road, passed out in his truck, drunk as a lord. Could smell booze on him ten yards away. And the gaso-line too. The dumbass splashed it on his clothes. Lucky he didn't torch himself along with the building."

"Lachaine burned the paper?" I asked.

"He's already admitted it. Says he was paid to do it. By Megan Keyes."

Meg paled as though she'd been struck. "That's insane. Forgodsake, why would I want to burn my own paper?"

"Sounds crazy to me too," Wolinski admitted. "You might consider that as a defense. Marty says you hired him to kick up some excitement about this series you're writing. Torching the *Herald* was part of it. Woman dies in a fire a hundred years ago, you raise her body, and suddenly things start burning again."

"And you believe that?" I asked.

"I can't think of a reason he'd lie about it, Doc. Can you, Meg? Does he have any kind of grudge against you?"

"Stan, I've never had more than a three-minute conversation with the man, getting his side of whatever he'd been arrested for."

"What about that day you wound up in the hospital? He claims you two were drinking together and that's when you hired him. Did you?"

"I — no. I couldn't have."

"Couldn't have?"

"My memory's a little shaky about that day."

"I'm not surprised," Wolinski said coolly. "You were stoned to the bone

344

when we picked you up. But Marty says he can prove his story. Claims you paid him with a check."

"A check?" she echoed, incredulous. "Don't you see how nuts that is?"

"Shouldn't be hard to verify, Meg. It's either your check or it's not, you signed it or you didn't. He says he cashed it the next day, so it'll still be in the system. Maybe you talked to Marty while you were under the influence and he made more of it than it was. Could that have happened?"

"No! I don't know anything about this! Or him!"

"Okay, but we're talking about multiple felonies here, Meg. I can't just give you a pass. We'll have to keep you in custody until we clear this up. I'm sorry." He motioned Jessup over. "Take Miss Keyes downtown. Don't book her. She can crash on the couch in my office. But she's a collar. Understood?"

"Yes sir. Ma'am, would you come with me, please?" Meg went along but barely seemed to understand what was happening. Daryl watched without saying a word, her face as cold as an ice sculpture.

It was too much. I jerked Wolinski around. "This is a crock! The guy's lying to cover himself."

"By confessing to a felony? Not likely. And his story makes a whacked-out kind of sense. He and Meg got hammered together, they talked, she forgot about it, he followed through. And if you had any part in this, Westbrook, you'd better pack your bags. You'll either be moving on or moving into a county cell for a long stay. And don't ever put your hands on me again. Ever. Understand?"

I was a split second from taking a swing at him and we both knew it. "Don't," he said quietly, shaking his head. "You've got troubles enough."

He was right. I lowered my hands.

"That's better. Maybe you're not as dumb as I thought. But anytime you really feel frisky, take your best shot. Or maybe I'll take mine." Pointing his forefinger at me like a pistol, he dropped the hammer. Right through the heart. Then he strode off to talk to the firemen.

"What do you think?" Reggie asked quietly, watching the fire crews pack up.

"About Meg hiring this done? Wolinski's out of his mind."

"Is he? Funny, I can think of some adjectives for that cracker, but crazy isn't one of them. Neither is stupid. He has to run for election. He wouldn't bust a reporter for the town's only paper unless it was open and shut. Either way, I'm done."

"Whoa!" I said, grabbing Reggie's arm as he turned away. "You can't really believe Meg did this?"

"I don't know what to believe, Westbrook. I don't know if Meg's fried or being haunted by some firebug ghost or if you two are running a scam. I do documentaries, not Elvis sightings. I need facts and right now I can't tell what's true around here. All I know for sure is that Meg's in custody and I'm not flushing my career over her. Or you. I'll see you around campus, Doc."

He stalked back to his Cadillac.

I found Daryl standing away from the others, watching the fire gutter out.

"Are you okay?"

"Of course not. Don't be an idiot, David."

"Sorry."

"Did you know that the *Herald*'s been published since 1861? Never missed an issue in all that time. What am I going to tell my father?"

"The truth. There was a fire."

"And that Meg's been arrested for arson?"

"They'll cut her loose in the morning. She didn't do this."

"No? Marty Lachaine is a drunk and a troublemaker, but he had absolutely no reason to burn the *Herald*. Unless someone paid him to do it."

"Meg wouldn't do that."

"Why are you so sure? Are you sleeping with my sister?"

"No. And that was a stupid question."

"Then let's go back to the previous question. Why would Lachaine burn the *Herald*?"

"I don't know. Why don't I ask him? Wait here." I trotted toward the prowl car. Too late. Wolinski was already pulling away with Lachaine in the back. As the car passed, the prisoner glanced out the side window. Grubby face, stubbled, dark hair hanging in his eyes. His glance met mine for an instant, then he was gone.

Strange. I was fairly sure I'd never seen Lachaine before. But I was just as sure I'd caught a flicker of recognition in his eyes. He definitely knew me from someplace. And on some intuitive level I knew exactly where that place was. A dark, rainy hillside. When I'd glimpsed his eyes reflected in a windshield.

He'd been at the wheel of Meg's truck. I don't know how I knew it but I did. Bone-deep. Maybe running with the hunting pack was developing more than my leg muscles. Maybe it was awakening a dormant instinct or two. Cats sense whether people like them or not. So do dogs, though they're less perceptive than cats. Animals intuitively recognize their friends. And enemies.

I stared after the prowl car until its taillights disappeared.

Daryl was looking at me oddly. "What's wrong?"

"Nothing." But there was. My fists were clenched so tightly my arms were quivering. Daryl trudged slowly off to the house. Leaving me to make sense of the night.

I'd never met Lachaine, had no idea who he was. I certainly had no beef with him.

Until now.

Did Meg hire him as some sort of drunken prank? I couldn't believe that. But it really didn't matter. Lachaine had killed Vixen deliberately. And then Dancer.

I didn't give a damn why. But we were definitely going to talk about it.

Chapter 43

A long, restless night.

I kept my bedroom door ajar and left a lamp lit in the living room. In case the smoke came again. Or the woman. A pretty basic precaution. But whenever I started to nod off, I instinctively took a last glance at the window and door.

The woman was never there. Nor was there any smoke. But looking for it, that twinge of uneasiness, roused me enough to keep me awake awhile longer.

A ghost? I couldn't believe I was even asking myself the question. She was only a waking dream. A warped memory from the night Tipton was killed. Definitely not the ghost of Rachel Hayes. Didn't resemble Rachel's photo at all.

The heater was real, though. If I hadn't awakened when I did, we'd be history. The way the *Herald* was history. As dead as Dancer and Vixen.

When I wasn't brooding about the lady, I was remembering Meg's monster truck lurching across the fields after us. Lachaine had taken a serious run at us. If Dancer hadn't laid down his life, he would have killed us all.

But I had exactly zero chance of proving it. You can't pick a pair of eyes out of a lineup or make an identification based on a flicker of recognition with nothing to back it. If I tried to file charges, Wolinski would laugh me out of his office. But that didn't mean I was wrong.

It also didn't explain why. I'd never met Lachaine, let alone crossed him. Why would he try to kill me?

I was still chewing that one over as dawn slowly brightened the room.

At least the solution was simple enough.

I'd damn well ask him.

After a night in the slam, Lachaine should be sober enough for a conversation. He might even be eager for one. And I definitely was.

I dressed quickly, T-shirt and jeans, and headed for the door when I realized Milady was watching me from the couch. I called her, and she rose and stretched before hopping lightly down.

Exactly as she'd done the night before.

With the room full of smoke, she'd watched me blunder around, not bothering to stir herself until I'd started pounding on Meg's door. Frank hadn't budged either.

The day of the lumber fire, Frankenkat was already halfway down the stairs before I caught up with him. But last night he'd calmly stayed put on the couch with Milady.

The smoke I saw couldn't have been from the heater. Carbon monoxide is colorless, almost odorless. When the firemen arrived, there was no trace of fire or smoke. Only the faint scent of uncombusted kerosene. Not a sniff of smoke.

Nor could I recall smelling it in my bedroom. I woke, saw the haze, and assumed it was smoke.

But Milady and Frank knew better. They didn't fear it. So it couldn't have been smoke. So what the hell was it?

"Some watchdog," I grumbled as I trotted Milady down to the Jeep. She leapt up into the passenger seat, sitting up, taking in the sights all the way to Algoma. Regal. There was no other word for her. I felt like a chauffeur.

An angry one. By the time we hit the city limits, my hands were clenched on the steering wheel and my stomach was knotted. Lachaine was big and looked hard as a brick. Plus, he'd likely have a case of morning-after surlies.

Yet I was still itching to meet him, one on one. To chat about outlaw trucks and dead dogs.

As I drove into the parking lot behind the courthouse that housed the Algoma Sheriff's Department, Milady suddenly went rigid, her hackles rising.

I slowed, thinking she'd seen another dog in a car, but it was more than that. She was wired, hackles up, fangs bared, gathering herself to leap out of the Jeep. Grabbing her collar, I held her until I'd parked.

Lady was lunging against my hold, but there was nothing to see. No people in sight, no dogs, just a row of parked cars. Untying her leash from the crash bar, I climbed out. She leapt past me in a rush, hauling me across the parking lot to a battered red Ford pickup.

Crouching, alert, she circled to the driver's side, a freight train growl rumbling deep in her chest. But there was no one to fight. The truck was empty. It was also vaguely familiar.

As I peered into the cab, I caught the sharp tang of gasoline from the truck bed. That's where I'd seen it before. Last night at the fire this truck had been parked near the prowl cars. It had to be Marty Lachaine's truck. That's why it reeked of gas. And any doubts I'd had evaporated in that moment.

Milady had reacted this way when we'd found Meg's pickup on its side. She'd scented her enemy then. And she'd recognized his scent as we passed the truck.

Hauling her bodily back to the Jeep, I parked her on the passenger seat and tied her leash securely to the crash bar. Then I stalked around to the front of the building, took a deep breath, and did something I vowed I'd never do again.

I went back to jail.

Chapter 44

The directory arrows to the county jail pointed down to the basement. Appropriate. I trotted down the steps, fighting back the fear that rose from the cells below like miasma, the stink of disinfectant and despair.

I pushed through the doors at the bottom without slowing, knowing if I hesitated for a second I'd U-turn and run for daylight.

The tiled corridor ended at an information counter. The cells were beyond. Couldn't see them, didn't have to. A female deputy was on duty, dark hair pulled back in a taut chignon, ruddy complexion, no makeup. Surprisingly pretty, and not one I'd seen before. So far, so good.

"Good morning, I'm Dr. Westbrook. I'd like to see Marty Lachaine."

"Lachaine? We'll be cutting him loose before long. His lawyer's upstairs posting his bond."

"I only need a minute. Is he still in custody?"

"Sure. He's in a holding cell. Sign in here. I'll have to search you."

I entered my name in her log, raised my hands for a quick pat down. And realized I was smiling. Remembering other searches in other jails. Naked. Barefoot on concrete floors.

"Is something funny?"

"No ma'am. Just swallowing a wisecrack."

"Good idea. I've heard 'em all. Holding cell's at the end of the block. No physical contact with the prisoner is allowed. Stay behind the yellow line."

She hit a switch below the counter, buzzing the heavy steel door open. I stepped through and it slammed shut behind me.

Typical county lockup, medium-security cells for prisoners awaiting trial or serving minimum terms, six months or less. Cell doors of reinforced oak with narrow Plexiglas observation slots faced each other on both sides of a long concrete corridor. A bright yellow stripe ran down its center.

The only barred cell was at the end of the hall. The drunk tank. No mattresses, no privacy, shower nozzles mounted in the ceiling for wetting down the winos and rinsing their vomit away.

Lachaine rose when he heard me coming, facing me through the bars. If he was surprised, he didn't show it. Big guy, six-three, about two-sixty, thirty pounds of suet bulked up at his waist in a beer belly. Unshaven, he was wearing the same red plaid shirt and grubby denims from last night, hair hanging in his eyes.

But those eyes were clear. Dark as cocktail olives and just as dead. No tremors, no stench of booze. For a drunk, he'd made a remarkable recovery. I stayed well behind the caution line, eyeing him through the iron.

"What the fuck are you lookin' at?"

"Not much. Let's cut right to it, Marty. I'm here alone, on my own, no wires, no cops, just us. And you know why. I'm the guy you tried to run down."

"Not me. I never seen you before in my life."

"Sure you have. And I've seen you. I recognized last night at the Keyes place."

"Yeah? Cops didn't say nothin' about it."

"I didn't tell them. I wanted to be sure. Now I am."

"I'm shakin' in my boots. It's your word against mine, jailbird, and I got friends who'll say where I was that night."

"You don't know me but you know I've done time and know which night I'm talking about? Man, you're not smart enough for this kind of work. No wonder you missed me."

"I'll do better next time."

"How about right now? If you're up to it?" Stepping across the yellow line, I moved within easy reach of the cell. He glanced down the empty corridor, then lunged! Clutching at me through the bars!

A weekender move, amateur. I let him clamp onto my shoulder, then grabbed his wrist, yanking him face-first into the steel doorframe. Using his arm for leverage, I jammed him up, kicking him hard between the bars. Once, twice! Square in the gonads.

He went chalk white, doubling over, gasping. Pushing him back into the cell, I quickly backed across the yellow line as the cell block gate buzzed open.

"Hey, hey! What's going on?" The deputy came sprinting back to us, a nightstick in her fist, primed for action. Raising my hands, I backed flat against the wall.

"Lachaine fell. I think he hurt himself."

"Fell how?" She jammed the tip of the stick into my sternum, holding me at bay while she looked Marty over. He was on his knees on the cell floor, retching, blood streaming from a gash over his eye.

"Marty? Are you all right?"

"Fuck you, bitch! And fuck you, Westbrook! You're out of your league and this ain't over!"

"It is for now," the deputy snapped. "What the hell happened?"

"Bastard sucker-punched me."

"Is that right?" She turned to me.

"Are you kidding? The guy must outweigh me by a hundred pounds. We had words, he tried to grab me, hit the bars, and fell down. It was all a misunderstanding."

"How about it, Marty? Do you want to press charges?"

"Wait a minute," I said, indignantly. "He's the one who —"

"Shut up!" she said, jabbing me with the stick. "Marty?"

"Hell no, I ain't pressin' no fuckin' charges! I'll be outta here in a few minutes, asshole. Then we'll see who falls down."

"How about you, Westbrook?" she said, facing me, the nightstick hard against my sternum. "Do you want to file any charges?"

"No, ma'am. As I said, it was just a —"

"— misunderstanding. Right. But just so we don't have any more misunderstandings, jack, if you come back here again, it won't be for a visit. Understand?"

"Absolutely."

"Now clear the hell out!"

I cleared, but only as far as the parking lot. Trotting to the Jeep, I fired it up and hastily backed into the corner of the lot behind a police van. The Jeep was concealed now but I could still keep an eye on the lot and Lachaine's pickup through the van's side windows.

Milady circled twice, then flopped on the front seat and promptly went to sleep, a practical way to wait.

I was wired from the jailhouse scuffle, sweating, hands trembling. Part adrenaline, part fear.

Lachaine was bigger than I'd expected. One on one in a straight scuffle, I didn't like my chances against him. But jailin' taught me that running from trouble isn't cost effective. If I didn't take him now, he'd tackle me later at a time and place of his choosing.

Better to settle things head on while he was still banged up and hope my anger and cellblock smarts would be enough to win. It wasn't a subtle plan, but Dancer would have understood it. I didn't give a damn if I won. I just wanted a piece of him.

Forty minutes later Lachaine stomped out of the building with a slender man in a silver three-piece suit that matched his razor cut mane. Les Hudspeth. I slid down in my seat, peering through the corner of the van window.

Les and Marty were arguing about something. I couldn't tell who won, but Lachaine climbed angrily into his truck, cranked it up, and roared out of the lot, forcing Les to jump aside to avoid being run down. Les stalked off across the village square, probably heading to his office.

Firing up the Jeep, I gunned out of the slot, then instantly hit the brakes. Hudspeth had stopped to talk with a taller man in the park. Their backs were to me but the second man's ramrod posture looked familiar — Whitfield? He half turned as the two of them walked off. Definitely Gerald Whitfield, Rachel's great-whatever. What the hell was he doing here?

No time to wonder. Lachaine already had a head start and I didn't want to lose him. Racing out of the lot, I turned north. Didn't see him at first, then spotted him stopped at a light, a half dozen cars ahead.

When the light changed he made a jackrabbit start, screeching his tires, burning rubber. I thought he'd spotted me, but he never looked back.

He stayed on the main drag through town, tailgating the car ahead of him, blaring his horn impatiently. Road rage? More likely he was in a hurry to get to his favorite pub. Which suited me. Especially if I could catch him alone in a parking lot.

No such luck. He continued north out of Algoma. Heading for home? Or the hills. No way to tell.

But the further from town we got, the lighter traffic became and a Jeep's a poor vehicle for tailing anyone. A few miles out he glanced in his side mirror, then swiveled slowly in his seat to stare back at me. And nodded.

Damn.

It was his move now. All I could do was tag along until he was ready to make it.

It didn't take long. Turning sharply onto a gravel road, Lachaine roared off, fishtailing his truck as he matted the gas.

I hurtled after him, cranking the wheel into the skid, fighting to keep the Jeep upright, then flooring the pedal, eating his dust, trying to keep him in sight.

No chance. Lachaine's Ford was a V-8 and he knew the roads. I had a wheezy four-banger in dire need of a valve job. Couldn't keep up with him, couldn't even stay close.

Ten miles and ten minutes later I slowed. I'd not only lost Lachaine, I'd lost myself. I had no idea where I was.

Chapter 45

A Jeep. Tailing him? When Marty recognized Westbrook following him a few cars back, he couldn't fucking believe it. Guy had brass balls for damn sure.

Marty's first thought was to wheel his pickup around in a big U-turn and ram Westbrook's Jeep off the road at fifty freakin' miles an hour, then stomp what was left of him into bat shit.

Bad idea. Too many nosy people with cell phones on the road. Cops would nail him sure. Better to wait, catch him alone, take his time workin' Westbrook over. So he waited for an opening, then bailed out, cutting across traffic onto a gravel road.

Marty kept the pedal to the metal for the first dozen miles, skidding through the curves, the pickup's big V-8 easily outrunning Westbrook's battered Jeep. Grinning as the Jeep vanished from his rear view, Marty poured it on for a few more miles, then made a hard right turn, and then another, heading back the way he came at seventy plus.

Kept checking the rear view but there was no sign of the Jeep. Lost the bastard. Good. Now it was time for payback.

Keeping to the back roads, he circled around Algoma to Westbrook's half-built clinic. Drove past once without slowing, checking it out. No vehicles parked in front, no one around. Looked deserted.

Naturally. Since dumb fuck Westbrook was still chasing his tail in the boondocks.

Making a U-turn, Marty pulled up in front and piled out. Hammered on the door. No answer. Glancing around to be sure there were no witnesses, he reared back and kicked at the latch. Once! Twice! Splintering the frame with the third blow.

Inside, he quickly scouted the office. Empty, no one around. Great! Grabbing a claw hammer he started ripping at the paneling, tearing down ceiling tiles, smashing light fixtures, trashing weeks of work in as many minutes. And enjoying every fucking lick!

High as a kite on adrenaline and destruction, Marty didn't hear the vehicle pull up out front. Didn't realize he had company until the doorway darkened.

"What the hell?" Bass roared. "You sonofabitch —"

Enraged, Bass charged at Marty from the doorway. Whirling to meet him, Marty swung the hammer on reflex. Full force! The blow caught Bass flush on the temple, smashing him down, spraying the paneling with blood!

But even falling, Bass grappled for Lachaine, trying to drag him down. And Marty snapped. Blood and rage sent him over the edge, into the darkness. He kept swinging the hammer, ripping flesh, shattering bones, savaging Bass's broken body long after any need for it was gone.

Chapter 46

I rocketed around the back roads a good half hour, furious, frustrated. No luck. No trace of Lachaine. Not even a damned dust trail.

On impulse, I downshifted into four-wheel drive, then goosed the Jeep across a shallow ditch, gunning it to the top of a long rise, hoping to spot Lachaine's red Ford pickup from high ground.

At the top I popped the door and stood up, scanning the countryside. Not much to see: scattered patches of woods, dirt roads winding through the empty hills like crook-back snakes. Blackened skeletons was all that remained of the few abandoned farms. What had Bass called it? Rachel Hayes country? Something like that.

No sign of Lachaine's battered truck or anyone else. The only activity in sight was a dump truck pulling up to a distant gate. A guy with a clipboard waved the driver through into an area the size of three or four football fields encircled by a tall chain link fence. The grounds looked like a bombing range after a busy day. Gravel pit.

I tried to remember if we'd crossed the county line. Probably. So this should be the gravel pit Chris Sinclair managed.

It was worth a try. Maybe they'd seen him.

Easing the Jeep slowly off the rise — driving downhill is a lot trickier than climbing — I got back on the dirt road, made a hard right at the next crossroad, and raced to the gate shack.

A guy in coveralls and a yellow hardhat came out of the guard shack beside the gate. Red-faced and wind-burned from outside work, he was carrying a clipboard. And an attitude.

"Something you want, pal?"

"I was following a friend and lost track of him. Did a red pickup pass by the last ten minutes or so? A Ford?"

"No. Nobody passed here."

"Maybe he lives around here. Marty Lachaine?"

"Haven't seen him."

"But you know who he is?"

He hesitated. A split second, but it was there. "No. Don't know him. Name sounded familiar, that's all. Look, I got work to do, so —"

"Is Chris Sinclair around?"

"He's asleep and I'm only supposed to wake him for an emergency. Are you some kinda emergency?"

"Nope, I was just in the neighborhood. Tell him Dave said hello." I backed my Jeep out of the drive. Mr. Clipboard stood at the gate, watching until I was out of sight.

Maybe Lachaine hadn't been there, but I was sure the gate recognized his name. Why play dumb? It might be nothing. Most people who knew Lachaine probably pretended not to. Still . . .

A half mile from the gate, I pulled off the road, parked, then climbed a hill near the fence for a better look at the pit.

No trucks moving now. A ramshackle farmhouse stood off to one side of the property, windows boarded up, eyeless and abandoned. Place looked deserted.

It was bigger than I'd thought, a jagged moonscape that sprawled over seventy or eighty acres. Mounds of gravel stood beside open craters, some of them apparently deep enough to need pumps to keep them dry. Several gouges had spherical tanks beside them, taller than a man. The whole area was seriously fenced, eight-foot chain link topped with loose strands of bayonet wire.

The guard said Chris was sleeping. The whole place looked asleep to me. Maybe the guy was cranky because he was missing his siesta.

No trace of Lachaine. But as I turned away, a flicker of light caught my eye. Red. Next to the fence. Two dragonflies, mating in midair . . . There it was again. A glint of red flickering on their wings. A very familiar red flash.

Kneeling, I scanned the fence line, spotting them immediately. Small plastic knobs on every second fence post, painted gray to match the metal. Infrared relays. Protecting the fence with a nearly invisible laser beam, narrow as a needle.

The Department of Corrections used them on the perimeter fence of the work camp where I'd served the last few months of my sentence. It's not a high-tech system. Break the beam for a second and it relays a signal that something's near the fence.

It seemed a bit extreme for a gravel pit, but maybe their insurance required it. Some people will sue you for depleting the world's air supply. By breathing.

I drove the back roads around the pit in a complete circle, thinking I might blunder across Lachaine's truck. Didn't find it. Or anything else. Only a few more burned-out farm sites. Nearing the main highway, I pulled into a rundown one-pump party store, topped off my tank, and went inside. One room, crammed floor to ceiling with chips, pretzels, sodas, and beer. Road food.

The heavyset kid behind the counter had bleached hair styled with garden shears and a bad case of acne. Lost in a soap opera on a seven-inch black-and-white TV, he barely glanced up.

"Eighteen bucks gas. Anything else?"

"A little help," I said, handing him a twenty. "I'm looking for a guy who lives around here. Marty Lachaine?"

"Nah," he said positively, popping the register open. "Not around here. I was born ten mile up the road. Don't know no Lachaines."

"He may be working at the gravel pit."

"Definitely don't know him then." He counted out my change. "They don't hire locals at the pit, only ex-flyboys off the old airbase, the one that closed? None of them live around here."

"Are you sure?"

"Damn straight. Tried to hire on there myself awhile back. I grew up on a farm, been workin' with heavy machinery all my life. Wouldn't even take my application.

Said don't bother comin' back. Any chance your friend could put in a word for me?"

"He's not a friend, just a guy I know. Sorry."

"Yeah, right." He tossed my two bucks on the counter.

"I noticed a few farms have been burned out around here."

"So?"

"Any idea why?"

"Kids, I guess. Little bastards got no respect for nothin' nowadays."

"Kids? Not Rachel Hayes?"

"Who?" He was already zoned into his TV soaper before I was out the door.

Chapter 47

Trouble. I knew it the moment I met the police car. The black-and-white came howling out of Algoma, lights and sirens full on. Eyeballing me as he passed, he whipped the prowlie around, powersliding into a U-turn. I'd already pulled over and stopped when he screeched to a stop behind me.

I started reaching for my license, then froze. It was Jessup, but he wasn't approaching. Using his open door as a shield, he was covering me with a shotgun.

"Step out of the car, Westbrook, hands in the air. Now!"

What the hell? I hesitated, then did exactly as he said. Very, very slowly.

"Assume the position. You know the drill."

He was dead right about that. Placing my hands on the hood in clear view, I leaned against the Jeep, my ankles in an open stance. Apparently not open enough. Jessup kicked them farther apart before frisking me and slapping on the cuffs.

"Mind telling me — ?" I began.

"Shut up." Grabbing my collar, he led me to the prowl car, pushed me into the rear seat, slammed the door, and we were off again. Lights and sirens. And déjà vu.

Home sweet home. A ten by twelve concrete box of an interrogation room, gray floor, institutional green walls. Mirror in the metal door, probably two-way.

I sat at a battered conference table on a metal office chair, my wrists cuffed behind me. I expected Wolinski to do the honors, but it was the heavyset lady cop who'd answered my 911 call after I tangled with the outlaw truck.

She sat across the table from me. Jessup was behind her, leaning against the wall. Cool. Watchful.

It was all so familiar that the barn and clinic already seemed like a dream, fading fast. Keeler read me my rights, then began.

"Do you know why you're here, David?"

"Nope." But I could guess. Hudspeth must have filed an assault complaint for Lachaine —

"Do you know a Chester Arthur Bascomb, David?"

It took a moment for the unfamiliar name to register. "Ches— you mean Bass? What about him?"

"Just answer the question, please."

"Sure I know him, he's my uncle. And I also know the drill. Either tell me what's up or we're done talking and I want an attorney. Has something happened to my uncle?"

Keeler eyed me a moment, then shrugged. "He's dead."

"What?" The concrete floor rocked beneath my chair. "Dead how? What the hell happened?"

"We're hoping you can help us with that. Can you give me a recap of your movements today? Where have you been?"

"I was right here at ten o'clock. Then I . . . went for a drive in the country."

"Alone?"

I nodded, numb, still trying to absorb what she'd said.

"Did you see anyone? Talk to anyone who can confirm your whereabouts?"

I almost mentioned the gravel pit, but didn't. I had a gut feeling the gate guard wouldn't vouch for me. "I gassed up at a little country store just over the county line. The clerk should remember me."

"Which store?"

Couldn't recall the name but I described

it. Jessup nodded and left to make a call. I took a deep breath, steadying down. "Now. What happened to my uncle? Exactly."

"You know what happened. He was killed in your clinic. The way it looks, you two had some kind of an argument, Bass lost his temper, started wrecking the place. You tried to stop him and things just . . . got out of hand. Is that how it was?"

"No. I wasn't there. How did my uncle die?"

"Multiple blows to the head. From a hammer." She eyed me, gauging my reaction. "We found it at the scene. An Estwing 20-ouncer. Rubber handle. Yours?"

"Yeah." I swallowed, hard. The room was closing in. Shrinking. Down to cell size. Its weight was bearing down, crushing me. I couldn't breathe.

Jessup reentered the room, leaned over Keeler's shoulder, and murmured something to her.

"Is he sure?" she asked. Jessup nodded.

"Your story checks out," she conceded. "Which doesn't necessarily mean you're off the hook. Do you know anyone who might have wanted to harm your uncle?"

"No. If I did, I'd say so. Am I free to go?"

She hesitated, then shrugged. "For now. Uncuff him."

As soon as my hands were free, I headed for the front door. Someone called after me to wait but I didn't. Couldn't. I had to get away from that place. When I hit the street I took off running. Pounding blindly down the sidewalk through the village, passing shops, parked cars. Didn't know where I was going. Didn't care.

Sprinted a mile, then another, running nearly flat out. A car blew past, angrily blaring its horn. It barely registered. Somewhere along the line I veered down a side road, leaving the pavement behind.

Pounding along on the shoulder of a country road, my chest began constricting, lungs afire. Suddenly a cramp grabbed my right calf with fiery tongs. I stumbled, came up limping, but didn't stop. Hobbling along, trying to get as far as —

"David?" Meg called. "David, wait a minute." She pulled alongside in a little yellow Geo Metro convertible, the loaner she'd gotten from the dealership while her truck was being repaired. "David, stop. Please."

My leg made the decision for me. Knotting up, it dropped me to my knees in agony. I sprawled in the gravel, trying to knead the pain away.

Meg pulled over and walked back to me.

And I realized she was still wearing the pajamas she'd had on the night before.

"Are you all right?" she asked.

"Do I look all right? What are you doing here? I thought you were busted."

"I was. I am, I mean. They found a check made out to Lachaine with my signature on it. Wolinski sent it to the State police crime lab for examination. I'm out on bail. I'm very sorry about your uncle."

"Me too." I sat up, looking around, taking stock of surroundings. "What the hell's going on, Meg?"

"I don't know," she said, kneeling to help me up. "But we'd better find out."

Chapter 48

As we pulled into the driveway of the Keyes place, the savagery of the carriage house fire struck home. A skeletal wall in one corner was all that remained standing. The rest of the building had collapsed into a shambles of splintered timbers and melted blobs of office equipment.

Daryl was on her knees in hand-me-down coveralls, haggard, her face streaked with soot, pawing through the sodden ruins like a refugee after an air raid. A grubby cardboard box of scorched papers was all she'd managed to salvage. She glanced up as we climbed out of Meg's car, her eyes as vacant as the wreckage.

"I heard about Bass. I'm sorry."

"So am I. Let me help you with that," I said, taking the cardboard box from her. "We have to talk."

"About what? In an hour I'll have to call my folks in Florida and tell them the paper they ran for forty years is a total loss. And there's no insurance money because Meg's been charged with complicity in the arson."

"You know it's not true."

"All I know is my parents trusted me to run the paper and look after Meg. And here we are."

"This wasn't your fault."

"I know. Was it yours?"

"Mine?"

"Sheriff Wolinski thinks you're involved in this, that you and Meg hired Lachaine to sensationalize the Rachel series. A firebug ghost."

"Nuts," Meg said. "David never wanted publicity. Ex-cons can't afford it. Not that it matters now. Reggie's pulled the plug. The series is dead."

"So are Bass, Tipton, and the bodies in the well," Daryl said acidly. "Compared to all that, the death of a small town newspaper doesn't count for much."

"Of course it does. My God, Dar, do you think I wanted — ?"

"Hold it!" I broke in. "Before we start working each other over, I've got a quick question. You said you'd done stories on Marty Lachaine. What about?"

"Not stories, items," Meg said, still

380

glaring at Daryl. "Police beat stuff. An assault arrest after a barroom brawl. He was a finalist in a Tough Man contest a few years ago. Apparently it went to his head."

"Any arrests for driving-under-the-influence?"

"I — no, not that I recall, just the assault and battery bust. Which was the only time I ever talked to him. Why?"

"I went to see him at the jail this morning. He was cold sober."

"So?"

"Meg, he wasn't even hung over. Last night he was supposedly so smashed he only managed to drive a half-mile from the fire before passing out. He's a big guy. It would take a lot of booze to put him under."

"But after a night's sleep —" Daryl began.

"Lady, if there's one thing I know about, it's drunks. If he was really smashed last night, he should have been exuding alcohol this morning, on his breath, through his pores. I should have smelled him three feet away and I got a lot closer than that. He was stone cold sober. I think he was probably sober last night too."

"But the police —"

"Found him sleeping in his truck and smelled booze. He acted drunk, admitted to it, and they bought it."

"You've lost me," Meg said. "Why would he act drunk?"

"Because he wanted to get caught. So he could tell the cops you hired him to set the fire."

"But he went to jail too," Daryl objected.

"Only overnight. Les Hudspeth bailed him out first thing this morning. He'll cop a plea, pay a fine, and walk. Not bad for arson and murder."

"Murder?"

"Lachaine was the guy who took a run at me in Meg's truck. Which most likely makes him the guy who took Bass out."

"I thought you couldn't identify the driver of the truck," Daryl said.

"I couldn't. But I recognized him last night: his eyes, his look, something. And he definitely recognized me. Jailin' teaches you to read people in a hurry. He was driving that night and he likes his work. He went out of his way to kill those dogs and took a hard run at me. If Dancer hadn't gone for him, I'd be as dead as Bass."

"And what about Bass?" Meg prompted.

"I don't know. I tangled with Lachaine at the jail, trailed him into the boondocks, then lost him. He could have circled back looking for me and found Bass instead."

"Did you tell the police?"

"Tell them what? The last time I saw Lachaine he was twenty miles from the scene. All I've got is a serious gut feeling about him. I can't prove anything."

"And no motive," Daryl said, brushing a wisp of hair back, smearing soot on her forehead. "What reason would Lachaine have to do any of this?"

"None. And that's a problem. You had no quarrel with him and I'd never even met him. He had no reason to torch your place or come after me. Unless somebody paid him to do it."

"He says I paid him," Meg said evenly.

"He's lying."

"How do you know?" Daryl asked.

"I've been chewing it over. Lachaine claims you hired him the day you wound up in the hospital, right? What time was that?"

"I'm not sure. Sometime late that afternoon."

"Okay, let's say you hired him and loaned him your truck to give me a scare. He didn't come to the barn. He smashed through the fence at the far corner of the pasture, the perfect spot to take a shot at us. You couldn't have told him I'd be there, you didn't know. Hell, I didn't know. I decided to run the dogs at the last minute to beat the storm. But Lachaine was already waiting for us."

"What are you saying?" Daryl asked.

"Someone must have told him where I'd be. Someone who had me staked out. It couldn't have been Marty, he was busy stealing your truck. It had to be somebody else, maybe the person who hired him."

"Who?"

"I don't know. Les Hudspeth is Lachaine's attorney. He might have it in for me, but he'd have no reason to torch the *Herald* or kill anyone."

"Do you realize how paranoid you sound?" Daryl asked.

"Tell that to Tipton or Bass. Or run a story about it in what used to be your newspaper. Or I'll take you to the high ground where I buried my dogs. Explain it to them."

"I'm only saying it makes no sense," Daryl pressed. "Who would want to harm us?"

"What about Whitfield? Does he want to stop the series badly enough to set up something like this?"

"To protect his family honor? Hardly. If he didn't like the stories, he could sue us."

"Anyone else?"

"Rachel Hayes," Meg said quietly. "Hey,

don't look at me like that, I don't mean a damned ghost. But she's our only connection. Without her we wouldn't even know each other. Or Tipton or even Whitfield."

"Here we go again with the curse," Daryl snapped.

"Lighten up!" I said. "I don't know squat about ghosts, but no spook beat my uncle to death or paid Lachaine to burn this place. Marty's strictly the cash-and-carry type."

"He also takes checks," Daryl sniped.

"In the joint I knew guys who could turn a twenty into a c-note with a number two pencil. Meg's signature would be child's play. And she's right. Rachel's our only real link."

"But there's nothing left of her," Meg said. "Her body's gone, her grave's gone. I can't even tell her story. She was better off in the well."

"So were the rest of us," Daryl said bitterly.

"No argument," I agreed, "but she's out now and something about her is important enough to get people killed. Money? Is she worth anything?"

"Not after a century," Meg said, "and anyway, she had no heirs. Her only daughter died in the same fire."

"Do we know that? Her daughter wasn't in the well."

"The few accounts I found assumed Hannah and Rachel died together," Meg said. "If she turned up later, our only hope of proving it went up in smoke with the *Herald*. All the old newspapers and records were in the carriage house."

"Not all of them," Daryl said reluctantly. "There are a few boxes of photographs and files stored in the basement behind the darkroom."

"Whoa," Meg said. "What photographs?"

"Albums dad bought at estate sales, family pictures, yearbooks, whatever."

"And you didn't tell me about them?"

"With all that's happened — no, that's not true. The truth is I was afraid you'd ditch the paper to play TV star. And probably jealous. Either way, it was a crappy thing to do."

"Save the apology, Dar. I've been screwing up enough for both of us. But we're down to it now. If we don't find a reason for all this, we're done."

"What reason? What are you looking for?"

"I don't know," Meg said. "Maybe some factoid in my notes. I've been so focused on polishing the first few scripts I've barely scanned the rest of the data."

"What about land?" I asked.

"Rachel's farm couldn't be worth much," Meg said. "There's plenty of undeveloped land around there."

"Maybe she owned other property."

"County land records go back before the Civil War, so any holdings would still be on file. Why don't you check with the county clerk's office, David? I'll go over my files and Dar can sort through her photographs. Something about that bitch must be worth killing for. Because it's already killing us."

Chapter 49

The county clerk's office was a tiny cubicle in the courthouse complex: beige tiled walls, gray carpeting, Formica counter. No chairs for waiting, no room for them.

The clerk looked ancient enough to be one of Rachel's ex-boyfriends, seventy-five minimum, wispy halo of white hair. His eyes were bright though, with a glint of humor. White shirt buttoned to the throat despite the heat of the day.

"What can I do for ya?"

"I'd like to see a plat book for Algoma County."

"Which quadrant? The books are divided into four sections."

"The area around the north county line?"

"Sector two." He pulled a slim folder from beneath the counter, flipped through it expertly, opening it to the page I needed. "A few titles might not be current, but I know most of the landholders around here.

Any particular parcel in mind?"

"This eighty-acre plot? The one that says Jozwiak on it? It belonged to a woman named Hayes —"

"Yah, yah, the one that girl's been writing about in the paper. I looked it up a couple weeks ago for a fella. Black fella, said he had somethin' to do with TV."

"Reggie Laws?"

"He didn't mention his name. Not very likable. Kinda pushy. I got nothin' at all against black folk, you understand. But assholes come in all colors. Friend of yours, is he?"

"No. About the parcel . . . ?"

"Right. Anyway, I found the Hayes farm for him. Belonged to a family named Dealey before Jozwiak bought it, and the . . . Brights before that."

"You remember all that? Off the top of your head, I mean?"

"What do you do, Sonny?"

"I'm a veterinarian. David Westbrook." I offered my hand, and he shook it. His palm was hard as horn.

"Duff Sorenson. If somebody showed you a map of a dog, could you name off all its innards?"

"I suppose so."

"Well, I been readin' these county maps

near fifty years now, probably forgot more about this country than most folks will ever know. Hell yes, I remember the names on all the lots. What do you wanna know?"

"Would you know if Rachel Hayes owned any land other than her farm?"

"Two other properties. A beachfront lot, unimproved. Probably figured to build a cottage on it sometime but never did. Got kilt in the Great Fire. Terrible thing. Half the damn' county went up."

"You sound like you remember it."

"Nah, I don't, but my mama did. She was just a little tyke then, but she knew a lotta people who got kilt. Don't know if she knew the Hayes woman."

"You said Rachel Hayes owned two other parcels?"

"Owned some pasture land just outside of town, a hundred acres. Part of the McCrae estate now."

I froze, staring. Felt like I'd been sucker punched.

"Somethin' wrong?"

"No," I managed, swallowing. "You mean Senator McCrae's place once belonged to Rachel Hayes?"

"Part of it, yeah. Wasn't no house on it then —"

"But the barn was there?"

"Not the same barn. The first one burned down in the Great Fire. The one that's there now is some newer. Built during the First World War. Was a blacksmith shop for a while. Had kind of a funny name."

"The shop?"

"Nah, the Hayes farm. Women ownin' property in them days didn't generally hold it in their own names. The Hayes woman called her place . . . Ten Cities Farm? Something like that. Hell, maybe my memory's not as good as —"

"Tenacity?" I said quietly.

"That's it," he nodded, brightening. "Tenacity Farm. Kind of an odd name."

"Yeah. Definitely odd. Can you tell me anything else?"

"Not much to tell. There was another Hayes farm in Algoma County later on, but they weren't related to your Mrs. Hayes. Ojibwas from Escanaba. Moved here during the depression. One boy got kilt in Korea. Damn shame."

"Suppose Rachel Hayes had heirs? Would they have any claim at all on her land?"

"No way," he snorted. "Hell, Sonny, after the fire none of the burnt land was worth spit for years. The Hayes parcels reverted to the state for back taxes three different times. Mrs. Hayes couldn't claim it if she walked

391

through that door herself, which ain't likely." He flashed me a grin. I couldn't even fake a response. Nothing about Rachel Hayes was funny anymore. Not to me.

"That land ain't fit for much but walkin' on anyways."

"What about gravel?"

"Not even that. The Osterhaus pit's been buyin' up a few parcels in the back country, hit and miss. But they won't be taking any gravel out of 'em."

"Why not?"

"See this section here?" He indicated a darkened area with a sausage-sized forefinger. "Ten-thousand-acre Federal nature preserve. EPA'll never grant clearance to mine there, and Hudspeth knew that when they bought it."

"Les Hudspeth is the attorney for the Osterhaus pit?"

"He handled the paperwork for 'em, sure."

"But if he knew they couldn't use the land, why buy it?"

"Lawyers," he snorted. "Maybe Les figured he could weasel around the regulations somehow. Or get paid by the hour to try. Or maybe Jerry Whitfield's speculatin'. He's bought a few other parcels —"

"Whoa up. Whitfield? You said the

Osterhaus pit bought the land."

"Whitfield, Osterhaus, same thing. All the same family. They're old money, used to own a half dozen businesses in the county. Most of 'em are belly-up now: bad investments, bad management, who knows. Maybe the blood thins out after a few generations.

"The pit's bought several parcels over the last ten years, though, here, here, and here." He indicated widely scattered sites on the county map with a fingertip. "Odd lots, an eighty here, twenty there. Haven't developed none of 'em. Maybe they're waitin' on a big real estate boom or something."

"Or something," I said.

Chapter 50

Driving back through Algoma, I spotted Meg's little Geo loaner parked in front of a coffee shop. Meg was in a window booth, staring into space. She glanced up, startled, as I slid in across from her.

"You look weird. What did you find out?"

"Nothing useful." I waved the waitress off. "Bottom line, this can't be about Rachel's property. She couldn't claim it if she showed up in person. How did you do?"

"I don't know. Dar phoned me and said she might have something. I asked her to meet me here. I couldn't stay at my apartment."

"Why not?"

"It feels . . . haunted to me. I don't mean by a ghost. It's more like something horrible happened there. It felt the same way the day I left the hospital. I thought it would fade. Seemed worse though. I kept getting flashes . . ." She took a deep breath. "Flashes of me. With some . . . guy. The worst of it is that I can't remember anything solid. Just bits and pieces. And there's more. My notes and the background material for the series are gone."

"What do you mean gone?"

"I had boxes of stuff, books on the great fires, stats and articles I downloaded off the net. All gone."

"Somebody ripped it off?"

"Unless Rachel zapped it into the afterlife. It was there the day I got out of the hospital, so I know I didn't move it, drunk or sober. Why would anybody want that stuff?"

"I don't know. Did Chris know your notes were there?"

"Chris? Of course, but —"

"How much do you know about the company Chris manages?"

"It's a gravel pit. They dig up dirt and sell it. It's the same job I do, only more honorable. Why?"

"Did you know Gerald Whitfield owns it?"

"What?"

"Right. Whitfield. Rachel's long lost relative. Funny Chris didn't mention that. Does Chris ever work nights?"

"Sometimes. Why?"

"I was out there today around noon. The gate guard said he was asleep. And the morning he came to see you he looked rough, like he'd been up all night."

"Maybe he was."

"Why? Why would anybody dig —"

"— mine," she corrected. "They don't dig gravel, they mine it."

"Okay, mine it. But why at night? Especially when no one seemed to be working days?"

"I don't know. Chris never talks about his work. After flying jets it must seem pretty tame."

"It might be more exciting than you think. Security's tight there: barbed wire, chain link fencing with infrared tripper beams. The last time I saw fences like that I was locked inside them."

"What are you getting at?"

"I don't know. But Les Hudspeth represented the gravel pit when it bought Rachel's farm and he's also Marty Lachaine's lawyer. Since Les is strictly a white-collar type, I wonder how a stiff like Lachaine can afford him? Unless somebody with serious bucks is picking up the tab?"

"Whitfield, you mean? Why should he?"

"You're the reporter, you tell me."

"Chris wouldn't do anything illegal — oh, hell! Now what?"

An Algoma county prowl car screeched to a halt beside my Jeep, flashers going.

Stan Wolinski bailed out and hurried into the coffee shop, heading straight for our booth.

"Meg, I'm sorry but —"

"Damn it, Stan, I posted bail! You can't arrest me again."

"It's not that. Your sister's had an accident. Rolled her car. I'm on my way there now; you can follow me if you like."

"Is she all right?"

"Don't know, but it sounds serious. Let's go."

It was all I could do to keep Wolinski in sight as he blasted through traffic, sirens and flashers clearing our way. The crash site was only a few miles out; an EMT van and a prowl car were angle-parked, blocking the right lane.

Daryl's Saturn was on its side in the ditch, chassis facing the road, bleeding oil and transmission fluid onto the torn grass. A pair of EMT techs were strapping Daryl to a stretcher as we roared up. Meg vaulted out of my Jeep and ran to her before we'd stopped rolling.

I parked and followed at a trot, glimpsing Daryl's ashen face, eyes closed, as the techs carefully lifted her into their van. Meg leapt in after her for the ride to the hospital. I thought.

But a few moments later she stepped out again, spoke to one of the techs, then trudged woodenly to me, as shaken as I've ever seen anyone.

"She's um, they think she'll be all right. She's got a broken shoulder and some lacerations. Lucky. With her arthritis, she could have been crippled — God. Where's Wolinski?"

"Checking over the wreck."

"Good. We have to get out of here."

"Why?" I fell into step with her as she hurried back to the Jeep.

"Daryl was pretty groggy from the accident, but —" Meg swallowed, blinking back tears. "She said she was rammed! Somebody deliberately ran her off the road. A pickup. Red. An old beater."

"Lachaine?"

"She didn't see his face. The truck came blasting out of a side road and smashed her into a ditch. But after the crash, she heard footsteps, so she pretended to be unconscious. Whoever it was kicked in a side window, reached in, and took the folder she had with her. She said the original is still at the house in the photo enlarger. We have to get it."

"What is it?"

"I don't know. She was drifting in and out. She wasn't making much sense."

"What did she say?"

Meg took a deep breath. "That I saw the wrong ghost. She kept repeating it over and over. Rachel is the wrong ghost."

Chapter 51

"Do you have any idea what she meant?" I asked. We were in my Jeep, halfway to the Keyes house.

"No. Maybe she was hallucinating."

"That wreck was no hallucination. They're down to it now."

"But they're making mistakes." Her eyes were as hard as any lifer's. "Hurting my sister is a big one. They don't know what serious is yet. They're about to find out. Take a right at the next intersection."

"Aren't we going to your place?"

"Not by the front door."

Following Meg's directions, I threaded a maze of back country roads that eventually brought us to the rear of the Keyes property. Parking the Jeep in a grove of cedars, we worked our way to the edge of the field at the back of the house.

Life inside the walls taught me to melt into shadows, but Meg had played on these grounds as a kid. Using every bit of cover, she moved through the grass, silent as a stalking cat.

As we entered the yard, she ducked into a garden shed. She came out with an axe handle and tossed it to me, keeping a hatchet for herself. She looked ready to use it. So was I.

Slipping in through the back door, we paused inside, listening. Silence. Then we moved through the house, room-by-room, tense, weapons ready. Nothing.

We left Daryl's basement photo lab for last. Files were scattered around on the floor. I glanced a question at Meg.

"She may have left it like this," she whispered, "but things were out of place upstairs and Dar's a neat freak. I think somebody searched the house. I just hope they didn't find it."

The enlarger crouched on the counter like a mechanical praying mantis. Picking her way through the mess, Meg gently pulled out the tray. It held an old photograph, a group shot in faded black-and-white. Frowning, Meg examined it intently then showed it to me.

"I don't understand. It's just an old school picture. Looks like some kind of a Christmas pageant."

I scanned it. A group of kids were seated in chairs in a semicircle facing the photographer. They appeared to be middle-schoolers, nine to twelve years old. Some were dressed as angels, others like shepherds or wise men.

A row of adults stood behind them, women in dark skirts, blouses, high button shoes. No smiles, all very solemn. All of them long dead before we were born. From their clothing, I guessed it was taken sometime near the end of the nineteenth century. . . .

My God. There she was.

Halfway along the row, she was standing behind a chubby, ten-year-old blonde angel, complete with silken halo and gossamer wings.

I checked the legend at the bottom of the photo. Miss Schuyler's fourth grade class, Advent Pageant Day, December 17, 1870. It made no sense. But at second glance, I realized what I'd taken for a trademark at the bottom of the shot wasn't. It was a seating chart, hand printed on the photograph, the ink so faded it was barely visible. The names of the students in the picture.

Tracing the seats with my fingertips, I felt an icy chill of recognition, though I'd never seen the child before. Only the woman standing behind her.

"What is it?" Meg asked, reading my face.

I pointed out the pudgy angel, smiling primly. The legend beneath her chair read H. Hayes.

"H . . . ? Hannah Hayes?" Meg said.

"It must be. The guy at the plat office said they were the only Hayes family in the area at the time."

"But where's Rachel?"

"Standing right behind her. Look at the resemblance."

"That's not Rachel. It doesn't look anything like her."

"You mean it doesn't look like the picture Whitfield showed us. But it's Rachel. It must be."

She stared up at me a moment before the realization sank in. "The wrong ghost," she breathed. "That's what Dar tried to tell me."

I nodded, still focused on the faded blur of a face standing behind Hannah's chair. Because I knew beyond doubt that I'd seen her before. The night Tipton died, and in my room, in the smoke. I didn't want it to be true. But it was. I just didn't know what it meant.

"Funny, she almost looks familiar," Meg said, "like I've seen her —" I put my finger to her lips, cutting her off. Picking up a plastic jar of photographic talc, I sprinkled it on the counter and wrote "bugs" in it. Her eyes met mine and she nodded, then wiped it away.

"This is a waste of time," she said in a level tone. "Let's go."

Neither of us spoke again until we were well clear of the house, headed toward the Jeep.

"What makes you think the house is bugged?" Meg asked.

"Because Daryl's in the hospital. When she called you, they knew she found something. And they ran her down."

"Lachaine." It wasn't a question this time.

"Ramming her off the road would be his style. But this isn't his show. He's just hired muscle, a rent-a-thug."

"Hired by Whitfield?"

"I think so. He's definitely in it. The phony wedding picture proves that."

"I don't understand. Why bother to show us a faked picture?"

"It wasn't for us, it was for the coroner. He needed proof in order to claim her remains and have them destroyed."

"But why? Just to blow us off Rachel's story? Nobody's family honor's worth that much."

"I don't know but somehow, to some-body, Rachel Hayes still matters. The body count's too high. Suppose her story had played on TV as planned. What would happen?"

"It would . . . generate interest in her, I guess. Maybe wider press coverage. Tour-ists might visit her old home site. That's about it. Nothing worth killing for."

"Doesn't seem like it," I admitted. "But if this isn't about Rachel, that only leaves her land."

"But it's worthless."

"It can't be. Whitfield's company has bought a half dozen parcels near it, even though they can't get a zoning variance for mining. Did Chris say anything about that?"

"He never talks about the pit. I've never even seen it."

"A local gas jockey told me the employees are all ex-military, not just Chris."

"Whoa up. You don't think Chris is part of this?"

"His company bought the land, Meg. He made damned sure Tipton didn't get Ra-chel's remains that first day, then he filled in the well and pushed you to give up the proj-ect."

"I don't believe it. You think he's been

playing me? No way. He wouldn't do that."

"No? You trust him completely, right? So you've told him everything that happened the night you got hurt?"

"No, but only because . . ." She broke off, eyeing me like a stranger. "You bastard."

"Sorry."

"I didn't tell him about the miscarriage because things are rocky between us. That doesn't make him guilty of anything."

"You said once you had a thing for dangerous men. How dangerous is Chris?"

She started to bark at me, then slowly shook her head. "Okay. I'll admit it's possible. So where does that leave us?"

"Pretty much on our own. Unless you think we should bring in the law."

"You've got to be kidding. Wolinski thinks I'm a nut job and he likes you even less. What do we tell him? That somebody killed Bass and smashed up my sister to get rid of a woman who's been dead a hundred years? He'll ship us both down to Ypsi for a psych workup."

"Not both of us. My guess is it has something to do with the pit. And checking it out is a one-man job."

"And you expect me to hold your coat? Dream on. They tried to kill my sister, David. I'm going. That's it. The only question is whether you're coming along."

"Then I guess we go together. Back in Milan I used to fantasize about breaking out of jail a lot. I never thought I'd be breaking into one."

"It's not a jail."

"Wrong. If we get caught, jail's exactly what it'll be."

"Assuming they don't kill us instead."

"Right," I conceded. "Assuming that."

Chapter 52

Every con dreams of breaking out. Bedsheet ladders. Guns carved from soap, blackened with shoe polish. TV schemes that fade at first light when you face the reality of reinforced concrete walls and a thousand steel gates. Escape? Forget it. Breaking in, though? That could work.

For openers we needed a vehicle. My Jeep was too obvious and Meg's yellow Geo looked like a lollipop on wheels. Bass's old work van was still parked at the barn. I didn't think he'd mind.

He always left the keys in it. But taking it wasn't that simple. My office door was sealed off with yellow Police Line — Do-Not-Cross tapes. But I couldn't leave without seeing it.

Ducking under the tape, I unlocked the door and stepped in.

And swallowed hard, gagging down the bile rising in my throat. The room was a brutal shambles. All the weeks of work Bass and I had done, ripped and hammered to pieces. As Bass had been.

A chalked silhouette where he'd fallen. Dried blood on the floor, spattered on the walls. Savagery suffused the room like a scarlet mist. A murderous fury so strong I could taste it the way a dog scents blood on the wind.

The feeling was so overwhelming I couldn't tell if I was sensing death lingering in the air. Or the red rage roiling in my own heart. I had to get out of there. Before I grabbed a hammer and finished the job the killer had started.

I went through to the cool, dim interior of the barn, took a deep breath, inhaling the scent of curing hay, gathering myself.

The dogs were restless, whining in their pens. If I could sense slaughter in the air, so could they. Only more so. When it comes to blood, humans are amateurs. Hounds are professionals.

I turned them loose to stretch their legs in the corridor while I refilled their bowls with food and water, then put them away again. We wouldn't be running today. I had other business.

Climbing behind the wheel of Bass's van, I fired it up, then adjusted the seat forward.

My uncle was a bigger man than I am. In every way.

As I dropped the truck in gear, I noticed my clinic sign was down, torn out of the wall, thrown aside. Uncovering the older sign above the door.

TENACITY. The word was even blacker than before, and growing larger as it continued to bleed out through the fresh red paint.

Chapter 53

Bass's battered rustbucket truck blended into the back country like a faded flannel shirt. Unwilling to risk passing the pit's entrance gate, we concealed the van in a copse of blue spruce on a hillside at the back of the pit, then belly-crawled through the underbrush to a ridge crest overlooking the diggings.

Seen from high ground, the fence made even less sense. It wasn't protecting anything of value. The pit was exactly that, sprawling, rocky ground gouged with multiple excavations gaping like open sores in the earth.

Sleepy as a schoolyard in July. An occasional worker strolled from the rundown farmhouse to a truck or to one of the tanks to take a reading, but there were no other signs of life.

"So what is this?" Meg hissed. "Nothing's going on."

"That's my point. Cars in the parking lot, a guard in the shack. But nobody's working. I want a closer look."

"How do we get in?"

"The fence is the first problem. I knew an old con at Milan who claimed you could disable infrared beams with a mirror. He'd been jailin' six years before I got there, still had eight to go when I left. Made me a little skeptical about his theory."

"But this isn't a prison, it's only for keeping out trespassers. Look across the pit. The little stream coming out of that swampy ground on the far corner?"

"It's blocked. The fence stretches across it."

"But the bottom of the fence is a foot above the waterline, probably to keep debris from clogging it up. There's room enough for us to slide under."

No choice. We scanned the perimeter a full half hour without finding another gap. The back gate was locked with infrared units on both sides and the fence was eight feet tall topped with bayonet wire. The stream bed would have to work.

Night falls hard in the northern hills. Shadows lengthen, then the horizon suddenly gulps the sun and dusk turns black as a raven's wing. No street lights glowed in the back country, no yard lights from the burned-out farms. The only light was the faint glow of Algoma's city-shine on the sky-line.

The moon was a question mark flickering between scudding clouds when we began working our way down to the stream. Thick underbrush made the going slow. I was worried about Meg keeping up, but she moved through the cover like a lynx. North country girl, born and bred.

We heard the stream before we saw it. Whispering softly in the shadows, moon-light dancing on its surface, a silvery path to the fence line.

With no hesitation Meg waded into the shin-deep water, dropped to her knees, then rolled on her side. Holding her camera just above the surface, she snaked under the fence, slick as a lizard.

I followed. Icy water swirled around my legs. Swallowing a curse, I dropped to my belly and wriggled under the wire. My collar snagged. Had to back off then duck face-first into the muck of the stream bed to squeeze through. When I staggered out, Meg was crouched on the bank, her face intent.

"What's wrong?"

"Listen. What is that?"

I felt it more than heard it, a low rumble shivering up through the soles of our shoes. I put my hand to the ground. A definite vibration.

"Heavy machinery."

"In the dark? There isn't even a light on in the gate shack."

"Maybe they pulverize the gravel or something. At least we don't have to worry about being quiet."

Following the stream, we moved warily down the hillside onto the grounds. The rumbling grew louder but the sound was so pervasive I couldn't place its origin. The earth seemed to be grumbling in its sleep.

"Which way?" Meg hissed.

"The holding tanks first. Maybe the noise is coming from the pumps."

In the dark, the pit was a dead zone, cratered ground, the oblong tanks only vague shapes. We moved carefully, keeping low, using the shadows. Somewhere across the compound an engine suddenly cranked to life, a heavy truck from the sound of it. After idling a moment, it got underway.

I could hear the engine, hear the driver shifting gears, but couldn't see the damned thing. Until it rumbled past us in the dark, a massive shape no more than ten yards away, driving without lights.

"What the hell is going on?" Meg whispered.

I didn't answer. I was still swallowing, trying to control my fear. There was something about that truck looming out of the night that made my skin crawl. Took me back to the well and Rachel's bones — that was it. The stench of the well. Only worse. The truck stank like a death wagon stacked with the remains of ancient graves.

Gearing down at the gate, it rumbled off into the night, still driving without lights.

"What was that smell?"

"I don't know, but that truck wasn't hauling gravel. It was a tanker of some kind, stainless steel. Come on, I want a look at those pumps."

Skirting the edge of an open pit, we worked our way to the pumping station beside it. The pump was turbine driven, I could feel the hum on its metal casing, but the deep rumble seemed to be emanating from much farther down, somewhere in the depths of the pit.

Feeling my way along the tank, I found a steel ladder and scrambled up on the platform. I had a penlight, but using it didn't help. None of the gauges in an array were familiar, their markings made no sense to me. The only thing I recognized was an odor of decay, like roadkill rotting in the dark. The stench from Rachel's well.

From atop the tank I could see across the pit. A sliver of light gleamed along the door sill of the old farmhouse. Apparently it wasn't as abandoned as we'd —

"Hey you! Come down from there. You too, lady. Get over by the ladder. Move!"

A second too late, it dawned on me. The truck had slowed at the gate. He was driving without lights, but knew exactly where he was. So he wasn't driving blind.

The guy motioning me down the ladder wasn't blind either, though he could have passed for it. Even in the faint starlight I could see he was wearing goggles that gave him a bug-eyed, alien look. He was also holding a weapon, a rifle with an odd cylinder around the barrel. A silencer? I didn't wait to find out. I started down the ladder, carefully, no sudden moves.

"Come on, lady. Over here."

"I can't see —" Meg stumbled into the ladder and went down with a yelp of pain. The guard knelt to help her up — and she triggered her camera flash in his face!

"Ahhh!" Staggering upright, blinded, he swung his weapon at her head, catching her on the shoulder, laying her out. He was raising it to finish her when I tackled him.

Leaping from the ladder I hit him chest high, slamming him face-first into the rocky ground. His breath exploded in a whuff and his weapon spun out of his hands, but he still managed a twisting roll that threw me off.

Fighting from a crouch, he hammered me with two quick blows to the torso that folded me in half, then he grabbed me in a choke hold — and froze as Meg jammed the rifle muzzle into his spine.

"Let him go," she said quietly. The guard released me and I stumbled backward, dropping to one knee. "Raise your hands."

"Lady, you have no idea —"

"Shut up. Get his glasses off, David."

He tried to fend off my arm, a mistake, since I was still smarting from the body shots. I hooked him hard in the belly, ripping off his goggles when he doubled over.

They looked inert until I slipped them on. Contact with my forehead triggered a circuit that gathered any available light, brightening the pit to the equivalent of an overcast afternoon with a bilious green tint.

No wonder he spotted us. Wearing the goggles, the sliver of light under the farmhouse door glowed like a neon tube.

"You people are making a big mistake. This is a government facility."

"Really?" Meg said. "Which government?"

"Don't be stupid, it's a U.S. military base. You can be shot. Surrender that weapon while you still can."

"You're not in uniform, buster," Meg said evenly. "There are no warnings posted and my sister's in intensive care. So the only question is whether you're going to walk us into that farmhouse or —"

"Gimme that gun, bitch!" She did. As the guard lunged at his rifle, Meg clipped him sharply across the temple with the barrel, dropping him to his knees.

I reached for his collar, but he toppled face down without a sound. Kneeling beside him, I checked his carotid artery for a pulse. Meg was rifling his pockets.

"He's alive. What are you doing?"

"Looking for his identification. What are these?" She handed me a half dozen thin nylon ties.

"Poor man's handcuffs." Pulling his hands behind him, I strapped his wrists together. "Find anything else?"

"No wallet, no ID, no help. Now what?"

"Help me drag him next to the turbine. If he comes around and yells, it may drown him out."

"Then what?"

"We're already down for trespass and assault with nothing to show. Wanna add breaking and entering while armed?"

"The farmhouse?"

"I see a light showing under the door."

"Let's move."

In the goggles' green haze I could make out distant figures across the pit at a pumping station with a truck idling next to it. No lights. Something was definitely up, here. But what?

Keeping low, we sprinted to the shadow of the building.

The rear door of the ramshackle farmhouse had been replaced with a new steel unit, unlocked, fortunately. I slid inside with Meg right behind me.

Total blackness. I fumbled my way to a second, inner door; we eased through it. And stopped. Dead.

The interior of the farmhouse had been transformed. Gutted and remodeled, its gray cubicles could have been transplanted from any corporate hive.

Walls and floor were lined with sound-killing gray carpet and the windows were shielded with blackout drapes. The only thing left of the original structure was a worn wooden staircase by the front door that led to the floor above.

The building seemed deserted, but that was clearly temporary. Computers were humming in several cubicles.

Hurrying to the nearest console, Meg slid into the chair and began scrolling while I moved quietly down the hallway. Two rooms near the front entrance had closed doors.

Listened carefully a moment, then cracked the left one. A bunkhouse, six cots, neatly made up, military style. Empty.

A weapons rack on one wall held two rifles like the one we'd taken from the sentry, but had slots for six more. Which meant more guards were roaming around. Armed.

The door across the hall opened into a conference room, chalkboard at one end facing a long table and a dozen metal chairs. A Bunn coffee maker was gurgling on a cart in the corner.

Sidling to the back of the room, I listened beside a narrow door, then eased it open. Broom closet. Mops and buckets.

Retracing my steps, I stopped to scan a chart beside the slateboard. The graphs looked vaguely familiar. Couldn't think why.

Lines intersected other lines like a highway map or a phone system but the reference points made no sense and there was no legend at the bottom to indicate what any of it meant.

Giving up, I hurried down the hall to Meg, still working at a computer station. "Anything?"

"Work schedules, grocery orders. Nothing useful. It's all encrypted and I'm no hacker. How about you?"

"Some graphs I don't understand —"

We froze, listening. Footsteps and muffled voices were coming from the floor above. Moving toward the stairway.

Our eyes met for a second, then she coolly switched the computer back to screen-saver then followed me into the conference room, all the way back to the broom closet.

Utter darkness inside, barely room to breathe, pressed together close enough to hear each other's heartbeats.

A rumble of conversation echoed from the hallway. Couldn't make out words. A door opened and closed. Then silence.

We waited five minutes that felt like a year without hearing anything more.

Easing the closet door open, I risked a look. The room was empty, the door closed. All clear. We slid out, listening. Suddenly Meg held up her hand.

"Someone's keying a computer down the

hall. We're stuck here for now. Where are the charts?"

"By the chalkboard. Do they mean anything to you?"

"A network? One-forty? Voltage? Maybe an area code?"

"Why make your own chart?"

"Good point. What about these numbers, forty-eight, one sixty-three, twenty-seven —"

"Where's twenty-seven?"

"Here, the one with the red line through it. Why?"

"Rachel's well was twenty-seven feet deep. Until it was filled in."

"Cancelled by this red line, you mean?"

"Maybe. If this is a hydrology chart, these three dots could represent the wells here at the pit: seventy-one, one forty-eight and one sixty-three. Depths, maybe? The other lines could indicate the properties they've bought up."

"What the hell are they after? Oil? Ore, maybe?"

"Not oil. I've worked on oil rigs, these pumps aren't for crude."

"So they're working at night to avoid regulations?"

"But at what?" I said, exasperated, "if not oil . . . Whoa."

"What is it?"

"Rachel's well smelled like . . . I don't know. Death. I thought it was rank from being sealed up all those years. But a few minutes ago I caught a whiff of the same stench at that tank."

I broke off, listening. Footsteps. Coming down the hall. In the sudden silence, the aroma of fresh coffee registered. Damn! The coffee urn was brewing. And someone was coming for it!

Chapter 54

Too late to run! The door was already opening. Meg was quicker than I, flattening herself against the wall behind the door, clutching the rifle.

Chris Sinclair strolled in, headed for the coffee maker. Spotting me, he froze, his eyes widening in shock.

"Westbrook? What the hell are you doing here?"

"That's my line, Chris," Meg said, closing the door quietly behind him. "Raise your hands."

"What?" he said, whirling to face her. "What is this, Meg? What's with the gun?"

"It's not mine, I took it from one of your guards."

"What? Are you out of your freaking mind? You could have been killed!"

"Nobody shoots anybody over gravel, Chris," Meg said. "They don't put armed guards around it either. Or commit murder and arson. You've got some explaining to do. But first you'd better raise your hands."

"Meg, you've got to put that gun down and get out of here."

"Or what? We could get killed? I've got a flash for you, babe, Tipton and David's uncle are dead, Daryl's in the hospital, and none of them were anywhere near this place. I'll keep the gun."

"What are you saying? Something happened to Daryl and Bass?"

"Bass was beaten to death," I said. "Daryl was run off the road. She's badly injured."

"And you think I had something to do with it?"

"I don't know," Meg said. "That's the rock-bottom worst of it, Chris. I don't. You'd better tell us what's going on here."

"It's not that simple."

Meg paled, then shook her head slowly. "Boy, was that the wrong answer. Daryl getting smashed to hell makes it very simple for me — what's that?"

"My beeper," Chris said, switching it off. "Intruder alert. They must have found the guard you jumped. They'll secure the perimeter, then come busting in here. You've got to give it up."

"After what happened to Bass and my sister? No way."

"Damn it, Meg, you don't understand! They'll come in shooting. It won't matter if I'm in the way. They won't care."

"Okay, you've convinced me," I said. "We'll surrender."

"Are you nuts?" Meg snapped.

"Nope. We're guilty of trespassing. Call 911, get Wolinski or the State Police out here and we'll give it up, Chris. But only to them. Not to you."

"This is a federal base. They have no authority here."

"Bull. This is no base. It's some kind of drilling operation. I've worked oil rigs. The pumps and pipes are too small and the tank gauges are all wrong for crude. All that leaves is water. Is that why you bought Rachel's well? For the water?"

"Damn it, Westbrook, we don't have time for this!"

"Make time. That guard wasn't patrolling the fence, he was near a tank. What happens if I fire a couple of rounds into one of those tanks, Chris? They'd have to fix the leaks, right?"

"No," he said, taking a deep breath. "They'd be dead. And so would we."

"So it's not water? Then what the hell's in those tanks, Chris? What . . . ?" And suddenly I knew. Should have known all along.

"What is it?" Meg asked.

"Something heavier than water," I said. "That's why they're drilling for it. It sinks to the bottom of the water table. Some kind of chemical . . . Chemical weapons? My God. Is that it?"

His face told me more than I wanted to know.

"Chris?" Meg prompted. "For God's sake, tell us. We're not Russian spies."

"It'd be simpler if you were. Then I'd know what to do."

"Try the truth," I said. "We're down to it anyway. What is this place?"

"An accident," he said, massaging his arm above the steel prosthesis. "A dumbass traffic accident."

"What accident?"

"One damn truck. Twenty years ago, when the Cold War was still on, B-52 bombers flew out of the airbase at Oscoda. Great circle route up to Alaska, refuel in midair, then come back and do it again. Planes in the air twenty-four/seven. Some with nukes, some with chemical weapons. A truck carrying a toxic gel component cracked up, ran off the road in a rainstorm. Lost its load in the swamp at the back of this property."

"What was it doing out here?" I asked.

"Avoiding main roads," Chris said dryly. "For safety."

"But surely they cleaned it up," Meg said.

"Absolutely. They dispatched a decontamination team to the wreck ASAP and cleaned up every trace of it. Problem was, it was in a swamp in a rainstorm. And the gel is heavier than water."

"They didn't get it all?"

"At the time they thought they had. We figure now they got less than half. Their equipment was pretty crude by today's standards and they weren't environmental types, they were airmen. Their best just wasn't good enough. Fortunately, it happened in the boondocks. Nobody got hurt. At first.

"A few years later, local farm animals started developing birth defects. At which point the brass realized the cleanup crew missed some of the gel. So they bought this place and the land around it and started recovery efforts."

"Secretly," I said.

"Hell yes, in secret. If our enemies know which bases were storing chemical weapons, we might as well e-mail every terrorist wacko on the planet."

"Local people might not like it much either," Meg said. "But if it happened years ago, why are you still here?"

"Because the toxin isn't where they lost it anymore," I said. "Rachel's well is miles from here. The gel's heavy, remember? It must have worked down to the bottom of the water table. And now it's moving. Right, Chris?"

"No one knew about the old well on the Hayes place 'til you hauled the bodies out of it. We only bought the land as a precaution."

"But you didn't recover anything at the Hayes well. You just filled it in."

"To immobilize the gel. When things quiet down, we'll transfer equipment to the site and recover it."

"Quiet down?" Meg echoed. "As quiet as Bass, you mean? Or my sister?"

"Meg, I swear to you —"

I caught a faint click, realized the doorknob was moving, too late! It flew open and a young trooper in black fatigues burst through, rifle at the ready, with another man close behind.

"Freeze! Nobody move!" I was already moving. Snaking a forearm around Chris's throat, I pulled him in front of me, into the line of fire between Meg and the gunmen.

"Dammit, I said freeze!"

"Hold it, Sarge," Chris gasped. "Don't

do anything stupid."

"Shut up, Sinclair." Marty Lachaine was the second gunman, looking even rougher than he had in jail: unshaven, red-eyed, still wearing the same greasy flannel shirt. The M-16 carbine in his fist was the cleanest thing about him.

"You got one second to toss that rifle, lady," Lachaine grated. "Then we cut loose whether Sinclair's in the way or not."

"Belay that, Sarge!" Chris yelled at the young soldier. "You don't take orders from this civilian dirtbag."

"Shut the fuck up, Sinclair!" Lachaine raged. "What's your girlfriend doin' here anyway? Time's up, lady —"

Lightning exploded in my eyes as Chris head-butted me, smashing his skull back into my face! Blinded by pain, I hung on desperately. Lachaine lunged left, trying to get a clear shot at Meg, but went sprawling as Chris kicked his legs out from under him.

The kick thrust us backward, off balance. I hung on, carrying Chris down with me. Leaving Meg and the young soldier facing each other, wild-eyed, weapons ready.

"Jesus H. Christ!" a voice snapped from the doorway. "What the hell's going on here?" Gerald Whitfield edged warily into the room. Unarmed and undressed, clad only in navy boxer shorts, he took in the scene in a glance.

"Sergeant, lower that weapon. Miss Keyes, I'd appreciate it if you'd do the same."

"No chance," Meg said, swallowing.

Chris tried to rise but I held him back, tightening my choke hold. Hot blood was seeping from my nose down the back of my throat. I needed to spit but was afraid to move.

"Stay put, Chris," Whitfield said. "You too, Lachaine. Everybody just hold position. Is anybody hurt?"

"My leg," Lachaine groaned, "I think Sinclair busted my fuckin' kneecap."

"Suck it up," Whitfield said. "This is your mess, Marty. Now, everybody cool down. No one has to die here. Miss Keyes, if you won't lower that weapon, could you ease your finger off the trigger? Please? You have my word no one will harm you."

"Your word?"

"I'm a serving officer in the U.S. Air Force Reserve. Colonel Gerald Whitfield. My word actually does mean something."

"Not to me. And you'd better stay where you are."

"Of course. For what it's worth, I guessed the night we met at the mortuary you wouldn't discourage easily. I requested permission to bring you on board. I was overruled. I'm sorry."

"On board?"

"To inform you of the situation and get your cooperation. Now we'll have to do it whether Washington likes it or not."

"What kind of cooperation?"

"Discretion. Since you know what's at stake here, you must understand the need for secrecy. The decision to keep this operation under wraps was taken at the highest levels of the Defense Department. My orders don't leave me much leeway, but we'll try to make this right."

"How do you make arson and murder right?" I asked.

"What murder?"

"Tipton for one. Your toxin turns deadly when exposed to the air and after working at the well bottom his wet suit must have been saturated with it. When the suit warmed in his car, he never had a chance."

"The State Police determined that he fell asleep at the wheel. An accident. Can you prove it wasn't?"

"The proof went up in smoke. Like the *Herald*. Which your goon admitted setting. Daryl getting smashed up? And my uncle's murder? The attempt to gas Meg and me at my clinic? All accidents?"

"No," Whitfield conceded, "they were mistakes. Proof that amateurs can't be entrusted with sensitive work. Lachaine has already confessed to arson, a federal inquiry will likely find him guilty of the other charges. He'll be held accountable."

"What the hell?" Marty said, stunned. "You're giving me up?"

"You crossed the line, Marty," Whitfield said. "You've put the whole project at risk."

"I didn't do a damned thing I wasn't ordered to. You said stop her but she wouldn't stop."

"And Bascomb? Did he — never mind. You see my situation, Miss Keyes. We tried to discourage you harmlessly with a few small fires. But things are out of hand now. We have to work this out."

"How?" Meg asked.

"First, let me send the sergeant out to order the sentries not to rush this room."

Meg glanced at me and I nodded. It would be one less person to cover. "He leaves his weapon behind," I said.

"Agreed. Sergeant, lean your weapon against the door and back out slowly. No one comes in without a direct order from me, understood?"

With a curt nod, the crew-cut trooper

backed out of the room.

"And sergeant?" Whitfield added. "No one leaves either. Code Red."

"What the hell was that?" Meg said, centering her weapon on Whitfield's midsection.

"Your last chance, Miss Keyes. Reality check. You've stumbled into a situation involving the security of our country. Mistakes have been made, but we can put them right."

"How?"

"We'll compensate you for your losses, the fire, the accident. Say, a hundred thousand for each of you? Your sister will receive the finest care, cost no object. I know money's a poor payment but it's all I can offer. That and the gratitude of your government. What do you say?"

Meg's eyes met mine, and I caught the sad flicker of a smile. "There's a word for girls who sell out for money," she said quietly. "I don't know which is worse, Mr. Whitfield, that you think I'm a whore or that we're stupid."

"I don't understand," he said.

"Cut the crap!" Meg snapped. "I'm a reporter, not some hick. This isn't a government operation. It's a black contract, an undercover deal the feds make to keep from getting their hands dirty. You signed on to clean up their mess, only the job's too big for you. The poison's moving, corpses are turning up in your well, people are asking questions. So you tried to keep the lid on with arson and assault. And murder!"

"It's a matter of national security! The UN could censure us, every psycho environmental group would swamp us with lawsuits —"

"That's the bottom line, isn't it?" I said. "In Rachel Hayes's time, loggers didn't bother cleaning up the slash and a thousand people burned to death. What you're doing is even worse. Your toxin's in the center of the Great Lakes basin and it's moving. You didn't know about Rachel's well. If you've missed any others, the poison could already be in water supplies in Detroit or Chicago. You're risking millions of lives to save a few lousy bucks. Just like the last time."

"That's utter rot!"

"It's the truth," Meg said. "And it's a hotter story than Rachel Hayes would have been."

"If I were you, I'd forget about her and start worrying about how you're going to get out of this room."

"The same way we came in. We have a rifle and three hostages. We'll call in the law and let them sort it out."

"I can't allow that. You're no soldier, Meg. You won't shoot anyone. Westbrook, let Sinclair go. You have ten seconds. Or I'll order my men to rush the room. Fire that weapon or drop it, Miss Keyes. You're finished either way."

"You think I won't shoot after what you did to my sister?" Meg said, swallowing.

"Unless you release Chris and lower your weapon right now, we'll find out. Well, Doctor?"

No chance. I could read the uncertainty in Meg's eyes and the murder in Lachaine's. If they rushed us, he'd kill Meg while she was still deciding whether to fire.

"Okay," I said, easing my choke hold on Chris's neck. "I'm letting him go. Everybody stay cool."

Chris and I both rose. He stepped away from me, massaging his throat. I half expected him to pop me in the mouth. He didn't.

"Take her weapon, Chris," Whitfield said. Lachaine got stiffly to his feet, grinning, casually picking up his M-16.

"Give it up, Meg," Chris said, reaching for the rifle. "It's over."

She hesitated, but only for a moment. Whitfield was right. She was no killer. Gently, Chris took the rifle from her.

"We'll hold you in temporary custody while we sort this out," Whitfield said smoothly. "Lachaine, take Miss Keyes and Westbrook to the basement —"

"Not a chance," Chris said, leveling the weapon at Marty Lachaine. "Lose the gun, stud, and lace your fingers behind your head. You too, Colonel. Now."

"Chris, what the hell — ?"

"Save it, Jerry, I just heard your speech. Westbrook's right, things went out of control when you hired this jailhouse genius to handle the rough work. Arson was bad enough but I'm not going along with murder. Are you?"

"I'm down for whatever the job takes, Chris. Don't sell out your country for this little twitch!"

"You're not my country, Jerry. This land is and we fucked it up. It's time to warn people about it and hope to hell we can stay out of jail."

"Nobody's doin' time," Lachaine snarled. "Wise up, Sinclair. This cunt ain't worth it and I oughta know. I banged her myself. Hell, me and a bud took turns."

"You incredible piece of shit," Chris said, paling. "Are you looking to get your head blown off?"

"I can prove it! We took pictures. I got

one in my wallet. Been passin' it around for laughs. I'll show you!"

"Just turn around, Marty —"

"No!" Meg interrupted. "Let's see your proof, Marty. Show us."

"Meg —" Chris began.

"Give it to me!"

"Sure, take a look, honey," Lachaine said, flipping open his wallet and tossing her a snapshot. "That's Hemke in the saddle gettin' seconds. I had you first."

Blood drained from Meg's face as she scanned the snapshot. She turned away, eyes misting, swallowing rapidly.

"Meg, what the hell is this?" Chris asked desperately.

"Nothin' but a party," Lachaine leered.

"Meg?"

"While you were gone I got loaded and wound up in the hospital. Blackout. Couldn't remember a thing. Now I know why. You slipped me something, didn't you, Marty? A roofie, maybe? Because I've never been drunk enough to do this."

"Bullshit. I met you in a bar, you was half in the bag, just askin' for it. So we gave ya all you could handle."

"And the baby I lost?"

"Wasn't no baby, you was alone. Pictures don't lie!"

"You're right," I said. "Do you have any more? With other women?"

"What?"

"I'm just wondering if you're a sick bastard who takes pictures every time you get lucky? Or only when somebody pays you."

Confused, Lachaine glanced at Whitfield for help. A look as good as a confession.

Chris lost it! With a howl of pure rage he launched himself at Lachaine, slamming into him chest high, carrying him over the conference table with the force of his rush. Grappling for the gun as they fell, Marty caught Chris full in the face with his elbow, dazing him. Lachaine tried to bring the weapon to bear but Chris blocked his wrist with his steel prosthesis. Bone slammed metal with an audible crunch, sending the gun spinning. Lachaine hit the floor, curling into a fetal crouch with Chris on top, savagely hammering him.

In the confusion Whitfield lunged for Lachaine's weapon, grabbing it up a split-second before I tackled him from behind. He twisted as we hit the floor, jamming me in the throat with an elbow.

All I could do was clutch his wrist, gasping, trying to keep him from firing. But he was too quick, too well trained.

Rolling the other way, he wrestled me beneath him, jamming the weapon down across my windpipe, cutting off my air. I brought up a knee, hard. He grunted but didn't let up. Eyes glassy with rage, teeth bared, he bore down even harder. I couldn't breathe, couldn't even gasp. Room was blurring, going red —

Suddenly Whitfield's head snapped sideways as Meg clipped him with the butt of the sergeant's weapon.

"Get off him," she hissed, jamming its muzzle under Whitfield's chin. And I've never seen anyone more wired up and ready for slaughter than Meg at that moment.

Reading her eyes, he opened his hand carefully, dropping the gun. "Easy now, Megan, you'd better —"

I hit him flush on the jaw, hard and as true as a home run, driving him off me with the force of the punch. He was out when he hit the floor, eyes rolling back, mouth agape.

"The door," I managed. "Lock the damned door!"

Gagging, my throat aflame, I could barely stand. But I was in better shape than Marty. Chris was in a zone, pounding Lachaine into chopped meat, turning his face into a bloody shambles.

"Stop it, Chris," Meg said quietly.

"You're killing him. We need him alive."

Chris landed another blow, then hesitated as her words filtered into his combat trance. He stumbled to his feet, blood streaming from a gash over his eye.

"Are you okay?" Meg asked.

He nodded, looking around, dazed, wobbly.

"We have to get out of here," I said.

"Can't," Chris said, wincing as he touched the cut on his forehead. "Code Red means the guards will cut down anyone coming out. They'll already have backup on the way. When it gets here they'll toss in tear gas and rush the room."

"But we've got their boss," Meg said.

"Won't matter. Some are ex-military, but some are thugs like Lachaine. Militia types. They've been lookin' to shoot something since they signed on. They'll waste us."

"Can we run for it?"

"No chance. They'll have the doors covered. The second we show ourselves they'll open up."

"How about a diversion?" I offered. "I could run for it, make some racket —"

"You wouldn't get ten feet. But it's not a bad idea."

"It sounded like one to me."

"The diversion, I mean. An explosion.

Every building in the pit is wired for demolition. Controls are in the cellar. I'll go out the door, hands raised. They won't shoot me. Trap door to the cellar's in the first cubicle. If I make it, I'll blow the gate shack. Ten seconds later I'll blow something else. At the first blast, you're out the window running for the woods. Hard. It won't take them long to figure what's going on."

"And you?"

"I'll be okay. The game's up once the blasts go off. I think the guards will bail out. Either way, we'll make enough noise to blow the lid off the coverup. That's what counts now."

"No!" Meg said fiercely. "What counts is all of us getting out of here in one piece."

"Too late for that," Chris grinned, flexing his steel prosthesis. "Don't worry, I'm not looking to die in this dump. We'll get out, but not together. You ready?"

"Do you want a gun?"

"If I step out with a weapon they'll pop me. I'll have to baffle 'em with bullshit."

"Then you'll do fine," Meg said grimly. "If you were as good a flyer as you are a liar you'd still have both wings."

"Sad but true. We'll sort that out later. If there is a later. Yo! Guys! It's Chris! I'm coming out! Be cool, okay?"

Opening the door, Chris backed out, hands in the air. I kicked the door shut behind him.

Muffled voices from the hall, someone yelling at Chris to turn around.

"Coley," Chris said, "that you?"

A door slammed and a half dozen shots exploded in the hall. Footsteps thumped down a stairway below us. Meg started for the door.

"No! I think he made it. Let's go." Grabbing a chair, I set myself beside the room's only window. Meg held position, covering the door.

"How will we know —" She never finished. The exploding gate shack rocked the house like a hammer blow. I hurled the chair through the window, smashing it out.

"Come on!" I lifted Meg through the shattered glass, then dove through after her. She was already sprinting for the trees at the rear of the house. No need for night scopes now, the guard shack was ablaze, flames spiraling into the night sky.

I tried to count seconds from the first blast, lost track. It didn't matter. A steel shed across the compound erupted with a flat, percussive blast, then a split second later, a massive, mind-bending explosion hammered us off our feet, slamming us down on the torn earth, breathless, cowering as flaming debris pinwheeled out of the sky, crashing down around us.

Footsteps pounded past only yards away, men shouting, racing toward the burning shed. A guard stumbled over my leg, kept on running without checking to see if I was dead or alive. Just as well. I wasn't sure myself.

Then Meg was up, staggering toward the tree line, blood streaming down her face, dragging the rifle, her clothes shredded. I stumbled after her with the ground writhing beneath my feet, trying to buck me off into the flaming sky.

Meg made it to the fence, flattened by the blasts, before she dropped to one knee. I knelt beside her, panting, nearly spent.

"You okay?"

"I hit my head," she gasped. "What the hell happened?"

"Secondary blast. Must have been something in the shed Chris didn't know about. We've got to keep going. Can you walk?"

She could. Barely. Together we stumbled through the cedars like death camp survivors. Below us, the chaos continued as the guards began spraying water on the tanks holding the toxins. God only knew what would happen if they burst.

One step, then another, holding Meg up or leaning on her until we made it to Bass's van. Together.

Sirens were approaching, lights flashing. Police? Fire trucks? Couldn't tell. Couldn't seem to focus. Head down, panting.

"We can't stay here," I managed at last. "If we get arrested —" Suddenly another blast went off in the compound below, a thundering roar that shook the earth, sending a torrent of flames howling upward, as though a window of hell had burst open.

"My God," she gasped. "What — ?"

"Looks like one of the tanks blew."

"But Chris said we'd all be killed."

"He was talking about a leak. When they destroyed chemical weapons after the Gulf War, they burned them. We'd better hope it works. Either way, the coverup's over. Come on, we have to get out of here."

Chapter 55

The drive to Algoma flashed past in a blur. A half dozen fire trucks blew by us, heading out. Police cars too. No one noticed Bass's old van. We were invisible.

Meg was silent for so long I glanced at her to see if she'd passed out.

"We can't talk yet," she said quietly. She was holding a bloody handkerchief against her temple, lines of crimson trickling down her arm.

"What do you mean?"

"Whitfield and his bosses have covered up this mess for years, and he has major government juice. You're an ex-convict and I'm a certified mental case. If we just blurt this thing out, they'll bust us on bogus charges, bury us, then cover it all up again. Our only chance is to spread the story so widely they can't kill it. But we'll only get one chance. I'll contact all the media people I know — TV, radio, Detroit and Saginaw papers — to set up a press conference. Then get ready to get hammered."

"How do you mean?"

"They'll try to destroy your credibility by beating you to death with your past. Mine too."

"That doesn't matter now. I'm up for whatever it takes."

She squeezed my arm, leaving a bloody palm print.

At the emergency room Meg's bleeding head and torn clothing earned her priority. A nurse and an intern rushed her off for x-rays and stitches.

The admitting doctor checked the bruises on my throat where Whitfield jammed me with the rifle and said I might have a fractured larynx. If it started swelling, it could strangle me. I felt like it already was.

He sent me off for an ultra-sound. A very pregnant Latino technician waved a plastic wand across my throat while watching a color monitor. No talking, please.

After ten minutes of scoping my injuries from all angles, she said I'd suffered severe contusions but no fracture. I'd been lucky.

I didn't feel lucky. She said a radiologist would have to confirm her diagnosis but I didn't wait. I headed back to the emergency room to find Meg.

Found utter chaos instead. Hospital personnel rushing past, police and firemen clustered at the admissions station. I asked a harried nurse where they'd taken Meg. No idea. They were swamped with injured men from a gravel pit explosion.

She hurried off. So did I, hastily checking the ER cubicles for Meg. Some of the injured men were goons from the pit. Whitfield or Lachaine could walk in at any moment. We had to get the hell out of here.

The third cubicle was empty but as I turned to go somebody shoved me back inside. I whirled, fists up.

"Lose somebody, Doc?" Wolinski's face and uniform were streaked with soot. His hand was resting on his gun butt. He didn't draw his weapon. Didn't have to.

"I have to find Megan. Do you know where she is?"

"Second floor surgery, seeing her sister and getting a couple stitches herself. Nothing serious. You look worse than she does. Are you okay?"

"That depends. Am I under arrest?"

"Not yet. In a minute, maybe. Murder, attempted murder, felony trespass, felony arson, assault with intent, malicious destruction of property. How do those charges sound?"

"Like you take orders from Jerry Whitfield. Maybe you have been all along."

"Is Jerry his name? I thought it was Colonel. He stressed the colonel part. A lot. Colonel Whitfield tells me you broke into his gravel pit at gunpoint and blew the place to hell. Claims you're some kind of eco-terrorist. Are you an eco-terrorist, Doc?"

"I'd save a whale if I could. The rest is a crock and you know it."

"All I know right now is that somebody definitely blew up a gravel pit. Two buildings were leveled and they've got a helluva chemical fire going. It'll take special equipment to get it out."

"And you think Meg and I did all that? Hauled in the explosives? And the chemicals?"

"Whitfield makes a pretty good case and you two are already on my shit list. The Colonel almost had me goin' until he started hinting how grateful his company would be if I could lock you up for a few days. With no visitors."

"How grateful? Big bucks? Or a cushy government job?"

"Both. He was cagey about the cash, though. Made sure I got the idea without incriminating himself. Pretty slick. Good thing he was in a hospital or I might have put him in one."

"He's here?"

"Two cubicles down. Looks even worse than you do."

"Good. So? Are you going to take the bribe?"

"You don't like me much, do you?"

The question took me off guard. I scanned his face. He was serious. "No. Not much."

"I don't like you either, Westbrook. Not from day one. I worked in Lansing ten years before I hired on here. Took enough crap from smartass college punks to last a lifetime. And you do have a mouth on you."

"Are you adding that to the list of charges?"

"Nope. No law says we have to like each other. I wanted it out front because we need to get past it. I'll be honest, I'm over my head here. I've got Whitfield foamin' at the mouth to have you and Meg arrested and I'm tempted to do it on general principles. I've had two calls in the past twenty minutes from Defense Department heavyweights telling me this is a federal case. Clamp a lid on it and wait for the cavalry."

"Then why don't you?"

"Hell, Doc, I know you and Meg didn't

blow up that pit. I did two tours in Vietnam. I know what C-4 and thermite smell like and I know what they cost. You couldn't afford enough C-4 to blow your nose. So I checked the rest of the buildings out there. They're all hard-wired for demolition, military style. I know Whitfield's lying but I don't know why. Nobody from the site will talk to me. Neither will Meg."

"Why not?"

"She's making calls to set up a press conference. It's supposed to go in an hour but that may be too late. I need answers now."

"If she doesn't trust you, why should I?"

"Because the feds have already contacted the Algoma prosecutor, and when government lawyers start buddyin' up you'd best hang on to your shlong, sport. The feds want to seal the pit, put it off limits. I have to move before they do."

"What do you want from me?"

"Is there anyone who can back your side of things?"

"Chris Sinclair."

"Where is he?"

"Last time I saw him he was forted up in the farmhouse basement. Didn't you check?"

Wolinski shook his head slowly. "The house is gone, Doc. Burned to the ground.

Firemen said debris landed on the roof. Old building, went up like flash paper. Total loss."

"What about Chris?"

"Whitfield said the building was empty. The fire crews hosed it down then shifted their equipment to cover the tanks."

"My God. Didn't they search?"

"No point, there's nothing left. Who else can I talk to?"

"No one. The rest of them work for Whitfield."

"Then we're down to it. You have to trust me, Westbrook. I can't deal with this unless I know what really happened."

He was right. Wolinski was a small town cop. Whitfield could easily block him out and neutralize him. He was also right that I didn't like him much. For two long years I took a lot of crap from guys like him.

The question was, personal friction aside, did I think he was honest?

A tough call. He disliked me, but he'd never crossed the line to give me grief. Best guess? We'd never be buddies but he was probably straight. I'd have to settle for that.

So I told him. The whole thing, as quickly as I could. It sounded farfetched in the telling but he didn't interrupt.

When I finished, I half expected him to

slap cuffs on me. Instead he turned away, massaging his fist with his palm. A large fist.

"Most of what you say is speculation," he said at last. "Tipton's death, Meg being drugged, the Reddy-Heater being left on. Even Bass's death. There's no actual evidence against Lachaine. Whitfield saying he did it doesn't make it true."

"You don't believe me?"

"I didn't say that. All I know for certain is that you and Meg didn't run her sister off the road and anything Marty Lachaine's tied into has to be dirty. If he's working for Whitfield then Whitfield's wrong. Marty wasn't at the pit, though. I'll put out an all-points for him and I'll have the fire crews check what's left of the farmhouse for Chris's body."

"Look for two. Marty was still out cold when we ran for it."

"But if Whitfield got out, Marty must have."

"Maybe not. He was blaming Marty for everything that's gone wrong."

"So he left him to burn? That's pretty cold."

"A lot of Whitfield's problems seem to go up in smoke. Marty was in rough shape. Chris really worked him over."

"It'll take more than a beating to finish

Marty. He comes across like a saloon thug but he's a lot worse. Psycho to the bone. Always figured he'd kill somebody eventually. Sorry it was your uncle."

He turned away, thinking. For a crazy moment I thought he might thank me. Yeah, right.

"Here's how it'll be. I won't file charges against you now, but if the prosecutor orders it I'll have to pick you up. If I can find you. Lay low at your clinic. I'll get you to the press conference and make sure you get a chance to say your piece, then hold you for questioning after to keep the feds from grabbing you up. Are you okay with that?"

"Why are you helping us? You just said you didn't like me."

"Nothing to do with you. Algoma's just a small town, Doc, but it's my home. I live here. My kids go to school here. And if Lachaine and Whitfield and the rest have been doing what you say, they're gonna wish to God they never heard of this place. Or me. I'll pick you up at the clinic in forty minutes. Take off. And Doc?"

"Yeah?"

"Clean yourself up. You look like a freakin' Taliban." And then he was gone.

So was Meg. The second floor surgery was working on burn victims from the gravel pit. I checked the admissions desk. The nurse said Meg left with a friend.

"What friend?"

"One of the men from the pit explosion, I believe. He was covered with soot."

"What? You let him drag her out without —"

"Calm down. Miss Keyes obviously knew him. They were hugging like teenagers in the hall. I didn't get his name but he had a prosthesis, an artificial arm. If you're Dr. Westbrook, she left you a note here somewhere. . . ."

She handed me a yellow Post-it with Meg's familiar scrawl.

Daryl's okay, Chris is safe & he'll back us all the way! Gone to barn for clothes. See you there.

Chapter 56

The sun was rising as I wheeled Bass's old van into the clinic driveway. Chris Sinclair's Mercedes convertible was parked in front of my office and seeing it gave me a lift. Glad he made it, especially because we needed him badly.

With enough spin from Whitfield, Meg and I could be dismissed as crackpots. A one-armed war hero is a lot tougher to write off. He'd proved that by getting out of that basement alive.

Milady was out too, pacing nervously around the Mercedes. Parking beside the Benz, I climbed out and called the dog. "Here girl, come on."

She ignored me. What else was new? She was more interested in the Benz, snuffling at the passenger door, whining, her tail and withers quivering.

Her focus made her easy to catch. Seizing her collar, I started for the barn but she lunged away, trying to shake free.

Odd that she was so excited by a car. I checked the Benz. Zip. Empty. But as I turned away my subconscious registered something: a stain on the driver's seat. Dark red. I touched it. Blood. Still warm.

I yanked open the door. A body was crumpled on the passenger-side floor, half-jammed under the dash. Chris!

Seizing his shoulders I hauled him up onto the seat. Ashen, unconscious. But alive. Blood was dribbling from the corner of his mouth down his chin. Massive blood loss. His shirt was sodden with it.

Easing him onto his side, I opened his shirt to check for wounds.

"Chris! Can you hear me?" No response. His breathing was shallow, barely audible. Felt his carotid for a pulse. A faint flutter, no more. Milady was frantically leaping at the car door, wired up by the blood scent.

Chris coughed, spewing pinkish foam from his nostrils and at the same moment I felt a spongy mass of edema where there should have been bone. A small hole. Bullet wound, stab wound, no way to tell, but it had punctured a lung. Chris was drowning in his own blood! Had to get him vertical.

Hauling him upright in the seat, I packed his torn shirt against the wound, strapped the safety belt across his chest to keep the pad in place and hold him in position.

He'd be dead in minutes if he didn't get help, but I was more worried about Meg. What happened? Where the hell was she? I ran for the open barn door, heading for the tack room telephone.

Dazzled by the sunlight, I tripped as I burst into the darkened barn, sprawling headlong in the corridor, face-first.

Dazed, the wind knocked out of me, I staggered to my feet. The corridor lights were out. But by the faint light of the open door, I realized I'd stumbled over a dog.

A dying dog.

Blitzen was sprawled on his back, staring sightlessly up at me a few feet inside the open door. He was still breathing, gouts of blood bubbling through a hole in his withers.

Lung shot. Like Chris. I backed slowly toward the door, my eyes straining against the murk.

"Hold it right there, Doc." The voice came from an open stall a few yards down the corridor. Lachaine. In the shadows of a stall doorway. I started backing away — a slug slammed into the plank beside my head!

"I said don't fuckin' move! Look up instead, motherfucker! I got your girlfriend high as a kite."

I glanced up warily, trying to keep Marty in view. Something was moving overhead . . . God. Megan was up there! Twisting slowly in the shadows of the roof peak, she was hanging from the hook that hoisted hay bales up to the loft.

"Yo, Meg!" Marty shouted. "Speak up, darlin'. Tell your buddy how much fun we had waitin' for him."

No response. I glimpsed her face as she turned. Eyes glazed, her cheek was swollen like a grapefruit with a purplish bruise. Her blouse was torn and she was naked from the waist down. But she was alive. Writhing in agony.

I tracked the pulley's haul rope down from the dimness to where it disappeared into the first stall. Marty's stall.

"Got the picture, Doc? I'm holdin' that snotty bitch up. If I let go, she drops like a box o' rocks. How high's that roof? Forty foot? She might live, but she'll look like that busted up cat of yours."

I swallowed, trying to control my rage. And fear. As my eyes adjusted I could see farther into the stall. Lachaine had the pulley rope snugged around his left forearm. He was holding a rifle in his free hand, its muzzle aimed at my face.

Midway down the corridor the remaining hounds were loose, milling in front of their pens, growling and whining in confusion.

If I sprinted across the corridor, could I tackle Marty before he took me out? Maybe. But if he released the damned rope, nothing could save Megan.

"Just so you know, Westbrook, I came here lookin' for you. Payback time. Sinclair and his snatch showin' up was strictly gravy. How's it feel, knowin' you fucked up your friends?"

"Not good." I swallowed, my mouth dry as dust.

"I'm not feelin' so hot either. Tough night. I'm way too tired to hang onto a fuckin' rope. Should I let it go?"

"No! Don't do that!"

"Why shouldn't I?"

"Sinclair isn't dead, Marty, and they can't pin my uncle's death on you. With what you've got to trade about Whitfield's operation you can cop a plea, maybe even walk. But not if you kill Meg."

"Hell, I don't need a deal, Doc. I've got one. With Whitfield. A fat bankroll and a long vacation. All I gotta do is tie up the loose ends. Sinclair and the broad. And you."

"It won't work, Marty. Wolinski knows."

"So what? In a pissin' contest between a hick sheriff and the feds, who gets wet? Now get your ass over here and grab this rope. I'm tired of holdin' it."

I hesitated, scanning the hall for — anything. But there was nothing. No weapon, no help in sight. Taking a deep breath, I walked across the corridor.

Marty stepped out, grinning. Crookedly. His cheek and jaw were swollen, raw as butchered beef from the beating Chris gave him.

His eyes were wild, dancing. Stoked on something. Probably methamphetamines? And rage. He flicked his wrist as I drew near, unwrapping a coil of rope.

And then he let it go.

"Noo!" Lunging, I grabbed the line as it snaked past, but Megan's hurtling weight yanked me to the center of the corridor, lifting me a foot off the floor, then dropping me again as my weight counterbalanced hers. Marty leered up at Meg spinning wildly above us, then he kicked me!

Twisting away, I took the blow on my hip. Pain flashed down my left side, numbing my leg.

Circling me slowly, chuckling, Marty casually shook the circulation back into his left hand.

"Little twitch is heavier'n she looks, ain't she? Here, lemme help you out." Pulling a clasp knife from his hip pocket, he thumbed it open, then moved in.

There was nothing I could do. Hanging onto the rope, I could only back away a step. He crowded me, his face inches from mine. Pressing the blade into my chest, he carved a shallow "s" in blood. Then he seized the rope just below my hands, hacked through the slack, and tossed it aside.

"Know what happens now, Doc? You get tired and the rope starts to slip. Only you've got no slack. You lose the end and she hits the deck a second later. Bam! End of story. For both of you. Wanna know why?"

I didn't. He told me anyway.

"With your record, the cops'll figure it's a lover's quarrel. You freaked, killed your roommate and her boyfriend, then torched the place. If Wolinski wonders, so what? Won't be nobody left to ask. How you holdin' out? She gettin' heavier?"

I didn't answer. Couldn't. Megan probably weighed a hundred and twenty pounds, tops, but I was feeling every ounce of it, my upper arms going numb from the strain.

"Cat got your tongue, Doc? Funny, you

had plenty to say down at the jail —"
Pivoting, he drove his fist into my
midsection, doubling me over.

Clinging to the rope was all that kept me
from falling.

Lachaine glanced up at Megan. "Get
ready, bitch! Your wuss buddy can't hold
you much longer." He kicked at me again,
gashing my shin, knocking me off my feet.
The rope end was grating through my
hands, inch by inch, rasping my palms raw,
slippery with sweat and blood. Couldn't
hold it much longer!

Dropping to my knees, I clutched the line
to my chest, defending it as Marty circled,
kicking me, jamming me with the gun butt.
I was almost done, hanging on with my last
shreds of strength.

Marty knelt, his face close to mine,
checking me out. "Don't pass out yet, Doc.
I want you to see something. I never liked
dogs much. Especially when they try to fuck
me up like that crazy bastard that jumped
the truck that night. Paybacks are a bitch,
ain't they?"

He spat in my face, then turned and fired
down the corridor at the milling hounds.
The shot ricocheted off the floor, just
missing Prancer. The hounds froze, tails
down, knowing something was terribly

wrong but not what to do about it.

"Damn! Missed. Never was much good with guns. Never had to be. I work better up close."

Marty backed away slowly, watching my face. Enjoying my anguish. "Here, doggies! Come on to Marty. Come and get it!"

Frightened, but with nowhere to run, the hounds retreated to the only safety they knew, their pens. Sick with horror, I watched Marty stop at the open gate of Donner's pen. Taking casual aim, he turned to smirk back at me. Then fired!

Donner yelped and began to yowl, thrashing around in agony. The other hounds took up the cry as Marty moved onto the next stall and aimed again.

"Noooo!" With a roar more animal than human, I leapt upward toward the wall! Plunging straight down, Megan's weight yanked me higher as I scrambled up the corridor wall like a spider.

Tumbling onto the haymow, I rolled over on the rope, snagging Megan to a halt a dozen feet above me, whirling in a wide circle over the floor.

"Motherfucker!" Marty roared, charging down the corridor, firing up at her. As Meg's arc carried her above me, I released the rope, dropping her like a stone onto the stacked hay bales. Bouncing off the upper tier, she came rocketing down, hands tied, unable to slow her fall, hurtling toward the edge!

Somehow I tackled her, halting her plunge an instant before she shot over the ledge. A slug whistled past my face, whacking into the roof above us. Too close!

Grabbing the nearest bale, I pitched it over the side trying to throw Marty off balance, frantically scanning the loft for a weapon.

A hay fork was sticking upright in a bale near the ladder. Racing to it, I yanked it free as a slug splintered a plank above me.

Damn it, we were dead meat up here! Hay bales were stacked neatly on two levels the full length of the barn. As long as we kept back from the ledge they'd shield us. But I couldn't stop Marty from coming up after us.

Even now he was backing warily across the corridor, looking for a clear shot as the dogs spilled anxiously out of their kennels, yelping, frantic with fear and excitement.

Shouting to drive them back, Marty fired a couple of wild shots toward them. They shrank from the noise, whimpering, tails down, terrorized. Without a leader they weren't a pack, just a mob with no purpose, no heart.

I clawed desperately at Meg's bonds, trying to free her hands. Couldn't budge the knots and she was too dazed to help.

Unable to spot us in the gloom, Marty switched on the overhead lights, instantly erasing the shadows. And revealing our position. Grinning, he trotted to the ladder and started up.

Pushing Megan back to shield her, I dragged a hay bale to the ladder and kicked it over the side, hoping to slow Marty up.

No luck. He grunted from the impact but easily bucked the eighty-pound bale off his shoulder, then came warily on in a combat crouch, his rifle aimed upward.

If he made it up here, we were finished. My only weapon was a dull hay fork and he'd start firing before I could use it. No cover, no place to hide. . . .

Except in the dark. The power cable that serviced the fluorescent fixtures overhead ran along the back wall. Tossing the hay fork to the upper level, I scrambled up after it.

Didn't make it. Missing a handhold, I fell backward, pulling a half dozen bales down with me in an avalanche.

Couldn't move for a moment, stunned by the impact, choking on dust, half buried. Heaving a bale off me, I crawled clear, expecting a slug to rip into me any second.

But the bales crashing down had spooked Marty. Scuttling down the ladder, he backed out into the aisle trying to see what was happening, rifle at the ready.

The fallen bales formed a rough stairway to the top of the stack and I scrambled up again, snaking on my belly to the back wall, flat as a shadow.

"Quit fuckin' around, Doc!" Marty yelled. "You can't hide. C'mon, we'll work somethin' out."

I crawled to the electrical cable. Brand new, it was armored with a metal sheath. And visible from below. Marty would have a clear shot. Damn it!

I risked a quick peep over the edge of the bales. Marty was stalking the corridor trying to spot me. But he was too hyped on speed to play cat and mouse. Sprinting to the ladder, he started up again.

I had a few seconds, no more. Rising to my knees, I jammed the fork into the cable shield. It bounced off! The tines were too damned dull to pierce the sheath. Jabbing it again and again, I dented the metal shield but couldn't punch through.

And suddenly Marty was there, peering over the edge of the loft, raising the rifle to fire. Nowhere to hide and no time. I made a last desperate lunge with the fork. And pierced the metal shield!

Wiring exploded in a shower of sparks, shorting out, plunging the barn into darkness. Blown backward by the 110-volt shock, I tumbled down the stack, pulling a couple of loose bales with me. Somehow I managed to grab a support post as the bales catapulted over the ledge, crashing to the floor below.

Dazzled by the flash, my arms tingling from the shock, I clung to the post, trying to gather my wits. Megan was coming out of her daze, clutching her torn blouse together, looking around, baffled.

Superheated by the voltage, the hay fork handle suddenly kindled into flame with an explosive whuff. A dozen small fires were already smoldering amid the bales near the sparking cable. In their flickering glow I spotted Marty backing away from the ladder, knuckling his eyes.

Flash blind. Must have been looking at the cable when it exploded. Now. This was my last chance.

Crawling quickly across the bales, I crouched, ready to jump. If I could tackle him . . .

No chance. Aiming his weapon in my direction, Marty backed across the corridor. A psycho, an animal, but not stupid.

Suddenly he whirled, covering the barn entrance with his rifle.

Milady. Drawn inside by the noise or perhaps by Marty's scent, she was crouched near the door, snarling at him. The pack took it up, echoing her threat from the far end of the barn.

Marty fired a hasty shot at Milady that ripped into the floor in front of her. He was right, he was no marksman. And the dogs were definitely spooking him. After facing Dancer's fatal charge, he was afraid they'd rush him in the dark.

Good. Maybe he'd make a mistake, give me a chance to — I stifled a cough to keep from giving my position away. My lungs were raw and my eyes were tearing up from the smoke —

Smoke? Rolling over, I looked upward.

My God! The fires were spreading, flames climbing up the barn walls to the ceiling. Satellite blazes from flying sparks leapt across the bales as thunderheads of smoke roiled among the rafters, churning lower every second.

"Marty!" I yelled. "Give it up! The place is burning."

"I'm going, but I'll be outside. Waiting. Hope you roast slow, the both of ya!"

He disappeared through the door, leaving

us in a smoky, smoldering hell lit by the flames in the loft.

I waited to be sure it wasn't a trick, then snaked across the bales to Megan and began working on the knots on her wrists. Her eyes met mine but there was no recognition.

"Meg? It's me, David." The damned knot finally loosened, then gave way, freeing her wrists. But she shrank from me, cowering, terrified. "Megan?"

"Get away!"

"Please, Meg, it's me. I won't hurt you. We have to get out of here. The place is burning."

"I want my clothes."

"There's no time — okay, okay. Here." Peeling off my shirt I gave it to her. "Wrap this around yourself. Now let's go."

I reached for her hand, but she pulled back and made her own way to the ladder. Halfway down she froze, staring numbly up at the flames in the loft. "My God, David, what's happening?"

"The barn's burning down around us," I said, scrambling down the ladder after her. "Lachaine's outside, covering the door. Our only shot is to break through an outside wall. There are tools in the tack room. Come on!"

Sprinting to the tack room with Meg stumbling behind, I groped my way inside. Smoke was getting denser. Could barely see now.

Fumbling through the murk to the tool crib, I grabbed a shovel and jammed it between two planks in the barn wall. Loosened a board at the top but when I tried to pry it free the shovel blade snapped off! Damn it! Enraged, I started battering the plank with the shovel's butt end.

In the hallway the dogs set up a clamor, yelping frantically. I should have listened. But I was focused on that damned board, pounding it again and again. Suddenly it popped free at the top! I started punching it loose along its length with the heat rising every second. We had only minutes, get out, perhaps not even that.

"Forgodsake grab something, Meg! Help me."

Stumbling blindly through the smoke, Megan started toward the tool crib just as Lachaine burst into the tiny room! Backhanding Meg, he knocked her sprawling into the corner.

"Too much racket, Doc!" he roared. "Drop that shovel. Turn around. I want you to see it comin'!"

Stumbling to her feet, Megan grabbed the

first thing at hand, a bucket of caustic lime. And pitched it full in Marty's face!

Bellowing in agony, he stumbled back, firing blindly. I dove and rolled, pulling Meg to the floor to protect her.

Marty was howling, pawing his eyes with his free hand as the alkali began to smoke, chewing into his skin. But even with his face smoldering he kept on blasting away, crazed with pain and rage. Dead set on killing us, no matter what it cost.

Grabbing the shovel handle, I jammed it into his chest, thrusting him backward out into the hall. Meg slammed the door and I hastily rolled a feed barrel in front of it, locking Marty out. Trapping us inside.

Dazed, her mouth bleeding, Meg grabbed a chunk of two-by-four and began beating on the loose board. I joined in with my shovel handle, hammering until it splintered and we smashed it out. I kicked the next plank free, then another, opening a narrow gap to daylight.

Thrusting Megan through, both of us on our knees, coughing, lungs aflame.

Meg recovered first, staggering to her feet, looking around wildly.

"Where's Chris? Lachaine shot Chris!"

"He's alive," I gasped. "This way!"

Clutching each other, we lurched to the

front of the building, stumbling like rummies in an earthquake.

Sinclair was slumped in the car where I'd left him. Dead? No. His pulse was faint but palpable.

"He's hanging on but he can't wait. Can you drive him to the hospital?"

"What are you going to do?"

"I'm going back for my dogs."

"Are you crazy? Lachaine's got a gun!"

"They're trapped in there, Meg. I can't let them burn! Go on! Get Chris out of here!"

I was already tugging at the door latch as she roared off. Couldn't budge it. The mechanism was jammed, warped by the heat, paint blistering. Damn it!

Tongues of flame were licking greedily between the planks. Above the door the old sign was smoldering. TENACITY. Smoking like the gates of hell.

The interior was a furnace now, superheating. In a few moments the building would combust and explode like a bomb.

Helplessly, I staggered back, driven off by the heat. Best get clear while I could. Then from somewhere inside, over the roar of the flames, I heard the hounds howling. In agony.

Sweet Jesus, they were still alive! Frantically I looked around for a tool, anything. Couldn't see clearly, my eyes were streaming from smoke. And tears. To hell with this!

Sprinting to Bass's van, I scrambled in and fired it up, slammed it in gear, and matted the gas pedal. Tires shrieking, the truck leapt forward, smashing through the barn wall.

Flames engulfed the cab, fire everywhere. Jamming the van into reverse, I roared back out again, spilling flaming debris off the hood and roof. I leapt down and raced to the splintered opening.

Smoke poured out through the gap, blinding me. Couldn't see inside. Dropping to my belly, I crawled in, keeping below the torrent.

The heat was incredible. Where the hell were the dogs? And Lachaine? Only a few feet inside my clothing began smoldering. But I could see now.

Blazing hay bales were tumbling down, blocking the corridor with a wall of fire, pillars of flame roaring up to the roof, fueled by the rush of air from the smashed wall.

And in that hellish light, I spotted Marty.

He was on his hands and knees in the middle of the corridor, blinded, crawling, his body smoking from the fire and the caustic lime. And God, the hounds were on him, circling him, lunging in and out, fangs slashing at his legs and body.

Oblivious of the inferno around them, they were lost in a savage ballet, their blood singing, answering the call of their ancient heritage, a hunting pack closing on a wounded enemy, fighting to the death so their clan could live on.

I shouted, trying to call them off. Donner looked up at me, then returned to the attack. It was hopeless anyway. There was no way out for them. They were going to die and I couldn't stop it.

A gust of smoke blurred my vision and through my streaming eyes it seemed there were more dogs whirling and charging in the flames. Somehow Dancer had rejoined the pack, and Vixen, and other hounds I didn't recognize.

And they weren't alone. In the shadows beyond I saw the figure of a woman, watching the hounds at their bloody work. She looked up and our eyes met —

With an unearthly roar the loft exploded! The roof began caving in, bales and flaming timbers crashing down around me. I had to get out!

But as I backed away I saw Milady. Crumpled against a stall door, she was writing. Wounded. Marty must have shot her. Her coat was smoldering in the furnace heat as she tried vainly to drag herself away from the flames.

I had no chance of saving her, the whole place was going up, yet I found myself sprinting inside. A blazing timber slammed into my shoulder, knocking me sprawling. I rolled with the blow, scrambling back to my feet without losing a step. Trained by experts. Crazed by pain, Milady snapped at me as I gathered her up, reopening the gash on my injured wrist. It didn't matter. I had her now, cradled in my arms. Turning, I started back.

Too late. With a deafening roar the roof imploded, collapsing along its length, timbers bursting like cannon shots.

A rushing wall of fire and superheated air enveloped me, blasting me through the shattered opening in a hurricane of flames.

Somehow I stayed conscious, stumbling into daylight, stunned, gasping, my clothes afire. But with Milady still clasped in my arms as I staggered away from the inferno. I only managed a few yards, then toppled to the ground, sobbing for breath.

Before I could stop her, Milady squirmed free, reeling back toward the burning barn! Standing in the splintered doorway with her bloody coat smoking, she barked frantically into the blaze, calling the others out.

But there were no answers. And no sign of the woman. Only the thunderous rumbling of the fire. Deep-throated and ravenous. The sound of a great beast feeding.

Chapter 57

There wasn't enough blood. As I sliced through the shaved skin of the Red Setter's hip, a thin red line trickled down the incision into the drain of the stainless steel surgery table. But the gush of crimson that should have pulsed from the five-inch gash didn't occur. Edema was already restricting the circulation to the dog's injured leg.

"Damn," I said softly.

Bettina Holtz, the student assistant I'd hired for the summer, looked up, her pale blue eyes troubled above the surgical mask.

"It's worse than you thought, isn't it?"

"Welcome to the wide world of surgery," I nodded. "In the x-ray, it looked like the femur was fractured in three places, serious but repairable. What we've really got here is a shattered bone, fifteen or twenty small pieces, maybe more."

"Will we have to amputate?"

"Not today," I said grimly. "The hip

socket is still in good shape. I'm going to tweeze out the bone chips. I want you to scrape them to recover every bit of the cancellous bone, the spongy stuff inside of the marrow cavity. We'll shift the larger bone fragments around and reassemble the pieces into a usable femur, then use cancellous bone to fill the gaps like putty."

"Will she be crippled?"

"This leg will definitely be shorter than the others but she's only a year old with a lot of growing to do. If she makes a good recovery her gait might not be affected all that much. But we've got to —"

The telephone gurgled, startling us both.

"Sorry," Bett said. "I know I'm supposed to switch it off when we're operating."

"You're fired. Get out. Never darken my doormat again."

"Yeah, right." Bettina picked it up. "Westbrook Veterinary Clinic."

I glanced around as she listened. My temporary clinic is in a new shopping center on the outskirts of Algoma. Wal-Mart and a Rite Aid Pharmacy are my neighbors. Great foot traffic, the real estate agent said. She was right.

We've been busy from the day we opened. Still, I don't care for the place much. Immaculate, professionally equipped, it's technically perfect. But with no history, no character.

Maybe it will grow on me, eventually. But I doubt it.

The only personal touches are the signs. One is above the entrance, green with raised gold lettering. Scorched around the edges. Westbrook Veterinary Clinic.

The other is above my office door. A charred piece of old barnboard that simply says: TENACITY.

A few people have asked about it. I say I inherited it from a friend. It reminds me that you can't lose if you never, never quit. Tenacity. A word to live by.

My new office is fully paid for. With a federal cashier's check. Compensation for the loss of the barn. And my uncle's life. And the dogs.

One government lawyer objected to paying for the dead greyhounds. He argued that since they were orphans, they had no actual monetary value.

I didn't actually attack him, but I came out of my chair, blood boiling. And he suddenly changed his mind. In the end they agreed to pay a thousand dollars for each animal.

I donated the check to the Algoma Humane Society.

Milady is recovering slowly. With luck she'll soon be well enough to run — Bett was staring at me.

"What's up?"

"That was the funeral home," she said, retying her mask. "Mr. Mallette said your gravestone's arrived."

It didn't register for a moment. Then I started to chuckle as I began probing the wound with forceps to salvage the bone fragments. Bett eyed me oddly above her mask.

"It's not my stone," I explained. "I just chipped in for it. I'd forgotten we ordered it."

"For a relative?"

"No. Not exactly."

Epilogue

Dusk was falling as I drove my Jeep through the gates of Holy Cross Cemetery.

A gleaming new blue Chevy Blazer was parked near the entrance. Meg had traded her wrecked outlaw pickup for it. Memories included. No extra charge.

She was waiting for me at the end of one of the tiled lanes near a new grave. She'd changed a lot in the months since our raid on the pit and its terrible aftermath.

Emotionally, she seemed recovered. Stronger if anything, with a deep reservoir of righteous anger about what had happened to us, and to the truth, and to the land.

She'd aged visibly, added wren's feet around her eyes and a few silvery highlights in her hair.

I liked the effect. She'd never be mistaken for a kid again, but her true character was emerging. She was a woman grown now, bright and focused. Formidable.

"Hi." She rose on tiptoe to give me a peck on the cheek. "I thought I might have to borrow a sick cat to see you."

"The new clinic's been really busy. I've met a lot of nice animals and a few nice people. How's Chris?"

"Good. Well, better anyway. He's up and around. Prognosis is positive. He's tough as a tree, but. . . ."

"But?"

"It's over with us, David. He tried to do the right thing in the end, almost died trying. But he went along with the cover-up too. And he lied to me. From the beginning. Funny, I could probably forgive a crime. But not the lies. Too many terrible things happened because of them. How about you?"

"I'm living like a monk. Selflessly devoted to the care and repair of injured critters."

"Uh-hunh. I heard Yvonne broke it off with Les."

"That was about his involvement with the pit and Whitfield. Nothing to do with me."

"But you've seen her, right? Talked to her?"

"Yeah. Once."

We'd met in a conference room in the Algoma State Bank, to work out a settlement for damages to her barn and my clinic with a team of government lawyers. Three of them. Short, medium, and tall. Federal drones in gray suits similar enough to pass for uniforms. I didn't bother to get their names straight nor did I pay much attention to the negotiations. I studied Yvonne instead.

Couldn't tell if she'd dressed for the occasion or not. Her blue suit and ecru blouse looked expensive, but she would have been every bit as elegant in jeans. Or so it seemed to me.

I noted she had a new attorney, a stout, balding bulldog from Lansing. He did most of the talking.

After an hour of haggling, Von whispered to her lawyer and he suggested a break, pointedly ushering the trio of government types out. Leaving Yvonne and me alone. Eyeing each other across an oaken conference table. Like strangers.

"Would you mind not staring at me, please?" she said.

"I'm trying not to."

"Well you're not doing a very good job. How have you been?"

"If you'd answer my telephone messages, you'd know."

"I'm sorry. I've been . . . a bit confused."

"Good."

"Confusion is good?"

"Sure. It means you're upset, which means, despite all that's gone wrong, you haven't decided to tell me to get lost. Yet. Or have you?"

"I don't know."

"See? Confusion can be good."

"Not necessarily. Sometimes — no, most times — I don't understand you at all. The way you think, I mean."

"If you mean we're not much alike, you're probably right. That's not necessarily a bad thing either."

"David, I did a lot of thinking out west. I like you and I won't deny I'm attracted to —"

"Can we skip the let-Dave-down-easy part and just cut to the but? The suspense is killing me."

"All right. But, after all that's happened, I can't see things working out between us."

"Who says so? Your friends?"

"If you think that, you really don't know me at all."

"You're right, I don't. But we can fix that. Why don't we —"

"— change the subject," she said. "From what I've heard so far, I think you'll get a substantial settlement from the government. What will you do with it?"

"Open a clinic."

"In Algoma?"

"Of course. That's why I came here."

"But with the money, you can —"

"— go anywhere? News flash, I didn't just fall off a turnip truck and land here. I came to this town for a fresh start. It's where I want to be. Especially now. Do you want me to leave, Yvonne? Is that it?"

"It might — simplify things if you did."

"You want things simple? Fine, tell me to get lost. Just say you don't give a damn about me and never will. Tell me to take the settlement money and disappear."

"And if I do, you'll go?"

"Hell no. Not a chance."

"I don't understand."

"Neither do I, but there it is. Look, I know we're an unlikely match. I don't blame you for having major doubts, I have a few myself. But I think there's a chance that we might be really good together. And I don't want to miss that chance. So. Marry me."

"What!"

"Marry me, Yvonne. Please."

"David, that's crazy."

"No it isn't. Hey, I'm not quite penniless anymore. Bass left me his farm, plus I'll

486

have whatever we score in this settlement. I can afford a ring, a church, whatever. I've even figured out how to settle the 'Cadillac eyes' thing. Ask Les Hudspeth to draw up a really nasty pre-nup agreement for you. And whatever it says, I'll sign it. Blind-folded. In front of a hundred witnesses. Is that foolproof enough?"

"Yes," she admitted, smiling. "But I can't marry you."

"You're right. We hardly know each other. So let's work on that part. I won't ask you to meet me in the meadow in the moon-light. I'll settle for lunch. Or a phone call. Let's talk, Yvonne. Just talk. How much trouble can you get into over the phone?"

"With you? A lot, I think."

"And would that be such a bad thing?"

"I don't know."

"See? Confusion can be good."

"Then I must be in great shape, because I'm thoroughly confused."

"Me too. It's been a — complicated summer. To be honest, I'm not sure things will work out for us. I can't even promise to make you happy. There's only one thing I'm absolutely sure of."

"What?"

"It won't be boring."

She had burst out laughing, a wonderful,

cascading laugh that brought her lawyer peeking through the door. "Is everything all right in here?"

"Yes," she had said, still smiling, her eyes glistening. "Everything's fine."

"And?" Meg asked, snapping me back to the cemetery reality. "What's been happening?"

"We've been talking. A lot. We've gone on a few walks. She's a tough sell. And she's right, in some ways we're a terrible match."

"Because she's older? Or because she's richer?"

"If I cared about money I wouldn't be a small town vet. The rest means even less to me."

"What are you going to do?"

"Wear her down, I think. I learned a lot, running with those hounds. They never quit. Ever. It's like they don't know how. Which isn't a bad lesson."

"Poor Yvonne. I don't think she stands a chance."

"I hope you're right. How's Daryl doing?"

"Terrific. Bitchy as a bear, harassing the poor bastards rebuilding the carriage house. With luck, they'll finish this week. I'm going to help Dar get the computers for the *Herald* up and running, but then I'm off to L.A. An offer I can't refuse."

"From Reggie?"

"Even better. The network offered me Reggie's job."

"A little payback?"

"I'll admit it sweetens the deal, but after all that's happened, revenge on Reggie doesn't seem very important."

"Maybe that's the ultimate revenge. Indifference."

"Whoa, that's pretty heavy, David."

"Graveyards tend to make me thoughtful. Or maybe it comes from working with characters like Frankenkat. He's doing fine, by the way. A little scorched, but otherwise okay. He has an incredible spirit. Animals are better than we are in so many ways. More loyal. Definitely more honest."

"I haven't seen much honesty lately. I've been interviewing too many bureaucrats and lawyers, all trying to weasel out of responsibility for the gravel pit. Trying to blame everything on that bastard Lachaine."

"Is anybody buying that?"

"No chance. The governor's furious at the feds for keeping him out of the loop. The state's launching its own investigation and Chris is cooperating with them. Whitfield will definitely do hard time, maybe his bosses will too."

"Good."

"I guess. And yet here we are. In the uproar over the killings and the chemical spill, Rachel and what happened to her have been forgotten all over again."

"Maybe that's as it should be. She's been gone a long time."

"I'm not so sure," Meg said, with a flash of her old mischief. "I still can't remember what I saw the day I cracked up Chris's car, but I did see a satellite photograph of the Hayes property a few days ago. Know what? Even at maximum magnification Rachel's well is just a damned dot. A dot. With all those hundreds of acres to run in, how did that kid manage to fall through a hole two feet wide? Unless . . ."

"What?"

"I think Rachel wanted to be found. To warn us that what happened to her was happening all over again. What do you think?"

I'm not sure why I didn't tell her. About the woman I saw the night Tipton died. Who woke me with smoke to escape the monoxide. The woman in the fire that last day. But I didn't. Her wounds are too fresh. So are mine.

"I think it's a nice headstone," I said.

"It is," she nodded. "Should we say a

prayer or something?"

"I wouldn't know what to say."

"Me either." Meg knelt beside the grave for a silent moment. I didn't. I'm not religious. I've been thinking more about such things lately, but I doubt I'll ever understand what happened to us. Or why.

But with all my heart I wished Rachel Hayes and her daughter well. And her dog too. Wherever they are.

Around us, the cemetery stretched away to the foothills. The only other mourner was an elderly woman in a dark raincoat. Far off and lost in her own thoughts.

After a bit, Meg said her goodbyes. She promised to call me when she's settled in L.A. Maybe she will.

I lingered as the shadows lengthened, reluctant to leave.

I was waiting for . . . Something. A sign, I suppose. Some indication we'd done the right thing. That the pain and the lives lost were worth it.

But nothing happened. I'd hoped burying Rachel's ashes in a proper place might give me a sense of closure. Lay some of my ghosts to rest.

It didn't though. Maybe the cynics are right and the grave really is the end of things. But it didn't feel like an ending. The sky was clearing as the sun lowered, the Black River Hills rolling into the dusk like ebony waves. In the waning light, they seemed to glow from within, as if the fires that once consumed them are still burning. Somewhere.

As I turned away, I noticed two figures in the distance, walking in the shadowed hills. A woman and child? Couldn't be sure. Too far off.

A dog was dancing around them, frolicking in the sunset. Having a wonderful time.

A collie, I think. Ginger colored.

About the Author

Author of seven novels and more than eighty short stories, Doug Allyn's background includes Chinese language studies at Indiana University and extended duty in Southeast Asia during the Vietnam War. Later, he studied creative writing and criminal psychology at the University of Michigan while moonlighting as a songwriter/guitarist in the rock band Devil's Triangle. He currently reviews books for the *Flint Journal* while maintaining a full time writing schedule. His short stories have garnered both critical and commercial acclaim and have been awarded numerous prizes, including the Robert L. Fish Award for best first story, the Edgar Allan Poe Award, the American Mystery Award, the Derringer Award twice, and the Ellery Queen Readers Award six times. Doug counts among his career highlights drinking champagne with Mickey Spillane and waltzing with Mary Higgins Clark.

The employees of Thorndike Press hope you have enjoyed this Large Print book. All our Thorndike and Wheeler Large Print titles are designed for easy reading, and all our books are made to last. Other Thorndike Press Large Print books are available at your library, through selected bookstores, or directly from us.

For information about titles, please call:

(800) 223-1244

or visit our Web site at:

www.gale.com/thorndike
www.gale.com/wheeler

To share your comments, please write:

Publisher
Thorndike Press
295 Kennedy Memorial Drive
Waterville, ME 04901